S targazer!" Torius drew his sword a̶─ rush of adrenaline surging throug̶─

Two flags flew up the mainmast, ─────────────── on a blue-and-gray shield, and directly beneath it, *Stargazer*'s own long black-and-silver pennant bearing a serpentine silhouette of a naga with flowing white hair. Thillion's archers leapt up from hiding to rake the galley's forecastle with a deadly volley. The crew of the enemy ballista fell, riddled with arrows. *Stargazer*'s deck shuddered beneath Torius's feet as six ballistae cracked in perfect unison. The bolts cleared the galley's rail by mere inches, and the triggering tethers came taut, detonating the ceramic warheads. Blue-white liquid splashed forth onto the astonished slavers, encasing them in freezing alchemical ice. Grogul and his boarders boiled up from the main hatchway, heaving grapples to pull the two ships closer.

"Celeste, Dukkol, Windy, Kalli, with me!" The helmswoman and bosun's mates drew weapons and ran with him to the rail, but Celeste didn't move. When he glanced back, she just stared at him with a questioning look. "Come on!"

"*Que towlre nokta?*" Celeste gaped at him wide-eyed.

Torius stared at Celeste, trying to interpret what she'd said. "Celeste! Come on!"

She blinked at him, uncomprehending, and spoke again, but her words came out as a string of gibberish.

What the hell language is she speaking?

The two ships met with a crash. Torius couldn't wait, even for her. He leapt the rail onto the enemy quarterdeck, parrying a pike thrust even before his feet touched the deck. Windy gutted the pikeman as she landed beside him, and parried a cutlass with her hook. Kalli lunged to skewer a slaver officer through the neck with her rapier. Dukkol bellowed a curse as he took a pike in the leg, but his axe clove through his opponent's arms in riposte. More slavers closed in on them, pressing them hard. Torius parried wildly, glimpsing the slaver captain beyond the flashing blades . . .

The Pathfinder Tales Library

Pirate's Prophecy

Chris A. Jackson

A TOM DOHERTY ASSOCIATES BOOK
New York

PATHFINDER TALES: PIRATE'S PROPHECY

Maps by Crystal Frasier and Robert Lazzaretti

A Tor Book
Published by Tom Doherty Associates, LLC
175 Fifth Avenue
New York, NY 10010

www.tor-forge.com

Tor® is a registered trademark of Tom Doherty Associates, LLC.

Library of Congress Cataloging-in-Publication Data

Names: Jackson, Chris A., author.
Title: Pirate's prophecy / Chris A. Jackson.
Description: New York : Tom Doherty Associates, LLC, 2016. | Series: Pathfinder tales ; 31
Identifiers: LCCN 2015040152 | ISBN 978-0-7653-7547-6 (trade paperback) | ISBN 978-1-4668-4734-7 (e-book)
Subjects: LCSH: Pirates—Fiction. | BISAC: FICTION / Fantasy / Epic. | FICTION / Media Tie-In. | GSAFD: Fantasy fiction.
Classification: LCC PS3610.A346 P57 2016 | DDC 813/.6—dc23
LC record available at http://lccn.loc.gov/2015040152

Our books may be purchased in bulk for promotional, educational, or business use. Please contact your local bookseller or the Macmillan Corporate and Premium Sales Department at (800) 221-7945, extension 5442, or by e-mail at MacmillanSpecialMarkets@macmillan.com.

First Edition: February 2016

Printed in the United States of America

0 9 8 7 6 5 4 3 2 1

This novel is for my father, Robert Donald Jackson, who passed away while it was being written. Fisherman, boat-builder, craftsman, and Kipling's proverbial *Thousandth Man*, he taught me to value friendship, and that you could love something that occasionally seemed bent on your destruction; namely the sea.

Inner Sea Region

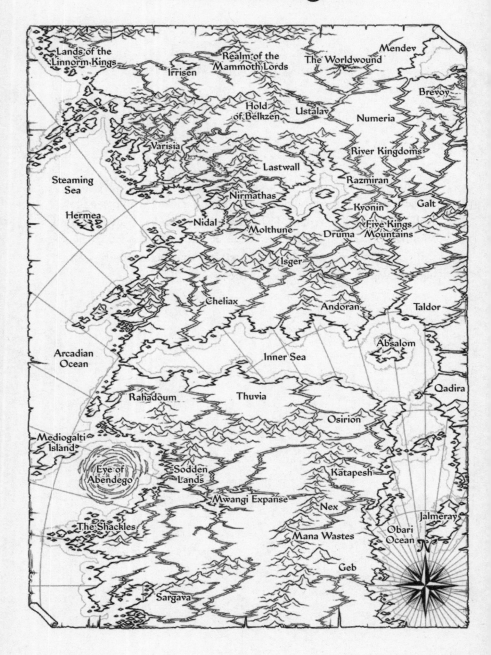

Stargazer

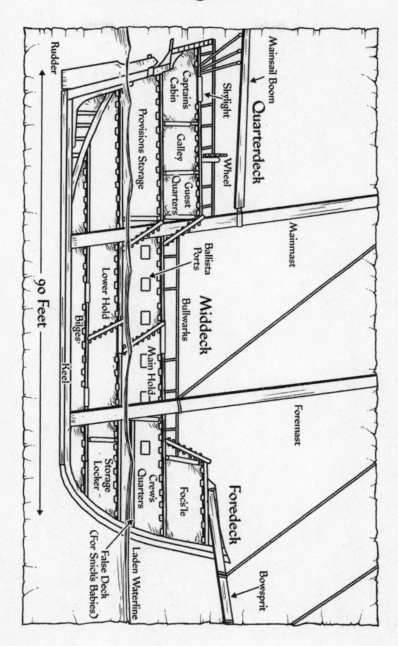

1

New Places, New Faces

Captain Abidi Ben Akhiri's boots brushed the thick planks of the Ostenso wharves a step behind the heavier tread of his half-orc bosun. The Akhiri disguise felt natural now, long-practiced in the five months they'd been spying on the Chelish fleet stationed here.

Spying for Andoran had taught them all caution, and the tension between the devil-worshiping nation of Cheliax and the abolitionist republic of Andoran bred espionage like filth bred the plague. Consequently, though the pair wasn't exactly trying to be stealthy, they kept to the narrower streets and alleys, shying away from the few flickering streetlamps that dotted the wharf district. For the most part, their passage went unnoticed—this late in the evening, most of the populace was already at home and asleep—but the tread of heavy boots and the clatter of armor told the sailors they were not without company.

"Damn!" The bosun stopped and cast around for someplace to hide. "There?" Grogul pointed to the recessed alcove of a shop's front door, shadowed from the pearly glow of the moon and sallow streetlamps.

"Go! We don't have time to deal with the city watch." The Ostenso constabulary patrolled the wharf district relentlessly after dark, questioning everyone they encountered.

The pair hurried into the alcove. Unfortunately, its depths proved shallower than they'd hoped. When the troop of guards rounded the corner, Grogul's bulk still protruded into the light.

"Thillion should have come! He's thinner!" The captain's whisper barely reached his bosun's ear, but was edged like a razor.

"Sorry." Grogul tried to pull back farther, but his boots still stuck out into the light.

Five guards clad in mail marched down the street behind a broad-shouldered sergeant wearing a breastplate emblazoned with the city crest. Their eyes darted about with professional scrutiny, sharp and attentive, their hands never far from their swords. If they spotted the pair, there would be questions at the very least, and the last thing Abidi Ben Akhiri wanted right now was to supply any answers.

"Run for it?" Grogul whispered.

"No. Just hold still." Breathy words issued from the captain's lips, and first Grogul, then the captain himself faded completely from view.

The squad clattered past, keen eyes sweeping over them. Steel whispered against leather as Grogul drew his kukri.

One of the squad stopped, staring right at their hiding place. Whether she had heard the faint noise or caught some anomaly of light and shadow, her attention transfixed them like a spear. The pair held their breath.

"Something?" The sergeant pulled his patrol to a stop with a raised fist. The entire squad turned and stared into the shadows.

"Nah. A rat maybe." The guard shook her head and rejoined her fellows. With a clatter of armor and weapons, they continued down the street.

When they were gone, a gusty breath escaped the half-orc's cavernous chest. "That's a handy trick."

"You have no idea. Now take my hand." They fumbled around until Grogul's huge hand enclosed the captain's smaller one. "Good. Now lead on."

"Just hope that spell lasts," the half-orc muttered. "This is embarrassing."

"Are you saying you'd be *ashamed* to be seen holding my hand?"

"Um . . . no . . . it's just that . . ." Grogul cleared his throat. "There's some rough types around the wharves, you know . . . and I got a reputation to uphold with the ladies."

The captain chuckled low. Grogul had indeed earned a reputation with the ladies of the local pubs and pleasure houses. Evidently, they liked scars. "Your reputation's safe with me. Just keep quiet and hurry. We're late already."

"Right." Grogul tugged, and they continued on through the planked streets and alleys.

Finally, the bosun stopped at a nondescript pub. The signboard swinging above the door displayed two spinning copper coins and a faded name: The Two Pinches. "This is it."

"Okay. Let me just . . ." With a quick glance to make sure no one was in sight, then a few whispered arcane words, they blinked into visibility. The captain straightened his jacket and fez and looked up at his bosun. "How do I look?"

The half-orc scowled at his companion and muttered, "Perfect." He led the way through the door into the pub's main room, his captain close on his heels.

The place gave a whole new definition to the word dreary. With plain wooden walls, simply built tables and chairs, and dim lamplight, this could have been any pub in any city in Avistan. It was perfectly anonymous, which was just what both the visitors and the regulars wanted. A few locals swept curious gazes over the pair and looked away. Grogul and Captain Akhiri had been here often enough that there would be no questions, no rumors, and no trouble. The bosun strode directly to the door to the left of the bar. The barkeep gave them a glance and a nod. Arrangements had been made.

The back room was even more bereft of decor than the common room, sporting nothing but a bare table, four chairs, and two dour thugs with cudgels. They reached for their clubs, then recognized their visitors and relaxed.

"How does this place stay in business?" the captain whispered.

The half-orc flashed him a stern glance, then faced the two thugs. "Nobody follows us." Grogul rounded the table and kicked back a threadbare rug to reveal a small trapdoor.

"Nobody follows. Got it," one of the bruisers agreed, crossing his burly arms.

Grogul lifted the trapdoor and descended into the dark and wet-smelling hole in the floor. His voice floated up from the gloom. "Careful. The boards are slippery and the ceiling's low."

"Right."

Grogul's warning turned out to be both accurate and welcome. Akhiri's boots found slippery purchase on the slimy ladder rungs. The trapdoor thumped closed overhead, plunging them into darkness. The captain settled onto the damp wooden platform gingerly. Wavelets lapped at its underside, too close for comfort, and the stench of rotting seaweed made it difficult to breathe without gagging.

"This way." Grogul's voice seemed to come from nowhere.

"Wait. I can't see." Akhiri's dagger whispered from its sheath, barely audible above the lap and clap of water on wood. A single arcane word brought light to the drawn blade, illuminating their surroundings well enough to see. "Okay. Go ahead."

Grogul shaded his eyes from the glare of the glowing dagger and led the way. The narrow walkway, barely two feet wide and slick with algal growth, flexed under his weight. Long practice walking on a pitching deck made such a traverse an easy affair for the bosun. Akhiri followed more carefully, eyeing the dark water with concern.

The way branched and forked several times as muted thumps and voices filtered down from the buildings overhead. A few other ladders could be seen in at the edge of the circle of light, egresses back to the world above. They passed them all by without a glance. Grogul turned this way and that, unerring in his choice of paths, until finally they came to a set of low steps that led up to a small trapdoor.

"Careful here. The boards are really slick, and you do *not* want to fall in the water."

"Just get the door open." There was trepidation in the captain's voice, now that the imagined horrors lurking beneath the dark water might not be imagined after all.

Grogul knocked three times, then once, then twice. With the loud clack of a bolt being thrown, the hatch opened. Warm yellow lamplight poured forth—a welcome sight indeed. The captain sheathed the glowing dagger, dousing the magical light, and followed Grogul up the steps into the low room above.

"About damned time." The diminutive form of Twilp Farfan backed away from the trapdoor, squinting suspiciously up at the two. "You're late!"

"Much later and you'd have missed your tide." An identical Captain Abidi Ben Akhiri rose from where he sat on a dusty bedroll and smiled at the pair. "Akhiri's supposed to be *my* disguise, Vreva. But I must say that you're looking very fine this evening—or should I say, *I'm* looking very fine!"

"And your sense of humor is as bad as ever, Torius Vin." Vreva dispelled her disguise with a snap of her fingers. Shaking out her long black hair, she smoothed her skirt and frowned at the algal slime marring the toes of her shoes. "And don't call me Vreva. It's Virika Korvis. If you confuse me, I might slip up."

"Virika. Right. Sorry. Well, you do look very fine, even as Virika."

"Thank you, but I still don't quite recognize myself when I look in the mirror." Vreva cringed inwardly as she remembered the numerous surgeries she had endured to change her face from that of the now-notorious Vreva Jhafae. Waking up swathed in bandages, only to be magically healed, then doped with opium again for the next go-round had been an onerous torment, but necessary to assume her new identity. There were too many people across the Inner Sea who wanted to hang her former persona. Other changes were easier. She ran her fingers through her hair, no longer elegantly coifed, but loose and curling about her shoulders. After so long as Vreva Jhafae, high-class courtesan to the slavers of Okeno, she had thought it would be difficult to become Virika Korvis, local Ostenso business owner, but she was actually enjoying her new persona, and Virika was certainly less expensive to maintain than Vreva had been.

Torius looked to Grogul. "Any trouble?"

"Not really." Grogul shrugged. "She had some persistent customers, and we met up with a watch patrol on the way, but we ditched 'em."

"Customers? That's good." Torius looked back at Vreva. "Business is picking up?"

"Quite a bit since your last visit, yes. The Officers' Club is finally getting a reputation as *the* place for all *sorts* of entertainment." The Twilight Talons, Andoran's covert organization of state-sponsored spies, had gone to great lengths to set Vreva up as the proprietor of the new social club. What better venue from which to spy on the Chelish navy. The immense Ostenso fleet and legendary naval shipyards were a constant threat to Andoran's young republic, and saber-rattling rival nations traded spies like fighting mastiffs traded fleas.

"Good." Torius waved Twilp forward, and the halfling approached. "We better hurry. I wasn't kidding about the tide. Half an hour and you'll be wading back to the Two Pinches."

"I don't know why we couldn't do the exchange at my place." Vreva frowned at Twilp. "All this sneaking around is ridiculous."

"No, me walking into a public house crowded with Chelish military officers with stolen merchandise under my arm would be ridiculous." The halfling crossed his arms. "My risk, my rules."

"You got it, I presume." Vreva eyed him hopefully.

"I wouldn't be here if I hadn't." Twilp pulled a waxed canvas bag from beneath his jacket and withdrew a slim, leather-bound book secured with a locked brass clasp. "In fact, I'd probably be dead if you hadn't told me exactly how to find this thing. Even knowing where it was hidden, it was all I could do to find the secret catch for that compartment. Really top-notch job of concealment there."

"Thank you." Vreva had taken great pains to hide the journal.

"Quopek has a new tenant in your old suite, you know."

"Good. That means they've stopped looking for my hidden caches." Vreva held out a hand for the book.

"Um . . ." Twilp drew it back, his eyes narrowing. "The other half of my payment, please."

Vreva dropped her hand. "After I confirm it's genuine." Her fingers brushed the handle of the hand crossbow hidden beneath the frills of her dress. At this range, she could fire the weapon right through the material with little chance of missing. And with the poison she'd put on the bolt, she wouldn't have to hit anything vital. Of course, Torius might not react well if she murdered Twilp for her codebook, but she'd sleep with Asmodeus himself before she walked out of here without it. "That's what we agreed on."

"Oh, all right." Twilp held it out again. "But I'd be a fool to try to hand you a forgery."

"Yes, you would, but I'm not saying *you* would have forged it." Vreva took the book and examined it carefully. "If the Okeno slavers found it, they might have decoded my cipher and put a forgery in its place to throw me off." She withdrew the poisoned needle that would shoot out of the spine if a key—any key—was inserted into the lock, or the clasp forced. Only by removing the needle would the book open. Holding the deadly needle between her teeth, she flipped open the clasp.

"That was really trapped?" Twilp squinted at the dark stain on the needle and swallowed hard.

"I *told* you it was." Vreva flipped to the third page and scanned the text. The first two pages were gibberish to throw off any attempt at cracking the code. She decoded the first line, the cipher long committed to memory, and found it accurate. Three more dated entries that she remembered matched as well. Her detailed notes from five years of spying on the Okeno slavers had been recovered and were safe in her hands. With a deep sigh of relief, she smiled at Twilp. "It's genuine."

The halfling stuck out his hand. "Now, my money?"

"One moment." Vreva reset the trap, slipped the poisoned needle back in place, latched the priceless book, and handed it to Torius. He already had orders to deliver it to Marshal Helena Trellis, commander of the Twilight Talons in Almas. Withdrawing a small leather pouch from a pocket in her dress, she tossed it to Twilp. "The sum we agreed upon in mixed gems, though I don't think we have time now for you to appraise them."

He caught it easily and bounced it in his palm. "I'm not going to insult you by saying I trust you, but I *do* know where you live, so cheating me would be pretty stupid." The halfling tucked the bag away. "And you don't strike me as stupid. Crazy, maybe, but definitely not stupid."

"I've been called worse." In fact, Vreva had been called many things in her life—prostitute, poisoner, sorcerer, and spy, among others. Being called crazy was almost a compliment.

"By me, in fact." Torius laughed as he tucked the book under the belt of his trousers beneath his shirt, then looked down at the bulge under his clothes and cringed. "That needle won't go off by itself, will it?"

"Not unless you try to pick the latch while it's tucked in your pants." Vreva raised an eyebrow. "And if you can do *that*, I can put you to work at the Officers' Club!"

"No, thanks. My dance card's already full." His nose wrinkled with a look of disgust.

"By the way, how *is* Lothera Cothos?" Vreva might have sympathized with Torius's plight, fielding the amorous attentions of the brusque harbormaster every time his ship arrived in Ostenso, if she wasn't playing the same game with inebriated naval officers every day.

"Actually, she didn't meet us when we arrived this time." Torius's countenance brightened. "I'm hoping she's losing interest."

"I hope *not*!" Vreva didn't elaborate. Twilp didn't know Vreva and Torius were Twilight Talons, and she didn't want to provide any clues that might help him make the connection. Besides, Torius knew what she meant.

"We better get moving, sir." Grogul lifted the trapdoor.

"Right. Time and tide wait for no one, and I don't feel like getting my feet wet." Torius gestured Vreva forward. "Ladies first."

"Right." She cast her disguise spell again, adjusting her gait and mannerisms reflexively. From the expression on Twilp's face as he looked back and forth between her and Torius, she knew that her Abidi Ben Akhiri facade was perfect. She pitched her voice as closely as she could to match her disguise. "Who's going to escort me back to the Officers' Club? At this time of night a lone man's a target for cutthroats, and I'm no fighter. I need someone along who can wield a sword, or at least be a distraction long enough for me to cast a spell."

"Well, I can't if you're going to wear my face." Torius peered at her and shook his head. "I don't suppose you'd take my place the next time Lothera—"

"No, I will *not*! My disguise won't hold up under *that* kind of scrutiny. Grogul, can you come with me?"

"I'll go with you, if you want company," Twilp offered, rattling the pouch of gems in his pocket. "I'm not carrying your book anymore, and I'm feeling lucky."

Vreva thought for a moment, then nodded. She could do a lot worse than to have a light-fingered halfling around. Besides, she knew he was trustworthy, or at least, as trustworthy as a burglar could be. "All right, then, let's go. But I'll warn you, when we get back to the club, don't bet on black twice in a row on the wheel of chance. The table's rigged."

"You're admitting to *cheating* your customers?" Twilp stared at her in exaggerated shock.

"On the contrary. I find it brings in more customers if I arrange for certain talkative gamblers to win more than they might on their own." She shrugged. "Just good business."

"You're my kind of businesswoman, Virika!" Twilp started down the steps.

"Akhiri in this disguise, please. Don't confuse me. A slip could be lethal." Vreva turned back to Torius. "Be careful with that book. And try not to alienate the harbormaster." Lothera Cothos really was a valuable source of information. It was unbelievable luck that she had become enamored with Abidi Ben Akhiri, obsequious toad though he was.

"And you don't forget who you're impersonating on your way home, please." Torius hitched up his belt and winced. "If rumors start flying around about Akhiri, I'll know who to blame."

"Don't worry, Torius. I don't like being Akhiri any more than you do." She drew her dagger, cast her light spell on it once again, and followed her halfling companion down into the secret byways beneath Ostenso's wharves.

Celeste swayed her long serpentine body to the silent rhythm of the heavens. With every twinkle and pulse of the stars, the celestial song sang in her mind, her blood, her every muscle and sinew.

She could sense their hidden message, feel it surging through her veins, but she couldn't quite understand.

So close . . .

Still swaying with the song, the lunar naga stretched toward the skylight over her head. Her coils brushed aside the pillows arrayed on the cabin floor. She couldn't recline, couldn't simply relax and enjoy the view as she had so many thousands of nights before. Not when she was so close to understanding. Her tail flicked with her frustration. She felt as if the answer lay on the tips of her forked tongue, but she couldn't speak it.

Please . . . tell me . . .

Something intruded upon her reverie, a faint sound like the buzzing of an insect. Celeste ignored it. The stars' message hovered in her mind, a guiding light shrouded in fog. *Closer . . . Please . . .* She could almost feel it. A faint caress, a touch, a prod . . .

A sharp poke, and a shrill voice.

"Celeste! Wake up!"

"What?" Celeste twisted and reared back, flaring her upper body in preparation to strike.

"Hey! Careful! It's me!" Snick stepped back, her hands out in impotent defense.

"Sorry." Celeste eased her posture but couldn't fully relax, her coils still writhing in time to the celestial song humming in her veins. "I was just . . . thinking. You startled me." The lie fell haltingly from her lips. The truth was that she'd been utterly lost in the heavens, entranced, oblivious to her surroundings. *Not again.*

"No kidding." Snick glared as dangerously as a gnome with blue hair could glare. "You damn near bit my head off!"

"I said I was sorry. Next time, don't poke me!"

Celeste didn't mean to snap at Snick, but her inability to understand the celestial message frustrated her to no end. As with any lunar naga, she had been born a stargazer, but lately her fascination had become so intense that she would slip into a kind of waking dream, straining to understand the message she could almost hear, yet never quite grasp. These episodes were not only frustrating, but worrisome. During their recent passage from Almas, the trance had occurred almost every night, every time she gazed at the starry sky. Several times Torius, Grogul, or the first mate Thillion had to jostle Celeste out of her reverie to remind her to take a navigational fix.

"I only poked you because I knocked, then called your name three times, and you didn't answer. You were really lost." Snick peered up at the skylight. "I don't understand what's so interesting about the stars. They're the same ones every night, you know."

Celeste's tail twitched at the gnome's shrewish tone. Snick was in a foul mood, and the whole ship knew why. They'd just dropped off Twilp Farfan, and Snick was already pining. Celeste considered pointing out that they'd be back in Ostenso in a month, and the gnome could renew her fling with the flighty halfling then, but expecting Snick to listen to logic would do no good.

"Instead of telling me my infatuation with the heavens is silly, why don't you tell me why you're here, Snick?"

"Oh, well, it's the harbormaster. She's here."

"Lothera Cothos?" Just saying the woman's name made Celeste's tail quiver in irritation. Every time they arrived in Ostenso, the harbormaster blustered aboard and ordered Torius away to her villa for the evening. She didn't even look at the ship's forged papers anymore, just greeted him, gave him that look, and told him to expect her carriage that evening. Then Torius would go off to be with her.

They never spoke of what happened, but Torius was always upset when he returned. He usually spent the rest of the evening drinking. Celeste knew he was having sex with Lothera—her sense of smell was too keen to miss it—but she could say nothing against it. Not considering that the first time they'd sailed into Ostenso disguised as Thuvian merchants, she'd actually encouraged Torius to go with the harbormaster to avoid unwanted scrutiny. At the time, an evening's dalliance seemed a small price to pay to avoid trouble. Now it was part of the interminable spying they'd agreed to do for the Twilight Talons.

No. The spying that Torius *agreed to do.* She often cursed the day that Vreva Jhafae talked Torius into helping her spy on the Okeno slavers. The deceitful courtesan had neglected to mention that his role would involve joining the Twilight Talons until they were all in up to their necks.

Only *Stargazer*'s officers knew Torius's secret. As far as the rest of the crew was concerned, they were simply being paid to run information and supplies to Vreva, originally in Okeno, and now under their old disguises as Thuvian merchants in Ostenso. The sailors weren't stupid, and probably suspected some kind of cloak-and-dagger mischief, but they were all loyal, and the pay was good. As a bonus, they still hunted slavers under an Andoren letter of marque, albeit surreptitiously—but even that was a deception, a means for them to sail in and out of Almas. Celeste had to admit that it felt good, working to disrupt the vile machine of sentient-trafficking, but it also meant that she had to watch the man she loved leave her for the intimate company of another woman every month or so.

By the stars, I hate this sometimes . . .

Celeste shook off her fit of pique, and realized what Snick was saying. "Why are you coming to me about Lothera? Isn't Thillion back yet?"

"Nope. He's still out with that wine merchant, and probably won't be back until dawn. They were going to sample some northern reds, and you know how *that* goes. Sometimes I think that half-elf has wine running in his veins instead of blood. And before you ask: No, Torius and Grogul aren't back yet either."

"You mean *I* have to talk to her?" Celeste had never spoken with the woman before. Lothera had no interest in the ship's navigator, and Celeste liked it that way.

"Well, *someone* better talk to her, and she's not going to be satisfied with me." Snick plucked at the breast of her cabin-gnome outfit, her disguise while the ship was in Ostenso.

They all had their roles to play in this dangerous game. Just as *Stargazer* became the Thuvian merchant ship *Sea Serpent*, every member of her crew also had their alternate identities. If anyone identified them as the now-notorious *Stargazer*'s crew, their necks would all be in the same noose.

"But . . ." Celeste knew she could deal with the woman, but should she? She looked up at the skylight, wishing she could just go back to her stellar musing.

The song of the heavens roared in her mind, and a sudden feeling of confidence flushed through her, a sense of rightness. She *should* do this. There was nothing to worry about.

"Fine. I'll come on deck. Why is she here, anyway? We're already checked in."

"She's looking for Torius, of course. Or rather, Akhiri. You know what I mean. And she's *not* happy."

"Lothera's *never* happy."

"Yeah, what's she got to be *happy* about?" Snick's sarcasm lashed out like a full broadside. "She only controls every bit of merchant shipping in Ostenso. She's rich and powerful, and wields her influence like a blunt weapon. If *my* life was like that, I'm sure *I'd* be a surly bitch, too!"

"I'll be right out. Tell her I was sleeping." The lunar naga slithered to the closet and opened the door with a flick of simple magic so familiar that she didn't even have to think of the spell.

"I'll tell her, but don't dawdle. I don't think she likes me much." Snick hurried out.

Celeste scowled as she surveyed the contents of the closet. While in Ostenso, she couldn't freely share the master cabin with Torius. In her guise as *Sea Serpent*'s human navigator, Celeste bunked in the guest cabin, and that was where she kept most of the clothes that she only really needed when she used magic to take on human form. She dared not risk going to her cabin in her natural form—or worse, unclothed as a human—in case the harbormaster happened into the sterncastle. She floated a robe out of the closet.

Celeste cast the spell that transformed her into human shape. Arms detached themselves from her body, and her tail split into legs. Other than for making love to Torius, she used the spell primarily to interact with people outside the crew. Lunar nagas were rare, and drew too much attention and prejudice for her to slither about looking like herself. When she didn't have to touch anyone, she could use a simple illusion, but Cothos might want to shake her hand or something. Long practice made the transformation easy, but she took special care this time, for she wasn't assuming her more common human countenance. Her naturally pale skin and long, flowing white hair were too conspicuous to be seen in Ostenso.

The transformation complete, Celeste gazed into the mirror, right into the eyes of a dead woman.

The dusky skin, deep crimson hair, and incongruously light hazel eyes were hauntingly familiar. They had belonged to Cammy, a shipmate killed by an Osirian mercenary cecaelia more than a year ago. Celeste still remembered the startled look on Cammy's face as the spear pinned her to the deck. *So many friends dead and gone.* The life of a pirate wasn't safe, and those of privateers and spies were no better. Celeste had little doubt that more friends would die in the course of their work for the Andoren abolitionists. She believed in what they were doing, but the lies within lies that they were all forced to weave sometimes wore on her.

Will we ever be done with it?

No answer came to her. She would just have to deal with her misgivings and play her part. Shaking off her morose thoughts, she slipped into the robe and left the cabin. She locked the door behind her, then walked past the silent galley and her own cabin to the door onto the deck. She cinched the robe tight, rubbed her eyes and mussed her hair, and strode forth to lie yet again.

Lothera stood just abaft the hatch to the main hold, arms crossed, a look of profound displeasure on her hard, angular features. She glared over the top of Snick's head at the crowded harbor, ignoring the fuming gnome. Scores of ships, most of them Chelish naval vessels, lay at anchor or docked around the protected bay. Anchor lanterns swayed atop the innumerable masts like constellations of low-hanging stars as the ships rolled on the gentle swell. This was the harbormaster's own personal fiefdom, but she scowled upon it with a mien of contempt.

"Harbormaster Cothos." Celeste curtseyed and made a show of straightening her hair. "Please forgive my appearance. I was asleep. How can I help you?"

"*You're* the navigator?" Cothos raked her from head to foot with her eyes.

"Yes, ma'am. Celeste." She curtsied again. "I'm sorry, but the captain and first mate are off the ship."

"Yes, this . . . menial told me that Captain Akhiri was away." The harbormaster didn't even look at Snick, which was just as well. The murder on the gnome's face would have probably started a fight. "Where is he this late at night?"

"I don't know, ma'am." Celeste shrugged helplessly. "He didn't tell me where they were going. I'd be happy to give him a message for you."

Lothera pursed her lips for a moment, and one eyebrow arched slowly. "I'll leave him a note." Without further explanation, she strode for the sterncastle door.

Unable to stop the woman—angering the harbormaster would certainly make their task here more difficult—Celeste could do nothing but follow. In fact, Lothera's strides were so long that she had to hurry to catch up. The harbormaster's progress halted at the locked cabin door, however. She rattled the handle so hard that Celeste was afraid she'd break it off.

"Damn it! I forgot that Abidi keeps his cabin locked."

"Not to worry, ma'am. Let me get that for you." Celeste fished the key from the robe pocket and worked it in the latch.

"You have a key to the captain's cabin?"

"All the officers do, ma'am." Celeste opened the door, and stepped inside to wave the harbormaster in, offering a weak smile. "If something should happen, we might need to get to his charts."

"I see." Lothera strode past her to the chart table strewn with Celeste's books, instruments, star charts, and astrological tables. Lothera reached for a sheet of blank parchment, then stopped and turned to Celeste. "If you're the navigator, why are the navigational instruments here? Shouldn't they be in *your* cabin?" The suspicion in the harbormaster's voice was thick enough to cut with a knife.

"Oh, those are the captain's instruments, ma'am." Celeste ducked her head disarmingly and waved toward the beautiful silver sextant that Torius had bought her. "I could never afford such fine tools. He lets me use them, of course."

"Of course." Lothera snatched the pen from the inkwell and scrawled a note on the page in her hand. After signing, she straightened and looked around the cabin. Her eyes narrowed as they settled on the nest of pillows beneath the skylight. "And what else does the captain let you use?"

"I'm sorry, ma'am?" Celeste followed her gaze and cursed herself for leaving her things out, but she hadn't thought the harbormaster would insist on coming to the cabin.

"The captain's pillows are misplaced. The last time I was here, they were stored in that nook beneath the stern gallery windows." Lothera picked up one of the astrological texts. She glanced at the open page, then looked back to Celeste, accusation plain in her eyes. "And I don't recall Abidi ever telling me he had an interest in *astrology*."

"He doesn't, ma'am. The books and the tables are mine." She shrugged, feigning nonchalance. "I was using the captain's telescope, a much finer instrument than my own, to view the planet Bretheda and her moons."

"So, you thought you'd lie back on his pillows in your *robe* to view the stars through the skylight in his cabin? Why not go outside?"

"I wasn't stargazing in my robe, ma'am." Celeste pulled her robe tightly closed. *Why is she so suspicious of me?* "I was using his telescope here because he doesn't allow me to take it up on deck when he's not around. It's very expensive, as you can see, and if something happened to it, I'd never be able to pay for it. As for the pillows . . ." It galled Celeste to have to deny her own possessions to this prying woman, but she bit back her anger and lied smoothly. ". . . well, they're more comfortable than lying on the cabin sole."

"Oh, really?" Lothera glared at her.

"Yes, ma'am." Turning, she grabbed the pillows and shoved them into their customary place. *Enough of this nonsense.* Celeste knew one way for certain to quell the woman's surly attitude. Mumbling a spell beneath her breath that would ease the harbormaster's mind, she tucked the last pillow in place. "I'm sorry, ma'am, but I don't understand why you're upset with me. If you don't believe me, you can confirm what I've said with Captain Akhiri when you see him next."

"Oh, I *will*. You can count on it." She rolled up the note as if it offended her and started searching around the chart table.

Celeste concentrated to make sure her spell had taken effect. The woman's mind seemed to be under the influence of her magic, but she wasn't acting very friendly. "Can I help you with something else?"

"Yes. A length of ribbon or string to tie this up."

"Here, ma'am." She brushed past Lothera to open the slim drawer under the chart table. Among the dividers, rulers, and rolled charts lay a spool of fine ribbon. She snipped off a length with a pair of scissors and held it out to the harbormaster.

Lothera snatched the ribbon and tied the rolled parchment so tightly that it crinkled the paper. Evidently, even charmed, Lothera Cothos remained brusque to the point of rudeness. Maybe some more assurance would help.

"Please, Mistress Cothos, let me assure you, there's nothing inappropriate about my being in the captain's cabin and using his telescope. He's given me permission."

"Has he, now?" Lothera dropped the note onto Torius's bunk. When she turned back, her face was set in a mask of hard planes, the muscles bunched at her jaw and her lips pressed in a thin line. "I'd like to believe you, Celeste, but let me tell you how this looks to me. You said you were sleeping, and I come here to find the lights turned low, the pillows placed, and you in naught but a robe. If this isn't a picture of seduction, I don't know what is!"

"Seduction!" So Lothera did suspect her. Celeste would have laughed out loud at the irony if the situation weren't so dangerous. "Mistress Cothos, let me assure you that nothing could be farther from the truth."

Lothera's skeptical scowl faded as the spell worked on her, soothing her ire and easing her fears. "Again, I'd like to believe you, but the evidence suggests otherwise. I will *not* be cuckolded by you, Celeste. Do you understand?"

"I understand perfectly, Mistress Cothos." If the charm spell had brought out Lothera's best, Celeste would hate to see her at her worst. "Rest assured, ma'am. Captain Akhiri isn't my type. Or, rather, I'm not his."

"Oh?" An eyebrow arched in question. "How so?"

"He prefers . . . strong women, ma'am, and I'm anything but that." She shrugged meekly and looked down. "He likes capable, powerful women like you. I'm afraid I don't have anything to offer him beyond my skills as a navigator, so you have nothing to worry about."

"Then why were you here in your robe?" There was still a hint of suspicion there.

"I wasn't. I did some stargazing, then went to bed. I forgot to put my books and the pillows back. That's all."

"I see." The harbormaster bit her lip. "I seem to have made a fool of myself."

"Not at all." Celeste smiled disarmingly as she gestured toward the door. "Your suspicions were based on the evidence you saw, and they show you have feelings for the captain. I can't blame you in the slightest."

"You won't . . . tell him I made such a scene, will you?" The spell was obviously working on her fully now, for Lothera to ask a favor.

"Oh, of course not. I'll just tell him you were concerned that he wasn't here. He'll be flattered." Celeste followed Lothera from the cabin and relocked the door. When she turned back, the harbormaster was giving her a very curious look.

"I . . . didn't mean to be accusative, you know. In my line of work you learn to suspect the worst of people."

That was the weakest apology Celeste had ever heard, but she smiled and took it for what it was worth, a charm-induced admission of lousy social skills. "I understand completely."

The corners of the harbormaster's mouth twitched upward in something that might have been a momentary smile. Then the expression passed. Lothera nodded, turned on her heel, and left without another word.

Celeste waited until she heard the night watch usher the harbormaster off the ship before returning to the cabin. Shrugging off the robe and hanging it in the closet, she dispelled her transformation and coiled back into her familiar form. A deep breath helped to settle her nerves, still jangling from her efforts to deal graciously with Lothera. She didn't envy Torius having to associate with the woman on a close personal basis. Not in her wildest imagination could she picture the two of them being intimate.

Which is just as well. If I ever did imagine Torius having sex with that woman, I'd probably bite them both.

2

Whispers in the Dark

Torius stepped out of Lothera Cothos's carriage, tugged his dress jacket straight, and steeled his nerves. He looked up at the classically hewn Chelish architecture of her villa and thought he would rather face a broadside from the biggest warship in the harbor than step through those doors.

The villa stood upon the crest of the Custodisce Break, a rocky peninsula that jutted a half mile into the Inner Sea, creating a protective arm that sheltered Ostenso's deep inner harbor. From its vantage, the house commanded views of both the open sea to the east and the city and bay to the west.

Ostenso framed the bay like a pair of cupped hands. The vast Chelish naval works dominated the western shore with its shipyards and supply houses, mills and smithies, quays and piers. The more modest city docks huddled on the northern shore, near the city's center of commerce. The wharves there were lined with chandleries and warehouses, as well as pubs and more elaborate establishments to entertain transient sailors.

With the darkening evening, lights had begun to flicker to life both ashore and among the anchored and docked ships. Torius did a quick count of the warships, more out of reflex than any need to verify what they already knew from an earlier survey. Eight first-rates, a score of line-of-battle ships, and swarms of accompanying frigates and galleons packed the harbor so tightly that little room remained for merchant shipping. In fact, one of the first-rates sat squarely upon the commercial pier with two frigates moored alongside. That was unusual, as the military generally kept to its own area, both for security and to minimize the impact of the naval presence on trade.

The Chelish navy had burgeoned in recent years, and the naval shipyards continued to launch warship after warship. Vreva monitored the strength, complement, armament, and state of readiness of the fleet, and Torius relayed those reports to Almas. She also kept track of the nearshore and offshore squadrons that continuously patrolled the sea-lanes along the border with Andoran, the squadrons that Torius took great pains to avoid on his circuitous trips between Ostenso and Almas. Torius finished his count: two more ships than they had counted earlier that very day.

Is something brewing, or is it just more saber rattling?

"Abidi!"

Torius turned to find Lothera standing in the door of her villa, hands on her hips. She was backlit from within, so he couldn't see her face, but he knew it was fixed in a scowl. Rarely were her features ever *not* fixed in a scowl, glare, or some other mien of discontent. He re-girded his nerves and went to her.

"A very good evening to you, Lothera." Torius assumed the rolling Thuvian accent and obsequious manner of Abidi Ben Akhiri as easily as picking up a familiar sword. Pausing to bow at the foot of the three shallow steps, he painted on a doting smile. "Thank you for the invitation. I'm sorry I wasn't aboard *Sea Serpent* to receive it personally."

Her "invitation" had consisted of exactly a dozen words: "Dinner at my villa tomorrow. My carriage will retrieve you at sunset." *Retrieve, like a stick thrown for a playful dog . . .*

Torius climbed the steps to the pillar-framed entry and saw that his presumption had been correct. Her face was set in the hard, humorless expression he had come to know all too well. Forgoing the chainmail and sword she wore when on duty, Lothera always dressed in a gown when he visited. Tonight's was deep blue embroidered with gold, sporting short sleeves and a slim waist. Though the clothes made her look more feminine, Lothera wore even the prettiest attire like armor, and exuded all the charm of a cavalry regiment.

"Where were you?"

And all the subtlety, too. Celeste had told him of the harbor-master's late-night arrival, her displeasure at his absence, and her supposition that the navigator and captain were having an affair under her nose. That didn't bode well for the night's mood, but months of association had taught him how to deal with Lothera, and Torius had already prepared himself to diffuse her displeasure.

"Business, my sweet Lothera." He shrugged in helpless acqui-escence. As with most dominant personalities, surrender yielded better results than confrontation. "A merchant captain's duties are never done. When I didn't see you upon our arrival, I assumed you had plans for the evening and endeavored to conduct my business quickly so I would have tonight free to spend with you."

"Business?" She looked skeptical. "So late at night?"

"Alas, when one deals with wine merchants, one must partake of their wares."

"So you were out drinking."

"Tasting, yes, and I woke with a thick head as a result." He shrugged again and glanced around at the porch. "Could we step inside so that I can apologize properly for not being aboard to greet you as I wished?"

"Oh, I suppose, though I ought to make you stand out here for making me deal with that strumpet of a navigator of yours." She turned partway and extended a hand to him. "She was parading around your ship in naught but a flimsy robe, you know! You ought to be careful about her."

"Oh, I am *very* careful about Celeste, my dear."

Wondering how Celeste would react to being called a strumpet, Torius bent low to kiss Lothera's hand, then walked with her into the lofty entrance hall. As the thick carpet of Qadiran silk muffled their footfalls, a silent butler closed the front door behind them. The light that had spilled out the door shone down from a chandelier wrought of gold and a thousand multihued crystals enchanted with magical light. The walls, papered with thick brocade of deep blue accented with gold, matched her dress perfectly. What Lothera lacked in poise, she made up for with money, and though her personal sense of decor and fashion might be wanting, she had the sense to hire the best decorators and tailors that her considerable fortune could afford.

"I admonished her just the other day for leaving my navigational instruments and her ridiculous astrological books lying about on my chart table, but she seems incapable of cleaning up after herself." He sighed despondently. "If she weren't such a good navigator, I'd have dismissed her long ago."

"You *should* let her go." Lothera cast him a look of suspicion, tightening her grasp on his hand. "She seems like the type to take advantage of your generosity. You didn't even *have* a navigator when we first met."

"Yes, but I discovered that my own skills were rather lacking when we were blown off course by a storm some months ago, and I found myself halfway to the Arch of Aroden by mistake." They walked past the double doors of the dining room, but Lothera didn't pause. Torius suppressed a twinge of worry as she led him to the wide, marble-balustered stairs. "Are we not having dinner, my dear?"

"On my balcony." She mounted the stairs without pause. "The night's pleasant, and the view is . . . well, you can look out over your beloved ocean."

"How very thoughtful of you."

She looked at him almost as if she thought he was mocking her, but then looked away. She seemed distracted, as if something other than the incident with Celeste had piqued her. Lothera wasn't the type to hold back where her temper was concerned, so he suspected it had nothing to do with him. That meant it had to do with her job, for little else occupied the harbormaster's mind. That, of course, was one trait that made her such a good source of information. It took little to set Lothera ranting on about the tribulations of her position, her lack of authority over the movement of naval ships, and the continued disrespect levied at her by the admiralty. Torius recalled the crowded harbor, and planned a simple conversation in his mind. A little sympathy and subtle prompts usually yielded an outpouring of useful details.

They entered the familiar sitting room of Lothera's suite, tastefully adorned with a mahogany breakfast table, gilded chairs, divans, coffee tables, ornate credenzas, and sideboards. They strode through a pair of glass-paned doors and out onto the wide balcony. Pale glow crystals set in sconces beside the door and along the railing provided diffuse and, he had to admit, romantic lighting that gleamed off of the porcelain, silver, and crystal of the table set for two. The sea breeze wafted across the expanse of marble in fragrant eddies, and he breathed deep, unable to suppress a smile.

"Very nice."

"I thought you'd prefer it." She released his hand and strode to the table. "Wine?"

"Please." Lothera usually had two or three servants hovering in the dining room, ready to fulfill their every need, but tonight they were alone on the balcony and she was pouring the wine herself. This was not usual, and put Torius on alert for trouble. He strolled to the table and accepted his glass from her. "Are you all right, my dear? You seem troubled."

"Do I?" She quaffed a third of her glass of wine and scowled. "I'm that easy to read?"

"Not at all." He reached out and touched her shoulder with a well-learned gesture of concern, careful not to seem too inquisitive. "But I've come to know you quite well. I can tell when something's bothering you."

She glanced down at his hand, then into his eyes. "You're very observant, Abidi." Turning, she waved a hand toward the harbor. "The reason I couldn't meet your ship yesterday sits right there at the main pier. The *Devil's Trident*, a gods-damned *flagship*, no less, and the navy's not paying a single gold sail for dockage. I could put *three* merchantmen in that space, and I'm not being compensated for it at all!"

"That hardly seems fair." The prompt brought her around so fast wine slopped over the edge of her glass.

She cursed, changed hands, and drained her glass, then snatched up the bottle of wine. "Not only is it not *fair*, it's impeding trade and usurping my authority! I had to sit and smile at a gods-damned admiral all afternoon, and listen to him yammer on about 'the good of queen and country,' and how 'the needs of Her Infernal Majestrix outweigh those of simple merchants.'" She filled her glass, banged down the bottle, and took another long swallow. "It made me want to *vomit*!"

"I can't blame you for being put out." Torius had also learned that Lothera became mean and demanding when she drank too much. In the interest of self-preservation, he put his glass down and took her hand, kneading it tenderly to ease the strain there, and brought it to his lips. "But I'm here to take your mind from these problems. Am I not?"

"Yes." She stared down at their conjoined hands, then gave him a disconcerting look. "You understand what the constant interference from the admiralty does to my position here. People laugh about the harbormaster who isn't the master of her own harbor. It's like I'm a damned *servant* or something!"

"No one is laughing, Lothera." Torius had discovered early in life that people who wielded power lived in constant fear of losing it. "Let's have a nice, relaxing dinner, and you can tell me about this pompous prig of an admiral."

"Dinner can wait." Lothera downed the rest of her wine and slammed the glass down so hard the stem broke. She let it go and the glittering glass rolled off the table to shatter on the stone balcony.

Uh-oh, Torius thought. He'd seen her like this before, and it didn't bode well.

"I need you to distract me, Abidi." Her strong fingers grasped his belt and pulled him close, her urgent, husky whisper scented with wine and stale cigar smoke. "I need you to remind me that there's more to my life than dealing with posturing admirals and cocksure commodores."

"I can do that." Torius summoned an easy smile, knowing there was no forestalling her. Saying no to Lothera was like saying no to a summer squall. It would come anyway, and seem twice as violent for every ounce of resistance. *Best to reef sails and run before the wind . . .*

"Good!" Her smile showed little real affection. In fact, it reminded him of a hyena he'd once seen closing in on an injured camelopard calf.

What we do with our bodies need not reflect what we feel in our hearts, he reminded himself as Lothera drew him into a violent kiss, thrusting him against the balcony rail. The hard stone met with the small of his back, and he stifled a yelp of pain. He'd have a bruise there in the morning. Torius loathed this part of his job more than any other, but training and practice had taught him how to deal with it. He focused his mind on a pleasant image of shining platinum hair and pale, soft skin . . .

Celeste . . .

And did his duty.

Admit it, you love this place. Mathias nuzzled Vreva's shoulder from his perch on the second-floor balustrade.

"Love it?" Leaning on the rail, Vreva swept her eyes over the main floor of the Officers' Club.

As a nod to the principally naval clientele, the V-shaped bar jutted like the prow of a ship into a sea of tables. Four bartenders served libations from all around the Inner Sea, from mugs of cheap local ale to goblets of pricy Irriseni icewine, or for those flush with coin and an appetite for the exotic, a thimbleful of top-shelf pesh brandy imported from Katapesh.

On the stage above and behind the bar, ladies in frilly skirts and men in snug trousers danced in a chorus line. An imp fluttered toward one of the men and tucked a gold sail deep into the dancer's pocket, then winged back to the shoulder of a Chelish captain at the bar. The imp spoke into his mistress' ear, pointing at the bulge of coins in the dancer's pocket, and the two of them laughed. The dancer leered and blew a kiss.

Even higher, above the stage, huge gilded letters hung from the lofty rafters, the name of the club rendered in gold-painted splendor. A beautiful woman sat within the "O", swinging and kicking her heels in a flutter of skirts. A gaggle of junior lieutenants took turns tossing silver coins to her. Snatching one of the coins from the air, she flipped down and hung by her knees to bestow a kiss on the skillful tosser. Her skirts turned out like a frilly white flower, exposing long, garter-clad legs and eliciting a cheer from the throng of officers.

Another cheer went up and bells rang out from the gambling pit as someone won a game of chance. Vreva breathed in the heady fog of pesh smoke, perspiration, a dozen varieties of alcohol, and a hundred colognes and perfumes, simultaneously cloying and exhilarating—and smiled.

Here at the Officers' Club, Chelish formality and order broke down into bawdy revelry. Here, naval officers, merchant captains, and an occasional member of the noble aristocracy came to play. And Vreva had made it all happen. She'd transformed a dilapidated warehouse into the most popular club in the district. It was all hers.

"Yes, I love it a little." She scratched her familiar under the chin. She had no fear that anyone would hear them above the din, and even if someone used magic to eavesdrop, none could understand their private language. They had long practice at carrying on covert conversations, and anyone close enough to notice would only think a doting pet owner was whispering nonsense to her cat. "And it's finally starting to pay off. Word is that the Gray Corsairs intercepted that galleon full of slaves being delivered to Absalom on the information we provided."

Excellent! Mathias licked his whiskers and lashed his tail.

The thought of the deadly Gray Corsairs, Andoran's elite naval arm, swooping down on a hapless slave ship made all Vreva's work worthwhile. The only good slaver, in Vreva's opinion, was one that had passed through the digestive system of a shark. "By the way, do you have any good gossip for me?"

Mathias twitched his tail and yawned widely, teeth gleaming. *Nothing yet tonight, but I did finally catch that rat that's been gnawing on the linens. I left him at the foot of your bed.*

"Thanks *so* much!"

All part of the service. He nuzzled her shoulder again, purring loudly.

Vreva quirked a smile at his enthusiasm. Whereas her late beloved familiar, Saffron, had been spoiled and refined, Mathias was always up for a scrap with a rival tomcat or a wharf rat that weighed almost as much as he did. What was more, he truly enjoyed his work. Most public houses had cats to keep the vermin under control, especially this close to the docks, so no one thought twice when Mathias meandered beneath tables and chairs. Nobody had a clue that he was actually eavesdropping on conversations, picking up juicy tidbits of gossip like fat little mice, which he then delivered to his mistress. He was a fighter, a survivor, and loyal to a fault. She loved him dearly, but he wouldn't let her get maudlin about it for one minute.

Mathias hopped down and sharpened his claws on a baluster. *I guess it's time to go to work!* He lashed his tail and trundled down the stairs, a streak of shadow lost in a forest of legs.

"Right." Vreva adjusted the low-cut bodice of her dress, assumed a confident smile, and descended the stairs with a haughty swagger and practiced bounce. "To work!"

She passed a couple on their way up the stairs, one of the club's ladies escorting a blushing young midshipman to one of the private rooms. Vreva gave the woman a smile, and received a covert wink in response. Her companion couldn't have been more than eighteen. The sailors seemed to get younger every day. *Or perhaps I'm just getting older . . .*

"Virika, my *darling*!" A portly officer met her at the bottom of the stairs, his face flushed scarlet from drink.

"Commodore Tiras!" Vreva offered her hand and he bowed to kiss it. "Enjoying yourself?"

"Immensely! But I'd enjoy myself more if you'd spend the evening with me." He leered and hitched up his trousers, though his bulging belly pushed them right back down.

"You've a warrior's appetites, Commodore!" She laughed, grasped his free hand to keep him from groping her, and leaned in to kiss his sweaty cheek. Tiras was a squadron commander, and she always got good information from him, but first she had to make her rounds. Fishing a golden chit from a pocket, she pressed it into his palm. "Duty calls. Perhaps later. Have a run at the gaming tables."

"You're tormenting me, Virika." He pocketed the chit and bowed, kissing her hand again. "I'll be back to claim my prize."

"Commodore! You make me blush!" Vreva pressed a hand to her breast and laughed easily. The chit would keep him occupied at the gaming tables for hours, and her pit bosses knew better than to let a commodore lose. She left him and worked her way through the throng, greeting people she recognized, introducing herself to a few flag officers she didn't know, and laughing at the antics of the gaggles of young officers eager to catch her eye.

If this keeps up, I'm going to have to hire more people.

The dancers finished their routine, and the fellow with the bulging pocket performed an astounding flip over the bar, landing next to the Chelish captain with the imp familiar. Vreva gave them a wide berth. She didn't like imps; they saw too much.

The trill of a flute and the flutter of pastel veils announced the next act. A pair of Qadiran dancers clad only in translucent silks tumbled onto the stage. Every eye in the room turned to take in this new spectacle, as the muscular man whirled his lithe companion in colorful arcs. In a country where it seemed like the height of culture was listening to a wailing opera or watching some poor wretch die in the abhorrent Theater of the Real, such tastefully sensual displays were a rarity.

Vreva used the distraction to scan the crowd, her gaze targeting epaulets and rank insignias. *Who should I—uh-oh.* One of her enforcers was striding purposefully toward her. From the look on his face, she knew something was wrong. Meeting him halfway, she leaned in close for his whispered message.

"Woman at the door asking for you. Says she's the harbormaster. She doesn't look happy."

"Lothera Cothos?" Vreva's eyes snapped to the door. There stood the woman herself, dressed in her customary surcoat emblazoned with the city crest over mail, sword at her hip.

Her garb suggested business, but she had no jurisdiction here, and from what Torius had told Vreva, the woman had no desire to socialize with naval officers. In fact, Lothera's eyes seethed with contempt as they swept the room.

Vreva patted her enforcer's shoulder. "Don't worry, Nonny. She never looks happy. I'll take care of it."

The mistress of the Officers' Club wound her way between the tables of men and women ogling the dancers, grateful for the distraction. Vreva knew that Torius had gone to Lothera's villa the previous evening, and couldn't imagine why the woman would be visiting her club. Regardless, she needed to keep her wits about her; the harbormaster wielded considerable power in Ostenso.

Her composure faltered, however, when she felt a compelling surge of urgency. Glancing casually around, she spied Mathias beneath a table, his tail lashing impatiently. He must have over-heard something interesting and wanted her to come over. Vreva sent him an empathetic nudge; she had more pressing concerns right now.

"Harbormaster Cothos." Vreva curtsied in precise deference to the woman's station and smiled disarmingly. "To what do I owe the pleasure of this visit?"

"*You're* Virika Korvis?" The harbormaster's eyes raked her from head to foot, lingering here and there.

"At your service." Years of spying had taught Vreva how to read people even without the aid of magic. She noted Lothera's flushed cheeks and the way her hand clenched the hilt of her sword. *A woman relying on strength to hide her insecurity, maybe*? Vreva could deal with that. "Can I help you in some way?"

"Yes." Lothera's eyes slipped past Vreva for a moment, swept the room, and she licked her lips, looking obviously discomforted. "This is a . . . personal matter."

"Of course." Vreva gestured toward the stairs. "If you'd prefer a private conversation, my chambers are just—"

"No!" The refusal came out loud enough to draw glances from nearby tables. Lothera noticed the attention and the muscles of her jaw clenched. "No, I don't want rumors to start flying around about me going to your chambers. I need to speak with you, but here will be fine."

"A secluded table, then?" Vreva gestured to a dimly lit corner booth far enough from the cacophony of the stage to allow some privacy, and not far from where Mathias still stalked about a table of officers. Maybe she could knock down two birds with the same arrow.

"Fine."

"This way, if you please." Vreva led the way, and Lothera followed, her boots pounding the floor as if it had offended her.

As they passed the bar, Vreva signaled one of the bartenders, who quickly dispatched a waiter with a bottle and two glasses. Another surge of urgency thrilled up Vreva's spine as they passed the table where Mathias was prowling. A group of lieutenants who were obviously well into their cups conversed in hushed tones. Mathias looked up at her with an *It's about time!* look in his eyes. She sent him a silent urge to be patient. She would have to deal with the harbormaster first, but there might be a way to find out what Lothera really wanted and eavesdrop on the lieutenants at the same time.

Vreva cast a silent spell and immediately felt the presence of dozens of minds around her. With the expertise of long practice, she narrowed her focus. By the time they reached the booth, she had sorted through the confusing background thoughts to pick out Lothera's.

"Please have a seat, Harbormaster Cothos." Vreva gestured toward one side of the booth and slipped into the other, which gave her a clear view of the lieutenants' table. *Perfect!* She caught a glimpse of Mathias under the table, rubbing up against one of the officers' legs as if begging for attention. "Can I offer you wine?"

"Yes, you can." Lothera unclipped her sword from her hip and leaned the heavy blade against the edge of the table before she slid into the padded seat. *I need a drink to deal with this.*

The waiter placed two glasses on the table and presented the bottle for inspection, a hearty Longacre red that was older than Vreva by a decade. She nodded, and he expertly drew the cork, filled their glasses, and slipped away.

Vreva smiled at her guest. "I must say, I'm surprised to see you in the club, Harbormaster."

"And why *wouldn't* I come here?" *How dare she suggest this place is too good for me!*

The pointed question and the clear thought behind it took Vreva by surprise, and she didn't like surprises. Torius had told her that Lothera was a blunt, strong, and commanding woman, not given to sentiment, and undaunted by virtually anything. Evidently, Vreva had been correct about the insecurity that lurked beneath the bluster. She made a mental note to let Torius know her discovery.

"Frankly, I didn't think you'd be interested." She waved at the uniformed patrons. "Most of my clientele haven't achieved your social standing, and I took you for a woman who would pursue more—" A cheer at the loss of one of the dancer's veils offered a timely comparison. "—shall we say, more *cultured* pursuits."

"Yes, well, *that's* true." Lothera glanced at the stage and looked away. "I don't usually frequent houses of frivolous debauchery."

"And frivolous debauchery is a specialty of the Officers' Club. Hence my surprise at your visit." Vreva sipped her wine, concentrating on the harbormaster's thoughts. The muddle of spiteful snippets—*strutting menials . . . rumors about me coming here . . . pompous tin soldiers*—offered little substance. "You're obviously here for some important reason, and you said it was personal. Please, how I can help you?"

Lothera frowned and sipped the wine. Her eyebrows rose in surprise at the rare vintage. *Is she trying to impress me with this?* The harbormaster's jaw clenched, and she looked up from her glass. *I've got to know if it's true.*

"A particular friend of mine, Captain Abidi Ben Akhiri of *Sea Serpent*, was one of your customers the night before last. I'd like to know why he was here."

So that's it! Someone must have noted Vreva in her Akhiri disguise coming and going from Vreva's chambers, and run to tell the harbormaster. Vreva had assumed the guise of Abidi Ben Akhiri on multiple occasions. Fortunately, she and Torius had long ago agreed on a pat excuse for the merchant captain's presence in the club. If anyone asked questions, they would have the same answer.

"Captain Akhiri was trying to impress one of the local wine merchants." Vreva raised her glass in emphasis. "He's quite a shrewd businessman, you know. He asked if he might reserve a private room."

"And this private room just happened to be your chambers."

"I had . . . other plans for the evening, and all of my other private rooms were booked, so I offered my own sitting room."

"I see." Lothera's eyes narrowed, her thoughts roiling with suspicion. "And you didn't . . . *entertain* him yourself?"

"A *merchant* captain?" Vreva laughed and shook her head. "No, my dear, I did not, and let me assure you that I do not *entertain* anyone under the rank of Commodore. I let Captain Akhiri use my chambers because we've known each other for years, and I owe him a debt of gratitude. He told me about the ripe opportunity for a club like this here in Ostenso. I made the investment, and it's paying off."

"Did he have anyone else attend him?"

"I don't know." Vreva lifted her wineglass and swirled the vintage within. She was walking a fine line here. She didn't want to damage the relationship between Akhiri and Lothera by suggesting that Akhiri might have been disloyal, but she also didn't want to relent too soon and make the harbormaster suspicious. *First, the stall.* "Harbormaster Cothos, I make it a rule not to confirm or deny any of my customers' activities while they're in my establishment. My livelihood relies on my discretion. You must understand what would happen to my business if I started gossiping about what passed between consenting adults behind closed doors."

"And *you* must understand that I'll not leave this place until I find out if my paramour is a whoremonger."

Vreva met the woman's hard stare with a careful mien of affront. It was all a ruse, of course. Allowing Lothera to intimidate her into telling of her lover's activities was nothing but a subtle manipulation. She sipped her wine, and put the glass down with exaggerated care, clenching her jaw in feigned exasperation. *Now, the capitulation.*

"Very well." She signaled for the waiter. When he arrived, Vreva said, "Send word for Kelipri."

"Yes, ma'am."

As the man hurried off, Vreva reached for the bottle. "More wine?"

Lothera drained her glass. "Please." *She should know better than to spar with me.*

Vreva refilled both glasses, thinking that she might achieve more here than to simply assuage the harbormaster's fears. She could help Torius in the bargain. "As I said, Captain Akhiri and I have known each other for years. I know the type of woman he likes, and it didn't surprise me when he said you and he had gotten together."

"He *told* you about me?" The wine rippled in the harbormaster's glass. *I'll be a laughingstock!*

"Nothing personal, I assure you. He simply asked me for some advice."

"Advice about what?" Vreva didn't need a spell to read the suspicion in Lothera's eyes.

"He has a weakness for women who . . . well, women such as you are. He simply . . . sometimes feels that you don't appreciate him."

"He *told* you that?" Lothera's thoughts roiled. *Next he'll be telling her how I am in bed!*

"Please." Vreva held up a hand in a forestalling gesture. "Try to understand his point of view. He enjoys his time with you, there's no *doubt* about that, but he can only visit once every few weeks, and each time he's summoned to your villa in a coach." She shrugged and looked at the harbormaster. "How would *you* feel?"

"I don't *summon* him!"

"No?" Vreva shrugged again. "Take the advice of a woman who knows men, my dear. Their egos are easily bruised. Sometimes a little coddling can yield untold riches."

"So, I should—" Lothera broke off as a dark-skinned gnome approached the table and bowed, her broad-brimmed, pink-tasseled hat cocked jauntily atop shocking chartreuse hair.

"You sent for me, ma'am?"

"Yes, Kelipri. I'd like to know if Captain Akhiri and his friend had any private entertainment when they were in my chambers the night before last."

"None, ma'am. They ordered wine, that's all."

"Thank you, Kelipri."

The gnome bowed and left.

Lothera stared down into her wineglass.

I'm such an idiot! Vreva heard clearly. She almost felt sorry for Lothera, but this chink in the woman's armor was simply too good to pass up. Played carefully, she could help Torius immeasurably.

"If you'd like to know anything else about Captain Akhiri, I suggest you ask him directly. He'll appreciate your concern. And if I might make a suggestion, treating him a little more like a man and less like a convenience might help."

"I do *not* treat him like a . . ." Lothera's voice faltered, and she gulped wine. *Do I?* "I didn't know he thought that of me."

"And you did *not* learn it from me!" Vreva's laugh brought the woman's eyes up. "Remember what I said about my business.

If word got out that I was telling secrets, I'd be ruined. I'm not your social equal, but I do know men. I hope you take my advice to heart."

"I will." The harbormaster downed her wine, stood, and clipped her sword to her belt. "Thank you for speaking frankly with me. I'm afraid I tend to come on too strong sometimes."

"You're simply forthright. I appreciate that." Vreva stood and held out her hand. "If you'd ever like to just talk about Akhiri . . ."

When Hell gets snow! Lothera's smile looked as false as the sentiment behind it. She took Vreva's hand and very nearly broke bones with her grip. "I may someday, but I'm a little uncomfortable talking about . . . such things."

"I understand." Vreva reclaimed her hand, and was startled to hear, *She's nicer than I thought she'd be.* She curtsied appropriately and hid a smile. "Goodnight, Harbormaster Cothos."

"Goodnight, Madame Korvis." Lothera gave a stiff bow, turned on her heel, and stalked off.

Oh, Torius, you poor, poor man . . . Vreva had dealt with enough clients like Lothera to know what he was putting up with, and felt an honest pang of regret for bringing him into this in the first place.

Vreva sat back down, topped up her glass, and turned her attention to the table of drunken lieutenants. A glance confirmed that Mathias still lurked under the table. Good—he could fill her in on whatever she'd missed of the spoken conversation. The thoughts came fast and furious, and Vreva matched each with a face.

He's such a whiner! Complaining just makes it worse. If I were posted to the flagship, I'd make the best of it.

So ask for reassignment, you pampered wimp! Another lieutenant downed his ale and waved to the waiter for another round.

Vreva focused on the fellow they seemed to be listening to. Young, well bred, and obviously discontent from the stream of disrespectful thoughts of his commander, Admiral Ronnel, that passed through his mind.

Vreva knew of Admiral Ronnel, of course, though she'd never met him. He commanded the Chelish fleet in Ostenso, and held a minor title to boot. He hadn't ever been in the club. Vreva's mind-delving spell lapsed, and she immediately recast it, sitting back and gazing at the wine in her glass while focusing on the disgruntled young lieutenant.

I should have known better! Apply for a post on the flagship, Father said. Old man Ronnel will treat you right, he said. Now I'm nothing but a babysitter for that filthy Kellid witch and her weapon!

Weapon? Vreva swirled her wine. *That's interesting. And a Kellid witch on board a flagship is unusual.* Though the Chelish navy employed numerous arcane casters, witches included, they generally preferred to work with those sworn to Asmodeus, the devil-god. The Chelish also harbored a firm dislike of Kellids, whom they thought of as uncouth savages. Vreva had seen the prejudice herself when she was a girl in Egorian. Though Vreva didn't share their disdain—in her opinion, the nomadic Kellids were simply a hard people shaped by a hard land—she also knew that Kellids distrusted magic, which made a Kellid witch that much more unusual. Perhaps she'd been exiled by her tribe.

The junior officers' thoughts had wandered to assignments, orders, duties, punishments, and every sailor's continual gripe— navy food. There was no more about witches or weapons, and Vreva wasn't about to stoop to covertly interrogating junior lieutenants. They might talk too much, but they rarely knew details. Vreva shook her head and ended her spell.

No. I'll set my sights higher, I think. She finished her wine and rose from the table.

Once again fixing a welcoming smile on her face, Vreva circulated through the room, greeting and chatting with patrons. Something rubbed up against her leg, and she felt an empathic

rush of pleasure. She reached down to scratch Mathias affection-
ately behind the ears.

"Well done, my love," she whispered in their secret language.

So, you heard all that? he purred in reply.

"I heard enough. We'll compare notes later."

Right. Mathias stopped suddenly, whiskers twitching.
I smell a rat! He dashed off into the crowd, tail high, darting
between legs like a deer through a forest.

Vreva didn't worry about Mathias. He was more than a match
for any rat in the district. Continuing her rounds of the club, she
greeted and gossiped and complimented, but her mind wasn't on
the work at hand. All the while, she wondered about what might
be going on aboard the Chelish flagship. Why would the navy
contract a Kellid witch, and what kind of weapon might one wield?
There was one obvious way she could find out, but that brought
up another question: how could she lure Admiral Vaetus Ronnel
into her clutches?

3

Prophecy and Deception

Water as dark as a devil's soul slipped past *Stargazer*'s hull. The hiss of foam, creak of wood, and occasional flap of canvas would have been soothing to Celeste if not for the low scudding clouds that blocked the moon and stars. She felt stifled, as if a blanket of ignorance had been pulled over her head. Even the steady, familiar scuff of Torius's boots as he paced the quarterdeck couldn't assuage her frazzled nerves.

Without the stars, I'm blind.

They were following their usual indirect route to Almas, first sailing southeast toward Osirion to avoid any encounter with the Chelish navy, but had yet to make their turn northeast toward their true destination. Unfortunately, with the continuous low overcast, Celeste had been unable to accurately fix their position for several days. She only knew that they were approaching the Garund coast. Dead reckoning put them somewhere north of the Alamein Peninsula, but without the stars, her estimate could easily be off by fifty miles. Even if they missed the peninsula itself, such an error could put them on the unforgiving rocks of the Coast of Graves.

Who names places like that? She stared southward and saw nothing but blackness. Where was the light at Djedefar? *Could the monks have let it go dark for some reason?* Celeste tried to keep her tail from twitching. Generations of mariners had used the light of the tower for navigation—not because it was a designated lighthouse, but because monks faithful to Irori kept the Stepped Tower lit for their own inscrutable reasons. Had she missed some significant date or convergence of the stars that would signify a darkening of the beacon? Not seeing the stars for two days was bad enough. Approaching an unseen shore only made her more nervous.

Torius paused behind her, so close she could taste his intimately familiar scent on her sensitive tongue. The brush of his hand along her smooth scales eased her anxiety a little.

"Don't worry, love. The mercury in the weatherglass has been rising since sunset. The stars will show themselves soon." The confidence in Torius's voice might have been affected, but it was welcome."

"Right now I'm more worried about rocks than stars. I hate approaching a shore in the dark with no solid navigational fix."

"It's quiet enough to hear surf from a mile off, and we can tack in a heartbeat if we spot the shore. I just want to get a solid position fix so we can set a proper course."

"I know." Without the stars, a sighting of shoreside landmarks was the only sure way to know where they were. "It concerns me that we haven't seen the light of the Stepped Tower. If there's fog on the coast—"

"There!" Torius pointed low on the eastern horizon. "A break in the clouds."

Celeste caught sight of a single star glimmering to the east through the overcast for a moment before it vanished. More gaps in the clouds gave tantalizing glimpses of the heavens, but were too fleeting to distinguish constellations or identify individual stars. Celeste glanced at the rack of hour and minute glasses she used to keep time, and quickly calculated where the planets would be in the sky. Those she could identify even without constellations, but none of them shone through the overcast yet.

Bretheda, Verces, Castrovel . . . where are you, my dears?

Celeste floated up her silver sextant in preparation. All she needed was a clear sighting on two of the three planets, and she would have their position.

"There!" She caught sight of Bretheda and raised her sextant to take a sighting.

A glint of red light on the instrument's polished silver caught her eye. At first she thought it was a reflection of the lamp from the binnacle compass, but the helm was behind her, blocked by her body. Lowering the sextant, she stared into the darkness, scanning the invisible horizon from windward to leeward. *Nothing. What the . . .* Then she looked up. A faint glow pulsed red through the thick, low clouds directly in front of the ship. Even as she opened her mouth to cry out a warning, the color shifted to purple, and Celeste knew exactly what it was.

"Torius! The Hor-Aha light!"

At the same moment, the lookout shouted down, "Light off the port bow! Up in the clouds!"

The Hor-Aha tower loomed out of the heavy mist not four ship-lengths ahead. Deadly stonework soared hundreds of feet high, a line of white surf frothing about the razor-sharp rocks at its base.

"Wear ship!" Torius thundered. "Sheet in the main! Man the braces!"

"Helm's hard astarboard!" Windy Kate called out as she hauled the big wheel over.

The crew responded like a well-oiled machine. Feet pounded down the deck, and callused hands pulled frantically on lines. Surf rumbled over black rocks a stone's throw off the port side. The deck leveled briefly as *Stargazer* turned downwind, then the heavy mainsail boom swept overhead with a lurch, and the deck heeled sharply to port as they rounded to the north. The rack of finely calibrated sand glasses and the small leather bag with Celeste's instruments started to slide toward the edge of the deck. She snatched the bag up with magic, and slithered to block the heavier rack of sand glasses with her coils.

As the brigantine steadied on her new course, slipping easily through the sea once again, Celeste watched Hor-Aha's lurid red shift to deep purple, then vanish into the mists in the ship's wake. The ancient lighthouse had once served as a navigational aid and warning for pending storms to Osirian ships, but the light had gone dark ages ago. Only recently had the light renewed, though it now only showed red and purple, the chromatic code for violent gales. Rumors about haunts and curses abounded, and the weather and currents around the spire were unnatural and unpredictable.

"Well, *that* was close." Torius plucked the rack of sand glasses from Celeste's coils and put it down on the upwind side of the quarterdeck. Nervous laughter sounded around the middeck as the crew settled from the near catastrophe.

"Too close." She put her bag of instruments down beside the rack, and glared down at the chart she'd pinned to the deck. "We're forty miles *east* of where I had us plotted. There must have been a countercurrent off the Alamein Peninsula that pulled us off course."

"Don't fret about it. I told you we could turn in a heartbeat." Torius caressed her scales and smiled.

Celeste fought to still her pounding heart as she looked to the east. More stars winked in the sky along the horizon as the overcast broke up. "Of course, *now* I can get sightings, since I no longer need them." She snatched a pencil out of her bag and marked an X on the chart right next to the symbol representing the ancient lighthouse.

"Gozreh's luck." Torius brushed her cheek with the back of his knuckles. "Good eye spotting the light."

"Thank you." Celeste smiled and leaned into the caress. Between her lover's touch and the stars now twinkling overhead, her stress slowly ebbed away. She drew a deep, calming breath and gazed skyward.

"After days of clouds, it's no wonder you're tense . . ." Torius pulled her close. "I'll leave you to enjoy the stars. We're headed for open sea, so I won't need a fix for the rest of my watch."

"Very well, my captain." Grogul wouldn't come up for the morning watch for an hour, so Celeste tucked her instruments back into her case.

Raising her face to the sky, she took in the beauty of the emerging stars. As the blanket of clouds swept to leeward, the heavens unfolded like a mound of glittering treasure. Overhead marched the constellations of the Cosmic Caravan, the planets scattered among them like brilliant escorts. For a little while, she tried to put aside her worries and just enjoy the view.

Spies . . . Never had Celeste thought that they would one day be trafficking secrets in a covert war for freedom. She remembered when freedom meant sailing the sea in search of plunder, taking fat merchant ships, stealing their illicit or smuggled cargo, and selling the ill-gotten prizes in Katapesh's dark markets. Now freedom meant fighting to free others, sailing the same circuitous route from Almas to Ostenso month after month, living in a ship full of lies. Glancing at the crew toiling about the deck, she wondered if any shared her misgivings. Torius's choice to get involved in Andoran's covert war against slavery had very nearly destroyed them all, but not a single member of the crew had abandoned ship.

They'll never abandon their captain, and neither would I, but . . . is this the only life for us?

Panged by guilt, Celeste gazed up at the stars. She often sought guidance in the heavens, seeking answers among the paths of the planets among the constellations. She had faith in the cosmos. It wasn't capricious or vindictive, and didn't take sides in right and wrong, good and evil. Its message might not always be easy to interpret, but the stars never lied. Tonight, Bretheda—the Cradle—shone from within the Stargazer, Celeste's birth sign, which had no immediate significance, and Castrovel approached the Lantern Bearer, which was Torius's. Celeste smiled. She'd never really noticed an increase in her lover's libido when the planet of lust and fertility crossed his sign.

Perhaps I'll start taking data.

The only other planet in the sky, Verces, glimmered between the constellations of the Stranger and the Follower. *Interesting . . .* Verces, the Line, signified choice. *Between a stranger and a follower? How might that apply to us?* The answer was there, if only she could discern it. *If I could just see it clearly in the stars, hear it in the song of the heavens.*

The celestial chorus sang through her soul . . .

"Sails!"

Celeste blinked. To the east, the sky glowed with the light of dawn. Hours had passed since Torius had left her to her musing. She'd lost herself among the stars yet again, oblivious to the bustle of sailors around her, undisturbed even by the changing of the watch. *Damn it . . .* Celeste felt as if a piece of her life had been stolen away, angry at her lapse, but also frightened at her loss of control.

"Where away, and what type of sails?" Grogul's bellow to the masthead lookout rattled Celeste's eardrums.

"Southeast," came Lacy Jane's answer. "Lateen rig. Two masts, but it's too dark to tell the color. She's hull down. Could be a felucca or a galley."

A felucca meant a merchant or fisherman. A galley could be a slaver.

Celeste opened her case and lifted out her telescope with a flick of magic. It was a far finer instrument than any other aboard. "Grogul." She floated the telescope to him. "Do you want to send this up to Lacy?"

"Sure, if you promise not to bite me if it goes overboard." He knew she cherished the instrument, and obviously appreciated the offer.

Celeste knew he was joking, but smiled to show her fangs. "I promise. I haven't bitten anyone in *days*!"

"Thanks." Grogul turned to his bosun's mate. "Kalli, run this up to Lacy."

"Aye!" Kalli the gillman tucked the telescope through her belt and climbed up the ratlines, her webbed hands and feet sure on the ropes.

In moments, Lacy Jane called down, "Galley! Yellow sails! She's turning north!"

"They're turning to follow us."

"Seems that way." Grogul's predatory grin spoke volumes. He shouted orders to the crew. "Maintain course, but slack the sheets to slow us down a bit. Someone wake the captain."

Celeste looked to the sky, but the light of dawn had already dimmed the stars. She would get no more guidance from there, but she remembered her earlier observations. *Verces between the Stranger and the Follower. A choice* . . . As usual, the signs could be interpreted numerous ways. If the ship they'd spotted was the follower, who was the stranger? Or perhaps the choice wasn't between a follower and a stranger, but between fleeing or fighting the stranger who followed them? If they chose to fight, they risked more than the ship and their lives, for they carried Vreva's coded logbook, a repository of secrets invaluable to the Andoren cause. They could never let slavers get their hands on that book.

Torius and Thillion hurried up to the quarterdeck. Snick followed, rubbing her eyes, her sea-green hair sticking up at all angles. She dyed it blue for her disguise in Ostenso, but insisted on washing it clean every time they left port, just like she insisted upon changing the identity of the ship from *Sea Serpent* to *Stargazer*.

"Looks like an Okeno slaver, sir," Grogul reported. "Still hull down, but they've turned to follow. I slacked sheets to slow us, and in this light wind, they'll catch up quickly. We should get a better look soon."

"Thanks, Grogul."

"Couldn't you have waited until after breakfast to bellow like a bull elephant?" Snick glared up at the bosun and tried to smooth her hair.

"Sorry to interrupt your beauty sleep. I know you need it." Grogul grinned down at her, showing his tusks.

The gnome made a face. "You should get some, too."

"We could lure them in and take them, Captain." Thillion squinted to the south, his elven eyes sharper than theirs by far. "Unless she turns out to be as big as the *Bloody Scourge*, of course."

Celeste could only agree. That ship had very nearly been the death of them all.

"We may have to let this one pass." Torius squinted at the sea and sky, obviously gauging the variables that might affect their chances. From his frown, he was also undoubtedly thinking about Vreva's logbook. He turned to Celeste and cocked an eyebrow. "Unless you have some insight from the stars?"

"I don't . . ." Celeste paused and considered the choice that faced them. *Should we fight and risk Vreva's book?*

"Yes." The answer came out of Celeste's mouth before she knew what she was saying. She had no idea where the overwhelming feeling of promise had come from, but it couldn't be denied. The song of the heavens sang it loud in her soul, a familiar rightness, just as when she'd considered facing Lothera Cothos.

Everyone looked at her in surprise.

"You *do* have some guidance from the stars?" Thillion sounded dubious.

Torius had learned to respect her astrological prophecies, but knew better than to ask for specific information. Long experience had taught him that her predictions were fraught with uncertainty, often only becoming clear in retrospect. The rest of the crew still often saw her prophecies as more troublesome than accurate. But this time, she was certain.

"Yes, I have. The choice is clear. We should take them."

"Captain!" Lacy Jane called down from the foretop. "She's hull up! One deck of oars, and she's pulling hard! They're coming after us!"

Torius turned to Celeste. The slaver wasn't so large that *Stargazer* couldn't take her, but there was still doubt in his eyes. "You're *sure*?"

"I'm sure, my captain." Celeste reared up, more sure of this than she had been about anything lately. "We should take that ship. Trust me!"

Torius grinned. "I was hoping you'd say that." He turned to his officers. "We take them! Thillion, I like your idea of luring them in. Let's make like we're a merchant fleeing in panic. Grogul, something aloft is going to break. Nothing catastrophic, just enough to foul the rigging and kill our speed. You'll command the main boarding party amidships."

"Aye, sir!" The half-orc hefted his axe and thumbed the razor edge.

"Snick, put the *Sea Serpent* placards back on, and load your babies with the usual tricks. We'll take them by surprise."

"Surprises are my specialty, Captain!" The gnome scurried off to tend her ballistae. *Stargazer* would look like a benign merchant until the cunningly disguised firing ports opened and the tips of six of Snick's specialized ballista warheads nosed out.

"Thillion, you and your archers will rake their deck from our forecastle as they come alongside, then board and continue the barrage from their own foredeck."

"Yes, sir."

"Celeste, you, Windy, and the bosun's mates will board aft with me. Once we've cleared their quarterdeck, I want you to rake their middeck with your spells."

"It'll be my pleasure." Celeste's heart raced in anticipation of the battle. Having suffered in chains herself, there were few things in life she enjoyed more than blasting slavers with destructive magic.

"Good! Windy, start steering wild. Grogul, tell the crew to handle the sheets and braces like lubbers. Thillion, pick your archers and stand ready. Remember, we're merchants until the trap is sprung!"

Canvas and tangled cordage flapped in the wind, and sailors scurried around the deck in apparent panic. The slaver was closing fast, near enough now that Torius could read the placard on her bow. The *Golden Chain* bore a figurehead of a woman bound in gilded manacles and a collar.

"Keep coming, you bastard." Torius lowered his glass and turned to shout panicked orders to his crew. They had to play this right. If the slaver got a whiff of the trap, they would rake *Stargazer* with arrows and ballista bolts from afar. But Torius had learned how to play on slavers' greed by appearing vulnerable. To traffickers in flesh, sailors were potential merchandise, not to be damaged unless they resisted. Few merchantmen could offer much of a fight. Most would choose slavery over death.

Torius knew better. He'd die before he became a slave again.

"Yaw to starboard, Windy. We're panicked, remember."

"Shakin' in my boots, sir." She grinned at him and hauled the wheel to starboard, her strong right hand working in concert with the hook-and-pike combination that had replaced her left. A slaver had taken that hand some months ago. Already, Windy had filed five notches in the pike for the slavers she'd killed as payback.

"*Sea Serpent!* Heave to and nobody dies!" The bellowed command from the bow of the *Golden Chain* brought a cold smile to Torius's lips.

Glancing over his shoulder, Torius assessed their foe. Slavers armed with nets, grapples, and cutlasses crowded the galley's middeck, ready to board. On the forecastle, a ballista crew stood ready beside their engine, but the adjacent catapult wasn't even loaded. There were no archers. There were, however, more slavers than Torius had counted on. He hoped he hadn't underestimated this foe.

"Kalli, ready the colors. I want to scare yesterday's breakfast right out of those bastards!" The instant the slavers saw Andoran's flag, they'd know they were in for a fight, and *Stargazer* had a deadly reputation in Okeno. "Dukkol, pass the word down to Celeste. Two minutes."

The two bosun's mates hurried to comply, the gillman clipping the flags to the mainmast halyard, and the one-eyed dwarf thumping down the stairs to where Celeste hid inside the sterncastle door. Moments later, the dwarf returned, and Torius heard the rasp of scales on the deck beside him.

"Ready, my captain." Celeste's disembodied voice sounded like music to his ears.

"Good. You know your target."

"Anyone who looks like they're about to cast a spell."

"Right." Recently the Okeno slavers had begun contracting powerful wizards to protect their ships. Torius winced as he recalled the Gray Corsair *Gold Wing*, sunk by a blast of magic before their eyes. That was another reason he chose to lure their prey in for the kill. Up close, a caster was an easier target. With any luck, Celeste could neutralize the threat before they had a chance to blast *Stargazer* to kindling.

Torius glanced over his shoulder again, trying to look scared as he gauged the angles and distances between the two ships. He muttered a prayer to Gozreh that Celeste's guidance on this battle would prove true. They were taking a serious risk in this venture. He'd probably catch hell from Marshal Trellis for putting Vreva's logbook at risk, but they did have to maintain their reputation as privateers. That meant actually taking on a slaver now and then. Besides, Torius never tired of killing slavers and freeing slaves. The looks on their faces—the horror of the slavers and the amazement of the slaves—when they realized what was happening made him feel more alive than just about anything else in the world.

"Yaw to port, Windy! Keep them guessing."

"Aye, sir!" *Stargazer* slewed to port. The slaver shifted course accordingly.

"*Sea Serpent!* Heave to, or we'll fire on you!" The crack of a ballista backed their threat, but the warning shot flew harmlessly overhead, a holed sail the only damage.

"Don't shoot! We surrender!" Torius dashed to the taffrail, waving his arms in a panic. "Let fly sheets! Helm to windward!"

Stargazer turned to starboard and *Golden Chain* back-paddled her starboard sweeps to come alongside. Torius scanned the galley's deck, noting the satisfied smiles and laughter among the slavers. *That's right, just keep laughing* . . . The two ships closed to barely ten yards.

"I have the caster, Torius." Celeste's voice came from right beside him.

"Do it."

Arcane words flowed, harsh and garbled to the captain's ear. Celeste materialized as lightning lashed out toward *Golden Chain*'s quarterdeck. The bolt struck a robed woman there, blasting her to the deck in a flutter of smoldering cloaks.

"*Stargazer!*" Torius drew his sword and thrust it high, the familiar rush of adrenaline surging through his veins.

Two flags flew up the mainmast, the golden eagle of Andoran on a blue-and-gray shield, and directly beneath it, *Stargazer*'s own long black-and-silver pennant bearing a serpentine silhouette of a naga with flowing white hair. Thillion's archers leapt up from hiding to rake the galley's forecastle with a deadly volley. The crew of the enemy ballista fell, riddled with arrows. *Stargazer*'s deck shuddered beneath Torius's feet as six ballistae cracked in perfect unison. The bolts cleared the galley's rail by mere inches, and the triggering tethers came taut, detonating the ceramic warheads. Blue-white liquid splashed forth onto the astonished slavers, encasing them in freezing alchemical ice. Grogul and his boarders boiled up from the main hatchway, heaving grapples to pull the two ships closer.

"Celeste, Dukkol, Windy, Kalli, with me!" The helmswoman and bosun's mates drew weapons and ran with him to the rail, but Celeste didn't move. When he glanced back, she just stared at him with a questioning look. "Come on!"

"*Que towlre nokta?*" Celeste gaped at him wide-eyed.

Torius stared at Celeste, trying to interpret what she'd said. "Celeste! Come on!"

She blinked at him, uncomprehending, and spoke again, but her words came out as a string of gibberish.

What the hell language is she speaking?

The two ships met with a crash. Torius couldn't wait, even for her. He leapt the rail onto the enemy quarterdeck, parrying a pike thrust even before his feet touched the deck. Windy gutted the pikeman as she landed beside him, and parried a cutlass with her hook. Kalli lunged to skewer a slaver officer through the neck with her rapier. Dukkol bellowed a curse as he took a pike in the leg, but his axe clove through his opponent's arms in riposte. More slavers closed in on them, pressing them hard. Torius parried wildly, glimpsing the slaver captain beyond the flashing blades. The officer knelt over the smoldering form of the fallen wizard, a blue glass bottle in one hand. The caster reached up for the bottle with one charred hand.

"The caster's still alive!" The Stargazers were holding their own so far, but if the slaver captain healed the wizard, they'd be in trouble. "Celeste!"

Torius couldn't break through the flashing blades before him, but the answering crackle of lightning was all he'd hoped for. The bolt caught both the wizard and the captain in its fury. The caster was reduced to a smoldering corpse, but the captain rolled to his feet and drew a pair of hooked silvery hand axes from his belt. Ignoring the smoke trailing from his singed jacket, the man charged to the attack.

Torius pressed his opponent hard, slashing through her guard to open a horrible gash in her leg. The woman stumbled, and Windy took the opening to slash her cutlass across the slaver's neck. The helmswoman took a cut to her other arm from her own opponent, but Kalli put her rapier in the slaver's ribs. Dukkol, though limping, guarded their flank as more slavers charged up the steps from the middeck to reinforce their officers.

Torius kicked away the twitching corpse and met the captain's attack, parrying one gleaming axe and dodging the other. The man was quick, however, and Torius missed his next parry. The slaver's blade ripped through the fine mail beneath his shirt, gouging a furrow down his ribs. Pain took his breath away and weakened his knees.

"Gozreh's guts!" Torius was no stranger to injuries, but this felt like he'd been plunged into boiling oil. He managed to evade the other axe and slash at the man's legs, driving him back.

The slaver captain grinned maniacally and flourished his weapons, which glimmered strangely. "You're no match for—"

A beam of searing energy from Celeste caught the man square in the face. The axes clattered to the deck and a horrible scream rose from the slaver captain's blistered lips, his hands clawing at eyes charred to cinders in their sockets.

"Match that, asshole!" Torius silenced the captain's screams with a slash of his sword. Clutching the wound in his side, he clenched his teeth against the excruciating pain and turned to face the enemy charge.

Then Celeste was beside him, her scales shimmering with a starry radiance. At first, Torius thought it was the mesmerizing shimmer she often used to distract an enemy, but the effect was different. Instead of her scales shimmering, it looked as if she wore a luminous cloak of glittering motes. A slaver lunged at her, and

Torius thought the cutlass would surely rake her, but the starry nimbus turned the blade before it touched her side. Celeste struck like a viper, sinking her fangs into the slaver's throat. His screams died in a gurgle, and she flung the twitching corpse aside with a twist of her body.

Torius spared a moment to assess the battle. Thillion and his archers had taken the foredeck, and their bows sang a song of death, shots picking off slavers as they struggled against Grogul's boarders. Two Stargazers had turned the enemy ballista around to fire down upon the slavers crowding the middeck. Snick's ballista crews now fired crossbows from the conjoined rails, and Torius spotted the shock of the gnome's green hair as she scrambled toward the enemy forecastle. The surprise of their assault had given them a foothold, but they were still outnumbered. Here on the quarterdeck, slavers poured up two flights of steps to oppose them. Even with Celeste's aid, they were being pressed hard.

"Rally!" he called out in encouragement. "We've got to take the quarterdeck!"

Celeste shouted something unintelligible, but her tone bespoke urgency.

"I can't understand a word you're saying, Celeste!" Had the wizard gotten off a spell to tangle her tongue? Torius swallowed his worry for her and slashed to drive the enemy back. If they could take the quarterdeck, Celeste could rake the middeck with her spells, but not while fighting at close quarters.

A flight of glowing motes shot from the naga to riddle the enemy, and Torius breathed easier. Two dropped their weapons, and were instantly skewered, and Dukkol hacked the legs out from under another. The Stargazers surged forward, and Torius drove his opponent over the forward rail.

They had taken the quarterdeck.

Lightning lashed out from Celeste, arcing the length of the deck to blast a furrow through the enemy force. Arrows streaked from the rear of the slaver ranks in reply. Kalli took a shaft in the shoulder, and Torius felt a burning sting as one creased his thigh, but the one aimed at Celeste glanced off her starry shield.

"Nice spell, Celeste!" He slashed at another slaver trying to regain the quarterdeck, sending her tumbling down the steps. "Dukkol, block the stairs! Don't let them get a foothold! We've got to give Celeste cover!"

Celeste yelled something else, but still he couldn't understand her. Fortunately, she knew her role. Another searing bolt of lightning blasted the enemy force. Grogul and his fighters were pressing the slavers against the far rail now, so reduced were their numbers. Celeste slithered quickly to the port side of the quarterdeck.

"Guard the stairs!" Torius commanded the others. "Nobody gets—" His orders died on his lips as a burly slaver with a hooked falchion leapt down at Celeste from the ratlines. The full force of the man's falling mass backed the two-handed stroke. "Celeste! Look out!"

Celeste turned to Torius, eyes uncomprehending as the blade fell like a guillotine toward the back of her head.

An iron-tipped ballista bolt struck the slaver the instant before the blade would have cloven her skull. The heavy falchion sheared away a lock of the naga's platinum hair, then skittered down her scales. The glancing blow brought her around in a flash of fangs, ready to strike, but the shaft had spitted the slaver through the chest. Her would-be assassin lay twitching on the deck, clutching the wrist-thick bolt and gasping for breath.

With a sigh of relief, Torius traced the bolt's trajectory back to the foredeck, where a grinning gnome leapt with delight at her life-saving shot. He'd have to remember to thank Snick, but the battle wasn't over yet.

"Celeste!" Torius pointed to the deck, since in her current state she seemed incapable of understanding him.

Celeste turned away from the dying slaver and cast her light-ning yet again, blasting the tightly pressed slavers and thinning their remaining ranks by half.

The devastation shattered the enemy's waning morale. Some dropped their weapons to plead for mercy, while others, rightly assuming that none would be given, leapt over the side. This proved a poor tactic, however, for the school of sharks that often followed slave galleys had been alerted to a pending meal by the blood running from the ship's scuppers. The water roiled, and shrill screams rose above the din of battle.

The surviving slavers fought grimly on—ravaged by Grogul's boarding party, Thillion's archers, and Celeste's spells—until the last fell in a welter of blood. A cheer rose up from the Stargazers, and Torius thrust his bloody sword to the sky in triumph.

"Grogul, search the ship and free the slaves! Snick, see to the wounded! Thillion, pick a prize crew and take stock of all she's carrying. You'll be taking her into Almas as usual." As the three hurried to follow his orders, he turned to find Celeste coiled over the slaver who had attacked her. She had ended his suffering with a bite to the throat, a kindness Torius doubted the slaver would have returned. Her cloak of starlight had vanished, and her black scales were spattered with blood, but she seemed unhurt. "Celeste! Are you all right?"

She turned to him with a startled look. "I'm . . . fine." She glanced down at the gash in his side. "You're bleeding."

"I'll live." He winced as he flexed his side. It still hurt abom-inably, but the crippling pain was gone. The blade had skittered across his ribs like a stick along a picket fence, but the wound wasn't life-threatening. "What happened to you? I couldn't under-stand a word you said."

"I . . . don't know. I couldn't understand you, either." She gazed at the charred corpse of the slaver wizard. "Maybe she cursed me."

"Well, it's lapsed, at least." He ran a hand down her truncated hair. "Though it cost you a haircut."

"Yes . . . I didn't see him." She looked forward. "Snick saved my life."

"Yes. She's certainly got a way with ballistae. That was an amazing shot. I'll have to give her a bonus. But that cloak-of-starlight saved you as well. That's a handy spell." He laughed, but was surprised to see that his mirth wasn't mirrored in her eyes. Instead, she looked rather shaken. "You sure you're okay?"

"Just a little rattled, I think." Celeste smiled weakly. "Close call, you know. But we won."

"That we did." Torius surveyed the deck. "Your prophecy was spot-on!"

The Stargazers were hard at work, and already the deck looked less like a slaughterhouse and more like a ship. Snick and her ballista crews tended the wounded with a satchel full of potions for those close to death and bandages for the rest. At a glance he saw only two dead Stargazers. They'd be in Almas in just a few days, and there was enough in the death fund they all paid into to have them brought back by the priests there. Torius looked over his crew with a surge of pride; taking on such a superior force with only two deaths was an amazing feat.

He cleaned his sword on a dead slaver's shirt and slipped it into its sheath. "Yes, it's a good day to be a pirate."

"*Privateer*, you mean," Celeste corrected.

"I suppose." He gave her his best piratical grin and laughed. "Doesn't have quite the same ring to it, but I must admit there are advantages."

The first of the freed slaves stumbled onto the deck, pale and blinking in the sunlight. That look of delighted astonishment on their faces made all his pain worthwhile.

4

Invitations

I still think I should go in with you.* Mathias rubbed up against Vreva's leg and lashed his tail. *You might need my help.*

"Not this time, love." Vreva took a calming breath and peered out the window of the carriage as it turned onto Ostenso's waterfront. She loved Mathias and might have used his help, but having him along would distract her. In the belly of a Chelish flagship, surrounded by a thousand sailors and marines, the last thing she needed was a distraction. "It's just dinner. I'll be in and out in a trice."

*Dinner with you is never *just* dinner.* Mathias knew better than to be put off by her assurances. *Tell me you're not planning to befuddle his brain with your feminine charms, drug his wine, break into his mind with magic, and steal his every secret right down to his mistress's favorite color.*

"Mathias!" She reached down and scratched him behind the ears. "Never *all* of that on the first date."

Right. He didn't sound convinced.

The truth was, Vreva didn't have much of a plan other than to make her best possible first impression on Admiral Ronnel. She'd done some digging on him, of course, and deemed him a hard man, a brilliant naval tactician, a political hawk, and—thank Calistria—a ladies' man. The only way she could get more information about him and this Kellid witch and her weapon, neither of which they had seen in several days of Mathias spying from the waterfront alleys, was to meet him in person. Unfortunately, her letter of introduction and invitation to a private dinner at the Officers' Club had been answered with regrets and an explanation that his duties would not let him leave his ship—but also with a return invitation to visit him aboard his flagship, *Devil's Trident*. If she got him alone, and detected none of the magical precautions so common among the powerful and paranoid, she might risk casting a spell on him or drugging his wine. Then, with some careful suggestions, she might attempt to discover what this secret weapon was. Vreva was experienced enough to know that things like this took time. Besides, the admiral wasn't going anywhere soon. Rumor had it that *Devil's Trident* would be tied to the dock for some time yet awaiting an unknown deadline.

The carriage rumbled to a stop, the iron wheels sounding hollow on the thick wooden planks of the wharf. Vreva smoothed her dress, and then cast a spell on Mathias that made him vanish from sight. Her familiar would skulk about the docks within range of her empathic messages. If something untoward occurred, at least he would know.

Vreva stepped from the carriage and tamped down her trepidation. She'd been in many dangerous places in her career, but never had she stepped aboard such an intimidating ship. This close, the sheer immensity of *Devil's Trident* made her feel as if she stood before the ramparts of a castle. Looming over lesser ships, the flagship's four towering masts soared so high they seemed to pierce the evening sky. Three rows of ballista ports checkered the hull, more than she'd ever seen on one ship. The gangplank looked more like a drawbridge than a simple ramp, sporting gilded rope handrails and carpeted steps that led up to a wide boarding hatch on the middeck.

Vreva approached with an easy, fluid gait that belied her tension. She had taken great care with her attire for the evening, remembering one of her very first lessons as a courtesan: you have only one chance to make a good first impression. Her gown—deep crimson silk brocade with gold accents—plunged low at both neckline and back, though a shawl clasped at her throat currently hid the full effect.

Security around the ship was tight, especially since it was docked not at the naval pier, but rather at the main commercial pier of the port. A score of Chelish marines were stationed all along the dock, and another ten in formation at the base of the gangplank, all of them resplendent in black-and-red uniforms. An army couldn't have easily breached the flagship's defenses— but Vreva could. She'd done some careful reconnoitering earlier in the day, looking for magical defenses, wards, traps, and the like. Though she'd found none, her skin crawled with unease. She had no doubt there were spellcasters aboard. For this first incursion, she'd taken great care to leave all of her magical trinkets and lethal poisons behind—nothing that would raise suspicions if discovered.

The marines at the gangplank snapped to rigid attention, but couldn't hide their covert glances at the admiral's guest.

"Madame Korvis." A tall lieutenant bowed stiffly, his face a mask of propriety. "Lieutenant Draell of the Imperial Marines at your service. The admiral's expecting you."

"And he's supplied me with quite a dashing escort." She proffered a silk-gloved hand. "Delighted to meet you, Lieutenant Draell."

He took her hand in a formal fingertip grasp and bowed again, his unsmiling face flushing slightly. "You'll excuse the formality, ma'am. We're under very strict security." He placed her hand on his arm and gestured to the gangway. Four of the marines fell in around them, their faces chiseled from stone.

"Well, I'm honored to receive such royal treatment." She wasn't really. Five soldiers surrounding her meant she couldn't make any haphazard observations en route to the admiral, but that wouldn't stop her from learning as much as she could. "I've never been aboard a *flagship* before. Perhaps you could point out a few things on the way."

"I'd be happy to, ma'am."

At the boarding hatch, another squad of marines stood around a man in a black jacket with two silver emblems on his lapels, a pair of crossed lightning bolts and a junior officer's insignia. He was young and good-looking, and Vreva knew instantly that he was a spellcaster. Here, it seemed, was the magical security.

"One moment please." The darkly clad caster stepped forward and held up a hand, his fingers bent in a crooked gesture as a whisper of arcane words issued from his mirthless lips. His hand shimmered briefly in the dim light of the deck lanterns.

"Magic?" She cocked an eyebrow at her escort. "You *are* being very careful, aren't you?"

"Just a precaution, Madame Korvis." Draell's face remained impassive. "I'm sure you understand."

"I understand perfectly." She fixed her features in a facade of mild affront. "Will there be a search of my *person*, as well?"

Draell looked momentarily horrified. "No, ma'am. We just look for magic."

That's good to know. She sighed as if mildly put out.

"Nothing." The caster nodded respectfully and tipped his tricorne, but remained impassive. "Your pardon, ma'am."

Vreva smiled sweetly at him, then turned back to Draell. "Now, about this wonderful ship, Lieutenant . . ."

Vreva feigned rapt interest as Draell happily spouted nautical mumbo-jumbo, drowning her in meaningless details about buntlines, cat-harpins, and double-preventer stays. Only once they entered the lofty sterncastle did the deluge of sailor-speak ease to a trickle, and her attention sharpen. She memorized every twist and turn of the corridors in case she had to make a quick escape. Surviving such an escape, however, seemed unlikely with all the sailors and soldiers about. Dour marines stood at many of the doors, and every passage branch. If she had to flee, she'd need to sprout wings and go out a porthole.

Finally, they came to a pair of double doors guarded by two more marines and narcissistically emblazoned with the crest of the Admiral's house. Cheliax's queen had granted Ronnel the title of baronet for his service to the empire, which barely qualified as nobility. At Lieutenant Draell's knock, a white-jacketed steward opened the door and stepped aside.

Draell escorted Vreva inside, and executed a crisp military bow. "Milord Admiral Vaetus Ronnel, Madame Virika Korvis."

A slim man of perhaps fifty years wearing an immaculate dress admiral's uniform turned from the broad expanse of stern gallery windows. "Madame Korvis, how very delightful of you to accept my invitation." Ronnel approached with a smile and a conspicuous brush of the golden epaulets atop his shoulders. "I regret *terribly* that I couldn't meet with you at your establishment, but the duties of command never end, and my presence is required here." The admiral executed a precise quarter-bow, the proper formality for a noble greeting a guest of lower standing.

Ronnel was surprisingly handsome, which didn't matter in the slightest. What did matter was his obvious arrogance. She could use that to her advantage. From her youth in Egorian, Vreva was all too familiar with the propriety and pomposity of the new nobility. She'd be living in that world still, had she not abandoned her true name, family, and heritage. She also knew enough about Ronnel to be on her guard. The man was skilled, intelligent, and ruthless. He was also an idiot when it came to money. Without a war to supply him with prize money from naval conquests, his lavish habits had resulted in a considerable debt. Lastly, and perhaps most importantly, he enjoyed female company.

"Milord Admiral." Unclipping her shawl, Vreva handed it off to the steward and curtsied gracefully, giving the admiral a delicate smile and a perfect view of her daring neckline. "It's such a pleasure to finally meet the commander so highly spoken of by his officers. I'm thrilled to be invited aboard such a *fabulous* ship!"

The last part, at least, was the absolute truth; she was thrilled by this opportunity to spy on a fleet admiral, and the ship was indeed fabulous. The great cabin was nothing short of palatial. Polished brass lamps hung from every beam, bathing the teak-paneled walls in a soft golden glow. The decor was both masculine and military. A large desk stood to the right, emblazoned with yet another coat of arms, a pair of crossed swords displayed on the wall behind it. A table set with burnished silver plates and sparkling crystal stood in front of high, gilt-framed windows that arched along the entire back wall, providing a glorious view of the harbor. White-gloved servants stood behind each chair, ready to attend.

Not exactly intimate. I'll have to get him alone somehow.

"Everything's so lovely and bright." She beamed at Ronnel and placed her hand on his proffered arm. "I expected a military vessel to be stuffy and cramped."

"We keep *Devil's Trident* in fighting trim," he said, puffing up his chest, "but I also enjoy my comfort. As Admiral of the Ostenso Fleet, I *do* require accommodations to entertain guests." He dismissed Draell with a wave and gestured toward the table. "A glass of wine before dinner?"

"I'd prefer whiskey, if you have a single malt handy."

"Whiskey?" Ronnel looked at her as if she'd asked him for a cup of freshly drawn blood. "Really?"

"*Really*, Milord Admiral." Vreva curved her lips in a licentious smile. Her request had caught him off guard, accomplishing exactly what she intended. "A dear friend introduced me to the pleasure of a finely crafted single malt whiskey." Memories of that friend and their ill-fated romance muddled her mind for a moment, but she thrust them aside and focused. "The flavor is so very . . . *smoldering*, don't you think?"

"I've never really tried whiskey, but I think my steward might be able to find something you'll like." Dragging his eyes away from hers, the admiral snapped his fingers and his steward hurried off, doubtlessly to delve the flagship's cellars. "You're a woman of eclectic tastes."

"Eclectic?" She shrugged and squeezed his arm. "Not to my thinking. I like my liquor like my men, strong and straight up."

Ronnel gaped at her for a moment, then laughed out loud. "By the stones of Asmodeus himself, you really *are* something!" He laughed again, fully and without reservation. "Quite refreshing! Quite refreshing indeed after so many simpering shrews. A *real* woman, not afraid to speak her piece to someone above her station. Quite refreshing!"

"Why, thank you, Admiral." *First task accomplished.* Vreva had just set her first impression in stone, distinguishing herself from any other woman the admiral might entertain. Squeezing his arm again, she joined in his laughter. "Not every man has the self-assurance to recognize me for what I am, but you've hit the proverbial nail on the head with the first stroke. No doubt one of your officers has told you of me."

"They have not. I swear it on my honor." Ronnel placed his hand over his heart and bowed. "Please, let's forget all this propriety and simply enjoy ourselves. I can't think of a single person with whom I'd rather spend an unabashed evening of frivolity."

"Unabashed frivolity just *happens* to be one of my favorite pastimes, Admiral." Vreva beamed up at him, enjoying the blush that rose to his cheeks. She had him exactly where she wanted him: mirth up, inhibitions down, and his libido ready to jump out of his pants and prance around the cabin.

"Very good!"

The steward arrived with a bottle that looked like it had spent several years rolling around the ship's bilge. The label was barely legible, but when the steward proffered it for inspection, she recognized the crest of a New Stetven distillery in distant Brevoy.

"Ah, you have good taste, Admiral! Let's give it a try."

"Damn the ballistae and full sail ahead! Ha ha!" The admiral snatched up two tumblers from the sideboard and clapped them down on the table. "I do believe I'll join you!"

"Please, allow me to serve your first taste!" Vreva plucked the bottle from the startled steward's hands, expertly cracked the seal, and twisted the stopper free with a resonant pop. She poured a measure into each glass and held one out to Ronnel. "To a night of unabashed frivolity."

He took his glass and glowed at her. "To that, Madame Korvis, I will drink!"

And they did.

The heady flavors of smoky peat and malt exploded in Vreva's senses, but she was prepared for the shock of it. She gasped in a cleansing breath, enjoying the liquid fire that warmed her throat and stomach. The admiral's gasp evolved into a fit of coughing, his face turning an astonishing shade of scarlet before he managed to draw a full breath.

"Rather takes you off guard, doesn't it?" She relieved him of his tumbler before he dropped it.

"Like a summer squall!" He coughed again and tried to smile.

"It's an acquired taste."

"I think I'll stick with wine." Ronnel motioned the steward forward.

"To each his own poison." Vreva strolled around the vast cabin, brushing her fingers lightly over the requisite portrait of Queen Abrogail II, and peering in admiration at the crossed swords mounted on the bulkhead behind Ronnel's broad desk.

"This cabin is positively lovely! Would it be possible to get a tour of the rest of the ship?"

"After dinner we can take a turn on deck, but I'm afraid most of the ship's off-limits to visitors." The admiral joined her, sipping a glass of deep-red wine. "This cabin is for formal dinners and meetings, mostly. I sometimes host dinners for the captains of the fleet here, but I generally use it as an office. I have more intimate quarters for entertaining . . . special friends."

Not too subtle, are we, Admiral? Vreva gave him a sultry smile. "I'd love to see them."

"After dinner, then." He guided her back to the table with a hand at the small of her back as two stewards entered bearing several covered dishes. "I've arranged quite a feast for us. I have one of the finest culinary slaves money can buy, you know."

"Really?" Vreva wondered about people who used slaves as their personal chefs. Didn't they realize how easy it was to poison someone?

Hoping that tonight wasn't the night the enslaved chef decided to rebel, Vreva took the seat a servant held for her. Just as Ronnel took his own seat, however, a knock sounded at the door. When the steward answered, a harried lieutenant burst into the cabin, gasping for breath and dabbing a handkerchief at four parallel scratches etched across his cheek. Vreva recognized him from the Officers' Club—the disgruntled lieutenant.

"Milord Admiral!" The officer saluted stiffly. "I beg your pardon, but there's an emergency, sir."

The admiral flushed crimson, the veins in his neck and face bulging. "Pardon me for a moment, my dear. The drudgeries of command again, I'm afraid."

"I understand perfectly, Admiral." Vreva smiled sweetly and sipped her whiskey as her host thrust himself out of his chair.

Ronnel stalked over to the injured lieutenant and backed him up against the door, his voice harsh and low. "This *better* be important, Lieutenant Emero, or you'll be scrubbing the bilges for a month!"

"It's that *witch* again, sir!"

Vreva could just make out the officer's hushed words. She gazed out the window as if entranced by the view, covertly watching the two men's reflections in the glass. She longed to cast a mind-reading or eavesdropping spell, but didn't dare with a servant hovering at her elbow. Even casting a silent spell might be noticed.

"What's she done now?" the admiral demanded.

Emero lowered his voice further, and Vreva strained to hear.

"She's . . . with that . . . and that bloody devil hit my . . . the infirmary . . . and when I . . . blood on my . . . immediately . . ."

"Right now?"

In the window's reflection, Vreva saw the admiral cast her a quick glance, then turn to glare at the poor lieutenant.

"I'm sorry, sir, but she . . ."

"Oh, *fine*! Wait here." Ronnel returned to the table and bowed to Vreva. "I'm very sorry, my dear, but I'm afraid I'm being called away."

"Oh, how *dreadful*!" Vreva put on her best pout and stood. "Can I wait for you here?"

"I don't know when I'll get back, but if you like, please stay and enjoy the meal. I'll be an hour, at least, but could be longer."

"Oh, I could never accept your hospitality without the pleasure of your company, Admiral." Vreva leaned forward to brush his cheek with her own, her voice a sultry whisper. "There's no hurry. An unabashed evening of frivolity must be done properly, you know." She trailed her nails down his taut waistcoat.

"Oh, I agree." Ronnel stepped back and took her hand in his, bending to kiss it. "I'll arrange another dinner, and we'll do it properly. You have my pledge of honor."

"I'll hold you to it, Admiral." Vreva curtsied again.

"Jensen, escort the lady off the ship and hail a carriage." The admiral cast Vreva one more longing glance before stalking out of the cabin, Lieutenant Emero at his heels.

Well, that was a waste of time! Smiling sweetly despite her disappointment, Vreva accepted her shawl from the steward and wrapped it around her shoulders. She looked wistfully at the dishes on the table. The covers hadn't even been removed, but the tantalizing aromas made her mouth water. Maybe she should have taken Ronnel up on his offer and dined alone, but it would have given the wrong impression. She'd done the right thing. She did, however, finish her whiskey before she followed the steward back through the labyrinthine passages. She caught the faint sound of distant raised voices, and considered what she'd overheard. *Devils and witches and blood, oh my . . .*

As her carriage approached, Vreva felt a surge of urgency. *Mathias.* She sent him a nudge of affirmation, and feigned a misstep as she boarded the hackney. Her marine escort caught her arm, and she pressed against him long enough for Mathias to slip ahead of her, his black fur rendering him virtually invisible in the darkness. Thanking her escort, she stepped up and settled into the carriage.

What the hell happened? Mathias mewed as they jerked into motion.

"The admiral was called away. Something to do with this witch of theirs. There might also be a devil involved, too, though it could have been just a turn of phrase."

*Are you kidding me? This is Cheliax! If someone says devil, they're probably talking about a *real* one!*

"Regardless, I think we need a different strategy."

A little feline reconnaissance?

"Exactly." Vreva scratched Mathias under the chin, but he was already purring with excitement. "One more ship's cat should go unnoticed, though getting you aboard might be tricky. They scan everyone who comes aboard for magic."

*As long as you don't use a *cat*-apult, I'm in!*

"Oh, my love, that was dreadful." She picked him up and nuzzled the back of his neck. Born an ordinary cat, Mathias had only been speaking since becoming her familiar less than a year ago, and was still learning the finer points of language. Unfortunately, he was also learning how to pun. "Stick to chasing rats."

*I'm so unappreciated . . . *

"Celeste?"

Something brushed through her hair, shattering the song of the heavens into a thousand shards. Celeste whirled and lashed out, fangs extended.

"Celeste!" Torius jerked his hand back. "Gozreh's guts! What's gotten into you?"

"Torius!" She slithered back, her panic receding, though her heart still raced. Then she saw the blood on the back of his hand. "By the stars! Torius, I'm sorry! I didn't . . . Clean it! Quickly!" If any of her venom got into his bloodstream, his addiction might flare back to life. Lunar naga venom was dangerously habit-forming, and that dependency had nearly destroyed their relationship once before. He'd all but accused her of trying to enslave him, and she'd thought he wanted to be rid of her. The last thing either of them wanted was to go through that again.

"I'm fine. It's just a scratch." He wiped the tiny trickle of blood away and sucked on the wound. "Be more careful, will you?"

"You startled me!" Dread descended on her like a shroud. Once more, she'd lost herself so deeply in the stars that she'd been oblivious to her surroundings. *What's happening to me? Maybe I have been cursed . . .*

Celeste didn't know what to think. Her inability to speak or understand a word of Taldane during the battle with the slavers might have been a spell cast by the dying wizard, but she wasn't sure. The shimmering cloak of stars that shielded her from enemy blades and arrows, however, had come from within her. She had felt the magic arise from deep inside her. It hadn't been a spell, at least not in the way she was used to casting spells, but something . . . internal. The magic might have protected her, but it also scared the hell out of her. And now she had bitten Torius.

"You're sure you're okay? How do you feel?"

"I'm fine." He sucked again at the tiny scratch and spat over the rail. "No venom got in. Believe me, I'd know."

"Thank the stars!" She felt a flood of relief, but still the nagging worry. *Cursed* . . . "Don't touch me like that when I'm stargazing. You startled me."

"Well, you can bet your scaly tail I won't do it again!"

"I *said* I was sorry."

"Forget it. No harm done." Torius reached out to touch her again, but she reared back out of reach. He stopped and stared at her. "What's *wrong* with you?"

"Nothing. I'm just rattled, I guess." Celeste glanced around the quarterdeck, but nothing seemed amiss. They were still sailing northbound, though the lights of Almas weren't yet visible. In fact, the only lights other than the stars were those of the captured galley following a mile in their wake. "What's going on?"

"Nothing serious. I just need our position. It's almost midnight."

"Of course." She had apparently been lost for hours again, and hadn't even heard the ship's bell tolling the watch change. *Cursed* . . . She took quick sightings on Bretheda and Castrovel, and ran through her calculations, grateful for something to occupy her mind for a while. Only after marking the chart and jotting down the time did she realize that Torius was staring at her. "What?"

"Nothing. You just seem jittery." He noted their position on the chart, ordered a minor course change, then returned to her. "You're sure you're all right?"

"I *am* a little jittery, I guess. I don't know. Perhaps that close call aboard the slave galley unnerved me." She wanted to tell him about the strange spell, that she felt it might be linked to her inability to communicate during the fight, but couldn't force herself to form the words. Celeste glanced about the quarterdeck at the sailors bustling about in their duties. Sailors were notoriously superstitious, so later might be better, when they could talk privately. Or maybe she shouldn't tell him at all. *Should I tell him about this?*

A curious feeling washed over her. The song of the heavens resounded in her mind, but unlike the feeling of rightness she'd felt when she suddenly knew taking the slave ship was the correct thing to do, she now felt a swirling uncertainty, a morass of good and bad, benefit and detriment, boon and bane. She shook her head at the strange sensation, and thought for a moment she heard musical laughter. She twisted, scanning the deck for the source, so clear and loud, but it wasn't any voice she'd ever heard. *Now I'm hearing voices in my head! What the hell's happening to me?*

"Celeste!" Torius reached out to her again, and she couldn't shy away. Not from him. His warm hands felt good on her scales. Soothing. Familiar. "What's wrong? You look like you just saw a ghost!"

"I . . . don't know." That was the truth at least. *Hearing voices, strange spells, speaking in tongues . . .* Her mind whirled with potential causes, none of them good. *Is this what it feels like to be possessed by a spirit or demon?* "I just . . . feel strange. I can't explain it."

"Just try to relax." He pulled her into a comforting embrace. "We'll be in Almas today, and it'll take at least a couple of days to get the ship straightened out. Snick said we sprung a few joints coming up against that galley, and they'll need to be repaired. We can afford to take a little time for ourselves."

"Time—you mean a few days off?" Maybe that was all she needed.

"Sure. We'll have to meet with our contact, of course, but after that . . . how about a night on the town? Almas is a big city. There are lots of places you haven't visited yet."

"That would be nice." Celeste smiled and leaned into Torius's warm arms. Almas also undoubtedly had innumerable wizards and clerics who might be able to discern what was wrong with her. *Maybe I can even find someone to lift this curse . . .*

5

Eyes in the Dark

After you, my dear." Torius pulled open the heavy mahogany-and-brass door of the People's Gallery of Fine Arts and ushered Celeste inside. Knowing her form was an illusion gave him a strange double view of her human shape superimposed upon her natural serpentine form. Thankfully, the same beautiful face and long alabaster hair adorned both. She couldn't slither Almas's streets as a naga, but she needn't wear another person's features to avoid attracting attention. He followed her through the door, careful not to tread on her tail. They'd gotten pretty good at maneuvering around one another to keep her illusion looking natural.

"Thank you, Torius, I— Oh *my*!"

Torius looked to where she was staring and caught his breath. A tornado of flame and crystal swirled up from a wide marble plinth to the apex of the gallery's pillared entry hall. The mesmerizing juxtaposition of colors and textures drew them toward the display. Upon closer inspection, he saw that the opposing elements were actually swarms of winged fire and ice creatures all soaring upward in conjoined spirals. At the zenith, they plunged down through the center of the sculpture to rejoin the rising throng. It was a true piece of living art.

"Welcome, citizens." A blue-robed attendant approached and nodded in greeting, a knowing smile on her wrinkled, cherubic features. "This is your first visit to the People's Gallery, I see." She waved a hand at the massive sculpture. "Our centerpiece often elicits awe. I'm Prissa Hambly, assistant curator."

"It's beautiful!" Celeste slithered forward, and Torius mentally thanked Gozreh that she'd managed to maintain her illusion, so enraptured was she with the art. "Is it . . . alive?"

"Oh *no!*" The curator looked aghast. "They're illusions, of course. To bind sentient creatures in such a display would be tantamount to slavery, and anything less would have them running amok and destroying the art."

"Oh, of course." Celeste circled the huge illusory sculpture, still gazing up in fascination.

Torius thought it was interesting, but after the initial shock, he was less than awestruck. It reminded him of some of the arcane works of art he'd seen in the merchant Benrahi Ekhan's private collection in Azir. To squander magic just to make something pretty seemed extravagant to the point of arrogance. For courtesy's sake, he kept his opinion confidential and nodded to the curator.

"You're right, this is our first visit to the gallery." They had reasons other than art appreciation for their visit, but Torius had no intention of letting the attendant know they'd been directed here by a message from Helena Trellis, head of the Twilight Talons. "We've heard that the collection's amazing. Especially the sculptures by Hasmir Taliff."

"Oh, yes, *The Tears of Fey* is one of our biggest attractions."

"So we were told."

Celeste finished her circuit of the sculpture and rejoined him, positioning herself so that Torius stood between her and the curator to avoid any accidental physical contact. Almas had a reputation for egalitarianism, but rumors of a lunar naga masquerading as a human might cause problems. She gestured around the entry hall with one illusory hand. "This place is immense. Is there a map?"

"No need." The curator motioned to the nearest of six passages leading away from the chamber. "Just start anywhere and your path will eventually lead back here."

"And the Taliff exhibit?" Torius asked.

"The shortest path is through there." Hambly pointed to the third passage from the right. "Enjoy yourselves."

"Thank you." Torius held out his arm for Celeste and her illusory hand rested there like a ghost.

The passage took them past paintings and sculptures both magical and mundane. They paused to admire each, though for Torius it was more out of the desire to appear inconspicuous than in true appreciation. He preferred genuine seascapes, starscapes, and sunsets to mere paintings of them.

Eventually, the hallway opened into a dim chamber. A single glowing crystal levitating overhead illuminated the room's centerpiece. At first glance it looked to be nothing but the stump of a great tree. A few people circled the roped-off exhibit, gesturing and speaking in hushed, reverent tones.

"That's art?" he whispered to Celeste.

Her only answer was a scathing glance. She slithered forward for a closer look. Not knowing what else to do, he followed and they circled the sculpture. On the opposite side, he espied a placard: *The Tears of Fey*. Squinting in the dim light, he leaned over the velvet rope for a better look . . . and saw her.

The title was apt. Curled in a fetal position between two of the stump's great roots lay a woman carved of the same piece of wood as the stump. Garbed in vines and flowers, her hair a crown of autumn leaves, she lay turned away from the viewers, her arms embracing the remains of the dead tree. Even though he couldn't see her face, somehow Torius knew that tears wet her cheeks, and that her forlorn expression would break his heart.

"Profound, isn't it?" A woman joined them at the rope barrier to look down at the sculpture of the dryad.

"Very . . . powerful." Torius didn't know what else to say, surprised that the sculpture truly moved him, and troubled him as well. His beloved *Stargazer* was built of hewn timber. Not every tree had a dryad, of course, but he'd never before considered where the wood had come from, or whose soul might have been riven by its cutting. Forcing his mind back to his task, he turned to the woman who had joined them. "It's so real, I would have expected a songbird to perch on it."

"Oh, there are no songbirds here." The middle-aged woman smiled at him, her eyes sharp in the dim light. "Only hawks and doves."

"But which are which?"

"Sometimes it's hard to tell." The woman pulled up her sleeve a couple of inches and muttered a word. A black eagle tattoo swam to the surface of her skin, then faded away.

Torius discreetly lifted his left sleeve and mouthed the name of his father. Since Torius barely remembered the man from the earliest years of his childhood, before his life had descended into pain and slavery, it was a sure bet that no one else would ever guess this password. The same tattoo surfaced upon his forearm, then faded.

"Torius. Celeste. Good of you to come."

"Helena." He nodded to Marshal Helena Trellis, the enigmatic leader of the Twilight Talons. "For you to come yourself, this must be important."

"It is." She withdrew a small lacquered snuffbox from a pocket and opened the lid. "And it needn't be overheard."

Torius had seen the magical box before, and knew its effect. The device would ensure that none of the gallery's other patrons would overhear their conversation or notice its absence.

"That's better." Trellis turned away and started strolling through the rest of the gallery. Torius and Celeste followed, staying close enough to be included in the spell's effect. "We've received a message from your friend in Ostenso. Admiral Ronnel seems to be up to something. He has some type of magical weapon aboard his flagship, and we don't know what it is."

"Ronnel?" Torius knew the name. Ronnel was commander of the Ostenso fleet, and a ruthless warmonger. The man pressed for military action at every provocation. If it was up to him, Cheliax would have invaded Andoran years ago. "That sounds like trouble."

"Yes, it does." Trellis flashed him a look that he couldn't read. "And what's worse is that none of our other operatives seem to know a thing about it. There are no rumors in Egorian about any weapon. This could be Ronnel taking his political failures into his own hands."

"You think he'll use it?" Celeste asked.

"I think if Admiral Ronnel thinks he has a weapon that will give him an advantage, he'd like nothing more than to plunge our two countries into war." Trellis's lips pressed into a tight line.

"Open war?" The standoff between Cheliax and Andoran had lasted decades with no more than posturing and border skirmishes. Andoran's Gray Corsairs preyed upon Chelish slave ships, as did privateers like Torius, but so far nothing had tipped the balance of power to either side's advantage. *Until now, apparently.*

"We don't know if its use will herald a formal declaration of war, or if it's intended to make us capitulate without a fight."

"Capitulate?" If Ronnel hoped that, the weapon was either immensely powerful, or he didn't know many Andorens well. From what Torius had seen, most Andorens would give up their lives before they gave up their freedom.

"What's the weapon?" Celeste asked.

"We don't know, but your friend's trying to find out." Helena stopped at a painting, peering at the image as if genuinely interested. Torius and Celeste strolled past without a glance and paused at the next display. "If Ronnel's involved, I'd bet it has something to do with a naval engagement, but we haven't gotten any good information. By the time you get back there, perhaps we'll know more."

"I see." The plan didn't need explaining. Vreva was a spy, not a warrior. She would discover what the weapon was, and Torius and the Stargazers would take it out. Using a former pirate turned privateer and spy to do this would make it easier to disavow if he was caught or killed than trying for a military intervention.

"Do we steal it or destroy it?" Celeste's question brought Helena's head around in a casual motion.

"Since we have no idea what *it* is, I can't answer that question specifically." Her gaze slid away, and she continued her stroll through the gallery. "Although stealing it would provide us with the best information, and possibly the same advantage they intend to use, we can't allow Andoran to be implicated. Even though we know they're planning something, they haven't technically moved against us yet, and we can't have it look like we struck first." She didn't look at them, but there was enough steel in her tone to make a glare redundant. "Do *not* let this come back to haunt us. We've got enough on our agenda without fending off accusations of espionage. Your primary objective is to neutralize that weapon."

"Understood." Torius and Celeste shared a glance as they paused to examine another painting. She looked more worried than he thought the situation warranted. He had faith in his Stargazers. They were used to sneaking around, and if destroying this weapon meant a fight, well, they could do that, too. "Sounds simple enough."

"*Nothing* is simple!" Trellis stopped beside them. "We can't afford a war right now."

Torius bit back an acerbic reply—*If Andoran can't afford a war, they shouldn't be pissing off half the nations of the Inner Sea!*—knowing it would only earn him Trellis's wrath. "I was speaking figuratively. We *can* be discreet."

"Can you?" She shot them a withering glance. "When are you going to start?"

He knew she was referring to their recent taking of the slaver galley. "We have to keep up appearances or certain people in Almas will start asking questions." A privateer that never took a prize would draw interest, and if anyone looked too closely, they might make the connection between *Sea Serpent* and *Stargazer*. "Besides, the opportunity was too good to pass up."

"You need to focus on the bigger picture, Torius. One slave ship will *not* win us a war. You risk too much for too little gain."

"I told Torius to take the slaver," Celeste interrupted. "The risk was negligible."

"And how could *you* know that?" Curiosity took the edge off of Marshal Trellis's question.

"I just knew." Celeste looked to Torius. "We should be going." She pulled a handbag from beneath her cloak.

Torius marveled at her use of her magical manipulation to make it look like her illusory hands were doing the work. She opened it to withdraw a hand mirror, then in an apparently genuine fumble, sent the bag tumbling from her grasp at the precise moment they walked past Trellis.

"Oh, I'm sorry!"

Torius and Trellis both reached for the fallen handbag. She reached it first, and handed it over.

"Thank you." Torius took the bag. It was lighter than the one Celeste had dropped, of course. That one contained Vreva's coded logbook, while this one rattled with scroll cases.

"My pleasure." Trellis smiled and turned away.

Handing the new bag to Celeste, he murmured, "Enjoy the light reading, Helena."

"I will." Trellis started to stroll away, but her last words reached them both clearly. "There are instructions, payment, and several communication scrolls in there. If you need naval intervention to prevent this weapon from being used, contact me directly, and I'll have a squadron of Gray Corsairs deployed from Augustana.

Anything less than a major attack will *not* warrant direct military action on our part. There's no time to waste. I expect you to sail on the morning tide, Captain."

"If our repairs are finished, we will." Torius brushed Celeste's scales with a hand. "But we're going to enjoy the rest of the gallery before we hurry off to do your bidding."

There was no reply. Trellis had either passed beyond the spell's range or refused to rise to Torius's barb.

"So much for taking a few days off." Celeste whispered something arcane, then said, "I made our conversation private—she can't hear us anymore. Torius, I don't *like* this."

Torius urged her to stroll on, more concerned by the worry in Celeste's voice than the mission. "Why? It sounds perfect to me. Neutralize the secret weapon, avert a war, thwart the evil empire . . . The only way it could be better is if we rescued a princess in the process."

"Don't joke, Toriusss!" Her hiss of irritation—a sign of anger that he'd learned to recognize at great personal sacrifice—quashed his humor. "This is serious!"

"I *know* it's serious, Celeste. I just don't know why you're so worked up about it." They paused at a sculpture of a succubus and an angel locked in a violently amorous embrace entitled *The Harder They Fall*. Torius admired the workmanship, but didn't care for the theme of the piece. "This mission could save thousands of lives."

"That's *exactly* why I'm worked up. It seems . . . too big for us." She sighed and hung her head. "Things were so much easier when we were pirates."

"Don't think I haven't told myself the same thing a hundred times." He pulled her close. "I believe in what we're doing for Andoran, but I don't always agree with their methods."

"Like throwing *us* under the grindstone to avert a war that *they're* instigating by interfering with the slave trade?" She looked at him and frowned. "I hate slavery as much as you do, Torius, but sometimes I feel like we're being used."

"I know what you mean." Trellis wielded her operatives like pieces on a game board. As any general in battle, she was playing to win, even if some pieces had to be sacrificed in the process. "We knew the risks when we signed up."

"No, Torius, *you* knew the risks when you signed *us* up!"

"Celeste! I—"

"No, hear me out, Torius!" Her lips stretched in a tight line. "I have a . . . feeling something's going to go horribly wrong, and I don't know what it is. I know every single Stargazer agreed to this, and you'd never force anyone, but the game's just gotten a *lot* more dangerous. Privateering and spying is one thing; taking on the whole Chelish fleet is something else entirely."

"You want to cut and run?" Torius was torn. He didn't want to make Celeste angrier, but he couldn't back down, either. It was a lose-lose situation. "You want me to break my word because you have a bad feeling?"

"No, Torius, I don't want you to break your word." She looked him straight in the eye. "I just want you to think of the consequences before you give it. I want you to tell the crew what the stakes are in this mission. If we fail . . ."

"If we fail, everybody I love dies." He fixed her with a hard stare. "You think I don't know that? After what's happened to us already, you think *they* don't know that?"

"I'll follow you anywhere, Torius, you *know* that, but we're in over our heads." She leaned in quick and kissed him, taking him by surprise and melting his anger with the spontaneous gesture. "Just let everyone *else* go into this knowing what we know. No more secrets."

"All right. No secrets." Torius nodded, wondering if any of the Stargazers would jump ship once they knew the stakes. Though guilt twinged him, he qualified his promise. "Once we're at sea, I'll tell them what we could be up against. I can't tell them *everything*, of course, but I'll tell them we could be sailing into the middle of a war. But if Trellis ever finds out I told the crew about our mission, the Chelish navy will be the *least* of our worries."

Vreva swaggered down the dark waterfront, struggling to maintain her disguise through her roiling emotions. The irritating thing was, most of the muddle of fear, elation, intrigue, and pleasure didn't even belong to her. Mathias had been aboard *Devil's Trident* for hours, and the furry little bastard was having fun! Her own emotions—worry for her familiar and irritation with the recent dream message from Marshal Trellis—were easier to control. That this weapon was unknown to Trellis's spy network screamed danger. Ronnel might be going rogue, and taking Cheliax into war on his own initiative. She recalled what she'd learned of him, of his financial trouble, and knew that could be part of his motivation. Naval action would put a lot of gold in his pockets, since admirals got a percentage of every prize taken by their fleet. He wouldn't be the first to line his pockets at the cost of a few thousand lives.

"What's the goin' rate, dearie?"

Vreva sighed in frustration. This was the fourth proposition she'd gotten in the last half hour. *Maybe I should have picked a less attractive disguise.* She eyed the tall, dark-skinned woman and her shorter, hairier dwarf companion, and briefly considered giving Mathias a dose of his own medicine. "For just you, or the both of you?"

"Just me." The woman grinned, her teeth like a rows of pearls. "Jabber here likes to watch." The dwarf smiled through his bushy red beard.

Exhilaration shivered up Vreva's spine. Though she knew it was probably Mathias tumbling some saucy ship's kitty, it was hard to suppress. She drew in a breath to decline and caught a whiff of the woman's perfume on the sultry sea air: orange blossoms with an underlying tinge of cumin, slightly sweaty, flowers crushed under sun-warmed skin in the course of summer lovemaking. The familiar scent hit Vreva like a runaway coach. *Zarina*. A sweet memory of the woman she'd loved and lost trundled through her mind. Vreva bit her lip. Sometimes she thought Calistria tormented her just for entertainment. "Fifteen sails, and you pay for the room."

"Fifteen! Ha!" The woman's laugh rang out loud enough to draw attention from the marines guarding the flagship's gangplank. "I'll pay five, but you better cook us breakfast!"

Vreva felt a surge of urgency. Glancing past the tall sailor, she spied a tiny black shape hurtling from one of the flagship's open ballista ports to vanish among the crates and barrels piled along the pier. Mathias had made his escape. It was time to go.

"Suit yourself." She turned away and started to flounce off.

"Hey! Wait! Aren't you even gonna *haggle* a little?"

Vreva turned back to the tall woman and struck a lascivious pose. "I don't haggle, *dearie*, and I never, *ever* cook breakfast." She left the two gaping after her, and rounded a corner into a deserted alley. With a quick spell, she shifted her appearance from buxom, red-haired prostitute to burly longshoreman. Innately adjusting her gait and manner to match her form, she strode right back out of the alley, passed the befuddled sailors without a glance, and hurried to where Mathias waited.

"Well?" She glanced around, careful to keep her voice low. "Did you learn anything?"

Yes. Mathias leapt into her arms as she started up the street toward the Officers' Club. *I found out that the Devil's Trident has one badass tomcat ruling the bilges, and he didn't like the attention I paid to his cadre of kitties.*

"Well, you get what you—" Vreva started to scratch him behind the ears, but her fingers came away bloody. "Mathias, you're *bleeding*!"

*So is he, and it was *totally* worth it!* He flicked his tail and yawned, showing his teeth. *I think I'm in love. I just have to decide with whom.*

"I sent you aboard that ship to find out about the weapon, not chase tails!"

*And I *did* find out about the weapon—or as much as I could, anyway. The rest was a bonus!*

"You need to pay attention to your job!"

And you need to lighten up and have some fun once in a while. He bumped her chin with his forehead. *Take *pleasure* in your work for a change.*

"I . . ." She stopped the lie before it came out. She could never lie to Mathias. "I don't like to mix work and pleasure. It's too dangerous. Now, what did you find out about the weapon?"

*Mostly that it's being guarded by a whole *squad* of marines.* He tried to lick a bloody gouge in his neck and winced. *Ouch. I don't suppose you brought a potion along, did you? That bite is really killing me.*

"Of course I did." Vreva fished a vial from a pocket, popped the cork, and upended the contents into his mouth. "Better?"

Much better. Thanks. He bonked her chin again. *I also found out that Lieutenant Emero wasn't exaggerating about the devil. It *is* a real devil, and it's almost too big to fit through the door!*

"What does it look like?" Growing up in Cheliax, Vreva had seen more than a few.

Like a big blue eel with arms, and hands like nests of snakes. It's got four big yellow eyes, too. Ugly bugger.

"A drowning devil." She'd never seen one before, but she'd heard of them. The guardians of Hell's waterways, they were dreadful indeed, but hardly powerful enough to tip the balance of power between two nations. "It must be guarding the weapon."

It was, until it went to talk to Ronnel. I followed, and got close enough to hear some of it. They're definitely working together on something. Ronnel was irritated that they couldn't use magic to do something with this weapon they've got. The devil was worried that magic might ruin it or trigger something. Some of it didn't make sense.

Vreva wished she had been there. Mathias was smart, but his interpretation of events was skewed to the perceptions of a cat, and his memory wasn't that of a trained spy. "Emero mentioned a witch, too. Did you see her?"

Oh, yeah. She's a piece of work, let me tell you. A mouth like a sailor and claws like a . . . well, like me. I think the marines are more scared of her than the devil.

"She's human?"

Yeah. She's got scars and a bunch of bone piercings, and a disposition like a rabid dog. She wears a kind of . . . tattered leather corset that doesn't smell right. I saw a tattoo on one bit of it—I think it's human skin.

Vreva shuddered. "What about her familiar? If she's a witch, she must have one."

It's a snake! A nasty little green one. He gave a shudder, and she felt his innate revulsion toward serpents. It was a trait they shared, which made working with Celeste sometimes hard to endure. *She talks to it, but I couldn't understand them.*

"Of course not, love. Did you hear any names?"

Emero called the witch Bushatra. Ronnel only ever called the devil 'fiend.' The devil and the witch were calling each other names, but not proper ones.

"They were fighting?" Vreva considered the possibilities. If she could rouse suspicion or dissent between them, she might gain an advantage.

Only verbally that I could tell, but yes. The devil was raging at her for leaving the ship, but she said she had better things to do than play nursemaid.

"Nursemaid . . ." So, it sounded like the witch and devil were guarding the weapon, and the weapon was . . . alive? She shook her head in puzzlement. What type of creature could be so destructive that Ronnel thought he could start a war with it, yet fit easily into a ship's cabin? She had to find out what it was, and how to neutralize it. Two potential sources of information popped to mind. "I need to make another appointment with Admiral Ronnel, and you need to follow Bushatra the next time she leaves the ship. She might use a disguise, so you'll have to watch closely."

No problem there. I'll recognize her by the smell of that corset.

Vreva felt a little sick. "Be careful, love." She scratched him under the chin, dried blood flaking from his healed scratches and bites. "I wouldn't want her to eat you."

I'd tell you the same, but suspect Admiral Ronnel's gonna want a little nibble before the night's over.

"Don't *even* go there, Mathias!"

His empathic flush of libidinous humor buoyed her spirits. He always looked on the bright side of things, even when their lives were in danger. Maybe that's why she loved him so much.

6

A Star to Steer Her By

The sky blazed with fire, the dying light of sunset breathing life into the heavens. The first stars hove from the darkening twilight as crimson gradually faded to indigo, and Akiton's spark winked to life.

War . . .

Low in the sky at this time of year, the war planet shone for bare minutes before it dipped below the horizon, but the stars of the Cosmic Caravan never changed, and Celeste knew what constellation the red planet resided in: The Pack. These followers of the caravan could signify friend or foe, dutiful hounds or hungry wolves.

Or in this case, maybe a fleet of marauding Chelish warships.

Celeste watched Akiton vanish below the horizon and raised her eyes to the heavens. The song sang in her mind . . .

"Don't you ever get a crick in your neck?"

Snick's question snapped Celeste out of her musing. She turned to the gnome with a smile. "No. I'm pretty much all neck." She twisted her long sinuous body into a coil and then unraveled. "See?"

"Huh!" Snick twisted her body as if considering how she might match the trick, but gave up and looked up at the brightening stars. "So, you reading our future tonight, or just musing?"

"Musing, I guess. There's nothing new to read from a few days ago."

"Well, no news is good news when there's a war brewing."

"So, Torius told everyone?" Celeste knew he'd planned to inform the crew of what little they knew of their mission, but didn't know when.

"Yeah, at dinner." Snick gave a little snort of laughter. "Ruined a few appetites."

"Anyone leaving?"

"Well, not yet!" The gnome gestured at the wide expanse of sea. "Kinda hard to jump ship in the middle of the ocean. Not everyone's happy about it, though, and there were a few questions about what we'll do if there *is* a war. Captain said *Stargazer*'s not a warship, and he never intends to make her one. Also said if anyone wants to leave, he'll put in at Sothis, and they can go."

"Do you think anyone will?"

"Maybe a few." Snick shrugged. "Can't blame 'em."

"You're not . . ." Celeste looked at the gnome worriedly.

"Leaving *Stargazer*?" She snorted and ran her nimble fingers along the smooth taffrail. "Don't be daft. Ship'd fall right apart without me!"

"Right." Celeste knew it was Torius that Snick would never leave, not the ship. The gnome was one of the few Stargazers who had been with Torius when he instigated a mutiny and seized the ship from its slave-master captain. In fact, Snick had apparently saved his life during that fight, much as she had saved Celeste's only days ago. Snick was surprising in that way. Though the gnome didn't care for violence, she could be deadly when she needed to be. "I never got a chance to thank you for the other day, Snick. You saved my life, you know."

"Nah! Just a lucky shot." The gnome grinned. "You'd do the same for me."

"Yes, I would."

"Well, I'll leave you to your stargazin'. The compass is all boogered up again. Gotta swing it true."

"In the dark?"

"Only time I can." Snick grinned and pointed to the north where the gleaming mote of Cynosure hung in the sky. "Gotta have a true north, ya know."

"I didn't know you knew the stars."

"Don't. Just that one." Snick grinned and turned to her work, leaving Celeste to her musing.

Celeste often envied the gnome's simple, pragmatic view of the world. Nothing ever got her down for long. *Not even dying.* The naga shivered at the thought. Snick was what sailors called a gallows jumper, someone who had died and been brought back by magic. She didn't talk much about the experience, except that it had strengthened her faith in Desna and her devotion to Torius. Celeste found it ironic that the gnome looked to the goddess for both spiritual and practical guidance, since Cynosure was reputed to be one of Desna's palaces. She gazed up at the glowing blue-white mote and wondered if Snick had made the right decision to allow her soul to be brought back. Was the Great Beyond so terrible? Had shuffling off mortality—even if only for a little while—changed her view of life and death? Did the gnome have some purpose on Golarion that she felt compelled to accomplish?

Do I?

The song of the heavens sang in Celeste's veins, but no answer came. She considered getting out her instruments and making some astrological calculations, but twitched her tail in frustration. Previous attempts to analyze their situation had only confused her. She was tired of ambiguous prophecies, tired of trying to figure out the meaning of things, the purpose behind their struggles. *Why can't I just get a simple answer?*

Because there are no simple answers, Celeste. Laughter like chiming bells rang in the naga's mind.

Snick leapt up onto the rail and pirouetted on one toe, glittering stardust arcing in a nimbus around her. *You must muddle through, like all mortals do, to find your own purpose, to follow your own dreams* . . . The gnome winked and laughter chimed again, but her lips didn't move, and her voice sounded only in Celeste's head.

Celeste tried to speak, to ask Snick what she meant, but she couldn't move, couldn't even breathe. Suddenly she realized the wind had stopped and the sea around them was frozen in place. The very stars themselves had ceased to twinkle. Panic surged up as she realized that her heart wasn't even beating. She felt as if she were caught in some kind of spell or waking dream.

Yes . . . *Only you, Celeste.* Stardust trailed from the finger Snick pointed at her. *This is only* . . . *for* . . . *you!* The gnome's finger touched the tip of the naga's nose.

Celeste's mind expanded as the heavens rushed in: a billion shining suns, misty nebulae, brilliant supernovae, swirling galaxies, newborn planets, and pits of blackness so deep that neither light nor the captured gods imprisoned within could escape. Like a crescendo of her own thoughts, trillions of beings cried out to the heavens for guidance. In that instant, she and the universe were one. For that moment in time, she understood . . . *everything*.

Celeste blinked, and the world around her resumed. The breeze flapped the sails, the sea rolled past in foamy crests glowing with phosphorescence, and the stars filled the sky instead of her mind. The universe continued spinning, expanding, living, and dying around her. She no longer heard the pleas of trillions, no longer understood all the meanings of existence . . . but she knew that for a brief, intense moment, she had.

By the stars! What's happening to me?

With a glance, Celeste spied Snick still working beside the binnacle, her eyes intent on the compass as she fiddled with her tools. There was no way the gnome could have been dancing on the taffrail a moment ago, trailing stardust from her fingertips.

Now I'm hallucinating! She shook her head, and a flick of movement caught her eye.

There on the rail sat a beautiful blue butterfly slowly opening and closing its wings, completely unruffled by the strong breeze. This far offshore, it wasn't unusual for a weary bird to perch in the rigging until it had regained its strength, but a butterfly?

How odd. Celeste peered at it more closely.

It was unlike any butterfly she'd ever seen, its swallowtail wings spangled with stars, a sunburst, and a crescent moon. The patterns stuck a chord within her mind. *Where have I seen that before?* Then she remembered, and fear cramped her gut. This exact butterfly was engraved on the platform of the Observatory in Katapesh—a shrine to Desna.

Desna . . . What would the goddess of stars want from me?

Celeste blinked in wonder as the butterfly fluttered its fabulous wings and rose easily into the air, still unaffected by the wind. Laughter—remembered or imaginary—chimed in her mind as the creature wafted away into the darkness. Suddenly all the strange things that had been happening to her—the magical cloak of starlight, speaking in tongues, the stargazing trances, her questions seemingly answered, and laughter in her head—clicked into place like the pieces of a puzzle.

Could these be, not curses, but gifts from Desna?

The universe spun overhead, the stars sang, and Celeste finally had an answer.

"More wine, my dear?" Admiral Ronnel waved the steward forward.

"No, thank you." Vreva dabbed her mouth with a monogrammed napkin, then dropped it beside her plate. "Any more and I'll be positively tipsy, and that wouldn't do at all."

"No?" Ronnel smiled like a shark scenting blood in the water. He emptied his own glass, and the steward refilled it. "I thought tipsy would suit perfectly for a night of unabashed frivolity."

"Perhaps at the end, but not just yet." She was nowhere near tipsy, of course, but more wine might make her careless, and this was no time to be careless. "I prefer to have my wits keen. So much enjoyment is lost if the mind is befuddled with alcohol."

"Do you think so?" The admiral sipped his wine. "I find that wine sharpens my senses, rather than dulls them."

"Your warrior's constitution, no doubt." Vreva felt a tug of desperation. The evening was winding down, and she had gotten nowhere.

While the meal had confirmed the chef's talents, the conversation had been as bland as a bowl of gruel. Nothing but banal blather about his exploits and her fabricated past. The playful mood of their initial encounter had been stifled, and she wasn't sure why. No matter how she'd tried to draw him out, he remained withdrawn, as if holding her at arm's length. To complicate matters, the hovering footmen and steward prevented her from employing her magic or using the few drugs she had smuggled aboard. She needed to get him alone, but not the way he obviously wanted to be alone with her. If she gave in too easily to his lust, she could soon find herself back on the pier with a tainted reputation and no information for her trouble. *I've got to get him out of this room first.*

"The other night you promised me a turn on deck. A breath of fresh air would help this fabulous meal to settle."

"A capital idea, Madame Korvis." Ronnel stood. "The weather's fine and the moon's risen. The view from the poop deck should be lovely."

"My thoughts exactly." A footman held Vreva's chair as she stood and took the admiral's arm. Her beaming smile drooped into a pretty pout as she glanced back at the two footmen following a step behind. Squeezing his arm, she arched an eyebrow. "We don't need chaperones, do we?"

"Well . . ." The expression that flashed across Ronnel's face worried her: concern, maybe even a little suspicion. The admiral was no fool, but could he suspect that she was more than just a smitten businesswoman?

"No matter." Vreva shrugged and pressed his arm against her bosom. "I'm just not used to such luxury. Servants at your beck and call all day and night . . ." She sighed wistfully. "We live very different lives, Admiral." It seemed that there was only one way to get him alone.

Mathias is never going to let me hear the end of this. Her familiar was close enough to pick up on her emotions. If she bedded the admiral, there would be no end to his jibes.

"One hardly notices servants when one becomes accustomed to nobility." Ronnel smiled down at her as the steward opened the door. "I feel positively naked without a footman to serve my meals and a valet to help me dress."

"Do they even attend you in your private cabin?" *That would make things difficult.*

"Well . . . not *always*, of course." Ronnel paused and pursed his lips. "If you would prefer a game of cards in the privacy of the quarter gallery . . ."

"Cards?" Vreva smiled knowingly. "You *do* know I run a gambling house, don't you, Admiral? I wouldn't want to take advantage of you."

"Oh, and I was *so* hoping you would."

Vreva laughed despite her mood, caught off guard by his quip. *Maybe he's loosening up after all.* "A hand or two of cards sounds lovely, Admiral."

"This way, my dear." Smiling affably, Ronnel guided her down the corridor to the left. Where the passage turned to the right, he stopped before a closed door and withdrew a key from his waist-coat pocket. "This is actually my favorite cabin in *Devil's Trident*."

"Really? I'm breathless with anticipation!" Worry thrilled down Vreva's spine. She didn't like Ronnel's tone of voice, suddenly as slick as oil upon water, but this was her chance to get him alone. Once inside, she could use magic and drugs to ease his mind and delve his thoughts. As the key clicked in the lock, she readied a spell.

"After you, my dear." He ushered her through, and the footmen stationed themselves in the corridor like a pair of palace guards.

Finally. Vreva stepped into the room, scanning the environment with a practiced glance. Open windows lined two sides of the small chamber, and the scent of the sea wafted in on the light evening breeze. *Easy escape, if necessary.* The furnishings were opulent and cozy—richly upholstered settees, a small table, sideboards stocked with crystal decanters, all illuminated by the soft glow of lamps turned low. Ideal for intimate conversation. *Perfect!*

As the door clicked closed behind her, Vreva mentally recited her spell and discretely wove a complex pattern with her fingers. Before she could complete the last gesture, however, an unyielding hand grasped her arm. Ronnel jerked her so hard that an involuntary yelp of alarm escaped her lips and the spell spun from her mind. Her back slammed against the bulkhead with enough force to snap her head back into the hard wood. Before Vreva could gather her wits, he had her pinned up against the wall, his hands gripping her arms painfully.

"Admiral!" At first, Vreva thought this might merely be rough foreplay, but the look in Ronnel's eyes chilled her to the bone. She tried to move, but his hands grasped harder. Panic surged up, memories of chained wrists, pain, pleading. *Not again. Never again . . .* She fought to keep fear out of her voice. "What are you *doing?*"

"My exact question for you, Madame Korvis." His chest pressed against hers, his wine-scented breath warm on her face. "What are *you* doing here? Why did you ask me to your club? What do you hope to gain?"

He doesn't know. He can't know! "Gain?" Vreva tried again to break free, but he had a good grip and outweighed her by half. "Admiral Ronnel, release me this instant! I came here as your guest!"

"Yes, you did. What I want to know is *why*!" Instead of releasing her, Ronnel leaned in closer, inhaling her scent. "You run a gaming house and brothel, so you're not here because you crave male company. What game are you playing?"

So he doesn't know. He's just suspicious. She could use that. If she gave him a legitimate reason, something he could believe, he would let her go. *Then* . . . Vreva thought of the poisoned needle in her hair, but instantly banished the image of jamming it into her host's pulsing jugular. *You can't kill him, Vreva!* Explaining a dead admiral would be more than problematic. Naval justice was swift and harsh. Most likely, she would be strung up by her neck from a yardarm. She had to deal with him, still needed the secrets locked in his head.

Feigning exasperation, she said, "I'm not playing a game at all, Admiral, I'm conducting *business*!"

He leaned back and gave her an incredulous look. "If you think I'm going to pay you for—"

"*Please*, Admiral. Don't insult me." Vreva writhed expertly against Ronnel, stifling her fear of him with a sensuous smile. "You're very astute. If you release me, I'll explain."

"Very well." He took a step back and let go of her arms. "Why did you invite me to your club?"

"*Prestige*, Admiral Ronnel." She straightened her dress, noting how his eyes still drifted down to her cleavage whenever he wasn't speaking to her. "You're commander of the Ostenso fleet. To have you in my club would honor my humble establishment. When you declined and invited me here, I thought that a dalliance between us might accomplish the same."

"You hope to elevate your social status through our association." It wasn't a question.

"And drum up business, yes. Surely you didn't think our . . . association would remain a secret from the officers of the fleet." Vreva smiled at him cunningly. Strolling past him to the sideboard, she began exploring the decanters, removing one crystal stopper after another and sniffing each. She took the opportunity to cast the silent spell she'd attempted before, and was relieved to feel his mind soothed by her magic. *Now for a little something else.* Pretending to smooth her skirt, she ensured that the tiny vial of striped toadstool toxin was accessible. The drug would weaken his defenses and befuddle his mind. Then she could direct the conversation to guide his thoughts, and strip away his secrets. Decanter in hand, she turned to him and smiled. "Brandy?"

"Please." He joined her at the sideboard before she had time to drug his glass.

Frustrated, Vreva locked a smile onto her lips and handed him a snifter. "Do you think I'm a terrible person for using you so? You *did* say you hoped I would take advantage of you." Swirling her brandy in her glass, she inhaled the aromatic vapors before taking a tiny sip.

"Using me to advance your *business* prospects wasn't exactly what I had in mind." Ronnel's tone had shifted from accusative to introspective. The spell was working.

"It *could* be a mutually beneficial arrangement, Admiral." Vreva sidled up to him and ran a finger over his jaw, the slight stubble like sandpaper beneath her fingertip. "I use you, you use me . . ."

His hand closed on her wrist again, but gently this time, and his eyes searched hers. "You really are . . . something."

Vreva leaned forward and drew his hand closer until it pressed against her cleavage. "You have no idea, Admiral." She brushed his lips with hers in the promise of a kiss, then pulled away. His grip turned to water, and he let her go. "But if you'd rather send me away . . ." She turned and sauntered to the windows, keeping a keen eye on his reflection.

"What*ever* made you think I would send you away, Virika?"

Oh, so now I'm Virika . . . While the admiral bolted his brandy and turned aside to place his snifter on the sideboard, Vreva capitalized on his inattention to cast another silent spell, this one to delve his mind. Immediately, she felt the flicker of his thoughts like a nearby candle flame.

"We all use one another when the day is done. No one's innocent of it." He pursued her to the windows, his hands encircling her trim waist. "I was just suspicious of your motives. I'm sure you can understand."

"You frightened me rather badly, you know." She met his gaze in their reflection. "Are you always so suspicious?"

"It comes with the onus of command. I'm a powerful man, Virika. The entire Ostenso fleet and, by extension, the well-being of Cheliax herself rests in my hands." He pulled her close, his lecherous thoughts filtering through the haze of alcohol that clouded his mind.

"So much responsibility must be a dreadful burden."

With Bushatra and Anguillithek fighting over who gets to destroy Augustana first, you bet your sweet little ass it is. His thought came to her as clearly as if he'd spoken.

Augustana. She bridled her delight at the discovery. *So that's the target.* Augustana was the nearest Andoren coastal city to Cheliax, and the bastion of Andoran's naval might. If the fleet stationed there was devastated, or the city razed, Andoran would be at a serious naval disadvantage. That would be the perfect crippling stroke as a prelude to war. Should she warn Trellis? *Not yet.* If Chelish spies noticed an evacuation of the harbor at Augustana, they'd know news of the attack had leaked. Then they'd start hunting for the source of that leak. And that, Calistria forbid, might lead back to her.

"A burden, yes, and with responsibility comes caution." Ronnel crushed her against him, his lips on the curve of her neck, the stubble of his beard sending shivers down her spine. "And the need for a distraction."

"Is that all I am to you, a distraction?" She leaned back against him and pressed his hands to her bosom. "What did you *think* I wanted from you?"

Can't exactly tell her you thought she might be a spy, Vaetus. "I have more to lose than most men, my dear. I've a reputation to consider, and family in Egorian. You might blackmail me."

So, he had *suspected me of spying.* Laughing to hide her fear, Vreva sipped her brandy and moved in slow, tantalizing gyrations against him, encouraging his fondling. "I'm not a fool, Admiral, and I would have to be an incredible idiot to blackmail a man like you."

"Yes, you *would.*" He chuckled low. *And they'd find your pretty corpse floating in the bay.*

Nice. She reconsidered the poison needle in her hair. *Maybe later . . .*

"But I certainly can't blame you for trying to use me for your own ends."

"And what exactly did you think my *ends* were, Vaetus?" She turned in his grasp, her free hand wandering down to his trousers. "I'm not exactly after your *title.*"

"You wouldn't be the first." His fingers deftly loosened the laces of her dress. *If Narika ever finds out about her, she'll drag my name through the muddiest streets in Egorian, the simpering shrew. If I didn't need her money . . .*

Vreva committed the detail to memory. *So Ronnel's chasing a wealthy heiress.* That fed into her theories about him well. A man who would marry someone he despised for money might also start a war for it.

"I've worked very hard to build a reputation here as well, Vaetus." She teased his lips with hers. "Just like you, I've got a lot to lose. My very livelihood, in fact. We've all got our secrets to keep, demons in our closets. I don't care about yours, and you'd find mine incredibly boring."

"I doubt that." *She could probably tell some stories . . .*

"Honestly, though, I thought you would enjoy the Officers' Club." It was time to get his mind back on track, and off of her drooping bodice. She had him where she wanted him now. There was no rush. "We *do* have the best entertainment in town, you know. Don't you *ever* get to leave this dreary old ship?"

"In a few days, perhaps." *When that slug Robust gets here, and I can get that bloody thing off my ship! Damn that cuckolding rake Giavano. Probably out sailing in circles. The scrub never could navigate worth a damn.* "But we can have our own entertainment here, can't we?"

Vreva's mind spun to decipher his thoughts. "That bloody thing" must be the weapon. *Robust . . .* She remembered a galleon by that name from her lists, but it was nothing but an old cargo transport, not a warship. What were they planning with a scow like that?

"Oh, that's right!" She slipped out of his grasp, ignoring the loose laces of her dress. The neckline sagged near the point of indecency, but she ignored that, too. "We were going to play *cards!*" She spied a deck on the table and snatched them up. "What should we play?"

Bloody tease. "You pick the game, I'll pick the stakes."

"Very well." Vreva took a seat beside the table and shuffled expertly. "Drakes and lions is my game. What are we playing for?"

He removed his cravat and dropped it on the table. "Ante up, my dear."

I should have guessed . . . "Very well." Slipping off a shoe, she flicked it up with her toe. She caught it in one hand and placed it on the table. "I may have slightly deeper pockets than you."

"Then we'll have to think of something else to wager."

She didn't need to read his thoughts to know what he meant, but did it anyway, and fought to keep her composure. The man would make a satyr blush. She examined him professionally, and decided that he was definitely handsome. She remembered what Mathias had said about taking pleasure in her work.

Vreva won several hands—how could she not, with her magic exposing his thoughts?—then lost one as her spell ran out.

Finishing her brandy, she sent the admiral for a refill and recast the spell as soon as his back was turned.

"You must get lonely being in command." She rose from her seat and strolled to the window again, listening for his thoughts.

"Sometimes, but it has its rewards." *Like a governorship, when we rebuild Augustana.*

Rebuild? That didn't sound good. Was this weapon really so devastating they could destroy an entire city? If so, why transfer it from a man-of-war to a transport ship? She remembered Mathias's report about their worries concerning magic and the weapon, and realized what it must have been about. *Teleport . . . they can't tele-port the weapon to Augustana for fear of triggering it here.*

"All the politics and bureaucratic nonsense must be weari-some. How do you cope with it?"

He sidled up behind her and handed her the snifter. "I'm above most of it." *And I'll be even farther above it soon.* "And tonight's not so lonely."

"I get lonely, Vaetus. You might think it strange, but I do." Turning, Vreva caressed his stubbly cheek. Now that she had his mind soothed, she could put any suggestion she wished there, and she knew he'd accept it. "You needn't fear your reputation from me. You must know that I'd never risk your wrath."

You better not . . . "And you needn't fear me, my dear."

"And as your power grows, perhaps we can continue to . . . use one another?" She teased his lips with her fingertips.

"I'm sure we can reach a mutually beneficial arrangement." *Once Giavano completes his suicide mission, and my fleet swoops in to aid the devastated city, she can keep me company in Augustana. Perfect!*

That explained much. A suicide mission to deploy this weapon would allow Cheliax to deal a death blow to Andoran's navy without the inconvenience of taking responsibility for killing thousands. If the Chelish fleet arrived to render aid after the devastation, the locals would be in no position to refuse them. Once ensconced, the Chelish would never leave. She wondered what lever he had over this Captain Giavano. What could force a man into suicide?

"I'm not used to . . . men like you, Vaetus." That was true enough. She was used to men a lot worse than the admiral. He might be a lecherous, power-hungry devil worshiper, but he didn't seem truly sadistic.

"You've never met *anyone* like me, Virika." He slipped her dress off her shoulders with deft assurance, his grip hardening on her arms again.

She shivered, not entirely unpleasantly. "What about our card game?"

"I tire of games."

"Patience is a virtue, they say." She leaned in and gave him a lingering kiss. "Good things come to those who wait."

"I've waited long enough." Ronnel grabbed her glass, quaffed the brandy, and tossed the snifter casually out the open window. He crushed her against him, his teeth playing the nerves along her neck, sending shocks down her spine.

"Oh, Vaetus!" Vreva dismissed her thought-reading spell and let Calistria, goddess of lust, have her way. Vreva would get nothing useful from him for the time being. At least nothing from his mind.

7

Perilous Prophecies

Torius mounted the quarterdeck steps, yawned in a great lungful of sea air, and smiled. *At sea again* . . . The motion of the ship, the wind in his hair, and the creak and groan of the rigging never ceased to ease his nerves. Beneath his feet, the deck barely heeled. The seas were running about twelve feet, but *Stargazer* bore it easily, steady on a beam reach, stabilized by her full hold and towering canvas. A glance aloft confirmed that nothing had changed since his last watch; all plain sail with a reef in the main and forecourse. Since becoming privateers, they'd run with the usual white sails at all times, forgoing the black sails they formerly used at night while pirating. Though it made checking the sails easier in the dark, it also made Torius feel a bit like a bug on a white tablecloth. *One of the trade-offs for being legitimate, I guess.*

"Nothing on the horizon, Captain." Thillion met him with a casual salute and a smile. "Not a single light nor sign of a ship. Snick worked the bugs out of the compass, and we're on course."

"Good." A glance around showed only one thing missing. "Where's Celeste?"

"She went below." The elf shrugged. "She asked if I needed her, and since we're headed for open sea, I said that I didn't. Kortos was off our port beam at sunset, and we've been on a rhumb line for Sothis since then."

"That's odd. She usually waits up for my watch."

"She's not in your cabin? I thought . . . well . . ."

Torius waved off Thillion's unease. The whole ship knew that he and Celeste often reserved the early evening watch for private time. "No, she's not there, and I didn't see her in the galley." He glanced around the middle deck, but didn't spy her distinctive white hair. He grew uneasy. *She's been acting strange lately . . .* "Would you mind staying on watch for a few more minutes, Thillion? I'd like to find her."

"No problem, sir."

"Thanks. Oh, and you can ease off to the west a few points. We're not going to Sothis."

"Yes, sir!" The elf grinned. He knew that meant that none of the Stargazers had decided to jump ship.

Torius went to their cabin first, wondering if he might have missed Celeste curled up on her pillows in the dark, but she wasn't there. Nor was she in the galley or reading in the spare stateroom. The main hold was dark, so he lit a lantern and started exploring among the barrels and crates of herbs and spices, the scents of rosemary, sage, and other exotic herbs overpowering in the close confines. The cargo was well secured against the motion of the sea, and Snick's babies were stowed away, but no Celeste. There was nothing forward on this deck but crew quarters, and he knew she wouldn't disturb the sleeping sailors.

A great, dark hole opened before him: the open hatch to the lower hold. A cool breeze ruffled his hair from above. As was their usual practice when the weather was good, the main hatch had been replaced by a grating for ventilation. Moonlight filtered down through the gaps, the checkerboard of pearly light sweeping back and forth with the roll of the ship. Torius shone his lantern down into the lower hold. There weren't many places to hide aboard a hull only a hundred feet long. He descended the ladder and peered into the gloom.

Over the ship's creaks and groans, he caught a faint sound of scratching. *The ship's cat chasing a rat?* Torius worked his way forward, shining his lantern into the narrow gaps between the stacked crates of cargo. When he reached the forepeak bulkhead and the hatch to the storage locker, he heard the scratching again over the rush of the sea past the hull. Definitely from inside the locker.

What the hell? Torius hung the lantern on a hook, quietly drew his dagger, and reached for the latch.

Scratch, scratch . . . *Like a pen on parchment, or . . .*

He pulled open the door. "Celeste?"

The soft lantern light spilling into the storage locker illuminated the naga coiled among the canvas and cordage. Turning toward him, she hissed and blinked at the light. The pile of translucent, scaly skin beneath her confirmed his suspicion.

Celeste was shedding.

"Go away, Toriusss."

"What's wrong? I've seen you shed before. It doesn't bother me." In fact, she usually shed her skin in their cabin. Instinct drove her to seek a safe haven until she could rid herself of the sloughing scales. It was inconvenient, but passed quickly. *So why is she hiding away in the bowels of the ship?*

"I . . . I don't want you . . . to come any closer. Please. Just go."

"No." Something was wrong, and Torius was determined to find out what it was. He grabbed the lantern, stepped inside the cramped locker, and shut the hatch behind him. Looking closer, he saw patches of dry skin still clinging to her body. That was unusual; her skin usually shed in one complete piece. Only once had he seen her looking so splotchy: chained in the slaver dungeon when he first met and rescued her. Later she had told him that stress adversely affected her ability to shed well. From the looks of it, she was pretty stressed right now. "Tell me what's wrong. You've been edgy lately, but this is over the top. What's bothering you?"

"I don't . . . I can't tell you." She turned away, hiding her face in her coils. "You'll think I'm crazy. By the stars, *I* think I'm crazy!"

"Crazy? What are you talking about, Celeste?" Torius gently ran a hand down her cool scales and felt her shudder. "What's happened?"

"I don't *know*! I saw . . . something that can't be real!" She writhed her coils, scraping more of the old, dry skin off her tail with that distinctive scratching sound. "It *can't* be . . ."

"What can't be real? What did you see?" He knelt down and ran his fingers through her hair, trying to ease her nerves, though her behavior had him truly worried. He'd seen her upset before, even to the point of hissing and spitting venom, but this was different. Judging from her wide eyes and twitching tail, she was terrified. Her natural reaction to a threat was anger, not fear.

"I saw . . . Snick, but it wasn't Snick. It was like the whole world stopped around me, then she . . . changed." Her head rose from her coils and turned to him, blinking hard against the light, tears glistening in her eyes. "She spoke to me, in my head, and then she changed into . . . into a butterfly. Into *Desna's* butterfly!"

"She . . ." Torius swallowed his initial skeptical response. If Celeste said Snick turned into a butterfly, then he believed her. He'd never known her to hallucinate or have delusions. "What did she say?"

She fixed him with a hard glare. "You think I'm crazy, don't you?"

"No, I don't think you're crazy, but I don't know what happened, either." He ran his hand through her hair again, and she leaned into the caress. At least she still trusted him. "This could be some evil trick, or it could be exactly what you thought. It could have been a waking dream sent by Desna. She *is* the goddess of dreams, you know."

"But why would Desna talk to me, Torius? What did I do?" Celeste shook her head. "I've never prayed to any god in my life!"

"True." Though Celeste wasn't an atheist, she tended to rely more on astrology than any divine influence for her answers.

She believed the entire universe was a single immense consciousness, and that the motions of the planets among the stars sent
messages to those willing to pay attention and listen. But that
didn't mean one of the gods might not take an interest in her.
"But you did spend weeks at her shrine. Maybe you . . . caught
her attention."

"But I don't *want* her attention!"

"Why not?" Torius smiled, relieved to think that there might
be a simple, albeit astounding explanation for her vision. "I pray
for Gozreh's attention all the time. It'd be nice to know that she
was actually listening! Besides, you couldn't have picked a better
deity than the goddess of stars."

Celeste slapped her tail against the hull. "But I *didn't* pick her!"

"No, but maybe she picked you."

"But why?"

"Who knows? Because you already look to the stars for guidance, maybe? Now, maybe you can just ask Desna."

"But that's just it, Torius. She said that . . . that I had to find
my *own* answers."

"She did?" Torius considered for a moment. "Actually, that
sound exactly like something a deity would say. What else?"

"She . . . touched me." Celeste's eyes lost their fearful look and
assumed a far-off, wonder-filled sort of gaze. "And for a second, I
had the answer to everything, every question I could ever think to
ask. But now . . . I can't remember."

"Well, I'm glad of that, anyway!" Torius laughed.

"What?" Celeste looked horrified. "Why?"

"What would be the fun in living if you had all the answers?
No more exploring, no more discovery, no more adventure!" He
shrugged. "Kind of like knowing the end of a book you just started
reading."

"But . . . I think she does give me *some* answers." At Torius's
befuddled look, she explained. "That slaver galley, Torius. I was

wondering if we should fight, and suddenly I just *knew* we'd win. At the time, I didn't understand how I knew, I just *knew* I was right."

"You did?" He grinned at her and laughed out loud. "Well, that'll come in handy!" A sudden memory came to him of Celeste shrouded in starry light. "What about that cloak of starlight during the battle? I didn't recognize it as one of your usual spells."

"I don't know. I didn't . . ." Celeste closed her eyes for a moment, then opened them wide. "Maybe I did! I . . ." She blinked, and starlight shimmered around her. She looked down at herself in amazement. "Torius! I did!"

"Holy—" Torius bit his tongue. Blaspheming in the presence of a divine manifestation didn't seem wise. Reaching out a hand, he felt a cool pressure against his palm before his fingers penetrated the radiant aura to brush Celeste's scales. "How did you do it?"

"I just . . . asked." She closed her eyes again and the luminous barrier faded.

"Did you send it away?"

"Yes."

"Can you summon it again?"

"I . . . don't want to." She writhed her coils again, her agitation returning.

"What's wrong, Celeste? If these are gifts from Desna, you should use them."

"But I'm not a cleric! I don't worship Desna! I've got my own faith, my own beliefs. Why would she give me anything unless she wants something in return?" Celeste bit her lip and shook her head.

"But Desna's a good—"

"It doesn't matter! I didn't ask for it." She looked stubborn. "You don't give someone a gift out of nowhere and then ask for devotion in return. It's . . . *rude!*"

"This isn't like gifts at a birthday party, Celeste. Just because we don't know *what* you did to earn her thanks doesn't mean you didn't do something worthy." He pondered, wondering how he could help her, and realized that matters of religion weren't really his area of expertise. "Maybe you should talk to one of Desna's clerics. Or at least someone who knows more about faith than a pirate."

"Maybe." Celeste took a deep breath and shuddered down her entire length. "I guess it couldn't hurt."

"You'll probably have to wait until we get back to Almas. I don't remember seeing any shrines to Desna in Ostenso."

"What about Sothis? Aren't we stopping there?"

"No." He smiled broadly. "No need—the crew all decided to stay. We've already come off to the west, and I'm going to make our turn to the north early, since Trellis is in such an all-fired hurry for us to deal with this Chelish weapon."

"Thank you for telling them all the truth." Celeste slithered forward and brushed his cheek with her own. "And thank you for helping me sort this out."

"I didn't do anything." Torius ran his hands through Celeste's hair and held her close, her glossy new scales cool against his shirt. "I just listened."

"Sometimes that's enough."

A surge of urgency twinged along Vreva's nerves. *Mathias . . .* She cast her spell, and looked down to check her disguise: the rough-skinned hands of a sailor, feminine yet muscular arms, and the canvas trousers and wide-collared shirt of a Chelish sailor on shore leave. *Perfect.* Without a mirror, she'd have to assume her face resembled her chosen foil—one of the sailors she'd seen on her way to Ronnel's cabin. She wasn't worried; dusk was deepening, and in the dark one sailor looked pretty much like another.

Another empathic surge thrilled up her spine; Mathias was close. Before she could step into the open, she caught sight of him, a black blur dashing into the shadowed alley. He leapt up into her arms and nuzzled her neck.

She's coming up the street. She looks like the same Chelish sailor she did last time: skinny, with brown hair, a missing front tooth, and a scar on her cheek. He bonked her chin with his forehead, mewing in apology when she winced.

"Don't worry. It's healing." The bruise was from the armrest of the settee in Ronnel's private cabin. He had turned out to be what one of her earliest instructors called a rough trick. The admiral wasn't really a sadist, but made love like he was fighting a battle: hard and fast, no mercy, no surrender. Not Vreva's favorite, but she had given as good as she got, and he had a few bruises of his own.

I don't know why you didn't just kill that bastard outright! Mathias mewed quietly. *Without him, this whole plan to start a war falls apart. On second thought, let me go with you next time. You slip knockout toxin into his wine, and I'll chew off his balls.*

Vreva stifled a laugh. Her familiar tended to be protective, and hadn't liked it at all when she returned from the dalliance sporting bruises. "As tempting as that sounds, I can't kill him. Anguillithek could be the kingpin behind this, and if Ronnel ends up dead, the devil will know something's up. He's still a good source of information."

He's not that good a source. You learned that they're targeting Augustana, but nothing about the weapon.

"For some reason Ronnel didn't like to think about it, and it's a difficult subject to work into pillow talk. But if Bushatra's actually guarding the weapon as you said, delving into her mind might give me all the details I need." Vreva peered around the corner and saw a Chelish sailor striding up the street—skinny, brown hair, and scarred cheek. "You're sure that's Bushatra, and not a real Chelish sailor?"

I'm sure. Same bad leather smell. The only way she could lose me is to lose that corset! I had no trouble following her the other night. His ears twitched. *But then, I'm a cat. *You* should probably be careful!*

"Always." Dropping Mathias, Vreva peered around the corner again and cast her charm spell. Winning the woman's trust was essential before she started reading her thoughts. Between the magic and her disguise as a fellow sailor, she hoped to get Bushatra thinking about things more important than just what she was planning to have for dinner.

Vreva felt her spell wrap around the woman's mind, then fail, as if some interposing force brushed her magic aside. Vreva wasn't too worried. She cast the spell again, and once again it failed to take hold of the witch's mind. *Damn!* Spell failure was common to new casters, but Vreva prided herself on her arcane skills.

"Something's wrong," she whispered, ducking back into the shadows as Bushatra strode past her hiding place. "She's resisting my magic." Vreva watched carefully, worried that her attempts might have been detected, but the witch walked on without a glance, her steps fast, evidently intent on her destination.

Losing your touch?

Vreva shot her familiar a glare. "I'll have to try without the charm." She cast her thought-reading spell and stepped out of hiding. Instantly, numerous minds—astute, dull, and indifferent—flickered into her perception. Concentrating, she identified Bushatra's—a keen mind indeed, which might explain the witch's ability to shrug off Vreva's charm spell. Hastening her steps, Vreva affected the raucous manner of a Chelish sailor on shore leave.

"Hey, shipmate! Hold up there!" She slurred her words as if tipsy, and fished a pipe out of a pocket as Bushatra turned to face her. "Got a light?"

"Bugger off! I'm busy!" The witch turned away and continued up the street.

Vreva tried to delve her thoughts, but didn't get past a haze of irritation. "Too busy to light a shipmate's pipe? Well, that's friendly for ya!" She lengthened her stride to keep up as she focused on the woman's mind. She could feel it, but couldn't penetrate through to hear her thoughts. "Come on, mate. I lost my matches. Just a light."

The witch turned, glared at her supposed shipmate, and uttered a single arcane word. With a snap of her fingers, a spark ignited the bowl of the pipe. "There's your light. Now bugger off!"

"Whoa, nice trick!" Vreva puffed and blew a smoke ring. She slowed her steps and tried one final time to pierce the haze of Bushatra's mind. Nothing. "Thanks, mate!" She raised her pipe and grinned, but the witch didn't even look back.

"What a *bitch*," she muttered under her breath as she strolled off the street. Mathias joined her in moments.

I told you she was a piece of work. Mathias rubbed her leg as Vreva tapped out her pipe. When she'd tucked it away, he hopped up into her arms.

"Yes, you did, but something's wrong. I can't seem to get any magic to work on her."

Maybe she's just tough. Mathias lashed his tail, and she felt his revulsion for the witch. *Or maybe her magic is stronger than yours. She *is* a witch, after all.*

"Maybe . . ." Vreva stiffened her resolve. If she couldn't get information about the weapon from Bushatra's thoughts, she'd find another way. "Where did you say she goes?"

A house up on the hill. She meets some people there. Last time she stayed half the night.

"A coven, perhaps," Vreva mused. "Well, then, I think I need to check out her little circle of friends. But let's take a roundabout route. And hurry. I'd like to get there before she does."

Mathias squirmed in her arms, and she dropped him. *Follow me!*

Vreva cast a quick spell to render herself invisible and hurried after her familiar. A cat running up the streets wouldn't draw attention, but she didn't need curious eyes following her. She was breathless by the time they stopped, hunkering in the shadows of an alley in an unassuming neighborhood.

Right there, across the street.

"That's it?" The house didn't look like a witches' lair. With lacy curtains, a low wrought-iron fence, and white-painted ginger-bread moldings, it looked more like someplace a grandmother would bake cookies.

What did you expect, a spooky mansion with bats flying out the windows? Mathias's sarcasm tweaked Vreva's temper, but he was right. Witches weren't often the stereotypical hags that most people thought they were. *There she is!*

Still looking like a Chelish sailor, Bushatra approached the house. She pushed through the creaky gate, climbed the steps, and knocked on the door. A moment later, the door opened, and Bushatra dispelled her disguise. A tall blond man let her in without a word. Shadows passed the windows in the front of the house as the two figures were backlit by lamplight.

There's another one.

A man in a merchant's jerkin strode up the street carrying a satchel. He, too, went to the door, knocked, and was let in by the blond man.

"How many are there?"

Four, including Bushatra. Mathias lashed his tail. *The last one's a woman. Short with spectacles and curly red hair. I don't see anyone else coming, so maybe she's already inside.*

"There's one way to find out. Stay here." Vreva cast her invisibility spell once again. There were few people out and about, but the street wasn't deserted. She hopped the low fence to avoid the creaky gate, and slunk up to the window. Through the tiny gap between the drapes she spied a comfortably furnished room. The man who had brought the satchel was pouring wine into glasses and distributing them to two of the three people who sat around a low table. The red-headed woman was there, but she wasn't the one who caught Vreva's eye. Vreva got her first close look at Bushatra.

Mathias wasn't exaggerating. The woman's hair was wild, and bone jewelry pierced her nose, ears, eyebrows, and lips. Her deep tan and the livid scars that marred her face and arms confirmed her Kellid ancestry, the flesh bearing the evidence of a hard life. Bushatra wore closely fitted leather that might be, as Mathias had suspected, human skin. Vreva suppressed a shiver of revulsion as she spotted strange tattoos inked here and there upon it. No wonder the woman only left the ship in disguise. She would draw unwelcome attention in Ostenso.

Lips moved among the group inside the house, but Vreva couldn't hear a word. *We can fix that.* She whispered a complex spell, and bent her concentration on the room beyond the window. Shortly, their voices sounded in her mind as if she stood among the coven of witches.

"—lovely vintage, Tyfuss." The blond man lifted his glass and sipped daintily. "Are you sure you won't try some, Bushatra? I daresay it's better than the swill they serve aboard *Devil's Trident.*"

"I'm not here to sip wine and trade pleasantries, Pothario. I'm here to learn magic from the rest of you, and give you magic in return. Your ridiculous social interactions don't interest me."

"Well, I hope you don't mind the rest of us being ridiculous." The red-haired woman held out her glass for Tyfuss to top up. She pushed up her thick spectacles with a flick of her wrist, the gold charms on her bracelet jingling with the motion. "What else are we supposed to do while our familiars exchange spells? Remember, *you* approached *us* with this offer of collusion. Besides, what's your hurry?"

"*Fate* hurries us on. *Robust* is due to arrive any day, and I need to learn as much as I can before I have to go."

"Relax, Bushatra." Tyfuss picked up the bottle and poured a measure into the empty glass on the table. "Have some wine. We've made excellent progress, and as Keah said, there's nothing for us to do while we wait for our familiars."

Bushatra grasped the glass and drained it in a single swallow. "Sour grape juice . . . You should learn to make archi. It's better than this."

"No way am I going to drink fermented yak's milk." Keah wrinkled her nose and pushed up her glasses again. "I don't even like beer."

"*Chelaxians* . . ." Bushatra made a disgusted face.

"Why do I get the feeling I'm being used?" Tyfuss narrowed his eyes at Bushatra, possibly put off by her opinion of the wine, or his country. "So far, you've benefitted from this interaction more than we have. Why should we believe that you'll ever come back to give us what you promised?"

"Because I've *shown* you what you'll receive. Once I've fulfilled my promise to Ronnel and escaped the destruction of Augustana, he'll take over as provincial governor and grant me wealth enough to make you all rich! Don't worry; you'll all get what you were promised!"

So that's the price of destroying a city. Bile welled up into Vreva's throat. *How can they so blithely consider killing thousands for their own gain?*

"Or, you could be filling our heads with delusions of grandeur," Pothario said.

"I would *never* betray my coven!" Bushatra glared him down, dark eyes flaring with spite and pointed teeth flashing. "Enough blather! I'm here for magic, not talk." Bushatra flung her glass aside. The crash elicited a hiss and a squeak from a corner of the room hidden from Vreva's view.

Keah leapt to her feet and glared at Bushatra. "If you hurt my Woobles, I'll—"

"You'll *what*?" Bushatra bared those filed teeth again in a grue-some sneer. "I have more magic than any of you, and I'm offering to make you all *rich*. All you have to do is help me see far enough into the future to make sure my plans are still intact, and you'll get your reward. So shut up and finish your rotten grape juice. I want to cast another vision tonight."

"You've already shown us all our futures." Tyfuss drank more wine, seemingly unintimidated by the witch's rant. "Why try again?"

She can see the future? Vreva revised her assessment of Bushatra. She might be revolting, but she wielded some serious magic if she could see farther than a few days into the future. Of course, if she would risk a shouting match with a drowning devil, she was either powerful or insane. *Maybe both . . .*

"The future's always changing. Even as the course of a river may change with the rains a hundred miles away, the course of a prophecy may be altered by seemingly unrelated events. I want to make sure all is well with *Robust.* If something has gone wrong, your futures will change."

"You said nothing *could* go wrong," Pothario protested.

"Once the weapon's aboard *Robust* and we're under way, I'll be in control of the situation and nothing *can* go wrong. Until then . . ." Bushatra shrugged.

Vreva's mind spun with potential plans of action. Perhaps she could contact Torius by dream spell. If he could waylay *Robust* before the ship reached Ostenso, it might buy them more time to discover what the weapon was and how to destroy it. Or it might tip off the Chelish navy and blow *Stargazer*'s cover. Laying plans against someone who could see the future was a paradox waiting to happen. *Am I altering their futures just by listening in on their conversation?*

"I don't get why they can't use another ship. I mean, the navy's got dozens, right?" Keah's petulance drew Bushatra's glare.

"It has to be a merchant ship, Keah, not a warship. How else can they sneak the weapon into Augustana's harbor? A naval ship would never get past the Gray Corsairs. Besides, it's the captain of *Robust* that Ronnel wants more than the ship itself. Apparently, Ronnel holds some threat over his family—caught him cuckolding some count or something. If he doesn't go through with this, Ronnel will ruin his family name. They're not likely to get any other volunteers."

"Oh." Keah sipped her wine and heaved a gusty sigh. "Well, you can read my future again if you want. I never get tired of seeing myself rich and powerful."

"Good! Finish your spoiled juice and we'll go down."

"Let me set the wards first." Pothario put down his glass and stood. Withdrawing a tiny bell and silver wire from a pocket, he positioned himself carefully and began to chant. The bell chimed as he cast the spell, and the wire glowed and vanished in a shower of silvery sparkles.

Quickly, Vreva cast a spell of her own. To her dismay, she discerned a subtle magical aura that centered upon Pothario and encompassed most of the room, including the front door and window. Several other items among the coven glowed with brighter auras, the most powerful from Bushatra's tattooed leather corset. *Maybe that's why my spells failed.*

"Pothario, you're so paranoid!" Keah finished her wine and stood.

"It keeps me alive." Pothario tucked the little bell away and gestured deeper into the house. "Shall we?"

"Yes." Bushatra stalked out of Vreva's view and the others followed, exchanging glances behind her back.

Vreva slipped over the fence and hurried back to Mathias. "Well, that was interesting."

What? He hopped up into her arms.

"Their familiars are exchanging spells, and Bushatra's using the others to look into the future."

Their familiars get spells? Mathias sounded hurt. *How come I don't get spells?*

"Because you don't bring me any. Witches get their magic from pacts with strange powers, and their familiars are the conduits of that knowledge. My magic comes from inside. But I'm worried about the looking-into-the-future thing. How can we thwart them if they know what we're going to do?"

But if you know they're looking, can't you plan for that?

"What do you mean?"

If Bushatra sees their futures, make them see what you want them to see. Mathias flicked his tail. *Make it look like—*

The loud slam of a door drew their attention back to the house. Keah hurried through the gate, clutching something close.

The door opened again, and Tyfuss called after her. "Keah! Don't be ridiculous! I would never—"

"Let her go, Tyfuss." Pothario grasped his arm to keep him from running after the fleeing woman. "What she saw is between the two of you. Don't let it interfere with our plans." Tyfuss pulled him back into the house. The door closed, and Keah hurried up the street without looking back.

What the hell was that about?

"I don't know, love, but I think it just gave me an idea." Vreva dropped Mathias and prepared a spell. "Stay here, and follow Tyfuss back to wherever he lives. I'm going to follow Keah."

You're not going to kill her, are you?

"No, but I need to find out what scared her so badly." She cast her spell and vanished from sight. "It may give me the edge I need to outwit Bushatra."

8

Predators and Prey

"Harbormaster's barge comin' out to greet us." Grogul turned to his captain with a malicious grin. "If you ordered Snick to give 'em a full broadside, you wouldn't have to go to her villa tonight."

"Don't tempt me." Torius scanned the barge with his spyglass and tried not to grind his teeth. Beyond the barge, the huge Chelish flagship, *Devil's Trident*, still dominated the waterfront, her gruesome figurehead thrusting a huge iron trident forward from her bow. "I just hope we get a slip. Looks like they're taking about half the merchant pier with that behemoth."

"As long as they put us as far away from it as possible." Grogul hawked and spat over the side. "Any ship that can throw a sixty-ballista broadside makes me nervous."

"Come on!" Torius clapped his bosun on the shoulder. "That's only a ten-to-one advantage, and we could sail *circles* around that slab." He laughed at Grogul's scowl.

"Trouble is, they always sail with about a dozen of those." The half-orc nodded toward a sleek frigate rafted up alongside the flagship.

"I wouldn't give her odds against *Stargazer* in a race, but she doesn't look very friendly either, does she?"

Torius took a moment to admire the frigate's sleek lines and powerful rig. The ship bore the name *Fury's Crown*. Raising his spyglass, he took a closer look at the ship's namesake figurehead. A masterpiece of sculpted wood and metal, the black-winged erinyes gripped the ship's bobstay like an immense drawn bow, a glittering golden crown atop its head. Despite the figurehead's physical beauty, the face gleamed with a wanton cruelty common to all fiends. Torius snapped his spyglass shut with a shudder. *What is it with the Chelaxians and their creepy figureheads?*

Glancing aloft, he gauged the wind. "Thillion, furl everything except the jib and main. We'll heave to when the barge gets close. Oh, and pass the word to Celeste. She should already be in the guest cabin, but I want to make sure."

Thankfully, Celeste's mood had improved over the last few days. She had even resumed her nightly contemplation of the heavens, and hadn't been plagued by any more dreams or visions. At least, she hadn't told him of any. Torius was still worried about her, but short of taking her to a cleric, he didn't know what to do.

The maneuver went like clockwork, and *Stargazer*, once again wearing her *Sea Serpent* guise, lay as still as a stone when the harbormaster's barge clapped alongside. A boarding ladder went over the side, and Torius trundled down to the middeck to welcome Lothera Cothos aboard. That, however, was when he got a surprise.

"Captain Akhiri!" Lothera sported an incongruously wide grin as she stepped aboard, her usual guard escort left behind on the barge. She hurried up to Torius and embraced him, even planting a kiss on his cheek right there in front of the entire crew. "What a sight for sore eyes you are! You're early!"

"I am." He smiled, ignoring the astonished looks of the Stargazers, feeling thoroughly disconcerted. Lothera never displayed anything resembling affection in public, preferring to save her rough attentions for privacy. On top of that, she seemed positively cheerful. "We conducted our trade in Sothis in record time, and had favorable winds for our return."

She leaned in close with a crooked smile. "Tell me you hurried back because you missed me, and I'll make it worth your while."

"Of course I missed you." He gestured toward the sterncastle. "Come, you can look over the ship's books and have a glass of wine. The heat must be stifling for you in that armor."

"By all means. A cool glass of wine sounds lovely." Grasping his hand like a merchant clutching an exclusive contract, she accompanied him to the aft cabin. As soon as the door clicked closed behind them, she pulled him into another embrace, kissing him deeply.

"Lothera!" Torius gasped for breath when she finally broke their clinch. The kiss had been . . . surprising. Not only unexpected, but quite pleasant. She tasted of mint instead of her usual cigar smoke and, though forceful, she also exhibited a hitherto unknown passion. "You're very . . . eager today."

"Eager to show you how much I appreciate you hurrying back, Abidi." She pulled him in and kissed him again. "I *do* miss you when you're gone, you know."

"You do?" That was a first, too. *What the hell's gotten into her?*

"Of course I do, and I also recently realized how little appreciation I've been showing you." Lothera released his hands and began pacing a circle around the cabin. "I've been preoccupied, Abidi, and I'm afraid I've been short with you."

"Oh, don't worry about that, my dear." Torius went to his liquor cabinet and quickly poured two glasses of pale wine. "I know you're a busy woman."

"Yes, I'm busy, but I shouldn't let that make me so . . . abrupt with you." She sighed and smiled again, an expression so foreign to her face that it made her look like an entirely different person. Not an entirely unattractive person, either. "I *do* appreciate you, and I've been remiss in showing it."

"Well, I . . . don't know what to say." Sadly true. Her abrupt change in attitude had taken him completely by the lee. Torius settled for handing her a glass of wine.

"Say you'll come out with me tonight to a restaurant." Lothera took the glass and raised it in toast. "I'll treat you to a fine meal, ply you with wine, and we can hold hands under the table like a couple of university sweethearts. How's that sound?"

"It sounds . . ." *Like someone has replaced you with a doppelganger.* She'd never taken him out to a public place, let alone asked for a rendezvous in such a pleasant manner. ". . . nice. Different."

"Good." The harbormaster touched his glass with hers and they drank. "What time would you like me to pick you up?"

Yet another change. She had never before asked him what he would like. Whatever was going on, he could certainly work her good mood to his advantage. "Whatever time is best for you, Lothera. But I'll have to have my crew row me in unless there's room somewhere at the pier for *Sea Serpent* . . ."

"Oh, I can always find room for *you*, Abidi!" She grinned and gave him another quick kiss. "Shall we say eight, then?"

"That would be fine." Torius was baffled beyond the capacity to be glib. "I'll be ready. Where should we dock?"

"Second slip from the east end. There's a Taldan lugger there now, but they should be off the dock before sundown. They're sailing on the evening tide." Squeezing his hand, Lothera searched his face with her eyes as if memorizing every feature. "I'm . . . sorry I've been so abrupt with you, Abidi. I hope I can make it up to you."

"Well . . . if this is a preview, I'll enjoy letting you try."

"Oh, this is just a tiny taste, my sweet." She put aside her glass and playfully caressed him beneath his jacket, laughing when she found a ticklish spot. "Ah-ha! *There's* something I hadn't noticed before!" She tickled him again, giggling like a girl.

"Lothera!" What in the blazes had gotten into her? Was she smoking pesh instead of cigars now? "We shouldn't keep your barge waiting. We're hove to in the middle of your harbor, after all."

"Oh, I suppose you're right." She sighed and let him go, though her mirth remained undaunted. "But don't you think for a moment that I'm not going to pay you back properly for my poor behavior, Captain Akhiri." She leaned in again, her lips barely an inch from his. "And it'll be a very long, drawn-out apology, let me assure you."

Torius swallowed and forced a smile. Now she was scaring him. Lothera never apologized for anything. "I . . . I look forward to it."

"Good. Oh, I almost forgot! I got you a present."

"A present? Lothera, you shouldn't have done that. I don't deserve—"

"Hush." She pressed a finger to his lips and drew an envelope from under her surcoat. "It's nothing extravagant, just a letter of passage. I may not have much real power with regard the navy, but I can grant a few minor boons." She handed it over. "It'll preclude any nonsense from those military prigs, at least. If you get boarded by the navy, just show them this, and they'll send you on your way without giving you any trouble."

"Thank you, my dear." Torius looked at the envelope, a little awed. Sincerely gratified, though also feeling somewhat guilty to know that he had managed to earn her unequivocal trust, he set the letter on the table and took her hand, kissing it gently. "That's very kind of you."

"Just something to make your life easier, Abidi, as you've made mine easier by giving me something to think about besides my work." Her smile, bright and genuine, lit up her face once again. "I want you to know I appreciate you."

"The feeling is mutual, Lothera."

"Good." Sighing, she glanced around the cabin. "You know, I've never noticed what a cozy little room this is. Maybe someday you'll invite me to dine with you here. We could even try out your pillows . . ." Lothera raised an eyebrow suggestively.

"I . . ." *Gozreh's guts!* The last thing Torius wanted was to soil the memory of all the wonderful times he and Celeste had enjoyed each other's company on those pillows. *So how do I get out of it?* A desperate thought came to mind. He brushed her cheek tenderly with his fingertips, a gesture he had learned during his training with the Twilight Talons, the most uncomfortable couple of months he'd ever spent. "I wouldn't want to insult you that way, Lothera. I don't use them anymore, except to lie and look at the stars, but before I met you, I . . . entertained other women. I don't want those memories interfering with what I have with you."

"I see." The corner of Lothera's mouth turned down. "I suppose it's good to know that I'm not just another woman in another port."

"Lothera." Torius clasped her hands and poured every ounce of sincerity he could into his voice. "You're the *only* woman in *any* port for me." It was essentially the truth, since Celeste lived aboard the ship, not in a port.

"Abidi, I . . ." She cleared her throat and looked away. "I should go."

"Of course." Had he overdone it? Did she not believe him?

"But . . ." Lothera looked into his eyes. "I . . . thank you for thinking of me as special. It means more than I can say."

Torius heaved a mental sigh of relief. She believed him, and even more importantly, she actually seemed to consider him more than just a convenient indulgence. Helena Trellis would be pleased; the closer he could get to the harbormaster, the more information he could pry from her. His stomach clenched with guilt at the thought. *I'm using her, and she has feelings for me . . .* Never in a million years had he thought that he would feel sorry for Lothera Cothos, but there it was.

You're a spy, Torius. Feelings don't enter into the picture.

"Well, we should shove off and get into position for docking before the tide changes." He reached for the door.

"Yes, I should go." Lothera paused at the door to give him another peck on the cheek and an incongruous smile. "I've got to get ready for tonight."

"I can't wait." Torius followed her onto the deck and saw her down into the waiting barge, waving as the oarsmen rowed away.

"What the hell was that?" Grogul asked from his side. "She seemed almost . . . pleasant."

"Maybe someone put pixie dust in her tobacco?" Thillion suggested.

"Nah." Snick hopped up to the rail to peer at the retreating barge. "She's just finally fallen for the captain's suave manner and masculine wiles."

Torius, Thillion, and Grogul looked at the gnome for a moment before all three burst into laughter.

"What?" Snick pouted. "It could happen!"

"Gozreh strike me down with a lightning bolt if it ever does, Snick!" Torius turned away and heaved a steadying breath. *The last thing in this world I need is for Lothera Cothos to start having honest-to-goodness human feelings.*

A knock on the door brought Vreva's eyes up from the paperwork she was rushing to finish. "Come in."

Her assistant, Kelipri, entered, her tasseled hat replaced by a glittering golden turban set with amethysts. The gnome had more hats than Vreva had disguises. "You sent for me, Madame Korvis?"

"Yes." Vreva finished the letter, scrawled her signature at the bottom, and waved the ink dry. "Something's come up and I have to leave town for a few days. A business opportunity that I simply can't pass up."

It wasn't business calling her away, of course, but espionage. She'd been running herself ragged the last two days doing reconnaissance, devising schemes, entertaining the admiral once again, and praying to Calistria that everything would work out. Last night she had gleaned from Ronnel's thoughts that *Robust* was due to arrive tomorrow. Serendipitously, *Stargazer* had sailed into port this very afternoon. It was time to move forward with her plan for neutralizing the weapon. Unfortunately, she hadn't had time to let Torius know yet.

"And you want me to watch the club while you're gone?" Kelipri asked.

"Exactly." Vreva folded the letter, sealed it in an envelope with a drip of wax and a press of her ring, and placed it on the pile of other letters she'd just finished. "The paperwork to keep things running is up to date for now, but I don't know how long I'll be away." The truth was, if things went poorly she might never return, but she couldn't let fear of failure or death interfere with her plans. "You know the business as well as I do. Just keep the show going, and don't let anyone over the rank of captain leave without a smile on their face."

"Not a problem, ma'am. Shall I call a carriage?"

"I've already arranged it, thanks. If you could post these for me, everything should be set." She handed over the letters, then gestured to the trunk she'd packed. "And have one of the crew haul that down to the back door for me."

"Right away." Kelipri dashed out.

Vreva stood and checked her various preparations, flicking through the list in her mind to ensure that she'd forgotten nothing.

You ready for this? Mathias hopped up on her desk and flicked his tail.

"As ready as I'll ever be." Vreva completed her mental inventory and went to the window, opening it wide. "Meet me at Tyfuss's shop."

I'll be there. Mathias leapt off the desk and out the window.

Closing it after him, Vreva drew a deep, steadying breath. *The tipping point.* In every operation there was a point at which things took on a momentum that could not be stopped. Tonight, Vreva would push events beyond that point. From now on, the mission would be like a ride on a runaway coach. If things went as planned, she'd be back at her desk tomorrow evening. If they didn't . . .

Don't think about that. Just do the job.

Another knock on the door heralded a burly bouncer who hefted her heavy trunk with no problem. Vreva carried only a modest handbag as she followed the broad-shouldered woman downstairs and out the back door of the club to where a carriage waited.

"Ready, Madame Korvis?" Twilp Farfan grinned down from the driver's seat and tipped his coachman's hat. Her association with the wily halfling was paying off.

"All packed and ready to go!" She boarded with a smile and sat back.

As soon as the carriage lurched into motion, Vreva pulled the shades and stripped off her dress. Beneath she wore close-fitting garments of supple black cloth. From her bag she withdrew a wide belt that buckled around her waist. Lifting the leather flap in front, she checked to see that her various vials fit snugly into their pockets. *Good.* With extreme care, she dipped her hand back into the bag and withdrew her weapons. Pulling one dagger from its sheath, she checked the dark stain along the blade's edge—concentrated extract of sea urchin spines, the deadliest toxin she possessed. She sheathed the dagger and tucked it and its mate beneath her belt at the small of her back. Next, she buckled a soft leather bracer around her left wrist and peered beneath the buttoned flap to make sure the six poisoned needles rested in their sheaths. Lastly, she ran her fingers lightly over her pride and joy: a beautiful hand crossbow crafted in the shape of a wasp, her very own Savored Sting. She secured it in a leather holster strapped between her shoulder blades. A bandolier of envenomed quarrels she strapped to her thigh. She slipped her feet into a pair of soft leather shoes, then stuffed her dress and fancy shoes into her magically voluminous handbag.

Closing her eyes, Vreva steeled her nerves. Though she was no stranger to peril, what she intended to do tonight was unprecedented in her experience. *Calm . . . deep breaths . . . you're ready . . .*

The carriage passed from Ostenso's pier district to the cobblestone-paved neighborhoods. The horses labored up the hill to the crack of Twilp's whip. The halfling had impressed her with his professionalism. He didn't know what she was planning, and hadn't asked for details. She'd merely outlined his job and offered him payment. He'd haggled in return, and they'd reached an agreement. Simple and straightforward, no nonsense and no questions.

The carriage turned a corner and jolted to a stop.

Vreva concentrated on the remembered form of the red-haired witch, Keah, and cast her spell. Yesterday she had visited the woman's shop, a drab little place that supplied slaves for domestic chores. Trying to remain inconspicuous among the other customers, she had observed Keah closely, memorizing the way she looked and moved, her mannerisms, and the pitch and intonation of her voice. A glance into the tiny mirror from her bag confirmed that her face and dress resembled those of the witch. Now, her performance would be tested.

Opening the carriage door, she stepped out onto the cobbled street. "Thank you."

Twilp dipped his hat and pocketed the silver coin she handed up to him. "Careful on the streets, miss. It'll be dark soon."

"Thanks for your concern. I'll be fine." Vreva had spent enough time delving Keah's thoughts to get the gist of what had troubled her so. Now it was time to make the woman's vision of the future come true.

As the carriage clattered away, Vreva hurried up the street toward the alchemist's shop where Tyfuss did business. In the shadows of the adjacent alley lurked a scraggly black cat. A deep sense of satisfaction washed over Vreva, and she wondered what Mathias had been doing to feel so pleased. *If he's tumbling kitty cats in the middle of this operation, I'm going to kick his furry little ass!* With a quick glance around, she stepped into the alley and he leapt up into her arms.

You look just like her!

"I hope I *sound* just like her." He was damp, and his fur stuck up at all angles. "You're a mess! What have you been up to?"

"Oh, I rolled in a gutter. Gotta look the part you know. Alley cats don't prance around with slick fur."

"Oh. Well, okay then. Now hold still." With a murmured spell, she made him vanish. "Make sure you don't trip me up going through the door."

*I'm not a *dog*, you know! I know my job.* Mathias leapt unseen from her arms, his flush of confidence buoying her mood. Unlike his mistress, Mathias was a fighter by nature, and his presence gave her strength.

Vreva slipped out of the alley and hurried to the shop. If her timing was right, Tyfuss would be locking up soon to head off to meet the rest of the coven. At least she hoped they planned to keep their usual schedule. If not, her preparations would all be for naught, and her plan would explode in her face.

A tiny bell chimed as Vreva pushed open the door. Mathias's tail brushed past her leg. She had been in the shop a couple of times already in different disguises to familiarize herself with the layout. There was only one customer now. Vreva kept her distance while the man concluded his purchase and tucked a small bottle into his satchel.

"Good evening, miss," the customer said, tipping his broad-brimmed hat as he passed her on his way out.

"Good evening."

"Keah! What are you doing here?" Tyfuss rounded the counter, eyes narrowed with suspicion.

"I wanted to talk to you before tonight's meeting." Vreva waved her hand in Keah's manner and took a tentative step closer. "I . . . wanted to apologize for what I said."

"Apologize then." The man's tone was hard.

"I'm trying, if you'd just let me." She heaved an exasperated sigh and pushed up her illusory glasses.

Following Keah home from the coven meeting, Vreva had harvested many confused thoughts. Flames and a fear of Tyfuss dominated, muddled with regret and distress. By the next day, however, Keah's thoughts had sharpened to suspicion and anger. Instead of avoiding the coven, the witch planned to confront them, determined not to be denied her spoils from Bushatra's scheme. From this had sprung Vreva's plan. But first she needed to discover just how Tyfuss fit into Keah's disturbing vision, and what had occurred with the coven after Keah left.

She bit her lip as she'd seen Keah do, and faced him. "I was scared the other night, all right? I admit it."

"I can understand being scared, Keah, but I can't even *cast* a fire spell like that, and you know it!"

Keah's fear now made a bit more sense. Had the vision shown Tyfuss casting a fire spell at her? "How do you explain it, then?" She took another step closer, concentrating on her disguise. She had to put him at ease enough to get close.

"I can't, but I have absolutely no reason to betray you or the coven." He pulled a bottle of wine out from behind the counter. "We can ask Bushatra what happened when we get to Potario's. Come on. I don't want to be late."

Vreva frowned. The next step of her plan needed to be completed here in the shop. She had to stall him. "Do you think she might be deceiving us? Trying to pit us against one another with false visions?"

"It's possible." Tyfuss pulled down the blinds in the shop's two front windows, then lowered the lamps to a bare flicker. "She's a nasty woman. I wouldn't put it past her if she saw some advantage in it. But why now, right before she sails off to earn her fortune?"

"Maybe so she doesn't have to share with us." Vreva slipped a needle from her wrist bracer and held it ready between two fingers. "Did she read your future after I left?"

"Read *my* future?" Tyfuss stopped barely a foot away, his brow wrinkling in confusion as he pulled a ring of keys from his pocket. "She'd already read yours. You know she can only cast that spell once a—"

A sharp squeak sounded from beneath the witch's jacket, and the head of a small white rat poked out from around his lapel. The creature squeaked again, and Tyfuss's eyes widened.

"You're not—"

Behind Tyfuss, a bottle clanked to the floor. Whirling toward the sound, the man dropped the keys and reached into his jacket, pulling something free. The dim lamplight glinted on the slim silver wand in his hand.

Vreva struck, jamming her poisoned needle deep into his neck.

Spinning back around, Tyfuss lashed out with the wine bottle.

The heavy bottle caught her on the cheekbone hard enough to send her sprawling to the floor. She reached over her shoulder for her crossbow even as her eyes focused on the silver wand in the witch's hand.

Tyfuss aimed the wand at her and opened his mouth, but then collapsed to his knees as the poison diffused through his bloodstream. The wine bottle fell from his grasp and rolled away. A startled look widened his eyes, but he managed to lift the wand again until it pointed directly at Vreva's heart. His lips moved to form a word.

Dear Calistria, help me! Vreva's fingers finally grasped the handle of her Savored Sting, but before she could draw the weapon, the wand wavered, Tyfuss's eyes rolled up, and the witch pitched forward to the floor. The small white rat disentangled itself from his coat and scurried away.

"Mathias!"

Just before the rat reached the safety of a low rack of bottles, it tumbled wildly aside. Mathias materialized, rolling from his diving tackle. The rat squeaked horribly, then fell silent as sharp teeth pierced its spine with a crunch.

Vreva heaved a breath and lurched up to her feet. "Thank you, love."

Mathias meowed, his words unintelligible through a mouthful of rat. His flush of pleasure was clear enough, however.

"You saved me by knocking over that bottle." Vreva pressed her hand to Tyfuss's neck—no pulse—grabbed the ring of keys, and quickly locked the front door. It wouldn't do to be disturbed right now. "Too bad he figured out that I wasn't Keah before I got the information I wanted."

His familiar figured it out for him. Mathias prodded the dead rat with his paw and flicked his tail in satisfaction. *I'm guessing you don't smell right.*

"Of course. That might be a problem . . ." A solution came to mind. "Save the rat."

But I was going to—

"Hush, love. You can snack later. I'll need his familiar, and maybe something else from Tyfuss if I'm going to pass muster with the others." Vreva cast a quick spell and checked the body for magic. The silver wand glowed, of course. Rummaging through the witch's clothing, she confiscated an amulet and ring as well. Grasping Tyfuss under the arms, she dragged him behind the counter. There, she plucked the needle from his neck. The tiny wound didn't bleed at all, and would hopefully go unnoticed by whoever discovered the body.

Oh, all right. Mathias picked up the rat and padded over, dropping it at her feet before sniffing the dead witch. *But keep it for later. Killing witches makes me hungry.*

"Everything makes you hungry." Vreva perused the apothecary shelves and picked out a bottle of deadly nightshade.

Everything but eating.

"Very funny." With a knife from the witch's jacket, Vreva scraped the label off the bottle and popped the cork. She poured a measure into Tyfuss's mouth, then dropped the bottle next to his outstretched hand. With any luck, whoever found him would jump to the conclusion that he took a sip from the wrong bottle. Vreva wrinkled her nose as she picked up the dead rat, its fur wet with cat spit. "Do you think this will be enough, or should I take something else, too? His coat's too big for me. It'll interfere with my movement."

Let me check. Mathias sniffed the body again, more carefully this time. *Inside breast pocket. He's got a smelly old handkerchief.*

"Perfect!" Vreva reached in and withdrew the obviously used cloth. Holding it gingerly with her fingertips, she shook it, and a few rat droppings fell out. "Ugh! This should do." Stifling her distaste, she tied the rat up in the kerchief and secured both to her belt.

Don't forget the wine.

"I won't." She retrieved the bottle Tyfuss had dropped and returned to the counter. From her belt, she withdrew a syringe with a thin needle and a corked vial of knockout toxin. With the deft motions of long practice, she filled the syringe, plunged the needle through the cork, and injected the toxin into the wine. With any luck, the hearty vintage would mask the flavor of the toxin. Vreva put away her tools, then bent to examine the corpse up close once more, committing to memory every detail of his clothes, hair, and facial features. "Ready?"

Always, but you should put back the bottle I knocked over before we leave.

"Right." Thankful for her familiar's sharp eyes, Vreva replaced the bottle. The first task of the evening was done, the tipping point past. What awaited them at Pothario's house would be infinitely more dangerous, and she didn't want to forget anything in her anxiety. "Anything else?"

I think that ought to do it. Just don't forget to walk like a man.

"Walking isn't the problem." She cast the spell that would guise her in the form of the dead witch and headed for the door, keys in hand. "Talking like him, on the other hand . . ."

Well, I can't help you there.

"I've got something in mind." Vreva peeked out through the drawn shades as she worked the key in the latch. "Keep to the shadows, and I'll make you invisible again right before we go in."

Skulking in the shadows is my specialty. When Vreva opened the door, Mathias dashed out and vanished into the deepening night.

Vreva exited the shop and secured the door behind her as casually as if she did it every night. She dropped the keys into her pocket, then assumed a masculine gait and strode up the street toward Pothario's house, her thoughts fixed upon her disguise, and the bottle of toxin-laced wine tucked firmly in the crook of her arm.

9

Playing with Fire

Snick popped her head through the doorway to the captain's cabin. "Harbormaster's carriage is here, Captain." She sounded far too cheerful about it for Torius's taste.

"I'm coming." Torius looked once more in the mirror. As Abidi Ben Akhiri, he wore Thuvian garb: a close-fitting silk jacket of deep purple embroidered with gold, and a broad red sash that complemented the scabbard of his scimitar nicely. Turning to Celeste, he adjusted his fez and asked, "How do I look?"

"Too good for Lothera Cothos." She sounded sullen, which was usual when Torius visited the harbormaster.

"I have to go, love."

"I know." Her tail twitched. "But I don't have to like it."

"Neither do I." Kissing her quickly, he strode out of the cabin.

A deep breath calmed his nerves as Torius descended the gangplank and approached Lothera's carriage. Her driver opened the door, and Torius stopped in shock as a long leg entwined in thin strips of black silk emerged. The silk strips girded Lothera's muscular leg to mid-thigh, where a gold-hilted dagger was secured by an ornate strap. She stepped down, utterly resplendent in a red satin gown, modestly cowled in front but cut thigh-high on one side. He'd seen her in evening gowns many times, but never one like this. She looked startlingly sensuous, powerful, and completely Chelish, from her elaborately coifed hair to her high-heeled shoes.

"You like?" Lothera smiled and turned in a circle.

"Of course I . . . Oh . . . *my.*" The back of her gown left him gaping. It plunged down to drape gracefully somewhat below her waist, revealing a well-toned back. *Gozreh's guts! I hope Celeste isn't watching.*

"I'll take that as a yes." She held out a hand gloved in red silk. "Shall we go? I have quite the surprise for you tonight."

Torius automatically took her hand to help her into the carriage, the eyes of the crew tangible on his back. He wasn't sure how to handle this new Lothera. She startled him with her smiles, astonished him with her attire, and terrified him with her pleasing manner. Suspicion about what had brought on this strange behavior blossomed into paranoia. Had she discovered his deception? Was he being set up?

Torius struggled to maintain his composure during the short ride to the Iron Crown, one of Ostenso's most exclusive restaurants. The rumble of the carriage precluded quiet conversation, but she kept looking at him strangely—not leering or domineering, but something he couldn't place. He handed Lothera down from the carriage and escorted her through gilded doors held by a crimson-uniformed usher.

Inside, the maître d' bowed respectfully. "Your reservation?"

"I'm Harbormaster Cothos. I reserved a table for two."

"Indeed you did, Mistress Cothos." He waved a hand, and a waiter appeared to escort them. "Enjoy your evening."

"I'm sure we will." She flashed Torius a smile as she took his arm.

The restaurant sported a number of small rooms on two floors, an intimate atmosphere of dark wood with red and gold accents. Lothera matched the decor perfectly. As they climbed a curved stair and traversed a winding path between tables of diners, Torius noticed some of the Iron Crown's other patrons. The number of naval officers' uniforms among the landscape of silk and satin heightened Torius's paranoia. Torius Vin was well known to the

Corentyn armada, and naval officers made him nervous. If any of those captains had been reposted to Ostenso, one might penetrate his disguise. Indeed, too many eyes followed their progress, and whispers hissed in their wake like froth behind a ship.

Torius strained to listen, and found his fears allayed.

"That *can't* be her."

"Cothos in a gown like that? I don't believe it."

"I'd sooner expect devils to take up knitting!"

Well, at least everyone's watching her, not me.

By the time they reached their table, secluded in a dimly lit corner with a view out the leaded glass windows, Torius noticed Lothera wobbling a little on her heels, her grip hard on his arm. Evidently she was as unaccustomed to her attire as he. When their escort pulled out her chair, the harbormaster sat with more relief than grace.

"This place looks as if it were made for you." Torius took his seat. "Do you have a gown to match every restaurant in Ostenso?"

"Hardly." She fingered the loose cowl of her dress. "I had my seamstress make this up especially for tonight. Unfortunately, the shoes don't quite fit." She gave him that incongruous smile again—not her usual leer or sneer, but genuinely pleasant. "I hope you like it?"

"I do, very much." *A special dress for a dinner out with me?* The thought rekindled his paranoia.

"Good." When the waiter offered the wine list, Lothera waved toward Torius. "Why don't you pick the wine, Abidi? From what I understand, you're quite the connoisseur."

"I'm afraid all I know about wine is how to buy low and sell high, but I'd be happy to pick something out." He wondered where she'd heard this as he perused the list. She knew he hauled wine as cargo, but that hardly made him a connoisseur. "How about . . . the Seven Hills Estates, 4692."

"An excellent choice, sir." The waiter took the list with a bow and left.

"You seem in a positively festive mood, Lothera." Torius reached out to touch her hand, intending to draw her motives out. "Something good must have happened since my last visit."

"*Anticipation* of something good." She leered, then shifted her expression back to the simple smile as if catching herself in her old mannerisms. "Actually, aside from your arrival, that damned flagship will be off my pier soon."

"Oh?" He knew from Vreva's report that the weapon was aboard the flagship. He hadn't had a chance to speak to her yet, but this might mean that the Chelish were ready to put their plan into motion. "Did they ever give you a reason why they insisted upon using your pier for that thing?"

"Oh, it's all a pretense." Lothera glanced at the dining naval officers and lowered her voice. "They *said* they needed space enough to raft some slug of a supply ship between *Devil's Trident* and *Fury's Crown*. According to Ronnel, they're transferring some special cargo *from* the flagship *to* the supply ship, but I know what they're really up to."

"You do?"

"Of course! They're trying to bring supplies into *my* port without paying proper duty." She looked smug. "I told Ronnel as much, but of course he denied it."

Torius tried not to smile. In the harbormaster's mind, the world rightly revolved around Lothera Cothos. "The navy can't put anything past you, my dear." It made sense. Dockage in the naval yard was too limited to allow three ships to moor abreast. *But why transfer the weapon from the flagship to a supply ship?*

The wine steward arrived, and showed Torius the bottle. He nodded, and the fellow drew the cork and filled their glasses.

"But enough about work!" Lothera swirled her wine and examined its color in the lamplight. "How long will you be staying in Ostenso this time, Abidi?"

"Alas, time is money." Torius sipped his wine, swirling the flavors around his tongue before swallowing. "As soon as we sell our spices and load more wine, I'll be off to sea again. Perhaps to Katapesh this time. I have a buyer there who said he'd give me a good price on choice Chelish vintages."

"So far?" Lothera frowned. "I don't like it when you're away so long."

Another first; she'd never expressed concern about his absence before. "Well, perhaps we could make another run to Sothis. I wouldn't want to dampen your spirits."

"You would do that for me?" She sounded surprised.

"For you, my dear, yes." He raised his glass, feeling emboldened. "I don't know what exactly put you in such a mood, but I'm not about to risk losing it."

"*You* did, Captain Akhiri." Lothera smiled and grasped his hand. "By being someone I wasn't expecting—someone honest and true—you . . . opened my eyes."

"I did?" *What the hell is she talking about?* The last time he'd been in Ostenso, she'd been as brusque and demanding as ever. She'd barely said goodbye after sating her appetites.

"Yes." Opening her menu, she scanned the page as if unaware of his scrutiny.

He knew better than to badger her for information. If he simply remained silent and attentive, she always opened up.

After a while, she finally met his gaze and sighed. "Suffice it to say that I thought I had a reason to be jealous, and I was proven wrong. I've never been so glad to be mistaken in my life. A . . . um, acquaintance informed me that I . . . wasn't showing you how much I appreciated you. And I do." Beneath the concealing tablecloth, she ran the toe of her shoe up his leg. "I appreciate you very much."

"And I appreciate you, my dear." *Who the hell would tell Lothera . . .* The question didn't even form fully before he had the answer. *Vreva!* Torius didn't know if he would be cursing her or thanking her for her intervention, but he'd know soon enough.

"Good. I was worried that you might feel . . . obligated . . . to be with me."

"Lothera, I never—"

"Please, Abidi, I need to apologize for the way I've treated you. My position sometimes . . ." She fell silent.

"You're under a lot of stress, my dear, I understand."

"It's not that!" She shook her head, a sharp jerk, as if banishing the bit of the old Lothera that had shown through, then took a deep breath and a sip of wine. "My position sometimes lends me to take . . . liberties where they might not be welcome. When we first met, I did that."

"Lothera, I—"

"No, Abidi, I did, and I know it was wrong, but I . . . needed someone. You were new to Ostenso, and I thought we could help each other. I'm afraid I abused my authority."

Torius considered the first time they'd met, when Lothera demanded that he come to her villa for dinner. He hadn't wanted to go, but Celeste had insisted he appease her to avoid undo attention to his cargo and crew. That had been when they were simple pirates. Now, as a Twilight Talon, his relationship with the harbormaster was invaluable.

Sex for gain . . . just like mother. His gut wrenched with the memories of his pesh-addict mother, selling her body to strangers to support her habit until finally she sold her own son into slavery for a brick of her sweet pesh. *Have I really sunk so low?* But his association with Vreva had changed his outlook on people who used their bodies as currency. For some, it was the only currency they possessed. For others, like Vreva, sex was a weapon. Torius used his relationship with Lothera to further the Andoren cause, which meant freeing slaves. That made him different from his mother. *Or does it just make me a hypocrite?* And now that Lothera seemed to be developing true feelings for him . . . Torius buried his guilt deep. Thousands of lives were on the line. There was only one thing he could do:

Lie.

"Lothera, my dear, I did nothing that I didn't want to do."

"Really?"

"What pressure do you think you exerted over me?" He smiled and swallowed his self-disgust. "I had nothing to hide aboard *Sea Serpent*, and when a strong, capable woman came aboard my ship and suggested we share an evening at her beautiful villa . . . Well, perhaps I got more than I bargained for that *first* evening, but since then, I think we've built something . . . meaningful."

"I'm glad that you think so, Abidi." Lothera beamed at him. "I, too, think we've . . ." Her eyes suddenly focused beyond him, out the window to the city. "Father of Lies! What in the name of Hell . . ."

Torius looked over his shoulder. Farther up the hill, the city was lit by a glaring orange glow, flames leaping into the night sky.

Something big was burning.

Vreva knocked on the door of Pothario's house as an unseen Mathias rubbed against her leg. The touch was comforting, though her familiar's empathic anxiety accented her own.

Pothario answered the door with a scowl. "You're late."

Vreva pitched her voice into a hoarse hiss to accompany her disguise. "I had a mishap at the shop distilling acid, and got a lung full of vapors. Damn near killed me!" She edged past the witch into the entry hall and turned into the sitting room she'd espied from the front window.

Keah and Bushatra were already there. The red-headed witch eyed Vreva suspiciously, shifting her position so that she stood halfway behind Bushatra. Clearly, her mistrust of Tyfuss was still as strong as Vreva had perceived the previous day.

"Sorry I'm late. Accident at the shop." Vreva snatched up the corkscrew on the table, and stifled a shudder of revulsion. This was the closest she had been to Bushatra. That corset, obviously the skin from some humanoid, made her want to retch.

As she drew the cork, Vreva regarded Keah. "I'm surprised to even see you here after last time." Movement in the far corner of the room caught her eye. An elderly slave woman bent and withered by a lifetime of hard labor stood beside a door there. Vreva hadn't seen any slave or that door during her previous spying, but her vantage had been limited by the curtain. She wondered for a moment if she should wait for the woman to serve the wine, but had watched Tyfuss do so before, so continued. The slave merely stood there.

"I couldn't very well stay away," Keah said. "Not and get what's my due."

Vreva poured the tainted vintage into four glasses and handed one to Keah. She had considered using a lethal poison, but dismissed the idea. Bushatra seemed a reluctant wine drinker, and it wouldn't do to have the other witches keel over before she drank. Vreva picked up a glass and sipped the toxin-laced wine without fear, having already taken an antidote.

"Smart woman." Pothario picked up his own glass and settled into a chair. "I told you there was nothing to it. The vision spell must have gone wrong."

"It did *not* go wrong!" Bushatra's face flushed in anger. "The vision shows only one *possible* future, not the *only* future."

"Possible or impossible, I've put too much into this to just run away. I'm not going to be cheated out of my share." Keah drank down her wine and refilled her glass. "Besides, I still have spells to learn."

"We don't have time for our familiars to exchange spells tonight, and your spoiled grape juice makes me ill!" Bushatra waved away the lone glass of wine still atop the table. "We need to go down so I can cast the vision again."

Vreva stiffened. Though relieved that she didn't have to contrive some reason that Tyfuss's familiar was in no condition to exchange spells, she had to prompt Bushatra to drink the wine. Also, she wanted to learn more about the weapon before the poison took effect.

"Oh?" Vreva cast a suspicious look at Bushatra. "Why the rush?"

Bushatra glared at Vreva. "Because *Robust* arrives tomorrow, and Anguillithek must report to its master tonight. We can't leave the weapon alone for even a moment!"

"I don't know how you can trust such a creature." Pothario made a face. "Aren't you afraid it'll just kill you and take the weapon for itself?"

"No. We have a contract. If the devils value anything, it's a contract." Bushatra grinned horribly, her pointed teeth gleaming. "Besides, *I'm* the only one who knows how to wield the weapon."

Well, that's useful. Maybe I just need to get rid of Bushatra . . .

Vreva topped off Pothario's glass and poured a miniscule amount into her own. "When is *Robust* leaving? And better yet, when might we expect our just rewards?"

"*Robust* sails day after tomorrow. I should return in less than a week, and the contract will be fulfilled." Bushatra grinned in avarice. "I must look into the future one last time to ensure that all is well, then return to *Devil's Trident.*"

"I don't believe these visions of yours." The charms on Keah's bracelet jingled as her hand twitched. "How do we know you're not going to just sail off into the sunset without us?"

"Think about what you're saying." Bushatra crossed her arms, her mouth set in a hard frown. "I joined this coven because I can't look into my own future. I need to look into *your* futures to make sure my plan is going to work, and the only way I can do that is

chamber. Keah's eyes widened, her scream shivering the air for an instant before the mote detonated in a searing ball of flame that engulfed half of the room. Bushatra dove away from the blast, but could not evade the expanding inferno.

Keah's vision of the future had just come true.

I guess Bushatra's spell was accurate after all. But even as the grim irony registered in Vreva's mind, she heard a stream of arcane words from the fading flames. Spears of ice erupted from the floor beneath her, jagged shards tearing a bloody track across her thigh. Vreva sprawled away from the deadly ice, her dagger skittering out of reach. Rolling into a crouch, she cast another spell and vanished from sight. Blood dribbled down her leg from the deep gash, but she had no time to tend the wound. Clenching her jaw against the pain, she struggled to her feet and drew her crossbow.

Bushatra strode from the ashes of Vreva's spell like a devil from Hell, her leathers blackened, her hair trailing smoke. Unfortunately, her skin was only blistered rather than charred to ash. She glared around the room, keen eyes searching for her foe.

Vreva eased back the crossbow's string and slid an envenomed bolt from her bandolier. The tiny quarrel clicked into the groove of the weapon.

Bushatra whirled toward the slight sound and cast an arc of glittering dust from her hand. With a single arcane word, golden light exploded, causing Vreva to blink hard against the glare. As the light faded, Vreva looked down to see her invisible form outlined in shimmering gold.

"There you are!" Bushatra lunged, her fetid hair lengthening and lashing out as if the tendrils had lives of their own.

Vreva took aim and fired her crossbow. Though her aim was true, the envenomed bolt glanced off the witch's magical armor. Vreva dove to evade the lashing hair, but it grasped her like a sea monster's tentacles, tightening around her waist with brutal strength. She dropped the crossbow and drew her other dagger, slashing at the clinging hair. While she managed to sever several tendrils, others grew to replace them in the blink of an eye, winding around her wrists and throat.

"So, we have an infiltrator, do we?" Laughing at Vreva's impotent attempts to free herself, Bushatra withdrew a preserved eyeball and a needle from a pocket of her smoldering clothes. Arcane words flowed, and she stabbed the needle into the eye. Pain lanced through Vreva's head, wrenching a scream from her throat.

"Who are you? You're obviously not Tyfuss." Bushatra's hair lifted Vreva off the floor and drew her closer, dangling her just out of reach of the spy's slashing dagger. "Tell me, and you die easy."

Instead of answering, Vreva screamed out a spell, negating the brutal magic that inflamed her nerves. The pain faded, and she slashed again at the writhing hair, but to no avail.

"You have some skill with magic." The witch began chanting again, the sound of her voice pressing in on Vreva as if boring into her brain. "Answer me! Who are you?"

"No!" Vreva thrashed against the spell that was trying to take over her mind, but the magic continued to press in. If the witch gained control, all of Vreva's secrets would be forfeit. Her friends would perish, and Augustana would be destroyed. In desperation, she screamed out another negating spell. The intrusive magic vanished like smoke blown away by a cleansing breeze.

Bushatra cursed and drew a vial and a small black sphere from a pouch. Holding the ball in one hand, she dumped the contents of the vial onto it. Noxious smoke hissed forth, and the sphere melted into a mass of green goo that coated the witch's hand like a caustic glove. "Now, tell me who you are, or my slime will eat you alive!"

Vreva choked on the burning fumes, turning her face away from the putrid green mass.

A streak of black fur leapt up at Bushatra's face, claws raking at her eyes. As Mathias's claws slashed, however, a serpent struck from hiding beneath the witch's writhing hair. The cat twisted out of the way of the striking fangs and clamped onto the snake's body with his teeth. The two tumbled aside in a tangle of fur and scales, spitting and slashing.

Vreva grabbed the chance to cast another spell. Gauging the distance carefully, she sent a spark of flame streaking past Bushatra's ear. The spell detonated and an expanding sheet of fire rushed toward them. This time, Bushatra couldn't dodge the inferno.

Vreva screamed as her skin blistered from the searing heat, but her placement proved good. The witch took the brunt of the conflagration, her body shielding Vreva from the worst of the blast. Bushatra shrieked in pain, and the writhing tendrils of hair withered. As Vreva's feet touched the floor, she lashed out with her envenomed dagger, but the witch's slime-coated hand met her wrist. The gooey mass stuck like glue, burning her skin like acid.

Vreva tried to rake the witch's arm with her dagger, but the pain from the caustic slime was too much and her grip on the hilt failed. She jerked her hand free of the woman's burning grasp and rolled away from the writhing mass of smoldering hair that was already growing back from Bushatra's blistered scalp. The slime was spreading, oozing up Vreva's arm toward her elbow. She scuttled to the fire pit and thrust the afflicted arm into the blazing coals. Agony tore a scream from her throat, but the consuming mass of slime blackened and fell away. When Vreva pulled back from the coals, her skin was charred black, but she could still clench her hand.

At the sound of another hissed incantation behind her, Vreva dodged. A lashing whip of flame struck the cauldron, missing her by inches. Rolling to her feet, she gaped at the hellish whip of fire writhing from the witch's mouth. Like a long, fiery tentacle, the woman's tongue lashed forth again. Vreva tried to evade the flaming member, but it scored a burning track across her shoulder.

Vreva dove behind the only significant barrier available, the heavy iron cauldron. There, she considered her dwindling options. Her daggers and crossbow were strewn about the room, and the witch seemed somehow able to resist magical attacks. Vreva only had one other weapon, but to use it, she had to get close to her foe. As the tongue of flame lashed against the unyielding iron pot, Vreva cast her invisibility spell once again. Pressing her charred hand to the gash in her leg to try to prevent leaving a blood trail, she limped out of hiding, skirting the edge of the room as quietly as she could.

Bushatra looked as bad as Vreva felt—her writhing hair smoking, her face a mess of oozing blisters, her clothing nothing but charred scraps. Circling the cauldron and finding Vreva gone, the witch swallowed the writhing tongue of flame and cast another spell. The air buzzed ominously as a swarm of wasps materialized around the witch in a nimbus of venomous fury.

No matter, Vreva thought stoically. She would take a few stings, but that wouldn't save the witch. She glanced around for Mathias and saw a lump of black fur still entwined with Bushatra's serpent, both motionless. Her heart skipped a beat, but she hadn't felt the gut-wrenching lurch of her familiar's death, a sensation she knew all too well. Mathias might yet survive, but the witch had to be dealt with first.

Another incantation from the witch snapped her attention back to her task. A sheet of flame shot out from Bushatra's outstretched hands, but it missed Vreva by a wide margin. The witch was desperate, firing off spells without a target. Vreva steeled her nerves and flipped open the leather flap that covered her bracer. She withdrew the envenomed needles and gripped them in her fist. With a deep breath and a mental plea to Calistria, she lunged into the swarm of wasps. As Vreva plunged the needles into the witch's neck, she felt the wasps' stingers pierce her skin.

Screams from both women echoed through the chamber. The witch whirled, her hair lashing out like a mass of whips across Vreva's face, but as she began casting yet another spell, her words faltered. Her eyes widened in shock as the massive dose of poison brought her heart to a standstill. Bushatra collapsed in a noisome heap, the buzzing swarm hovering around her like a death shroud.

"Mathias!" Vreva hobbled to her familiar, the pain of her wounds stabbing her anew with every stride. Kneeling, she examined the two entwined animals. They were locked in an embrace of fangs, the snake's lodged deep in the cat's shoulder, Mathias's clamped just behind the snake's head, crushing the fragile spine. Vreva carefully pulled the serpent's fangs free and threw the creature aside. Mathias still breathed, but barely.

"Mathias?" She jostled him, and he opened an eye.

Got . . . bit. He licked his nose and flipped his tail weakly. *Dirty rotten reptile bit me . . . *

"Hold still." Vreva lifted her belt flap and pulled out a vial. Long experience with poisons had taught her to be prepared. An old instructor with the Twilight Talons had once told her that an ounce of prevention might be worth a pound of cure, but a handy cure was worth its weight in platinum. Popping the cork, she poured the contents into her familiar's mouth. "Swallow."

Tastes like rat piss! he complained, but his eyes flicked open and he breathed easier. *I feel a little better, though.* Mathias struggled to his feet and shook himself, then eyed her critically. *You look like crap.*

"Thanks." Vreva plucked out another vial and downed the contents. The deep wound in her leg and the horrible burns on her hand faded. She still ached all over, but she could walk without limping too badly. "Can you walk? We have to get out of here."

Mathias took a few wobbly steps. *Um . . . can you carry me? I can't seem to make my legs work right.*

"Sure. Wait one minute." Scouting around the room, Vreva retrieved her lost weapons. She cast one more spell, and grinned as several magical auras came alight in her sight. Keah's charm bracelet and ring were the first to go in her pocket. Next, she collected an amulet and a curious pair of polyhedral dice from Pothario. Lastly she looked to Bushatra. Deeply tattooed with runes, the woman's close-fitting leather garment glowed brightly with potent magic despite some charring. Surely this was what had interfered with Vreva's spells, but she was loath to peel it off the dead witch, let alone wear such a vile thing. Bushatra's dagger was also enchanted, and Vreva took it, along with a ring of keys and odds and ends from her pouches and pockets.

"Time to get to *Stargazer*." Gently lifting Mathias into her arms, Vreva walked to the stairs, then turned back. The flames from her fire spell still smoldered, the thick overhead timbers burnt nearly through. They couldn't take much more punishment before the entire house came crashing down into the cellar.

What are you waiting for?

Vreva recalled the slave Keah murdered, the plan to annihilate Augustana, killing thousands for nothing other than money and prestige. Cleansing the world of such vile pestilence with fire seemed just.

"Nothing at all." Vreva cast a spell, and watched the tiny spark of orange flame dance atop her finger. Flicking her wrist, she sent the mote streaking into the smoldering rafters. Flames billowed anew, engulfing the room. Without a twinge of remorse, Vreva hurried up the stairs. She still had work to do tonight. The tipping point was behind her, and there was no looking back.

10

The Devil's Den

"Celeste! Trouble."

Three hard raps snapped Celeste out of her stellar musing. She slithered to the door of Torius's cabin, muttering an oath. *What could have possibly gone wrong already?* They'd only just arrived, Torius was out with loathsome Lothera, and they hadn't even contacted Vreva yet. She flipped the latch on the door with a flick of magic and opened it a crack to peer through.

"What's wrong? Who—" A glance told her everything she needed to know. Behind Snick stood Grogul with one meaty arm wrapped around Vreva. His embrace seemed to be the only thing keeping her upright. Instead of her usual garb, the woman wore dark pants and shirt and various weapons. With tattered and bloody clothing, and several nasty burns, Vreva looked like she'd been run through a meat grinder, then thrown on a grill. She cradled a black bundle of fur in one arm, the cat's tail dangling limply. Celeste flung open the door. "Inside, quick! Did anyone see you come aboard?"

"Give me a *little* credit, dear," Vreva said with a tired smile. "They saw a drunken sailor stumble aboard, which I daresay is nothing unusual for *this* ship." She glanced around. "Where's Torius?"

"Out." Celeste slithered out of the way. "Snick, get your healer's kit. Grogul, put her on the bunk and go get Thillion. What happened to Mathias?"

"He was bitten by a viper. He's sleeping, but the venom's made him sick." Vreva winced as Grogul lifted her onto Torius's bunk. "Thank you, Grogul. You're a dear."

"You're welcome." Grogul ducked out of the cabin to fetch the first mate.

"Oh, stop being polite and tell us what happened!" Celeste snapped.

"I'd really rather wait until everyone's here. That way I only have to tell it once." Vreva pushed herself up on the bed and winced.

Snick returned with her satchel of potions and bandages, a blue bottle already in her hand. "Here you go!"

"Oh, thank Calistria." Vreva popped the cork and downed the contents. "Ah, much better."

"And if Mathias is sick from snakebite, this should set him up." Snick handed over another bottle, this one of green instead of blue.

"Oh, excellent! Thank you, Snick!"

Celeste watched anxiously as Vreva jostled her familiar awake and fed him the potion. She breathed easier when the cat perked up, yawned, and lashed his tail. She had known Mathias since the day he'd become Vreva's familiar, and had liked him from the start. Though she couldn't actually speak with him, she knew Mathias was one of the team, more family than pet. She smiled when he let out a yowl and lashed his tail.

"Be civil, Mathias. I carried you here, and you slept all the way." Vreva scratched his chin, and he sat down to tolerate the abuse. "Now, as to what happened—"

Another knock on the door heralded Grogul and a bleary-eyed Thillion. "Sorry. I was reading and must have dozed off. I didn't hear you come aboard." The half-elf looked around and blinked. "Where's the captain?"

"He's still out." *With Lothera* . . . Celeste banished the image of him stepping aboard the carriage with the harbormaster and focused on Vreva. "I don't know when he'll be back."

"Well, I'm afraid I can't wait for him to return. I've got a lot to tell you, and more to do tonight."

They all paid rapt attention as Vreva filled them in on everything she'd learned about Admiral Ronnel's plan. Though she glazed over her intimate encounters with the admiral, she provided all the details about the witch's coven and her battle with Bushatra.

Celeste's tail twitched. "Did you have to burn the place down? That's going to draw attention."

"I know, but there was no other way. If anyone identifies Bushatra's body, I'm dead." Vreva moved to sit on the edge of the bed and rubbed her eyes. "Now, did a trunk and bag arrive by messenger?"

"Oh, yeah. Twilp brought a couple of things." Snick grinned, obviously pleased by the halfling's visit. "Didn't say who they were for, so I put 'em in the hold. They're yours?"

"Yes, and I need to change and get some supplies before I go aboard *Devil's Trident.*"

"Before you *what*?" Celeste gaped at her anew. "With a *devil* watching over that weapon, you're just going to walk in and destroy it?"

"Um, I'll get the bags." Grogul ducked out of the room, obviously reticent about being around while the two got into another argument.

Celeste didn't understand his discomfort. *It's not like he hasn't seen us fight before.* Her long history of disagreements with Vreva originated with the courtesan's attempts to seduce Torius and culminated in her betrayal of the pirates. Of course, that was before they knew she was actually a spy for Andoran. Baptized together in a desperate battle against slavers, they now shared the same goals and risks. But that didn't stop them from disagreeing. *Especially when she comes up with stupid ideas like this.*

"That's basically the plan." Vreva shrugged and scratched Mathias. "Bushatra said that she was the only one who could wield the weapon, but we can't take any chances. If I can destroy the weapon while Anguillithek's away, I should be able to create some kind of catastrophic distraction and slip off the ship without too much trouble. I've got to do it before *Robust* puts to sea with the weapon aboard."

"Why?" Thillion withdrew a puzzle chain from a pocket and started working the links quickly through his fingers, his usual habit when applying his keen mind to a complex problem. "We can easily catch a galleon. We could take them at sea before they reach Augustana. Or we could simply inform the Gray Corsairs and have them destroy the ship."

"Because we don't know what Ronnel will send along as an escort. If they're surrounded by half a dozen warships—" Mathias interrupted Vreva with a yowl, which brought a smile to her lips. "And Mathias doesn't like sea travel."

"Fine!" Celeste conceded. "But if you insist on doing this, you need to tell us one more thing."

"What's that?"

"What you want written on your *tombstone*, because walking into a room with a devil is likely to get you killed! This is suicide!" Celeste rattled her tail against the table leg in irritation.

"There's no need to be insulting, Celeste. I *have* been in the company of devils before. I'm Chelish, after all, but I—"

The door opened, and Grogul entered, Vreva's trunk in his hands and her handbag looking comically dainty looped over his shoulder. "You two still goin' at it? Where do you want these?"

"Right there's fine, Grogul. Thank you." Vreva got up and opened the chest, then started rifling through the contents, talking as she worked. "As for my tombstone, if I get caught, they probably won't hand over my body for burial, so there'll be no need for one." Pulling out two vials, she popped the tops off and downed the contents. Shaking herself as if newly invigorated, she started removing her weapons and tossing them on the bed.

"If you get caught, they'll interrogate you," Celeste pointed out.

"I don't intend to let that happen ever again." Vreva fixed Celeste with a serious stare as she slipped off her shoes. "Once was more than enough, thank you. I've got ways of taking my life if they catch me."

Grogul growled deep in his chest and Celeste twitched her tail. They all knew what Vreva had gone through the last time she'd been captured. Celeste couldn't blame her for planning suicide rather than go through it again. "So if you're going to dance with the devil, what's our role in your plan?"

"If I *am* discovered and have a chance to escape, I'm going to need a quick way out of Ostenso." Vreva unfastened her belt and slipped out of her torn and bloody trousers and scorched shirt. She wore scanties and a snug camisole beneath that were less revealing than some of the gowns Celeste had seen her wear as a courtesan. Dampening a cloth in the washbasin, she scrubbed the blood and soot from her legs and arms as she spoke. "I may have to jump into the bay, so I'll need a way to get to *Stargazer* before they shoot me full of arrows or the devil comes after me."

"We can station Kalli under the ship while you're aboard," Thillion offered. "She can stay underwater indefinitely and help you if the need arises."

"Got one of those potions that let you breathe like a fish, too," Snick offered. "Kalli can give it to you if you have to jump in."

"That's all good, but . . ." Celeste frowned. Though she didn't want to be the one to bring it up, another subject had to be addressed. ". . . if you're discovered and you *don't* have a chance to escape . . . how will we know?"

"If Mathias returns without me, it means I'm dead." Vreva donned a clean shirt and pants, and secured her daggers and bandolier of crossbow bolts. Mathias yowled, but she hushed the cat with a wave of her hand. "If that happens, you'll have to destroy

Robust at sea, or if that's impossible, contact Trellis and have her call in the Gray Corsairs. But if I *am* caught, even if they get no information from me, they'll know their plan's been discovered. They might change things, or even lay a trap for you."

"What if you aren't caught, but need more time to neutralize the weapon?" Thillion's fingers were clicking through the puzzle chain at top speed. Obviously, he wanted to consider every possible eventuality. "You still have no idea what this weapon is, so it may take you some time to decide how to best disarm or destroy it."

"Have someone keep an eye on the ships. If you see Bushatra cross over to *Robust*, you'll know I'm still working on it. I'll contact you using magic to let you know what my plan is."

"I wish Captain Vin was here," the first mate said tightly. "He might have more questions."

"No time," Vreva said, an inscrutable smile quirking across her lips. "I've got to board *Devil's Trident* before Bushatra's overdue." She checked over her gear one more time and picked a few more items out of her chest, tucking them in her belt pouch.

"Don't know how you can go in there alone." Snick frowned, her usual ebullient mood quashed by the gravity of what the spy was proposing.

Mathias meowed loudly and thrashed his tail.

"See? I won't be alone." Vreva smiled and sighed. "Don't look so glum. There's no way to know if it'll work or not, so the best we can do is—"

"Wait!" *No way to know* . . . Celeste writhed her coils in agitation. She hadn't told anyone but Torius about her strange new abilities, though they had been on her mind constantly. She had even tried practicing, asking questions of the heavens to see if they deigned to answer. Most of the time she got no answer, but sometimes she did. *I have to at least try.*

"There might be . . ."

"Might be what?"

"A way to know. The stars might tell me."

Vreva flashed a condescending smile. "No offense to your skills, dear, but I don't think astrology will tell you whether or not I'll survive this."

"No, you're right, astrology won't help, but . . . something else might." Celeste bit her lip, hoping that her confession wouldn't alienate her friends. If she wasn't comfortable being blessed or cursed by a god, how might they see it? Sailors were superstitious by nature, after all, but if ever they needed to see into the future, now was that time. "I've had some premonitions and . . . a message. From Desna."

"You *what*?" Vreva stared open-mouthed, and Celeste felt a perverse satisfaction at shattering her poise.

"From *Desna*?" Snick positively glowed with elation. "Oh, Celeste! That's just . . ."

Mathias meowed loudly.

"Yeah! That!" Snick hopped over to the bunk and scratched the cat under the chin.

"That's how you knew we should attack the slaver." Thillion looked equally astonished, but had apparently connected the recent events more quickly than his shipmates.

"So you're some kind of seer, then?" Grogul sounded only slightly less skeptical than Vreva.

"Something like that. There are other . . . manifestations that I'm having difficulty understanding. I couldn't speak or understand Taldane during the battle, and I somehow cast a spell I didn't even know I had." The doubt in some of their eyes tweaked Celeste's ire. With a thought, she summoned the shielding cloak of starlight, smiling grimly as her companions stepped back from the shimmering radiance. "See?"

"Wait. Let me . . ." Vreva cast a spell and squinted at Celeste. "For the love of Calistria, you're right! This isn't even a spell, it's a . . . well, I don't really know what to call it other than a manifestation." Vreva blinked and shook her head.

"It scared me spitless the first time it happened." Celeste banished the starry aura.

Mathias meowed, and Vreva nodded. "Yes, love, I will. And you say you can see the future?"

"Sort of. When I'm stargazing I sometimes slip into a kind of trance. When I consider a question, I get a feeling whether something's a good idea or not. Sometimes it works, sometimes it doesn't. I could try, if you want me to."

"No, I—" Mathias meowed again, and Vreva rolled her eyes. "I'm *not* being stupid about this, Mathias, just cautious. I don't want to know if something bad is going to happen, because I've got to do this anyway."

"Even if you absolutely *knew* that you were gonna die?" Snick's brow wrinkled in surprise.

"Yes, even if I knew." Vreva shrugged. "Think of it this way: any of you would risk your lives for your captain or crewmates. If I have to sacrifice my life to save an entire city and prevent a war, I'll do it in a heartbeat."

"If you don't want me to ask the question, I won't, but it might help *us* to know if this has a chance of working. If it doesn't, we can send a message to Trellis sooner, and make sure she's ready for a naval action."

"There is that." Vreva pursed her lips in consideration then nodded. "Okay, Celeste. Give it a try, and we'll see what happens."

"All right." Celeste slithered to her favored spot beneath the skylight and looked up into the star-spangled sky. Her mind settled into the now-familiar trance, lulled by the song of the heavens.

Should Vreva go aboard Devil's Trident?

An upwelling of rightness surged through her, a definite feeling that this was the correct thing to do.

Thank you.

Celeste stirred from her trance and turned to the others. They all sat about looking at her expectantly. "You should go. It's the right thing to do."

"I'll survive?" Vreva stood, hope brightening her countenance.

Celeste cringed, realizing that she should have been more careful phrasing her question. "I didn't ask that. Sorry, but I just asked if you should go, and I got a good feeling about it. I don't know if it'll be good for you, us, or Desna, but *someone* will be happy about the result."

"Well, that's clear as mud," Grogul grumbled.

"Prophecies often are, but that makes it no less welcome. Thank you, Celeste. Please tell Torius what I'm doing, and not to do anything rash if I don't come back." Vreva smiled at Celeste and patted Snick on the shoulder. "No swashbuckling rescues this time. Neutralizing the weapon has to take precedence, even if things go awry."

"I'll tell him, but I can't control what he does."

"I think you have more control over Torius than you think." Vreva winked and hurried for the door, Mathias trotting along at her heels. With her hand on the latch, she stopped and looked back. "But don't tell him I said so. You know how he is about his freedom."

"Yes, I do." Celeste felt a sudden wave of guilt that Vreva was going into such peril while they would be safe aboard *Stargazer*, but she was going of her own choice, and there was nothing anyone could say to change her mind. "Be careful."

"Careful never won a battle, Celeste." Vreva grinned.

"Then, good luck."

"I'll take all the luck I can get. Thank you all." Vreva nodded and left.

"I hope she knows what she's doing." Thillion worked the links of his chain, shaking his head.

"She's got guts, I'll give her that." Grogul left, followed by Thillion. Snick, however, stood there staring at Celeste.

"What's wrong?"

"Dunno." Snick made a face. "Just trying to figure out an angle to use this new talent of yours. Maybe we could go to one of the gambling houses and fleece some nobles or something."

"I don't think so, Snick." Celeste wasn't quite sure if the gnome was joking or not.

Vreva strode up to *Devil's Trident's* gangplank looking not like Bushatra, but like the sailor whose face and form Bushatra had imitated. Despite the sea-worn countenance, however, she didn't smell like a sailor. She had delved several trash bins behind a tannery until her scent met with Mathias's approval. Unfortunately, there was no way to test it but to walk into a room with a drowning devil.

First, though, she had to get through the flagship's security. Mathias had taken his usual route aboard, scrambling invisibly up one of the massive mooring lines. He would meet her on deck to guide her path to the cabin where they kept the weapon.

"Password, sailor!" demanded the marine lieutenant on guard duty.

"Parasol," Vreva growled in Bushatra's harsh tone, thankful that Mathias had scouted ahead to learn the daily code word.

The second security team met her at the boarding hatch. A different wizard this time—a robed woman with the slightly pointed ears of a half-elf and a rapier at her hip—raised a hand.

"Hang on there." The wizard twisted her fingers and started to recite arcane words.

"Save your pitiful spell." Vreva stepped through the boarding hatch onto the deck and shifted her disguise to resemble Bushatra.

"Miss Bushatra!" The wizard's eyes widened, and she swallowed hard. "My apologies, but I have to check." She finished her spell.

Before the wizard could even interpret the result, Vreva inter-
jected, remembering Bushatra's caustic attitude even when dealing
with her own coven. "Of *course* you're going to see magic, idiot!
You think I'm here to improve morale? And I'm not about to walk
around this city without protection!"

"Of course, I . . ." The wizard swallowed again and took half a
step back. "I'm just following orders, ma'am."

"*I'm just following orders, ma'am,*" Vreva mocked in an infantile
tone. "Follow this one." She spat a vile and anatomically impossible
command, wheeled on her heel, and stalked away without looking
back. She had to get out of there before the wizard had time to
interpret what kind of magic Vreva was actually using. Since they
didn't shoot her in the back, her performance must have hit the
mark.

She passed two more marine guards at the door to the flagship's towering sterncastle and then paused inside. This was where
she was supposed to meet Mathias. She jumped with an involuntary start when something invisible brushed her leg.

Straight ahead, then left and down at the companionway,
Mathias meowed quietly.

Vreva followed his directions, memorizing the layout as she
went. She didn't know this part of the ship at all, since it wasn't
near Ronnel's cabin. Mathias had helped her draw out some rough
sketches, but he tended to navigate more by scent than floor plan,
resulting in inconsistencies between the map and what she was
seeing now. They descended another deck, and the space started to
feel confined, the walls closer, the overhead lower. It worried her
that they were going so deep into the ship. Escape would be that
much harder.

Around the next corner. Mathias sent her a nudge of confidence. *I'll be nearby, but I shouldn't go any closer.*

"All right." She kept her voice a bare whisper and took a deep
breath to steady her nerves. "If Anguillithek penetrates my disguise,

you should know soon enough." She rounded the corner and spied six marines and a lieutenant standing guard at a cabin door. They snapped to attention when they spotted her.

"Good evening, Miss Bushatra." Lieutenant Emero saluted.

Following Mathias's coaching on how Bushatra interacted with the sailors and officers, Vreva adopted a harsh tone. "Out of my way, and stop that ridiculous saluting. I'm not in your *navy!*"

"Yes, ma'am." The lieutenant stepped aside, though he was hardly in her way. "Sorry, ma'am."

Vreva fished from her pocket the key ring she'd taken from Bushatra. Of the five keys, two looked like they would fit the lock. The first one didn't turn, but the second did. She opened the door, stepped inside, and turned to slam it closed.

"Quiet! You make too much noise."

Anguillithek. Vreva felt her blood chill with the otherworldly inflections of that deep rumbling voice. This was the moment where her disguise would succeed or fail, and she would live or die. Steeped in the lore of devils since her childhood, Vreva knew how hard it was to deceive Hell's minions. Her life depended on her skill at deception.

"What does it matter how much noise I make?" She put all the spite she could in her tone as she turned to face the fiend.

Mathias hadn't exaggerated in his description, but seeing the drowning devil in the flesh was more daunting than Vreva had imagined. Perhaps fifteen feet from its fishy tail to the top of its sea-blue head, it overwhelmed the moderately sized cabin. Two muscular arms ended in nests of writhing purple tentacles. Needlelike teeth lined a lipless mouth framed by two long barbels that wiggled like snakes. Curved ram's horns framed that baleful face, four pupilless eyes staring at her like glowing golden orbs, turning her blood to ice water.

Its massive head tilted quizzically, as if the devil were sizing her up for a meal. Anguillithek waved one hand toward a bunk in the room's corner. "Yami is sleeping. If he wakes, *you* can listen to him complain all night!"

Yami? Who's Yami? Vreva spied a shape huddled under a blanket, and remembered her speculation from Mathias's report that the weapon might be alive. *Well, if it's alive, then it'll just have to die.* She let her irritation edge her voice. "How is he supposed to sleep with you slithering around the cabin?"

The devil ignored her comment and undulated toward her, exhibiting a sinuous grace despite its bulk. "What took you so long tonight? You know I have to report to Gorthoklek."

Gorthoklek. Vreva recognized the name of Queen Abrogail's fiendish counselor. *So Ronnel's plot is at least known by the queen.* The revelation didn't really surprise her. She also had little doubt that Abrogail would disavow any knowledge of the reckless plan if it failed. She stood her ground, enduring the devil's blank-eyed stare. "So leave! I'm here now."

"See that you *stay* here and watch over him until I return." With that command, the devil vanished with a pop of inrushing air.

Vreva breathed a sigh of relief. Her disguise had passed the devil's inspection, but then the devil's words revisited her. *Watch over him.* She peered at the shrouded form on the bed, a mop of auburn hair peeking out from one end of the blanket. *This has to be the weapon.* A cold resolve settled over her. She'd killed before to save Augustana. What was one more life to save thousands?

Flipping up the cover of her wrist bracer, she withdrew an envenomed needle and concealed it in her palm. Cautiously, she approached the bunk. She had no idea what to expect, but a creature that could destroy a city would undoubtedly be formidable.

"I wish you wouldn't leave me alone with that thing." The blanket shifted, and Vreva found herself looking into eyes like blue-white gemstones. The surrounding skin was marred by hard, lumpy growths like the chitinous shell of a crustacean. A hand sporting more of those shell-like growths and short clawlike nails reached up to pull the blanket aside. "It scares me."

The diminutive figure sat up, and Vreva stopped short. It was a boy. A strangely featured boy, to be sure, but other than the eyes and growths, he looked human, and barely out of childhood. He regarded Bushatra without a hint of fear or revulsion.

It doesn't matter. If this is the weapon, I've got to kill him, but . . . I've got to be sure. "Anguillithek's here to protect you."

"I know, but I still don't like it." Yami scratched idly at one of the odd patches on his face. "It just stares at me. It won't talk to me like you do."

He actually likes *Bushatra?* Given what Vreva had seen of the witch, she had doubted anyone would think of her as a friend. Even the witches in her coven had considered her a nasty creature. But Yami was looking up at her with honest regard. How could Bushatra have engendered such guileless trust? Magic, perhaps, but Vreva had no spell on him now, and he looked perfectly amiable and eager for her companionship.

"What would you like to talk about?" She sat beside him on the bed, the needle still at the ready.

"Oh, I don't care." He smiled and tucked his feet under him. "Tell me a story."

She told him stories? It didn't seem possible. He seemed so innocent. She wondered if he even knew what he really was. *It doesn't matter! Just kill him and escape. That's the mission!*

Vreva knew that was the logical thing to do, but curiosity niggled at her. There was something compelling about Yami. Not quite a little boy, but not yet a young man, his innocence touched her in a way she couldn't define. That innocence stayed her hand. She covertly tucked the deadly needle into her belt. *I've got to know more about him.*

"So, let's see . . ." She got up and went to a cubby where a pitcher of water and two cups rested in protective nooks. With her back turned to the boy, she whispered her thought-reading spell. Taking her time, she poured some water, strolled back to the bunk, and handed the cup to Yami. As his thoughts resolved in her mind, she said, "I was just thinking about how we first met. Do you remember that?"

Yami's face clouded over, and Vreva glimpsed a confusion of horrific images: a massive wave, flimsy houses torn from their frames and smashed against the shore, torrential rain soaking bodies that littered a beach, water running red with blood. *Mama! Papa!* A tide of crushing guilt rose up to overwhelm all else.

"I don't like to remember that." The cup trembled in Yami's hand. "You know I don't."

Vreva felt ill. Yami felt responsible for the destruction of his village, the deaths of hundreds of people, including his parents. *But why? What happened?* She had to know more.

"I know, but I was thinking of what happened later."

Yami looked up at her solemnly and said, "I remember. You found me after . . . after it happened, and healed my broken leg. You said you could take away the curse so that it never happens again, and . . . showed me what would happen if you didn't." *Never again. Never . . .*

Curse? Vreva pondered his remarks. What kind of curse could wreak such havoc? Had Bushatra discovered that Yami was responsible for some kind of natural disaster? Then the last statement registered:

. . . showed me what would happen . . .

Of course! Just like she'd showed Keah her future. That sounded exactly like something the vile woman would do: blackmail an innocent boy into destroying an entire city with his own fear and guilt. She'd given him a vision of his future, and tricked him into helping her make it come true. It was a nice theory, but she had to be sure.

"What I showed you . . ."

Once again, the boy's mind projected an image of vast destruction, but this time, Vreva recognized the location. It was, or had been, Augustana, Andoran's great naval seaport. The bay was littered with crushed ships, the city's waterfront torn to shreds, bodies strewn everywhere. It was so vivid, Vreva had to bite her lip to keep from gasping.

Please don't let it come true. Not again.

Yami's silent plea broke Vreva's heart. She wrapped an arm around the boy's shoulder. "I won't let that happen. I'm here to help you."

I'm here to help you . . . A memory washed over Vreva, taking her back to her youth. She'd said the same words to Delphie, her younger sister—her best friend—right before the girl had died in Vreva's arms. She'd been an innocent, cast out by their parents because she had no magic, sold into slavery.

Just as Bushatra, Ronnel, and Anguillithek planned to use Yami. Vreva trembled with rage.

But how could she help him? That was the question. She touched the poisoned needle in her belt. A painless end . . . *One sting, and not only is my mission accomplished, but he'll never have to feel that crushing guilt again. Killing him will save thousands of lives. It's the logical thing to do.*

But is it the right *thing?* Vreva thought for only a moment before taking her hand away from the needle. She couldn't do it. Even if Yami could be used as some kind of horrific weapon, he was innocent. "Don't worry, Yami. Now, drink your water and try to sleep. I'll tell you a story and watch over you."

"Thank you." Yami drained the cup and handed it back. By the time Vreva returned it to its cubby and replaced her poisoned needle in its sheath, he had rolled back over and pulled the blanket up over his shoulder.

To hell with logic. She sat on the bed, telling him an old children's story from her youth, watching him breathe evenly, and firming her resolve. *To hell with orders and spying and wars. I can't kill an innocent boy.* And if she couldn't kill Yami, there was only one other means of foiling the Chelish plans for Augustana. *We've got to steal him away.*

Vreva thought of using magic to transport them away, but even if she'd had the proper scroll, she wouldn't have dared use it. Bushatra hadn't wanted to use magic to take the boy to Augustana, for fear of triggering the weapon. They might currently be in Chelish waters, but Vreva wasn't about to trade one city's massacre for another. She could render the boy invisible and bluff her way ashore in Bushatra's guise, but could she count on Yami to stay quiet enough to bypass the guards? And then there was the devil to consider. If Anguillithek returned and raised an alarm before they escaped, she was as good as dead, and Yami would be all alone. If the boy truly could be as destructive as the vision showed, Anguillithek and Ronnel would stop at nothing to figure out how to wield him as a weapon.

Torture . . . They'd torture him for his secret. She couldn't let that happen.

When Yami's breathing deepened with sleep, Vreva explored the cabin, renewing her disguise spell when it lapsed and trying to figure out some workable plan. One of her keys opened the only other door into a small sleeping cabin. By the litter of personal items, she determined that it must be Bushatra's. She would rifle through the witch's things later, maybe find some clue to help her understand what had passed between her and the boy.

She had just relocked the door when a rush of displaced air announced Anguillithek's return. The devil's blank yellow eyes scanned the room, passing over the sleeping boy and settling on Vreva.

"He sleeps?"

"Yes, and so must I." She turned back to the door to Bushatra's room.

"What were you up to tonight?" It was more demand than question. "A building has burned in the city, and you smell of smoke. I hope you had nothing to do with it."

Vreva cursed herself for not washing more thoroughly and met the devil's glare with one of her own. Powerful fiends, she knew, were skilled at seeing through lies, but Vreva was long practiced in the art of disguising her falsehoods with truth. "As a matter of fact, I did. The coven and I had a disagreement. I had to eliminate them."

"I see." The devil's tail twitched in an agitated motion that reminded Vreva of Celeste. "You betrayed them."

"They intended to interfere with my plans. I couldn't have that. Leaving them alive would have ruined everything." All true enough from her point of view.

"Your *plans*! Did you dare to tell them about—" Anguillithek waved one tentacled hand toward Yami's bunk.

"I'm not *stupid*." Vreva sneered at the glowering devil. "I told them nothing about the plan! I merely used them. They wanted money and power, nothing more."

"Be glad you didn't betray our contract, witch." Apparently mollified, the drowning devil turned away to face the sleeping Yami. "Go sleep. I'll watch."

Vreva didn't have to be told twice. Her mind was dull with fatigue, and she needed rest to replenish her magic. *Not to mention thinking of a way to get Yami away from the Chelish, and telling Torius there's been a change of plan.* He wouldn't like that, but it wasn't his call.

Locking the door behind her, she shuddered at the thought of trying to sleep with that devil in the next cabin. Vreva projected a feeling of well-being for Mathias's sake. He'd probably picked up on her feelings already, and she didn't want him to worry. Yawning, she looked at the rumpled bunk and wrinkled her nose. The blankets reeked with the smell of poorly tanned leather.

11

A Change of Plans

Vreva stifled a sigh of relief as she and Yami emerged onto the deck of *Devil's Trident*. Maneuvering through the narrow corridors belowdecks amid a cordon of Chelish marines had wound her nerves tighter than a crossbow string. Though still surrounded, at least now she had a little breathing room. She blinked in the bright sunlight and surveyed her surroundings.

Robust lay rafted up between *Devil's Trident* and the frigate, *Fury's Crown*, thick lines binding them together like a child between two protective parents. The galleon wasn't much to look at—beamy and drab, without the grandeur of the flagship or the sleek lines of the frigate. She had been aptly named, built to haul vast amounts of cargo and withstand hard use, not to win any prizes for speed or aesthetics.

The frigate contrasted with the galleon in every respect. Trim and smart, her crew turned out in full regalia, *Fury's Crown* was one of the gems of the Ostenso fleet, fast and deadly. That the frigate would be their sole escort was both heartening and worrisome.

Admiral Ronnel had visited them first thing that morning to give them the details. "*Robust* has arrived, and everything's ready for the transfer. Captain Giavano has his orders, and Captain Lance of *Fury's Crown* has hers. We can't risk sending an entire squadron into Andoren waters, but *Fury's Crown*'s a crack ship. She'll follow close enough to protect *Robust* from mishaps, but far enough to look like she's not sailing in company. If an Andoren ship shows up, she's fast enough to evade."

That was the encouraging part. With only a single ship as escort, the plan forming in Vreva's head might just work. *If Torius is willing to go along.*

Vreva clutched Yami's arm and followed Anguillithek across the deck. Thankfully, the devil's attention remained focused on their surroundings, not Vreva. The longer she interacted with it, the more likely the devil would be to pierce her deception. Yami seemed to accept her disguise without question. They paused at the boarding hatch where the gangway inclined steeply down to the galleon's deck.

"I don't see why we have to go aboard a different ship." Yami sounded like any disgruntled youngster as he looked dubiously at the lesser vessel. "Why can't we stay on this one?"

"Because this one can't take us where we need to go." Vreva urged the boy across. The drowning devil rose off the deck and hovered in escort as they crossed, its iridescent finlike wings flapping lazily as its blank eyes scanned nonstop. Looking down the narrow gap between the two ships, Vreva briefly considered dragging Yami over the side with her. Kalli was down there somewhere to help, but with so many sailors and marines on deck, and the drowning devil, too, she knew they would never escape.

No, it's got to be at sea. That was the only plan that had a chance of success.

She caught a flicker of movement down in the shadow between the ships, a small black shape leaping from one of the flagship's open ballista ports to scrabble through a porthole in the galleon's hull. Mathias was aboard. Vreva felt a flush of annoyance, and knew he wasn't happy with her change of plans. Her familiar truly despised sea travel.

A squad of hard-looking sailors awaited them on the deck of *Robust*. At the fore stood a tall, attractive man—*Giavano*—dressed in a plain merchant's blue jacket with gold epaulets. She could see how the captain's good looks could get him into trouble with some noble's wife, but his chiseled features now bore the haunted expression of a man who knew he was destined to die and that there was nothing he could do about it. Vreva wondered if the rest of the crew knew this was to be a one-way trip. If she told them, maybe they'd mutiny and save her the trouble of killing the captain.

No, that won't work. She watched Anguillithek settle lightly to the deck. *The only way to escape is to kill the devil, and to do that I need Torius and his Stargazers.*

"Anguillithek." Giavano looked up at the devil with something just short of disdain. "I trust all's well in Egorian."

"Perfectly well, Captain." The drowning devil's rumbling voice brimmed with cold amusement.

There's no love lost there. Vreva wondered how well-acquainted the captain and the devil were, and if she could somehow use their animosity to her advantage.

Turning away from the devil, the captain doffed his bicorne hat and bowed shortly to Vreva, his eyes flicking curiously over Yami. "Welcome aboard *Robust*, Miss Bushatra. Your service to the Chelish Empire is laudable."

"Save your pleasantries, Captain." Vreva kept Yami close and glared the man down. She couldn't imagine Bushatra being swayed by his suave manners and good looks. She wondered at his comment about serving the Chelish Empire, however. *How high does this plot go?* None of Trellis's spies had caught wind of it. She felt sure the queen knew—only an idiot would undertake something of this magnitude without at least her tacit approval—but apparently few others did. Total deniability. "I hope you have our accommodations ready."

"Of course. We've walled off a section of the hold for your comfort and your things will be brought down directly. If you would follow me." He turned to the drowning devil and pointed toward the main cargo hatch. "Our passages are too cramped for you, Anguillithek. You'll have to fly down through there."

The drowning devil rose off the deck and descended through the gaping hatch without a word.

"Hyrich, see to the transfer of the ballast," Giavano ordered one of the sailors. "We sail on the morning tide."

"Aye, Captain." The man saluted and started barking orders.

"Why are you loading ballast, Captain? Wouldn't we sail faster with *less* weight?" One hand protectively on Yami's shoulder, Vreva followed Giavano into the stuffy confines of the sterncastle and down a passage to a steep companionway.

"We would, but merchant vessels don't sail without cargo. There might be suspicion if we arrived riding too high in the water. We're taking on enough stone to make *Robust* look as if she's fully laden."

"I don't understand," Yami said. "Are we trying to fool someone?"

Captain Giavano stopped and stared, first at Yami, then at Bushatra. "I'll let your mistress explain the details of our arrangement."

"Yes, you *will*, Captain. No one is to speak to Yami without my leave. Is that clear?" The last thing Vreva needed was for the boy to learn the truth about their mission.

Giavano's brow furrowed. "Your leave or Anguillithek's, you mean."

"No, I said *exactly* what I meant." Vreva put all the vitriol she could muster into her voice. "My leave *alone*, Captain. Clear?"

"Perfectly clear." He glared right back at her for a moment before turning and going on his way.

"I'll explain when we're alone, Yami. Don't worry. Everything's exactly as it should be."

"Yes, Bushatra."

Down another steep stair, the air became even thicker. They turned toward the bow and passed through a heavy double door into the ship's vast lower hold. To her left, a section of the space had been walled off with temporary bulkheads to form a large cabin. The door was oversized, large enough to allow Anguillithek to pass in and out.

"Here you are." Giavano gestured to the cabin, then to a pallet bearing the witch's trunks that was being lowered into the hold. "My sailors will see to your needs. I have duties to perform." He nodded, turned, and left.

Stepping into the cabin, she glanced around and deemed it adequate. It sported few amenities, but they were only scheduled to be aboard a few days. Thankfully, there was a separate cabin forward, which she assumed would be hers. There were even locks on the doors, but no ports or hatches for fresh air or easy escape. Anguillithek was already busy inspecting every nook and cranny.

Vreva sat Yami on the bunk in the corner and instructed him to stay out of the way as the sailors lugged in Bushatra's heavy trunks. "Put them in there," she ordered, pointing to the secondary cabin.

Vreva had gone through the trunks carefully that morning and found a few more magical trinkets that Bushatra had hidden away. She'd examined everything using magic, including the items she'd found on the other witches. She'd been able to figure out how some of them worked, and secreted them on her person. They might come in handy.

"Here, ma'am." The sailor in charge of the detail handed over a ring of two keys. "Keys to your cabins."

"Are there any duplicates of these?"

"Yes, ma'am. The captain has a set."

"Bring me those, too."

"But, ma'am, the captain has to—"

Vreva's backhanded blow caught the startled sailor square in the mouth. As he reeled back, she cast a simple spell, her hand flaring with a torchlike radiance. She thrust it at the sailor's face, Bushatra's long, dirty nails like claws ready to tear his eyes out.

"The next time you argue with me, I take off your head! Now go . . . get . . . those . . . keys!"

"Yes, ma'am." The sailor and his work crew hurried out, muttering beneath their breath.

Vreva slammed the door behind them and turned to find Anguillithek staring at her. "What?"

"You surprise me, Bushatra." The drowning devil undulated to the middle of the room and crossed its tentacle-tipped arms over its chest. "You're learning restraint. A week ago, you would have murdered the man for arguing."

"Don't be stupid, Anguillithek." Truth be told, Vreva was relieved that her action appeared restrained rather than overly harsh. Assuming alternative identities, she often had to be pleasant to unpleasant people. Now she had to be unpleasant to people who didn't deserve it. The change was proving difficult for her to get used to. If the devil thought that slapping and threatening a man was showing restraint, then Bushatra must have been a true horror. Even Yami seemed nonplussed by the violence. The witch must have used magic to win him over. Or maybe children could just get used to anything. "The crew's shorthanded, or hadn't you noticed? Killing one of them would have impeded our mission."

"And again you surprise me. Forethought and consideration of our mission above your own whims is something new for you."

She bristled. Bushatra would never back down from an insult like that. "Why don't you take that scaly tail of yours and stick it up your—"

"Bushatra?" Yami's voice cut off her invective. "Why's the crew shorthanded? And why is the captain loading ballast to make it look like we're carrying cargo when we're not? What's going on?"

"It's complicated." Vreva strode over to the sideboard and poured a cup of water, downing it in one long draught. The stuffy confines of the cabin had her sweating. *Or maybe it's facing down a drowning devil.*

"Then explain it to me."

Vreva took a deep breath and let it out slowly. She would have to proceed carefully here. She didn't know what Bushatra had told Yami, and with the devil in the room, she didn't dare cast a spell to delve the boy's thoughts. "We've talked about this before. What did I tell you about my removing your curse?"

"I know you said it would be easier to do it where the vision showed me it would happen, but why do we have to go on this ship, and not the big one?

"Because the place where we're going isn't friendly with Cheliax. They're a bunch of rebellious fanatics, and won't allow a Chelish warship in their waters. So the navy made this transport look like a merchant and ordered Captain Giavano to take us where we need to go." Vreva poured another cup of water and slipped a few drops of knockout toxin into it from a vial secreted in her sleeve. She stole a glance at the drowning devil as she took it to Yami. Anguillithek stared at her without expression, its chin barbels wriggling slowly. "They're shorthanded because the sailors on this ship had to be taken from real warships, and nobody wants to leave *them* shorthanded."

"Okay. I get it." Yami took the cup and drank. "So, when we get there, you lift the curse and get the magic."

Get the magic? What kind of lies was Bushatra feeding him? She had no doubt that the witch had played on the boy's ignorance of magic, but not knowing what she'd told him left her in a bad situation. She had to keep her answers ambiguous. "Yes, as I said. Everybody wins."

"Then we come back here and live in your big house with lots of servants!"

Yami's grin and hopeful expression broke Vreva's heart. She wondered if Bushatra even expected Yami to survive the destruction of Augustana. She'd spoken to the other witches about her escape from the destruction, but not Yami's.

"That's right. I'll take good care of you, Yami." She glanced at the devil. Anguillithek remained impassive, but Vreva knew she was pushing her luck. One slip and the devil would know she wasn't Bushatra. "Finish your drink."

"Yes, Bushatra." Yami drank the water down without hesitation.

Vreva replaced the cup and made a show of exploring their new quarters. In time, Yami slumped down on the bed to sleep.

"You drugged him?"

"Picked that up, did you?" She faced the devil, crossing her arms defiantly. "I was tired of his stupid questions."

"You astonish me with your capacity for lies."

Vreva's heart skipped a beat. She fingered the bracer that concealed her poisoned needles. If Anguillithek was onto her deception, one needle for Yami and one for herself would complete her mission and avoid an interrogation. Enduring torture at the hands of an inquisitor had very nearly shattered her sanity. She doubted devils would be so gentle.

"What the hell is that supposed to mean?"

"It means that I'm impressed. My lord Asmodeus, the Prince of Lies, would approve. Should our mission unfold as you've foreseen, you'll truly be an asset to Him . . . and Queen Abrogail, of course."

"Don't patronize me!" Vreva whirled away and retreated to her small sleeping cabin. Slamming and locking the door, she leaned against it and took a deep, calming breath. Dealing with the drowning devil was like dancing on hot coals; one misstep and she would burn.

A cold resolve settled over her. To rescue Yami, Anguillithek would have to die. To accomplish that, she needed Torius.

Tonight, Vreva realized. The ship is leaving in the morning, so I have to talk to Torius tonight.

"Captain! We've got company."

"What?" Torius glanced at the nondescript sailor coming aboard, then noticed Grogul's arched brows and jerky nod of the head. He didn't recognize this fellow, but his bosun obviously knew him. He trotted down the steps from the quarterdeck where he'd been discussing Snick's plan for a new rigging improvement. "What can I— Gozreh's guts! What's that *smell*?"

"It's *me*, Torius!" Vreva's voice from the slovenly sailor's mouth told him all he needed to know.

"This way." Torius spun on his heel and led her aft, trailed by Thillion, Grogul, and Snick. Celeste had filled him in on Vreva's visit and her suicidal plan to neutralize the weapon. Vreva's sudden appearance might mean that their mission was complete.

"Did you do it?" he asked once the sterncastle door had closed behind them.

"One second." The unfamiliar sailor waved a hand and morphed into the woman he knew, though she was garbed as he'd never seen her, in dark leathers and bristling with weapons. "I want Celeste to hear this, too."

Torius ushered Vreva and his officers into his cabin. Celeste lay coiled in her customary place beneath the skylight. As far as he could tell, she hadn't moved since he'd left the cabin several hours ago. She'd barely spoken to him since he came home early that morning, even when he'd tried to explain that he'd simply fallen asleep at Lothera's villa. All she had said was that she wasn't angry with him, but her subsequent silence spoke volumes.

"Where's Mathias?" Snick closed the door, looking worried. "He wasn't . . ."

"Mathias is fine. He's aboard *Robust*." Vreva began to pace the crowded cabin, her hands clenched at her sides. "And, no, Torius, I didn't neutralize the weapon. There's been a change of plan."

"What? Why?" Torius didn't like the sound of this, and from the sour looks on their faces, neither did his officers.

"Because of what the weapon is. Or rather, *who* the weapon is. I couldn't—"

"Stop!" Celeste slithered to the fore, her tail twitching nervously as she coiled.

Torius knew that posture; she was ready to strike. But why would she want to bite Vreva? "Celeste, what—"

"We need to know that you're really Vreva. I'm picking up all kinds of magic around you. We need to make sure you are who you say. If Vreva was discovered, you might be an impostor."

The others shifted, instantly wary, hands drifting toward weapons, and Torius realized that Celeste was right. The stakes were too high on this mission. If this was a magically disguised infiltrator, they could all end up dancing on the end of a yardarm.

"Of course." Vreva looked to Celeste and signed. "Ask me something only I would know."

"When we first met, what were you doing?"

"I was . . . entertaining a slave merchant in my suite in Okeno." Vreva smiled wryly. "Would you like a *detailed* description of the compromising position you found us in?"

"No. I've been trying to purge that image from my memory, actually."

"So have I. This should ease your suspicions." Vreva rolled up her sleeve and uttered a single word under her breath. The black eagle insignia of the Twilight Talons coalesced upon her pale forearm for a moment before fading.

"We can't be too careful." Celeste relaxed her coils. "So, why couldn't you destroy the weapon?"

"Because the weapon is a boy, not a thing." Fatigue and stress edged Vreva's voice, as well it might after spending a day in a cabin with a devil. "I couldn't murder him."

Torius couldn't believe what he was hearing. "Why not? One life to save thousands sounds like a good deal to me."

"Because he's innocent, Torius. He doesn't even know he's a weapon."

They listened while Vreva resumed her pacing and filled them in on all she'd learned. Torius went to his liquor cabinet and offered to pour something to calm her nerves, but she shook her head.

"Thank you, Torius, but no. I've got to hurry back and deal with Anguillithek. It was all I could do to convince the devil that I needed to leave the ship to pick up some spell ingredients. I need to stay sharp."

"So what's this new plan?" Torius put the bottle away.

"We have to steal him away."

"*Steal* him away?" Torius stared at her as if she'd told him his hair was on fire. "Just like that? From under the noses of the Chelish navy and a Gozreh-be-damned *devil*?"

"Come on, Torius. That's what you do best! You were a pirate for how many years?" Vreva stared him down. "Of course, we'll have to kill Anguillithek. And we'll have to do it before it can teleport away."

"And just how are we supposed to do that? I've never fought a drowning devil before, but I'm pretty sure they're tougher than your average slaver." Torius cast about for potential solutions to this suicidal plan. "Can't you—I don't know—slip some poison into its tea?"

"Most devils are immune to poison. No, we'll have to kill it using more conventional means. Fire's no good, but Celeste's lightning spell should affect it, and even devils aren't immune to blades and arrows."

"Got plenty of those," Snick offered. "But how do we convince the thing to stick around and fight?"

"Drawing Anguillithek into a fight won't be hard." Vreva resumed her pacing. "If you attack *Robust*, it'll defend Yami. The trick will be to kill it before it realizes that you're not common pirates, I'm not Bushatra, and that I'm stealing Yami away. If it discovers that, it'll blink away and call in reinforcements."

"You mean more fiends, don't you?" This plan was going from bad to worse. Fighting a drowning devil was bad enough.

If Anguillithek returned with other, more powerful fiends, they didn't stand a chance.

"Yes," Vreva agreed. "But I think there's a limit to what kind of support this mission can expect from the Chelish navy, or even Hell. I have a suspicion this was cooked up between Ronnel and Anguillithek. I don't know who Bushatra cut the deal with, or how much Abrogail knows, but I'm willing to bet my life that the queen can't offer any imperial support to the operation, not and maintain deniability if it goes wrong."

"She's covering her ass." That sounded about right for the Chelish queen. By all accounts, Abrogail was a brilliant strategist, ruthlessly plotting for every political advantage.

"Exactly." Vreva nodded.

"Why do *we* have to do this?" Celeste asked. "Can't we just call in a squadron of Gray Corsairs?"

"Once again, the problem is Anguillithek's ability to teleport." Vreva looked stern. She had obviously thought this through. "If we pull the Gray Corsairs in, not only could it start a war, but they'll know immediately that we discovered their plot and that *Stargazer*'s not just a pirate ship. Once the devil's dead, we can call in reinforcements."

"What about this weapon?" Thillion asked. "Is there a way we could use it against them?"

"*He* is a boy, and his name is Yami. But no, I don't think so. I don't know what this power of his is, or how to trigger it. Bushatra and Anguillithek are afraid to use powerful magic on him, which is why they're not teleporting him to Augustana, so magic might have something to do with it. That's why I can't just buy a teleportation scroll and steal him away that way, either. Yami doesn't even understand his powers, as far as I can tell. Or if he does, it's buried under so much guilt that I can't see it." Vreva sighed and rubbed her eyes. "I'm sorry, but I just couldn't kill him. He doesn't even know what's going on."

"Ever think of telling him?" Snick asked.

Vreva looked up. "What?"

"Tell him what's going on. Tell him Bushatra's dead, that she lied to him, and we're going to rescue him from an evil plot to destroy a whole gods-damned city and kill *thousands*!" Snick snorted derisively. "Sometimes the truth *does* work, you know."

"It would be one hell of a risk. He trusts Bushatra." Vreva made a face. "Though Calistria knows why. Gods, what a vile woman!"

"So, convince him to trust *you*." Grogul shrugged as if the entire problem was simple. "You're pretty persuasive. Show the kid what you really look like, use a little magic, and you'll have him wrapped around your finger."

"I suppose it could work, but if I admit to killing the woman who promised to help him, he might tell Anguillithek. If he does, I'm dead."

"And if we don't figure out some sure way to kill that devil, we're *all* dead." Torius bit his lip, trying to think of all the things that could go wrong. There were too many. "What about their escort? You say they're only sending one ship?"

"Yes, *Fury's Crown*, and she's to stand off a respectable distance. They don't want a chance mishap, but they don't want a Chelish warship to be seen escorting *Robust*, either."

"Well, one ship's better than a fleet, but that's a very fine frigate. Even if we do kill Anguillithek, we'll have a chase on our hands, and I don't know if we can outrun *Fury's Crown*." Torius shook his head ruefully. A ship that size boasted twice *Stargazer's* crew complement, and he would bet his last scarab that they had at least one caster aboard. There seemed to be no way out. "If we could just figure out how to use that weapon . . ."

"He's a *boy*, Torius, an innocent boy. If we use him, then we're no better than the Chelish!" Again she glared at him, but this time she dropped her gaze first. "But . . . I'll see what I can discover. I'll send you a message by spell if I learn anything valuable."

"Good." Mollified by Vreva's concession, Torius went to his chart table and pulled out a small-scale rendering of the coast between Ostenso and Augustana. "Now, they probably won't hug the coast. Gray Corsairs patrol that area. With the prevailing winds from the east, and not using coastal winds, they'll take a long tack out to sea, and—"

"I'm sorry, Torius, but I've got to get back." Vreva smiled and headed for the door. "Anguillithek's waiting, and it's not very patient. Besides, I don't really understand all this nautical mumbo-jumbo."

"Go. Celeste can inform you of our plans by spell. Be careful."

"Right." Vreva regarded them with a grateful smile. "Thank you all for understanding."

"I understand, Vreva, but that doesn't mean I agree." Torius bit back a surge of temper. As a pirate and privateer, he had to make decisions that cost lives as a matter of course. He'd watched his Stargazers die because of his orders, and he'd give those same orders again if he had to, because every life spent usually meant ten lives saved. One life to save thousands didn't even seem like a decision in his mind. "I was ordered to help you, so I'm helping. I can't say what I would have done in your place, and it doesn't really matter. We're in it up to our eyeballs now."

"Yes, we are." Vreva left without another word.

Torius felt the eyes of his officers upon him. Shaking off his cynical mood, he got back to business. It took some time, but they outlined a workable strategy for intercepting and taking *Robust* at sea, with some modifications to Snick's ballistae to increase their chances of success. When they all had their assignments, he set them to work.

"We'll sail on the end of the morning tide, after *Robust* and *Fury's Crown* are well out to sea. We'll dump our cargo as soon as we're out of sight of land. We'll need all the speed we can muster."

"Damn shame to waste all that wine," Grogul grumbled.

"Well, let the crew breach a barrel tonight, but not too much. We don't want any fuzzy heads in the morning."

"Aye, sir."

Snick, Grogul, and Thillion left, and Torius stowed away the chart. Celeste returned to her spot under the skylight, her stillness filling the room like an oppressive fog, pulling his spirits down even further. Finally, he could take no more, and broke the silence. "Can you use your new talents to find out if this plan is going to get us killed?"

"Not tonight." She glanced away from the skylight and regarded him with solemn eyes, then resumed her stargazing. "I discovered that it only works once a day. I'll try tomorrow night, but I can't promise an answer."

"I'm not asking for promises." Torius sat on the edge of the bunk and watched her as she peered up at the stars. Her long body swayed with the gentle roll of the ship at dock, sinuous and sensuous. He longed to embrace her, but wasn't sure what reception he'd receive. At least she was talking to him again. That was a start. "So you already asked one question today. What was it?"

"If I should question you about what happened with Lothera last night." When she looked at him this time, her eyes swam with tears. "I received the impression that it wasn't a good idea."

"Then I won't tell you." He pushed himself up and started for the door, self-disgust roiling his gut, then stopped and turned back. "I will tell you this, however: I did what I *had* to do. And I'll tell you that today I love you more than I ever have before. And tomorrow, I'll love you even more than that. And no matter what happens with Lothera or when we take *Robust*, every day I draw breath, I'll love you even more."

Torius reached for the door latch, but the hiss of scales on the deck stopped him.

"Don't you *dare* leave this room, Torius Vin!" He turned, and Celeste was there, so close that he stumbled back into the door.

Her upper body flared, and her tail twitched in a manner he knew all too well. Her temper was up. "You don't get to say that to me, then just walk away!"

"What do you want me to say, Celeste?"

"I don't want you to say *anything*!" She muttered under her breath. Before his eyes, arms and legs separated from her long serpentine curves, her pale skin fairly glowing in the lamplight. "Just shut up and make love to me."

Torius would have answered, but found his mouth suddenly too busy to speak. He decided he rather liked it when Celeste got the last word.

12

Consultations

The song of the heavens faded from her mind, and Celeste drifted back to the real world. The sea breeze cooled her scales and ruffled her hair, refreshing after the stifling atmosphere of Ostenso's harbor. Unfortunately, the breeze couldn't refresh her spirits. She felt strangely empty at Desna's answer, or rather, the lack of an answer. Shaking her head to clear the last vestiges of her trance, she turned to her friends. They all stood on the quarterdeck looking at her expectantly.

"I'm sorry. I didn't get an answer. Nothing."

"Well, getting nothing is better than getting 'we're all gonna be eaten by a drowning devil,' so I think that's as good as a win!" Snick grinned and went back to her work. The gnome and her crew had been busy dismantling the six starboard-side ballistae and reassembling them on the port-side quarterdeck and foredeck. By keeping *Stargazer*'s port side facing *Robust*, this would effectively double their firepower. If they had to fight Anguillithek, they were going to need it.

"Best not knowin' anyway," Grogul added with a tusky grin. "It wouldn't change the fact that we gotta do it."

"He's got a point." Thillion turned to Torius. "It's my watch, Captain. I'll see you at midnight."

"Thanks, Thillion." When the first mate and bosun had departed to their tasks, Torius came to Celeste's side and ran a hand through her hair. "Don't worry, love. I can't imagine the future is an easy thing to see, even for Desna. Maybe you'll have better luck tomorrow."

"Maybe. It's just so frustrating!" She smacked her tail against the rail. "I don't know if I'm asking the right questions, and why some are answered and others aren't. When I wondered if we should attack that slaver, it just felt so *right*! Now, when I asked if we should attack *Robust*, I get *nothing*!"

"You'll get used to it." Torius pulled her close, the warmth of his body like a furnace against her cool scales. "I'm sure there's plenty about these new gifts that you've still got to discover."

"There's even more than I've told you about now, Torius." Celeste rested her head on his shoulder and gazed out at the dark horizon. "My head is swimming with all kinds of new magic."

"Like what?"

"Spells to protect me, guide me." She glanced about to make sure no crew were about, and lowered her voice. "Even a spell to help someone who's near death."

"What, like a healing spell?"

Celeste shook her head. "No, not like that. It won't heal a wound, but if someone's bleeding to death, it'll keep them from actually dying. I haven't tried to cast any of them yet, but they're there."

"You usually enjoy experimenting with magic. Besides, this gift from Desna seems pretty good so far."

"Remind me how good it is during the fight with Anguillithek, when I can't understand a word you say." Rearing back, Celeste looked into his eyes, willing him to understand her fears. "These gifts . . . I feel like they're bait. I've never worshiped Desna, so why did she grant me these powers? By using them, am I placing myself in her debt?"

"When you put it that way, it does sound a little frightening. When we get back to Almas, we'll go to a temple of Desna and talk to one of the high priests. They'll have answers."

"I hope so."

Torius took her face gently between his hands. "Until then, if you're uncomfortable using these gifts, then don't. We've gotten by for a long time without them. The choice is entirely up to you."

Celeste smiled at his simple pragmatism. Torius was right. She needed to stop worrying about these new powers and either use or ignore them. She'd get her answers when they came, and not before. She gave him quick kiss. "So, since I can't seem to look into the future, we just continue with the plan?"

"Right. So far the Chelish are doing exactly what I thought they'd do." He pointed to the two faint points of light on the southwestern horizon. "They're tacking to the south with *Fury's Crown* about three miles behind *Robust*. We'll keep them both in sight with our tops'ls furled to keep a low profile. That way we can watch them and they shouldn't be able to spot us. When they turn to the northeast toward Augustana, we'll wait until dark and intercept *Robust*. We'll swoop in on their wake just like we used to do in the old days."

"The old days . . ." Celeste glanced up at the black sails overhead. With dark hull and sails, they could creep up in a ship's wake unseen. Of course, in the old days, they were usually after a piece of art or arcane trinket that they could sell to support themselves for a few more months, not a weapon that could destroy an entire city. "I miss those days."

"So do I," Torius admitted with a sigh. "Still, we're doing the right thing. I can't imagine letting those bastards destroy Augustana. If the Chelish cripple the Andoren fleet and gain a foothold in Andoran, the war against slavery is pretty much over."

"I know, Torius." Celeste shivered at the thought and made up her mind. People were dying every day for the Andoren cause. The least she could do was to use Desna's gifts to help. "I'll try asking my question again tomorrow night."

"All right." He yawned and rubbed his eyes. "Well, I'm going to bed. Try not to obsess, okay?" He gave her a playful nudge to take away the sting of his words.

"I'm not obsessive, I'm just . . . pensive. Don't worry. I won't let it drive me crazy."

"Good." He leaned in and gave her a long, lingering kiss. "See you at midnight, love."

Celeste returned his smile. "Midnight it is, my captain."

Listening to his footsteps fade, Celeste gazed into the heavens. The sky was so clear and dark that the constellations were hard to distinguish among the clouds of billions of stars. Suddenly she realized that, with all that had been happening lately, it had been more than a week since she had observed the positions of the planets in the zodiac to see what insights they might provide.

Akiton the Red was well below the horizon already, but she knew the war planet had moved into the constellation of the Mother, the nurturing heart of the Cosmic Caravan. *Peace.* That was a comforting thought.

Lifting her telescope out of her bag of instruments with a flick of magic, Celeste turned to her own birth sign, the Stargazer. A chill raced up her long, sinuous spine as she focused on a small planet glimmering within the constellation: Eox the Dead. The only planet with a retrograde orbit, it carried a sinister astrological association, a reputation not unfounded. Ancient astronomical tomes spoke of a time, millennia ago, when the planet suddenly flared with light, outshining all others for a short time before fading to its current, duller appearance. Since that time, Eox had been interpreted as an omen of self-destruction. Celeste shivered and turned away from the stars, refusing to consider what that grim harbinger might portend.

Two loud thumps on her door jolted Vreva out of a dead sleep. She cast her disguise spell even before pulling down her blanket, thankful again for the lock on the door. Lurching to her feet—she'd slept fully clothed and armed, tolerating discomfort over the risk of being caught unprepared—she went to the door.

It's the middle of the damned night! A hundred reasons why Anguillithek would wake her rambled through her sleep-addled mind, all of them bad. She jerked open the door and glared at the devil with all the malice she could muster.

"What?"

"I've been called away. Gorthoklek wants a report."

"In the middle of the night?" Vreva stepped into the outer cabin, suddenly wide awake. This was her opportunity to speak with Yami alone. "Don't you fiends *ever* sleep?"

"No." Anguillithek vanished without another word.

Vreva hurried to Yami's bed and quickly cast her charm spell on the sleeping boy. She needed to persuade him of her sincerity, even if it meant using magic to ease his mind. When she knew her spell had taken effect, she gripped his shoulder and shook him awake.

"Yami, wake up. I need to speak with you."

"What?" He rolled over and blinked at her in the subdued lamplight. "What is it? What's wrong?"

"I need to tell you something. Come with me." Urging him up, she guided him into her smaller cabin and closed the door. "Please. Sit on the bed. I've something to show you."

"What's wrong? You sound . . . different."

No doubt, Vreva thought. She wasn't disguising her voice, and doubted that Bushatra had ever used the word 'please' in her life. She didn't have time to be gentle with him. The devil could return any moment. "What's wrong is that you've been lied to and used, Yami. I need to show you something, but you have to promise me not to panic or cry out."

"What?" His strange blue-white eyes widened, his voice breathless.

"Just listen." Vreva turned up her lamp until all the shadows in the room were banished. "Anguillithek and Admiral Ronnel are using you. They're not going to remove your curse. They're going to use it to destroy a city. They're going to blame the disaster on you, and get away with murdering thousands of people."

"But *you* said you would remove my curse!" He stared at her in shock. "Were you lying?"

"No, *Bushatra* was lying to you." Vreva canceled her disguise spell. "I'm not Bushatra."

"What?" The boy scrambled back, his heels kicking the blanket onto the floor, horror plain on his face. "Who are you? Where's Bushatra?"

"Yami, please calm down." Vreva held her hands out in a peaceful gesture. "I was sent here to help you, to rescue you. Bushatra wanted to use you to kill people, but I'm going to keep that from happening."

"What happened to Bushatra?" His voice quavered with fear and disbelief.

"Yami, *listen* to me. Bushatra lied to you from the start. She never intended to remove your curse. She was using you as a weapon for her own gain. She was getting paid to destroy a city, to kill thousands of innocent people, just like your village. She saw what you could do and wanted to wield that power for herself."

"I . . ." Yami's lower lip quivered.

Vreva could see him trying to understand. Hopefully her charm spell would convince him that she had his best interests at heart. Unfortunately, Bushatra had done the same, and Vreva was now tearing down that trust. *I have to make him believe me, but how?*

"Where is she?" he demanded.

Sometimes the truth works . . . Snick's theory was about to be tested. "She's dead, Yami."

"Did . . . did you kill her?"

"Yes. I found out what she was planning to do, and killed her to take her identity. I had to get to you, to rescue you." Not exactly the truth, but close enough.

"Rescue me how? We're in the middle of the *ocean!*"

That was encouraging. At least he was asking an intelligent question, not screaming in panic. "There's a ship following us— friends of mine. They're going to attack *Robust* one night soon, and we'll escape." She held out a hand to him, praying to Calistria that he would take it. "Please, Yami. You've got to trust me." If he didn't trust her, he might tell Anguillithek what she'd said. Vreva slipped her other hand back to the dagger hidden behind her back. If he wouldn't trust her, she would have no choice. She would have to kill him.

He looked at her hand with narrowed eyes. "What's your name?"

"I'm sorry, Yami, but I can't tell you. If I did, you might slip up and use that name in front of Anguillithek. If you tell the devil about me, it'll kill me, and they'll still use you in their plot." She held her hand steady, open and imploring. "You need to call me Bushatra, or the devil will suspect."

"Oh." He reached out and slipped his hand into hers. His fingers were rough, the backs knobby with hard chitinous growths, but they were warm, and they gripped hers tightly. "I don't want to hurt anyone. I just want to go away where it'll never happen again."

"We'll find someplace like that, I promise." Vreva squeezed his hand and smiled. She sat beside him and patted his hand. "I knew you'd do the right thing. Now you have to help me. Okay?"

"Okay." He pursed his lips and his brow furrowed. "But if you're here to rescue me, why don't we just jump overboard while Anguillithek's gone, and your friends can pick us up?"

Vreva chuckled low. "Two reasons. The first is that I didn't plan for it. Anguillithek didn't tell me when it was going to be away, and my friends aren't close enough to pick us up. The second is that I don't swim very well."

"You don't *swim?*" He looked at her like she'd sprouted horns. "How can anyone not swim?"

"I just never learned." She smiled at his naivete. "What we have to do now is keep you safe and prevent the curse from activating. To do that, I need to know how this power of yours works. Tell me how it's triggered, and what happens."

Yami paled, his lips thinning in a tight frown. "I . . . don't know. It only ever happened once. There was yelling and pain, then this sound like someone hit a big drum, and . . . then . . . I don't remember. I only remember afterward. My whole village was destroyed, everyone killed. It looked like after a hurricane. Everything was torn apart."

A sound like a big drum could certainly have been some kind of magic spell. Maybe lightning or thunder triggered him. "You don't remember what caused the damage?"

"No. I don't want it to happen again." He squeezed his eyes tightly closed. "If it happens, you can't control it, and neither can I."

"I don't want to use it, Yami, but I need to know how it happens so we can prevent it." It wasn't exactly a lie. She didn't *want* to use his curse, even though they might have to.

"I don't know what causes it. All I know is that when I woke up, my leg was broken, and then Bushatra found me." He swallowed hard and sniffed back tears. "She helped me, healed my leg, and took me with her. And she told me . . . that I was cursed. That I killed everyone. She showed me the future, a whole city destroyed. Please don't let that happen."

"I won't, Yami. You have my word." Vreva sighed, feeling a strange sense of relief. Torius might not agree with her reluctance to use Yami's power, but now the point was moot. They were back to her original plan. They would have to kill Anguillithek without invoking Yami's curse.

"Thank you." The boy sniffed and looked at her, his mouth quirking into a hesitant smile. "I like you. You're pretty."

"I like you, too, Yami, but you have to promise not to tell Anguillithek any of this, or let on that you know anything."

"I won't say anything. But how are you going to get me away from it? The devil's really strong."

"My friends will help." Vreva squeezed his hand again and stood, pulling him to his feet. "They're going to kill Anguillithek, and take us away. Just focus on that and remember that I'm your friend."

"I will." He took a deep breath and smiled. "What do you want me to do to help?"

"Right now, just go back to bed. I'll give you something to help you sleep." She quickly cast her disguise spell again and cracked the door to check the outer cabin. Yami gasped. "Don't be afraid. It's just an illusion. I have to look like her, but you know it's really me. Come on."

"Okay." Yami followed her into the outer cabin and accepted the drug. In minutes, he was sleeping.

Hurrying back to her cabin, Vreva withdrew a small scroll from her secreted stash. She checked the outer cabin one more time, then quickly cast the spell. "Torius Vin," she whispered. After a moment, she felt as if a tether tugged lightly on her mind. The spell had taken effect. "We can't use Yami's curse as a weapon. He doesn't know how it manifests, and can't control it. Stick to the plan."

His reply came immediately, his ire resounding in her mind. "Marvelous! I think it'll be two nights from now. Be ready. We'll board on your starboard side."

The connection snapped and was gone. Vreva breathed a deep sigh of relief. She hurried out to the main cabin and paced the floor until Anguillithek finally teleported back in.

Feigning irritation, she snapped, "Well? Any news?"

"None. We continue the plan." The drowning devil undulated around the cabin once as if sniffing out some hidden threat.

Vreva hoped it couldn't smell the residual magic of her messaging spell—or worse, her disguise. "So you woke me in the middle of the night for nothing!" She whirled away and headed for her cabin.

"No, I woke you because I was *ordered* to do so." Its blank yellow eyes fixed upon her. "Don't think you're in charge here, witch. We *both* serve Cheliax."

She paused at the door and glared back at the devil. "I don't understand you fiends. Don't you *ever* get tired of being slaves?"

"We're all slaves to *something*, Bushatra. Some of us are simply wise enough to know it."

"Phah!" Vreva flipped a dismissive hand and closed the door, making sure it was securely locked, for all the good that would do against the devil. She sat on the bed and felt the comforting presence of Mathias somewhere nearby. His confidence buoyed her, and she sent him a nudge of reassurance. But as she lay down and pulled up the blanket, she considered what the devil had said, and wondered how true it might be.

13

Thieves in the Night

The wind ruffled Torius's hair as *Stargazer* slipped quietly through the water, all but invisible with her dark hull and black sails. The captain tugged his tricorne hat down and peered forward at the twin lanterns glowing from *Robust*'s sternposts: a pair of gleaming eyes in the night, easy to follow. The wind was brisk but steady, the seas moderate, and the moon not due to rise for another hour. Everything was perfect. Torius clenched his fists at his side and fought the urge to pace. He usually loved the stealthy pursuit before the strike, but not tonight.

"Worried, my captain?" Celeste's voice came as a warm whisper in his ear. "We've done this dozens of times."

"Not with a devil aboard our target and a Chelish frigate in our wake." Torius smiled grimly. He appreciated her attempt to ease his nerves, but sometimes he didn't think she really understood the burden of being in command. "It's my job to worry, remember?"

"Then *you* worry about your ship and crew, and let *me* worry about the devil."

"That's a deal." He gauged the distance to their prey—about two ship-lengths. "Easy, Windy. Just a touch to star—"

"Ship astern!" a shout rang out from ahead. "Black sails!"

"Damn it! They've spotted us!" Torius dashed to the forward rail of the quarterdeck, squinting at the galleon. "How the hell . . ." It didn't matter how they'd been spotted. All that mattered now was how to react.

They were close enough to fire the foredeck ballistae, but only the midship siege engines were equipped to fire grappling bolts. They would have to veer to bring those to bear, and could only target the larger vessel's stern. The plan was to board her starboard side.

"The galleon's turning downwind, Captain!" Thillion called back from the foredeck.

"Gozreh's guts!" It was going to be a chase, but they could still catch them. "Steer to follow, Windy! Grogul, slack the main and forecourse for a downwind run, and hoist the flying jib! We need speed!"

"Captain! They're jibing!"

"Where the hell's he going?" Torius cursed again and glanced to port. On the dark horizon bobbed the faint lights of *Fury's Crown*. "Of course! *That's* why *Robust* spotted us! They had a lookout watching aft to keep track of the frigate. Now they're running for their escort!"

Torius felt stupid. Long years of piracy had taught him that lookouts generally looked forward, but he had never attacked a ship under escort before. The frigate had been sailing about three miles behind the galleon. Now on convergent courses, the two ships would close quickly. Adding insult to injury, a flaming arrow shot into the sky from the galleon's foredeck—a distress signal. *Fury's Crown* would be on them in no time. They had to strike now.

"So much for the plan."

Torius considered the fleeing ship, her sails jibing clumsily, which wasn't surprising since they were shorthanded. Coming around to the galleon's starboard side now would put *Stargazer* in the galleon's lee. That would risk *Stargazer* being rammed by the heavier ship, not to mention taking far too long. *Fury's Crown* would be on them before they could finish the job. No, they had to board her immediately. There was only one option.

Cupping his hands, Torius shouted down through the main hatch grating. "Snick, be ready to fire grapples on my command! Point-blank!"

"Aye, Captain."

"Grogul, ready hand grapples. We'll board her over her transom."

"That sounds like fun." Grogul hefted a heavy grappling hook and scowled. The galleon's poop deck loomed twenty feet higher than *Stargazer*'s middeck.

"Thillion! You and your archers keep them pinned down so we can board her." Torius turned to Celeste. "You may have trouble getting aboard."

"No, I won't." A scroll floated up from one of the tubes she wore on her harness and unrolled. "Just give me the signal, and I'll fly over."

"Oh. Right." He sometimes forgot the varied spells she could cast with her collection of expensive scrolls. "Once the fight starts, you may not understand me, so listen for my whistle."

"I will." She leaned in for a quick kiss and smiled, showing her fangs. "For luck!"

"We'll need it." Torius turned to the helm. "Straight at 'em, Windy. I want to leave paint on their transom!"

"Aye, sir!" The steel hook that substituted for Windy Kate's left hand clicked on the wheel's spokes as she steered *Stargazer* toward the fleeing galleon.

"Trim sails and get ready to let fly all sheets!" They were closing fast—too fast. If they didn't reduce speed before Snick fired her grappling bolts, the shock would either snap the lines or rip the barbed heads free of the galleon's hull. Torius bellowed down into the hold again, "Snick, fire as soon as you have a target. Right in her transom!"

"Ready, sir!" Snick sounded far too cheerful for Torius's comfort.

"Grogul, throw hand grapples as we pass. We've got to ease the shock on the ballista bolts!"

"On it, sir!" Six stout sailors stood ready with grapples, the lines looped loosely around bollards to ease the tension without risking anyone being yanked overboard.

"If this doesn't rip the side out of the ship, we're good." Torius looked forward again and cringed. Windy Kate had evidently taken him seriously. At their current angle of approach, the bowsprit would miss the galleon's stern by mere inches . . . maybe. He cocked a warning eyebrow at the helmswoman. "Don't break my ship, Windy."

"Wouldn't *dream* of breaking your ship, sir!" She flashed him a dangerous grin.

Torius checked their progress with clenched teeth. His hands flexed in longing for the spokes of the wheel, but he had other duties. He had to trust Windy not to run their bowsprit through the galleon's quarter gallery windows.

Close enough. "Slack sheets!"

The sailors obeyed, slackening the lines so that *Stargazer*'s sails flapped in the wind. The ship slowed, but not much.

"It's gonna be close!" came a cry from the crow's nest. Lacy Jane had a better vantage than anyone else aboard.

Torius held his breath.

The tip of *Stargazer*'s bowsprit shattered the brass lamp hanging from the galleon's port stern corner post. Thillion swore loudly and inventively as glass showered the foredeck.

"Windy!" Torius admonished.

"You *said* leave paint!"

Torius braced himself. "This is gonna hurt!"

"Grapples away!" Grogul bellowed.

Stargazer swept past the galleon's stern close enough to spit on the weathered wood. A rippling volley of ballista bolts pierced *Robust*'s stern, and Grogul's team threw their grapples through the stern gallery windows. The ropes came taut with a horrendous jerk, wrenching *Stargazer* to port. The brigantine heeled so hard that her mainmast shrouds struck the galleon's taffrail. With a crack, one of the grappling lines parted, the line whipping back to knock a sailor to the deck. Thankfully, the others held.

Robust—far heavier than the brigantine, and still under sail—dragged *Stargazer* sideways through the sea, though the smaller ship's momentum pulled the galleon's stern to leeward. Both ships lurched as the galleon's bow pounded into wind and waves, killing her momentum.

"Haul away! Let her jibe!" The mainsail boom swept over Torius's head in an uncontrolled jibe, but with all the sheets slack, there was no chance of ripping a sail. *Stargazer*'s straining capstan hauled in the thick hemp lines attached to the grappling bolts. The two ships crashed together, shivering the deck and sending splinters flying.

A glance told Torius the best path to board their prey. "Grogul, follow me up the ratlines to cross!"

"Aye, si—"

"Archers!" Lacy Jane's warning came just as an arrow whizzed past Torius's ear.

Looking up, he spied several archers firing down from the galleon's taffrail. Before he could give the order, his own bowmen and the deck ballistae unleashed a murderous crossfire from fore and aft. The Chelish archers went down in a hail of arrows and bolts.

"Boarders with me!" Torius glanced back for Celeste, but she was already rising into the air. She shot forward like a silver-tipped arrow, wreathed in her protective cloak of starlight.

Torius leapt to the mainsail ratlines and swarmed up, his Stargazers right behind him. Barely five feet separated *Stargazer*'s shrouds from the galleon's taffrail, but it wouldn't be an easy leap with the conflicting roll and pitch of the two ships. With a deep breath and a short prayer to Gozreh, Torius leapt the gap, skidding across the bloody planks of the galleon's poop deck.

Downed archers lay strewn across the deck, including one wearing epaulets that he took to be the captain. There was no time to check them as several more sailors pounded up the stairs from forward with swords and pikes raised. As he drew his sword to face his closest adversary, however, a beam of searing energy from Celeste blasted the man in the chest. Torius ended the sailor's panicked screams with a quick slash of his scimitar. He raised his sword to parry a pike thrust, but Grogul's axe smashed through the weapon to take the man down.

Grogul grunted with satisfaction as he dislodged his axe from a sailor's chest. He looked around, but the pirates had taken the poop deck. "Well, that was—"

A torrent of seawater blasted the half-orc back, taking the bosun and two other Stargazers over the taffrail.

"Grogul!" Torius started to turn toward his fallen friend, but the source of that blast of water demanded his immediate attention. In the dim starlight, a sinuous shape rose from the galleon's middeck. *The devil.*

"In the name of Asmodeus—"

Torius never learned what the devil was going to do in the name of its god, for a bolt of electricity interrupted its tirade. The blast illuminated the drowning devil in a halo of blinding white light. The fiend writhed in the blast, blue scales scorched black, finlike wings trailing smoke in the wind, but it didn't fall. Despite the horrible burns across its chest, the devil turned to face the source of the spell.

We've got to take it down!

"Stargazers, fire all!" Ballistae fired from fore and aft, and a storm of arrows flew. Two of the ballista bolts hit their mark, and arrows pincushioned the devil's scaly hide, but Anguillithek wrenched the larger bolts free and ignored the lesser missiles.

We're in trouble.

"Boarding party, with me!" Torius and the remaining boarders leapt from the poop deck down to the quarterdeck, even as more Chelish sailors pelted up the stairs to meet their advance. The Stargazers fought with long-practiced coordination, hewing through the lesser force.

Ignoring the melee, the devil focused its attention upon its greatest threat: Celeste. Waving one tentacled hand, it conjured another blast of seawater. The naga was flung backward by the torrent, but since she was still hovering beside the ship, there was nothing for her to hit. Shaking the water from her hair, Celeste cast another scorching bolt of lightning. The drowning devil roared in agony and rage under the magical onslaught.

At least something can hurt this fiend.

The captain's satisfaction faded as Anguillithek bellowed in some unintelligible language, and a shimmering fissure opened in the sky. As Torius stared with a sinking heart, a second undulating blue form flew out of the pit of blackness.

"Criminy! Another one?" exclaimed Windy Kate.

The second devil flew at Celeste with a howl of rage. She met its charge with another bolt of searing electricity, but the spell failed to slow its advance. She dodged the devil's sweeping grasp, but could not get past it to direct her magic at Anguillithek. They hadn't planned to fight two of the fiends.

"We've got to end this now!" Torius dashed forward to launch himself from the quarterdeck rail at Anguillithek. Gripping his sword with both hands, he plunged it deep into the devil's thick blue hide.

Hissing in rage, Anguillithek grasped Torius in one huge hand. The writhing mass of tentacles enveloped him in a crushing embrace, stinging like nettles, the pain taking his breath away, sapping his strength. The devil jerked him back, tearing Torius's sword free of its flesh. He managed to keep hold of the hilt, gritting his teeth against the stinging embrace as Anguillithek raised its other massive hand to squash him like an insect.

Vreva's eyes shot open, a sudden sense of urgency surging through her mind. *Mathias.* A moment later, she heard muffled shouts from the deck.

It's time.

Celeste had contacted her by spell earlier in the evening, a short, succinct message warning her to be ready. Finally, her waiting was over.

Surging up from her bunk, she cast her disguise spell and took a deep, steadying breath. *Wait . . . Calm . . .* This would be the tricky part. If Yami inadvertently gave away their plan with a misplaced word, this would be the shortest rescue attempt in history.

She heard more shouts from overhead, louder now, followed by several sharp thumps that reverberated through the hull. Vreva jerked open the door and burst into the outer cabin. "What was that?"

Anguillithek swayed on its sinuous tail, head cocked, listening to the fracas above. "I don't know."

The ship lurched, and Vreva had to hang onto the doorjamb to keep her feet. Yami clung to the bunk, fear widening his eyes as they darted first to Vreva, then the devil.

Anguillithek vanished, then immediately reappeared. "We're under attack!"

"Attack? How could anyone be—"

"What's happening?" Yami tried to stand, but was thrown back into his bunk by another sickening lurch, even more violent than the first.

With a horrendous crash from aft, the ship jerked forward, knocking Vreva to her knees. That didn't bode well. The plan was for the Stargazers to board on the starboard side, but it felt as if

Robust had been hit from behind. Something must have gone wrong.

"Stay calm, Yami. We won't let anyone hurt you." She couldn't let him panic.

"Stay here and guard him, and keep the door locked!" Anguillithek vanished once again.

The yells and screams from the main deck grew louder.

"Is that—"

"Shhh." Vreva held up a cautioning finger and hurried to the door, hastily unlocking it and peeking out. As she had hoped, the hold was empty. Captain Giavano had not assigned a guard to the cabin. Shorthanded, he needed every crew member for sailing the ship. She beckoned Yami forward. "Come on!"

The boy hurried over, his face pale with fear. "How will we get past them to your friends?"

"Magic." Vreva cast a spell and faded from view. At his startled gasp, she said, "Calm down. It won't hurt you." At least she hoped it wouldn't. Bushatra hadn't wanted to use powerful spells on Yami, but this one wasn't that powerful—hopefully it wouldn't be enough to trigger his curse. There was no way to tell for sure, but they had no way to escape with him visible. "Now hold out your hand."

"All right." When he held out a hand, she muttered a quick prayer to Calistria, then cast the same spell again.

He vanished, and nothing untoward happened. With a sigh of relief, she reached out and grasped his trembling fingers. "Be as quiet as you can. If I have to let go of your hand, just stay put, and I'll come back for you."

"Okay."

Vreva pulled him through the door into the hold. Yells and screams filtered down through the main hatch grating. She hoped that it wasn't her friends dying out there. After relocked the cabin door behind them in case anyone came to check, she tugged Yami aft. Since she hadn't been able to explore *Robust*, and didn't want to get lost, she had planned to leave the way they'd come in. Besides, the sounds of fighting seemed to be coming from aft, which meant that was where the Stargazers were.

As she cautiously opened the door from the hold to the stern section of the ship, a tiny dark shape darted around the corner, tail high and fur bristling. *Where the blazes are you?* Mathias yowled. *I can smell you, but I can't see you.*

"Here, Mathias!" she hissed in their private language. "What's going on?"

*All hell's breaking loose outside! *Stargazer*'s tied to the stern. Follow me.*

"Lead on!" She tugged Yami forward, but he resisted.

"What was that? What were those noises you were making?" He sounded terrified.

"Nothing's wrong. The cat is my familiar, a friend." Now wasn't the time to explain the nuances of their relationship. "Just stay close."

Mathias led them up two sets of stairs, down a corridor, and up a third, the sounds of battle louder as they ascended. Finally, the cat stopped before a door. *The quarterdeck's just through there. Take a right, and go up the steps to the poop deck. We can climb down onto *Stargazer* from there.*

Vreva eased open the door. Several bodies littered the quarterdeck, thankfully all Chelish, and a number of Stargazers stood with weapons drawn, their attention forward. Beyond them, Anguillithek hovered in midair, a struggling figure clenched in one tentacled hand.

Gods! Torius!

The devil swatted at the pirate captain with its free hand, but Torius slashed with his scimitar, shearing away a mass of tentacles. The drowning devil was riddled with arrows and bolts, and scorched by magic, but still fought on. Vreva ducked back inside and shut the door. As much as she would like to help Torius, she couldn't. She had to trust the pirates to finish off the devil. She had other tasks to attend to.

Squeezing Yami's hand, she said, "Stay here. I've got to do something before we go."

"What? I can't just—"

"Yami, relax! It'll be fine. Just wait here and don't move. I'll be right back." She had to pry his hand away from hers, but finally he relaxed his grip. "Stay with him, Mathias."

*Kind of *hard* when I can't see him.* The cat's sarcasm came across clear and strong, but she knew he could keep track of the boy by smell and sound.

Vreva hurried back to the companionway. *Time to make sure there are no accidental survivors.* Conjuring a spark of flame on her fingertip, she flicked it down the steep stairs. She dashed back to her companions with flames roaring up the passage behind her.

"Yami! Take my hand!" She thrust out her now-visible hand. A warm but trembling hand gripped hers. "Time to go." Vreva cast another spell and vanished from sight, then opened the door.

Torius still struggled in the grasp of the drowning devil, hacking at the gripping tentacles. Lightning flashed from her left, illuminating everything in stark white light and drawing her eye. Out over the water, Celeste flew haloed in starlight, dodging and weaving to evade yet another drowning devil.

Well, at least there's plenty of distraction. Vreva tugged Yami's hand, and they raced up the steps to the poop deck, Mathias hot on their heels. Thillion stood there with a half-dozen archers, firing at both drowning devils as quickly as they could nock arrows. She skirted the pirates, pulling Yami along so that they weren't caught in the barrage.

"Bushatra!" Anguillithek's bellow shook the air and shivered up Vreva's spine. "Traitor!"

"Oh no!" Vreva whipped around and found the devil staring right at her. She started to summon a dense fog to hide them, but too late.

Anguillithek tossed Torius aside like a rag doll and gestured toward her with its slashed and bleeding tentacles. "Die, witch!"

Agony exploded within Vreva's chest. She tried to gasp, to scream, but only convulsed in a spasm of coughing. She collapsed to the deck, retching foul water from her lungs. Yami cried out, and she felt him tugging at her arm, but she couldn't even draw breath. As blackness descended upon her sight, she had one last desperate thought, and canceled the magic that hid her from sight.

A gout of seawater hit Celeste squarely, knocking the breath out of her lungs and sending her sprawling. She coughed and spat, then heaved a deep breath as the deluge subsided. Once again, the devil's spell had knocked her back from her goal.

This is taking too long! Her job had been to kill Anguillithek, but the summoned devil wouldn't let her past, and evading its attacks demanded her full attention. Now Anguillithek clutched Torius in its grasp, and she couldn't help him. She cast another destructive spell at her foe, but the drowning devil ignored the barrage of magical projectiles. It paused in flight and waved a tentacled hand at her in a strange undulating pattern.

Excruciating pain shot through Celeste's upper body, as if her insides were suddenly on fire. She convulsed, coiling and twisting in a desperate attempt to alleviate the agony. With a violent heave, she spewed out a torrent of foul water. Her sides ached as she gasped for breath, but she was able to choke out another spell as the devil charged her, once again riddling it with spheres of magical energy. Unfortunately, the spell didn't slow the devil, and recovering from its drowning magic had left her too busy to dodge.

A tentacled hand slammed into her, the stinging members gouging her scales. Its teeth snapped an inch from her throat.

She struck reflexively, plunging her fangs through its tough hide, feeling the hot blood well into her mouth. The devil pummeled her again, ripping her teeth free of its flesh and knocking her aside.

As she reeled from the blow, a hellish bellow came from *Robust. Torius!* Expecting the worst, Celeste glanced at the ship. To her relief, Torius lay on the deck, struggling to rise. Anguillithek now directed its attention toward the poop deck. Forced to pay attention to her nearer adversary or get swatted out of the air, she lost sight of what was happening aboard the ship.

"Celeste!"

The shrill call snapped her head around. Though she might not understand the rest of what people were saying, her name came through loud and clear. Snick was shouting from *Stargazer*'s quarterdeck, her hand on the trigger of one of the deck-mounted ballistae. She waved wildly, and Celeste noted with shock that all three ballistae were pointed right at her. With the memory of the gnome's life-saving marksmanship, she grasped Snick's intent.

Celeste paused to allow the drowning devil to charge her again, then suddenly soared straight up and out of the line of fire. All three ballistae cracked in unison. Two of the missiles struck true, their warheads rupturing to douse the devil in acid. The fiend howled in pain, its hide bubbling and hissing under the caustic liquid. It dove for the water, trailing smoke.

Oh no you don't! Celeste wasn't about to allow it to wash away the burning liquid and rejoin the fight. Her lightning spell lit the night as bright as day, lashing forth to strike the devil just before it smashed into the water. The long blue body convulsed once and lay there floating for a moment, its scaly hide scorched and black-ened, before vanishing.

Celeste whirled to streak toward Anguillithek.

The drowning devil charged the galleon's poop deck, ignoring the barrage of arrows from Thillion and his archers. Behind the archers, Grogul stood over a fallen shape, his battle axe poised to defend his charge. Then Celeste spotted a tiny black cat standing atop the motionless figure, hissing and bristling.

Mathias! That could only mean that the fallen shape was Vreva. A quick scan of the deck, however, didn't reveal the boy the sorcerer had been determined to rescue.

Regardless of whether Vreva had succeeded or failed, Celeste focused upon her own task. She flew straight at the devil, casting her last lightning spell ahead of her. The bolt struck Anguillithek, burning a gouge across its blue hide. Thillion and his archers continued to fire, raking the devil with arrows, and a well-placed shot from a ballista on *Stargazer*'s bow plunged through the devil's thick torso.

Howling in rage and pain, Anguillithek scanned its foes with cold yellow eyes, its mouth barbels writhing. Their attacks were finally taking their toll.

Celeste began to cast yet another spell, but before she spoke the final word, the drowning devil vanished. Anguillithek immediately rematerialized behind Grogul, but didn't attack the half-orc. Instead, it reached down and plucked at the air beside the fallen shape of Vreva. A high-pitched cry rang out, and a slim boy blinked into sight, batting at the grasping tentacles of the devil's hand as it lifted him off the deck.

The weapon!

"No!" Celeste finished her spell, sending a flight of magical projectiles streaking toward the devil, but Grogul was faster. His axe swept down, severing the devil's squirming fingers, and the boy fell beside Vreva.

As Celeste's spell struck Anguillithek, Grogul slashed again, but his axe clove only air as the devil vanished once more. Everyone looked around expectantly, waiting for Anguillithek to reappear, but the sky and deck remained clear. The drowning devil had finally fled.

"Damn it!" If the devil returned with reinforcements, they would be in trouble. Celeste shot down to the lower deck where Torius had managed to stand, leaning heavily on his bloody scimitar. "Are you all right? Can you understand me?"

"Yeah. I'm just weak." He dropped an empty potion bottle, though his face and neck were still crisscrossed with red wheals. "The damned thing got away. We've got to get out of here." He staggered forward, but she stopped him.

"Grab my harness. I'll fly you."

"Thanks. I don't think I could climb the stairs." He sheathed his sword and grasped her harness, and Celeste flew him up to the poop deck.

Grogul had rolled Vreva onto her back. Confusion showed on the faces of the Stargazers huddled around as they stared at the feral-looking woman. This was not the beautiful courtesan they all knew.

Torius raised an eyebrow. "Is that really Vreva?"

Mathias yowled and lashed his tail.

"It's got to be a disguise." Celeste said. "Mathias wouldn't protect anyone else like that. The magic doesn't just go away, even if she *is* out cold."

Grogul probed the woman's neck and frowned. "She's alive, but just barely. She's not breathing."

"Don't let her die! Please!" The boy kneeling beside Vreva wiped his eyes and sniffed.

"No time to treat her here. Get her aboard *Stargazer*, and we'll get a potion into her."

But as the others moved to follow Torius's commands, Celeste noticed water trickling from the corner of Vreva's mouth and knew from her own experience what had befallen the sorcerer. "Wait! She's drowning! The other devil did the same to me. We need to get the water out of her lungs."

"I got it!" Grogul lifted Vreva easily and clutched his arms together just below her ribs. One hard jerk sent a gout of foul water from the woman's mouth and nose. Vreva coughed, expelling more water, and drew a ragged breath. She remained unconscious, but she was breathing at least.

"That ought to hold her for a while." Torius waved a hand to urge the others off the ship. "We gotta go *now!*"

As if to emphasize her desire for haste, the galleon's stern windows blew out, scattering glass all over *Stargazer*'s deck and sending smoke billowing forth. *Robust* was going up in flames.

"All right, you swabs, let's get off this tub before she burns to the waterline! Smartly now!" Grogul flung the unconscious woman over one shoulder. Mathias yowled and leapt up to clamber aboard his mistress, reluctant to be separated. "Kalli, see to the pup there."

Only now did Celeste get a good look at the boy who had knelt beside Vreva, and his strangeness struck her. His skin looked mottled, almost like chitin in patches, and his eyes glittered like blue jewels. His hands clenched together, short clawlike nails pressing into his skin. He looked around at them with otherworldly eyes, confusion plain on his face. "Are you the friends she told me about?"

"That's right. Come on now. We've gotta go." Kalli guided him to the taffrail.

"Yes, we do." Thillion shouldered his bow and pointed to the southwest. "*Fury's Crown* is bearing down, sir. She's maybe a mile away."

"Step lively, people!" Torius staggered toward the rail.

"Grab hold again, my captain. I wouldn't want you to fall." Celeste flew him to *Stargazer*'s quarterdeck with only minor grumbling from her charge.

"Thanks." Torius steadied himself on the binnacle, shouting orders as the crew clambered back aboard and cast off from the burning galleon. The sails cracked full, and they bore away into the pitch-black night.

"Here, sir." Snick hurried up with two potion bottles for Torius, and passed another to Celeste. "Not many wounded, and you two look like you took the worst of it."

"Thanks, Snick. Go see to Vreva. She didn't look good."

"Aye, sir!" The gnome scampered off.

Celeste drank down the potions, enjoying the warm wash of healing and strength that suffused her body. "I'm sorry that I couldn't kill Anguillithek."

"You had your hands full. Well, not your *hands*, but you know what I mean." He brushed her wet hair off her forehead and smiled grimly. "We did our best, and we *did* get the weapon away from them. That's the most important thing."

Grogul and Thillion climbed to the quarterdeck. The bosun bore a nasty contusion, half of his face a mass of swollen bruises.

"One dead, Captain." Grogul rubbed his jaw. "Felchi McFannon broke his neck when he fell. I had the crew wrap him up and stow him below in case we get back to Almas in time to raise him."

"We're not heading to Almas."

They all looked at Torius like he'd told them they were going to surrender.

"If we only had *Fury's Crown* to deal with, we'd head for Augustana and have Trellis send the Gray Corsairs to take out the frigate, but we've still got Anguillithek to worry about, and we can't let word get back to Egorian that we're anything other than pirates. If they suspect that we're working for Andoran, there'll be hell to pay. Maybe even war." Torius peered into the night at the frigate's lights bearing down on the burning galleon. "They'll look for survivors, then for us. If we can't lose them before daybreak, we'll have to figure out a new plan. Until then, make all sail to the southeast. Celeste, I'll need you to plot a course to keep us well off the coast and evade *Fury's Crown*."

"And if Anguillithek returns with even worse fiends?" Celeste asked.

Torius sighed. "Well, we have to figure that out. We can't let them take the weapon, even if it means . . ."

Everyone looked away for a moment, avoiding each other's eyes. They all knew what he meant, but none of them wanted to actually say that they'd have to murder a helpless boy.

"I think we should consult Vreva before we do anything rash." Celeste slithered to the stairs. "Where is she, Grogul?"

"In the guest cabin. I don't know which is clinging to her tighter, the cat or the kid."

"All right. I need my navigation instruments, so I'll stop by and talk to Vreva."

Celeste hurried down to the guest cabin and opened the door with a flick of magic. Vreva sat up on the bunk, looking like herself once again, though still rather pale as Snick listened to her chest with an odd little device that looked like a tiny trumpet. Mathias lay curled in her lap, kneading her legs in contentment. The boy, Yami, sat on the side of the bunk.

"How is she?" Celeste asked Snick.

"Right as rain!" The gnome put the device into her medical kit and grinned. "Now I gotta go see if I can coax Grogul into drinking a potion. He's such a stubborn twit." She was out the door in a flash.

Yami looked at her with wide eyes and edged away. "What . . . What *are* you?"

"That's Celeste, Yami," Vreva said with a calming gesture. "She's a friend. You can trust her."

"I'm a lunar naga, if you want a real answer, but she's right. I *am* a friend." Celeste turned to Vreva. "Bad news: Anguillithek escaped."

"Snick told me." The sorcerer swung her legs over the side of the bed. Mathias meowed indignantly as he was forced to move, but she calmed him with some petting and rubbed her eyes wearily. "That *is* bad, but at least we got Yami away."

"Why is it bad?" the boy asked.

"Because the devil can teleport, and he'll return. Maybe with help." Celeste coiled and fixed Vreva with a meaningful stare. "If we can't lose *Fury's Crown* in the dark, we've got trouble."

"I know, Celeste." Vreva smiled at Yami and patted the bed beside her. "But for now, we're safe."

Yami sat without a word. Celeste wondered if Vreva had him magically charmed, or if he was simply that trusting. He seemed just like Vreva had said: utterly innocent.

"For now." Celeste uncoiled and opened the door. "Keep Yami close, and get some rest."

"I will. And thank you, Celeste. Thank Torius for me, too."

"You can thank us when we get out of this alive."

14

Devil and the Deep Blue Sea

A knock on the cabin door snapped Torius from a deep, dream-filled sleep. He opened his eyes to a dark cabin, the pearly gray glow of predawn just beginning to show through the skylight. He felt the cool length of Celeste next to him, and remembered that they'd retired to her pillows after his watch.

"Captain?" Grogul's voice from beyond the door sounded urgent.

Celeste stirred, hissing in annoyance. Morning wasn't her best time of day, considering her nocturnal nature. Also, last night had been anything but relaxing.

"One moment." Torius brushed a hand down her scales and got to his feet. "Go back to sleep, love. I'll take care of it."

"No. I want to know what's happening."

The haze of half-sleep swept clear from his mind as he realized why Grogul must be waking him early. *Fury's Crown* . . . Torius pulled on a pair of trousers and answered the door.

"Are they in sight?"

"More'n in sight, sir. They're only about four miles behind us."

"Son of a . . ." Torius grabbed his shirt and boots, struggling to put them on all at once. "How the hell did they follow us in the dark?"

"I was thinkin' about that, sir. Might be they sent that devil up high in the sky as a lookout. We were throwin' quite a wake last night, and there was more'n a little phosphorescence in the water. They must have doused their lights, else we'd have seen them earlier."

"Well, it doesn't matter now. Rouse all hands, and warn them to be ready for a fight. Tell Soursop to feed them as soon as he can. That devil could attack at any moment."

"Aye, sir. See you on deck."

When Torius turned for his jacket and sword belt, Celeste faced him.

"Do you want me to wake Vreva?"

"Yes. If that devil attacks, we might need her help." He clipped his belt and slipped a dagger into his boot sheath. "Make sure she knows that the wea . . . that *Yami* is not to be left alone. Not for a second."

"I'll tell her."

"Thank you." He left her with a kiss and hurried to the quarterdeck.

His officers were already there, as were the two bosun's mates, Kalli and Dukkol. Thillion slapped a spyglass into his hand without a word, and Torius trained it astern. *Fury's Crown* had indeed gained on them during the night. The frigate slammed through the seas, spray flying from her grim figurehead as she plunged into each wave.

Gozreh seemed to be playing her own hand in this chase. The seas were building, and the wind whistled loud in the rigging. *Stargazer* was fastest on a beam reach, so they might gain a little speed if they fell off the wind a bit, but she was already flying everything she could under these conditions. *Fury's Crown* could spread twice as much canvas as any brigantine afloat. She handled the building seas admirably, and could obviously match *Stargazer*'s speed and more.

There was one trick, however, that *Fury's Crown* couldn't match.

"Rig staysails and furl the squares. When they're set, we'll beat as close-hauled to the wind as she'll bear." With the fore-and-aft-rigged staysails, *Stargazer* could sail closer to the wind than any square-rigged ship on the sea. The maneuver would slow their speed, but to catch them, the frigate would have to tack, which would cost them miles. *I should have been sailing closer to the wind from the start! We'd be over the horizon by now!*

"Aye, Captain!" Grogul turned to his two mates. "You heard him! No lounging about!"

"You want me to try to disable their rudder, sir?" Kalli hefted a heavy crowbar and grinned. The gillman had done that very thing in a previous engagement with a slaver galley, but Torius deemed it too risky in this situation.

"No, Kalli. That drowning devil would be on you like ugly on an ogre, and we couldn't turn back to pick you up."

"Aye, sir." Kalli hurried after Dukkol, bellowing for the topmen to get to the perilous job of changing sails in a stiff breeze. One slip would send a careless sailor overboard, and with *Fury's Crown* hot on their heels, there would be no rescue.

"Thillion, have the off-watch shift stores to the port side to stiffen her up. Things are going to get trouncy when we start beating into the seas."

"Aye, sir."

"Snick, are your babies all back where they belong?"

"Snug as bugs in a rug, sir!"

"Good. If we have to fight that frigate, we'll need both sides of the ship armed with all your tricks."

"Got tricks nobody's ever *seen* before, sir!" She grinned and hurried off.

To Torius's surprise, Vreva passed Snick on the stairs and joined him on the quarterdeck.

"I said not to leave—"

Vreva raised a hand. "Relax, Torius. Yami's not alone. Celeste is with him." She squinted aft at *Fury's Crown* and frowned. "Will they catch us?"

"Not if I can help it." He nodded aloft. "We're turning upwind farther than the frigate can sail. With luck and Gozreh's blessing, we should leave them behind."

"I sent a message to Trellis, and got a reply. She's sending help, but we're way out here in the middle of"—she looked around at the limitless expanse of ocean—"*nowhere*. And now we're changing direction."

"I know exactly where we are." Torius didn't bother to hide his irritation. "I had to keep them thinking that we were pirates. If I sailed for Augustana, they'd know we weren't. No pirate would sail into a port full of Gray Corsairs. And unless you want that frigate to sail right up beside us, we've got to change course. Right now, I'm less concerned with *Fury's Crown* than I am with Anguillithek bringing in fiendish reinforcements. You think it will?"

"As I said before, I'm pretty sure that Anguillithek and Admiral Ronnel cooked this up on their own." Vreva's frown intensified. "If I'm right, they can't call in imperial forces, fiendish or otherwise— not if there's a chance anyone might find out. If Anguillithek petitions for help, and Gorthoklek sends devils, there's no telling who might notice."

"And as far as they're concerned, we're just pirates, not Andoren agents."

"That helps, yes." Vreva looked grim. "If Anguillithek reported to Gorthoklek what happened last night, and the sky's not full of a thousand furies this morning, it's a pretty safe bet that they won't call in the forces of Hell to destroy us."

"But you can't guarantee they won't."

"I can't *guarantee* anything."

They stood silent for several minutes, listening to Grogul bellow orders from the main deck and the crack of canvas overhead. When the new sails were set, Windy Kate turned the wheel

232 CHRIS A. JACKSON

to windward, and *Stargazer* bore up another twenty degrees. Spray lashed the deck as they began to pound into the mounting seas.

Torius relished the cool mist on his face. *Life used to be so simple . . .* They were quickly running out of options. He needed an advantage, something he could use to kill a drowning devil and sink that frigate. "You had a couple of days with Yami. Did you learn anything more about how this 'weapon' works?"

"Not specifically." Vreva grabbed the railing as *Stargazer* slammed into another wave, and waited until the ship settled before answering. "As far as I can tell, some sort of natural disaster destroyed Yami's village. He was the sole survivor, but was injured. Whatever it was, Bushatra apparently convinced the Chelish that she could make it happen again, and use it to destroy Augustana. Then Admiral Ronnel would arrive with the Ostenso fleet to render *humanitarian aid*, prop himself up as governor, and in doing so, establish a foothold in Andoran. Bushatra was to receive a massive reward, probably seized from the occupied lands. With the Andoren fleet hamstrung, there isn't much we could do about it."

"What kind of natural disaster?"

Vreva shrugged. "Hurricane? Deluge and flood? Tidal wave? I don't know."

"And the boy causes it?"

"If Bushatra's to be believed, yes. He could transform into it himself, for all I know. He's obviously got some strange mutation or deformity. Perhaps it's some kind of primal elemental magic."

"And were you able to discover how he's triggered?"

"He said he remembered a loud sound, like a drum being struck, and Bushatra didn't want to use powerful magic on him for fear of triggering him. It may be that magic sets him off."

"Damn!" Torius gritted his teeth until his head pounded. "So we can't use him, we can't let the Chelish get hold of him, and *you've* decided that we can't kill him."

Vreva's voice turned cold. "Yes. It's my decision, not yours. Trellis tasked me with—"

"Trellis tasked you with *neutralizing* the weapon!"

"'Neutralize the weapon' is an awfully impersonal way of saying 'murder the boy,' Torius. I know we can't let the Chelish take him back, but I'm not going to kill him unless its *absolutely* necessary."

Torius didn't know what else to say. Never in his life would he have thought that murdering an innocent boy would be the right thing to do, but if worst came to worst that seemed to be their only option. *One life or thousands . . .*

Overhead, a spar creaked ominously, followed by the distinctive sound of ripping canvas.

"Gozreh's guts!" Torius looked aloft, wondering how they'd managed to rip a sail in only moderate winds. "Who's manning the—"

"Captain!" Lacy Jane cried. "It's the devil!"

A sinuous blue shape undulated through the rigging. It grabbed the main topsail in two tentacle hands and wrenched. The sail tore from luff to leech, tattered canvas flapping uselessly in the wind. Anguillithek was back, and it was ravaging his ship.

"Oh, dear Calistria!" Vreva cried.

Heads swiveled, trying to catch sight of any hellish reinforcements, but the drowning devil seemed to be alone.

Torius was already shouting orders. "Archers! Shoot that thing down!" He turned to Vreva. "It's alone!"

"I must have been right!"

Torius felt a thread of hope. So far, the devil seemed to be only attacking the topsails, not his crew, but every torn sail slowed them. He had to stop it somehow before it broke something they couldn't fix, and arrows didn't seem to be doing the job.

"Vreva, get Celeste! I need her spells! Stay with that kid!"

"Right!" Vreva dashed off.

"Look out below!"

Torius ducked reflexively and looked up. The devil had slammed into the main topmast with all its weight, and the wooden trestletrees that held it in place splintered under the onslaught. The main topmast toppled toward the quarterdeck like a felled tree.

"Down!" Torius tackled Windy Kate as the topmast smashed down. Splinters flew from both forward and aft rails, and tangled rigging fell atop them like a net. Torius lurched to his feet and hauled Windy up. The spar had missed them and the ship's wheel by less than a foot, but the fallen lines fouled the steering. "Man the helm, Windy! You there, cut this mess free!"

Sailors attacked the tangled ropes with their cutlasses, freeing the wheel in moments. Windy hauled them back on course. Aloft, Anguillithek continued to run amok, breaking and tearing anything it could reach. The devil flew to the foremast and started prying at the topmast shrouds with its massive hands. Motion caught Torius's eye, and he saw Lacy Jane climbing up to the railing of the crow's nest. She launched herself up to drive her dagger hilt-deep into its shoulder. As the devil roared in rage and surprise, she drew her cutlass and brought the blade down on the back of it head, shearing off one of the devil's curved horns.

"Lacy!" Torius looked around frantically for a way to attack the devil, but there was nothing at hand. Horrified, he watched as Anguillithek reached one tentacled hand to rip Lacy Jane from its back, then pulled her toward its open maw.

Listening to Torius pound up to the quarterdeck, hoping that things weren't as dire as Grogul had implied, Celeste slithered to the guest cabin. She entered as quietly as she could, nudging the door closed behind her with a gentle press of magic. The lamp was turned down, but she had no trouble seeing Vreva and Yami huddled together on the narrow bunk. The sorcerer slept with one arm protectively around the boy. Vreva had never struck Celeste as motherly, but something about Yami must have penetrated the spy's armor. Celeste looked more closely at Yami's strange features and wondered if his curse had any relation to his physical oddity.

Celeste nudged Vreva with another simple spell, and the woman's eyes flicked open. At her feet, a lump of shadow moved, and Mathias's eyes blinked open. Vreva lifted her head from the pillow and opened her mouth to speak.

"Shhh. I need to speak with you, but you needn't wake him." The naga kept her voice to a bare whisper, confident that the water rushing past the hull and the creak of wood would mask the sound.

Vreva nodded and eased out of the bunk with the grace of a cat burglar. Or a courtesan—Vreva had spent years spying in the guise of the best-known and highest-priced courtesan in Okeno, and undoubtedly had much practice slipping out of bed without waking her partner.

Vreva made a quiet mewling sound, and Mathias lay back down next to Yami. She then gestured to the far corner of the room, and they moved away from the sleeping boy. "What is it?"

"It's dawn, and *Fury's Crown* is on our tail, only a few miles back."

Vreva's face paled in the dim light. "Oh no."

"Oh yes. Torius is worried." Celeste nodded toward the bunk. "He said Yami's not to be left alone, even for a moment. We can't let them capture him."

"I know." As Vreva looked at the boy, her eyes softened, though her nervousness remained evident in the taut muscles of her neck and face. "He's innocent, Celeste."

"I know he's innocent, but he's also a death sentence for thousands more innocents in Augustana. If the Chelish recover him, those thousands are doomed."

"I need to speak to Torius. Can you stay with Yami for a few minutes?"

"Yes, but . . ." Celeste's gaze slid uneasily toward the bunk. "What do I do if he wakes up?"

"Talk to him. He's just a boy." Vreva slipped out of the room with barely a sound.

Celeste slithered to the side of the bed and relaxed on her coils. She considered their situation. Before their attack the night before, she had questioned the stars about their course of action: Should they attack *Robust*? The song of the heavens had resonated in her bones, an overwhelming sense of rightness. She wrinkled her brow as she wondered about the accuracy of that prophecy. They had Yami now, but Anguillithek had escaped. Would that doom them? As long as the boy lived, they were in danger.

Celeste watched the pulse throbbing in Yami's throat. She could kill him with one strike, solve all their problems with one dose of her venom. But no, that wasn't true—regardless of whether Yami lived or died, the Chelish would never let them get away. Besides, she couldn't betray Vreva's trust like that.

Overhead, Grogul shouted out orders for sail changes. The ship lurched, and Celeste felt the change as they began to pitch more. They'd altered course and were beating into the wind. The ship shuddered as her bow pounded into a wave, and Yami woke with a start.

"What's wrong? Vreva?" He blinked his odd blue eyes and drew a startled breath at the sight of Celeste.

"It's all right, Yami. Vreva had to go up on deck for a moment. She'll be right back. I'm just watching over you for a while."

"Oh." He sat up and shifted until his back was against the hull, his eyes still on her. Mathias meowed, and rubbed against the boy until Yami began to stroke him absently. The action seemed to calm him.

They stared at each other for a moment while Celeste wondered what to say. Finally, she decided to stick with the basics. "Do you want anything? Food or drink?" She turned up the lamp with her magic, and his large pupilless eyes blinked in surprise.

"How did you do that?"

"Simple magic." She lifted one of her books and floated it around to demonstrate. "Nagas don't have hands, but we have other talents."

"I've, um, never met a naga before."

"Now you have." She tried for a disarming tone. "I've never met anyone like you before, either. Were your parents like you? Your eyes and skin?"

"No." He looked away, his mouth set in a hard frown. "No, I'm different. They didn't know why, but I am. A lot of the other kids didn't like me. They hurt me."

"People are like that when you're different. I know." Celeste didn't need magic to hear the pain in the boy's voice. He must have had a difficult childhood, and now this. "They do it because they're afraid. Frightened people are dangerous. Some try to use you for their own ends, and some try to enslave you."

"I know." He looked at her and rubbed his nose with a sniff. "Vreva told me what Cheliax was planning to do with me."

"I've had people try to use me, too, Yami."

"And what did you do?"

Celeste smiled and bared her fangs. "I fought back."

"But I don't know—"

The ship lurched again, and a shout rang out overhead. When Celeste heard Torius bellow for archers, she knew it was serious. She twitched her tail in irritation. She needed to go see what was happening, but dared not leave the boy alone.

"What is it?" Panic edged Yami's voice.

Celeste could offer little comfort. "I don't know, but I'm here to protect you. Don't worry."

238 CHRIS A. JACKSON

He huddled on the bed. "Don't let them take me, Celeste. I don't want . . . I don't want what happened before to happen again! I can't let it!"

Celeste's curiosity got the better of her. What exactly could this boy do? "What happened before, Yami? Do you remember?"

"No, I . . . Just pain, and then a sound, and everyone dying. I don't remember, but I know it was my fault!"

"Pain? You were hurt *before*—"

Vreva burst into the room. "It's Anguillithek! He's ripping up the sails! Torius needs you!"

"This time I *kill* that fishy fiend!" Celeste raced out the door. The crash of something falling to the quarterdeck greeted her arrival on deck. She ducked under the shower of splinters, and looked back over the shattered rail. "Torius!"

He rose from the wreckage, alive and uninjured, but a spar lay the full length of the quarterdeck, having missed him by mere feet. She followed his gaze aloft, and caught her breath.

The devil flew high above, tearing at the sails and rigging, its long, sinuous body unmarred by their previous battle. Somehow, it was completely healed. *At least it's alone.* She slithered to the windward rail for a better angle, and started to cast her lightning spell to blast the devil. Before she could finish the incantation, Lacy Jane leapt up from the crow's nest, onto the fiend's back.

"Damn!" Celeste choked back her spell. If she cast it now, she'd likely kill Lacy.

"Hold fire!" Thillion ordered, evidently coming to the same conclusion. Archers lined the windward rail, bows and crossbows ready, all eyes trained on their embattled shipmate.

Lacy slashed, and one blue horn fell to the deck. Anguillithek reached back to tear its assailant free, holding her at arm's length for a moment as it opened its tooth-lined mouth.

Now! Lightning shot aloft, scorching a furrow through the drowning devil's scales. Anguillithek roared, arching and writhing in pain, and Lacy fell from its grasp.

"Fire!" Thillion ordered, and the archers let fly. A storm of arrows and bolts shot through the air.

As the shafts riddled the devil's hide, Celeste heard a splash beyond the leeward rail. At least Lacy had hit the water, not the deck. A cry and another splash followed, but Celeste dared not take her eyes from her quarry. Anguillithek ignored the hail of arrows, tearing at the foretopmast mountings with its powerful tentacled hands, flinging its heavy body against the spar to knock it loose. Celeste cast another bolt of lightning aloft, careful to avoid catching the sails on fire. The devil howled, but continued its onslaught. Finally, the bracings gave way, and the foretopmast toppled to leeward.

Sailors cried out and ducked as the spar hit the water trailing half a dozen lines. The deck erupted into activity around her as Stargazers fought the tangled cordage, cutting free the damaged rigging. Celeste kept her eyes aloft, but by the time she was prepared to cast another spell, Anguillithek was gone.

"Damn that devil back to Hell!" Celeste writhed in rage, scanning for any sign that Anguillithek had simply teleported to attack them from another angle, but the sky remained clear. "By the stars, I hate that fiend!"

"I think you've got company, Miss Celeste." Thillion slipped an arrow back into his quiver. "But we marked him well for the trouble he caused, and he didn't bring in a more powerful fiend to help, which bodes well."

"I suppose—"

"Heave, Stargazers!"

Grogul's bellow brought her attention to the rail, where the bosun and a team of sailors hauled a sputtering Lacy Jane and a grinning Kalli onto the deck. The gillman had a rope tied around her waist. Evidently, she had gone overboard after the fallen lookout—quite a daring rescue considering that they were sailing along at ten knots. The half-orc clapped Lacy hard on the back, expelling a surprising volume of water. Lacy coughed and spat, but seemed hale enough, despite the red wheals from the devil's tentacles that crisscrossed her face and arms.

"Damn quick rescue, Kalli!" Grogul praised.

"Can't let a good lookout go by the board so easy." The gillman grabbed Lacy's arm and hauled her forward. "Come on, then. Dry clothes and a tot'll put you to rights!"

"Grogul!" Torius's shout from the quarterdeck drew every eye. "Get this topmast swayed back up. Thillion, I want archers posted all around the deck and in the crow's nest. If that devil pops in again, I want it to look like a pincushion. Celeste, damn fine shooting with your spells. Can you stay on deck to keep lookout while we get this all sorted out?"

"Yes." She slithered up to the quarterdeck and looked astern. *Fury's Crown* sailed no more than three miles behind.

"The frigate's falling off to leeward," Torius pointed out. "But I don't know if we can get this damage fixed quick enough to get away, especially if that devil comes back."

"They'll never let us get away. If we start to pull away, you can bet that it'll be back to slow us down again."

"Well, I'm not about to just let them catch us!"

But Celeste was thinking beyond simple escape. "Anguillithek didn't bring in another devil. Why not?"

"I don't think it can." Torius edged out of the way as sailors swarmed the quarterdeck and began attacking the fallen rigging. "Vreva thinks this whole plot was covert. Abrogail can't commit imperial resources to an illegal act without political fallout, and destroying Augustana is about as illegal as it gets. Admiral Ronnel swoops in to render aid after the destruction, and they've won without a war. If Andoran does fight back, we're the aggressors. But if Abrogail sends official aid before-hand, the plot becomes public."

"That's good for us, I guess."

They watched as sailors rigged blocks and lines to haul the main topmast back into place. Dukkol, who often served as the ship's carpenter, and Snick were already hauling spare lumber from the hold and taking measurements for the new topmast trestletrees. Grogul and several others climbed aloft to rig the lines that would raise the spar. The procedure was tricky even at anchor; under sail in these conditions, it would be perilous, but they had no option. They needed all sails aloft to outrun *Fury's Crown*. Unfortunately, the foretopmast was gone, and they had no replacement.

Celeste floated Torius's telescope to her eye and watched the frigate pounding into the seas behind them. The view sparked an idea in Celeste's mind. "Torius!"

"What?" He didn't look away from the spar going aloft.

"Why do you think that Anguillithek just attacked our sails to slow us down? It could just as easily have sunk us from below if it wanted to."

"They want Yami."

"Of course, but it might be more than that. Once they have Yami, they've got to get him into Augustana Harbor to . . . do whatever he does. But they can't sail *that* in." She jerked her head toward the pursuing frigate. "They'd never get a navy ship past the Augustana fleet. They need a merchant vessel. With *Robust* destroyed, they want to take *Stargazer* intact so they can use her in their plan!"

"Over my dead body!" Torius bit his lip in thought. "If the devil's going to keep slowing us down so we can't outrun them, we need a plan. If they don't want to damage the ship too badly, that might give us an edge."

"We can certainly fight back," Celeste said. "Snick's got some surprises up her sleeves, I'm sure, and Vreva can set their sails afire."

"All of that's good, but we have to remember that they won't let us escape with Yami. I wish we could use his weapon or curse or whatever it is against them."

"Oh!" Celeste remembered her truncated discussion with Yami then. "I think I might know what triggers him."

"Really?" Torius looked stunned. "What is it?"

"I think it might be injury. He told me he remembered pain, *then* everyone dying, so I think he was hurt before it happened."

"But he still doesn't remember what happens."

"No."

Torius gritted his teeth. "We don't dare use it. We don't know if it'll destroy us, too."

"At least they can't sink us, right?"

"They might not want to, but they can always postpone their plan and get another ship to use. There's no substitute for their weapon. They want the boy. We've got to kill that devil. Then we can sail for Augustana and hope for help from the Gray Corsairs."

"Agreed," Celeste said. "And I think I know how we can get them close enough to kill that blue bastard."

"How's that?" Torius looked at her with furrowed brow.

"Offer them exactly what they want."

15

A Devil by the Tail

They're tacking, sir!" Thillion called out.

Torius squinted into the flying spray. The winds had picked up during the morning, and *Stargazer* slammed through the mounting swells like a bull through stained-glass windows. Despite the recently increasing distance between the two ships, the brigantine was going to lose the race. The frigate's greater mass, more powerful rig, and sleek hull handled the heavier seas better. Now that *Fury's Crown* had rounded to a northeasterly course, she would quickly close the gap that had been widened by their diverging courses. Torius went to the binnacle and gazed over the compass card at their foe, gauging the diminishing distance and unwavering angle. From what he could tell, they were now on collision courses.

"What do you think, Celeste?" He knew she could calculate their converging paths down to the second in her head.

"I think their captain knows her ship very well." She lowered her telescope and looked at him with a grim mien. "If we stay on this course, they'll cut us off to windward in about twenty minutes. If we tack, it'll give us more time, but they'll have even more sea room, and can bear down on us from whatever angle they want."

"Can you tell me which might benefit us more? Do we delay this, or just get it over with?"

"I . . ." Celeste bit her lip so hard that Torius feared she would draw blood with her fangs. She still wasn't comfortable with her new ability to glimpse the future, but even a hint would be helpful. "I'll try."

Celeste stowed her telescope and gazed up into the sky. Her body swayed with the motion of the ship, and her eyes lost focus.

"Captain?" Windy Kate's voice held no small amount of trepidation. The frigate was tearing toward them at a furious pace.

He held up a forestalling hand. He had to give Celeste time.

After minutes that seemed like hours, she stirred from her trance, shaking her head as if trying to wake up. Her tail twitched in a gesture that he knew meant she was frustrated. "I asked if we should stay this course, but the answer was ambiguous, both good and bad. I don't know what's best."

"We stay on course, then. Some good is better than no good at all. We're as ready for this as we'll ever be." He turned to a sailor. "Fly the pennant!"

"Aye, sir!"

The sailor clipped *Stargazer*'s long black pennant to the flag halyard and hauled it aloft. It unfurled to reveal the silver outline of a naga, white hair streaming.

Celeste nudged him with her tail. "You *know* that's a little embarrassing."

"Oh, but it strikes *terror* into the hearts of our enemies!" Torius grinned at her and ran a hand through her hair.

"So, I invoke *terror* now?"

"Only in our enemies, love." He strode to the forward rail. "Grogul, go tell Vreva that *Fury's Crown* is approaching."

"Aye, sir!" The bosun hurried into the sterncastle, axe in hand.

"Thillion, archers into position."

"Very good, sir. I'm aloft." The elf scrambled up the ratlines to the main top as nimble as a spider.

"All hands, prepare to heave to at my command." Torius leaned forward and yelled down to the hold. "Did you get that, Snick?"

The gnome's voice floated up through the main hatch grating. "Ready, sir!"

Torius rejoined Celeste beside the wheel, and they watched together as the frigate loomed larger, heading at them as if to ram the smaller ship.

Celeste twitched. "I feel so exposed. I'm usually invisible before a battle."

"No sense in wasting a spell," Torius reminded her. "Anguillithek already knows you're a naga."

"You're right, but that doesn't mean I have to feel good about it." She raised her telescope to her eye, holding it perfectly steady in her magical grasp as her body swayed with the roll and pitch of the ship. When the ships were about a quarter mile apart, she broke her silence. "There's a man in brown robes standing beside the captain. He's got to be a caster. They're talking and pointing at us."

"Good. Pass that on to Thillion," Torius snapped to Kalli, and the bosun's mate clambered up the ratlines. "And Anguillithek?"

"I don't see the devil." She lowered her telescope and peered around nervously. "It could be anywhere, just waiting to teleport in right on top of us."

"With any luck it will." Torius gripped the hilt of his sword and watched *Fury's Crown* approach. Her hull-side ports opened, and the gleaming tips of ballista bolts nosed out. Chelish marines, resplendent in their black-and-red uniforms, lined the rail, and sailors with crossbows manned the broad crow's nests on her three masts.

Grogul mounted the steps of the quarterdeck escorting a terrified-looking Yami.

Torius inspected the boy and nodded in approval. "You're good at that."

"I'm a spy, Torius." Vreva's voice came out of Yami's mouth. "I have to be good at this. I just hope they buy it."

"So do I. You ready?"

She took a deep breath. "Yes."

"And Mathias?"

"He's with Yami and Soursop. He's got his orders. I poisoned his claws. If all else fails . . . Mathias knows what to do." She turned away from him.

Torius wasn't about to tell her that putting a cat in charge of a destroying a weapon that could kill thousands made him a little nervous. He trusted her on this, and if she trusted Mathias, he had to.

When the two ships were within a hundred yards, Torius gave the order they'd all been waiting for. "Heave to!"

Shouts rang out across the deck. Windy Kate brought *Stargazer*'s bow through the eye of the wind while the sailors set about adjusting the sheeting lines. In no time, the ship stood with her bow just off the wind, her sails and rudder counteracting each other to bring them to a virtual standstill, her deck remarkably steady despite the brisk wind and choppy seas.

"Now let's see if they take the bait. Grogul, show them our prize."

"Aye, sir." Grogul hoisted the sham Yami up by the collar of his shirt, holding his axe as if ready to lop off the boy's head at the least provocation.

"They definitely see him." Celeste glanced at Torius, then looked back through her telescope. "They're gesturing and talking among themselves. There are men with tower shields lining up on the quarterdeck to protect the officers and the caster."

Fury's Crown was close enough now to clearly see the officers and marines on her quarterdeck. Torius watched as the captain gave orders, and the warship turned into the wind, her crew smartly heaving to. When the frigate floated steady barely twenty yards off *Stargazer*'s beam, a Chelish officer lifted a speaking trumpet and bellowed over the wind.

"Give us the boy and hand over Bushatra, or we sink your ship!"

"Empty threats don't impress us!" Torius bellowed back, grinning in challenge. "The witch is dead! Your fishy fiend killed her! Yami here belongs to us. Sink us and you lose your prize. Attack us, and we cut his throat!"

"That would be your doom, Captain! Kill the boy, and we destroy you!"

"And then you go back to your bitch queen with *nothing*! I'm sure she's a forgiving sort."

The captain—named Lance, according to Vreva, a tall woman with short-cropped black hair, her armor gleaming in the afternoon sun—spoke with the man in the robes. He nodded, then stepped forward, all but obscured behind the shield-bearing marines.

Torius tensed. *Where the hell is Anguillithek?* "Be ready. Here it comes."

"What do you want for the boy?" the officer shouted.

"Twice what you were going to pay Bushatra!" Torius shouted back without hesitation.

"We don't have that kind of treasure aboard!"

"Then have that devil of yours go get it!" Torius drew his scimitar. "No negotiations!" *Come on! Show yourself, you big blue bastard!*

Suddenly, Torius got his wish.

Anguillithek materialized only feet away from them, its huge tentacled hands reaching for the disguised Vreva. Grogul shoved Vreva behind him, and both the bosun and Torius stepped between the devil and its goal. Axe and scimitar swept aside the fiend's writhing grasp.

"Now!" Torius shouted, and all hell broke loose.

The hair on the back of Torius's neck crackled, and his ears rang as lightning flashed over his head. The bolt struck Anguillithek in the face, burning away its chin barbels and blackening one eye.

Torius's vision cleared from the blinding flash an instant before one of the devil's massive hands slammed him aside, knocking the breath out of his lungs and sending him skidding across the deck. His head smacked into the quarterdeck rail, and his skin stung from the devil's poisonous tentacles. He struggled to rise, but his head swam with dizziness from the impact.

Grogul stood firm against the devil, his axe carving gashes in the thick blue hide and fending off the sweeping blows. The staccato thrum of bowstrings caught Torius's ear as Thillion's archers unleashed their deadly missiles. The arrows and bolts flew toward the frigate, but wind suddenly howled up from nowhere to throw the missiles into the sky. Fortunately, Snick's ballista bolts didn't suffer the same fate. The heavier missiles arched over the frigate's deck and detonated in midair, raining deadly acid down on the massed Chelish marines. Screams shrilled across the water, but Torius didn't have time to gloat, for Chelish grappling bolts slammed into *Stargazer*'s hull, the deck shuddering beneath his feet with the impact.

As Torius pushed off the rail to rejoin the fight, a searing ball of flame blossomed upon the quarterdeck of *Fury's Crown*. Vreva had cast her first spell. Then, as he stared in shock, the flames miraculously died away. The Chelish spellcaster lowered his arms, the deck and sails overhead only singed instead of charred. Captain Lance and her officers had not, as they had planned, been incinerated.

Torius cursed and slashed desperately at the drowning devil. They had to kill Anguillithek before the Chelish discovered they'd been deceived. Their lives depended on it. He heard Thillion curse from high overhead, but couldn't spare a glance.

Beyond his foe, Torius saw the Chelish spellcaster raise his arms beseechingly to the sky. Lightning crackled down from above to blast *Stargazer*'s crow's nest, and two archers fell burning to the deck. Torius sliced a tentacled hand, and glanced up to where

Thillion climbed precariously to the very top of the repaired topmast. His arrows rained down into the line of shield bearers protecting the caster, over the impeding wall of wind. Two marines went down, victims to the lethal toxin Vreva had put on Thillion's arrows. Lightning crashed down again onto Stargazer's middeck, sending sailors sprawling, but before the Chelish caster could call another bolt, he staggered back. Even as he gaped down at the green-fletched arrow in his chest, another struck him in the abdomen. As he folded over, a third lodged into his back.

Yes! Thillion had just evened the odds a little. If Vreva's poison was as lethal as she said, the caster wouldn't be getting up.

Lightning blasted past Torius again, raking the devil as Grogul and Torius kept it at bay. Vreva, still in the guise of Yami, cast another ball of fire at *Fury's Crown*, this time at the mainmast crow's nest. Burning sailors toppled and fell, and the huge square sails burst into flames.

Blackened and slashed, Anguillithek stopped and stared at the presumed boy. "Deceivers!" The devil vanished.

Torius looked around wildly, his frustration mirrored by Celeste and Grogul. Anguillithek rematerialized in midair behind the ship and flew straight at the transom. Torius gaped in horror as the devil smashed through the stern gallery windows into his cabin. It was going after Yami! Torius whirled to bark out an order, but Celeste was already racing down the steps to the deck, her serpentine form shimmering with her starry cloak.

"Yami!" Vreva turned to follow Celeste.

"Vreva, don't you *dare* leave your post!" Torius commanded. "Celeste will deal with the devil. You've got a job to do!"

The sorcerer turned back to her task, hurling another mote of fire at the enemy ship. It detonated on the foremast crow's nest, incinerating more Chelish archers and catching sails on fire.

The deck lurched, and Torius stumbled. The frigate's grappling lines had come taut, and were pulling them in. Several of his crew lay sprawled on the deck sporting arrow wounds, shot by Chelish archers as they tried to cut *Stargazer* free. Snick's ballistae cracked again, the bolts flying the short distance to *Fury's Crown*, their blue-painted warheads detonating over the frigate and spraying liquid ice atop the enemy marines.

Lightning blasted out *Stargazer's* stern windows, sending shattered glass and splintered wood flying. Celeste was battling Anguillithek belowdecks, and the ship was taking a beating. *Just don't catch my ship on fire, love.*

Torius tried to focus on his own tasks. He had Chelish boarders to deal with. "Grogul, with me! Vreva, keep targeting their archers!"

The half-orc growled and followed. Vreva answered with another spell that engulfed the frigate's foredeck in flames. Cries of agony rose on the heat-blasted air as burning canvas fell onto the Chelish sailors and marines below. *Stargazer's* sails were untouched so far. If they could kill Anguillithek and break away, they might just be able to draw the frigate into a trap with the Gray Corsairs.

First things first! Torius joined his crew on the middeck, Grogul to his right and Kalli to his left, his scimitar comfortable in his grasp. He almost felt like a pirate again.

The two ships crashed together.

"Boarders away!" Captain Lance leapt down to the frigate's main deck with her officers, brandishing her sword as she egged her crew on.

"Stargazers, repel boarders!" Torius drew a fighting dagger to fill his off hand as the Chelish marines leapt across, and his world devolved into a chaos of steel and blood.

Celeste called upon Desna's gifts as she slithered down the steps to the main deck, desperate for every advantage she could get against the drowning devil. The spells that had been buzzing in her mind for days, but that she had not yet used, leapt forth now, musical laughter jingling in her thoughts. A divine radiance brightened her starry cloak, and a shimmering shield of energy formed before her. As she slithered into the sterncastle's long corridor, the door to the aft cabin flung open. Anguillithek emerged, undulating awkwardly forward into a passage barely wide enough to accommodate its bulk. Celeste flung her lightning spell down the hallway, wreathing the devil in searing energy. Instead of retreating from the electrical barrage, the devil countered with a deluge of seawater that slammed Celeste back against the door.

Sputtering and hissing, she caught her breath and charged forward, screaming out a spell that doubled her speed. The devil outweighed her, but the narrow passage prevented it from dodging, and Celeste had momentum on her side. She hit Anguillithek hard, burying her fangs in its scaly hide and forcing it backward into the aft cabin. She had to keep the fiend from the galley where Soursop and Mathias watched over Yami.

Devil and naga landed in a writhing heap of scales and flashing teeth. Anguillithek grasped her with its sticky tentacles, ripped her teeth free, and flung her into the chart table. Splinters raked her scales with the impact, but she ignored the pain. Before the devil could reach the door, she blasted it with lightning yet again, slithering into its path as it reeled back.

Anguillithek roared something she couldn't understand and lunged at her with squirming tentacles and gnashing teeth. Shimmering starlight flared between them, deflecting his grasping hands and snapping jaws. She slithered aside to keep from being pinned against the wall and cast another spell, riddling the devil with motes of magical energy. It whirled and lashed out, its massive arm smashing into her like a sledgehammer.

Celeste slammed into the bulkhead, the coppery taste of blood filling her mouth. The ship lurched beneath her, and she wondered if the sensation was real, or dizziness from the blow. The crunch of wood and battle cries overhead told her that she hadn't been knocked senseless. The two ships had come together. They were being boarded. Torius undoubtedly had his hands full on deck. She longed to be beside him, but she had to keep Anguillithek from taking Yami. If she failed, all their troubles would be for naught.

To that end, she slithered between the devil and the door. Her lightning spells spent, she cast another flight of magical projectiles at it. A shrill cry from behind startled her, and she whirled. Yami burst into the cabin, a kitchen knife in one hand, his face a rictus of terror and determination.

By the stars—I told him to fight back! "No, Yami!"

Anguillithek slammed her aside and reached for the boy, but a flashing cleaver flew through the doorway to lodge in the devil's broad chest. Soursop lunged into the cabin wielding another cleaver. The ship's cook shoved Yami out of harm's way and pulled a long butcher knife from his belt. Behind Soursop, the tiny furry shape of Mathias skidded to a halt in the doorway, his yellow eyes wide with terror. Unintimidated by Soursop, his kitchen implements, or the bristling feline, the fiend knocked the cook sideways and reached once again for the boy.

Knowing that none of her remaining spells would stop Anguillithek, Celeste struck, burying her fangs in its flesh and bowling the devil over. Unfortunately, her shield of starlight could not keep its tentacles from wrapping around her. The poisonous members stung like fire as the devil ripped her teeth free and threw her off. Celeste felt her long tail strike something soft and heard a high-pitched cry.

Yami!

As the impact smashed the boy against the cabinetry, his arm twisted with an audible crack. Yami's scream of pain shivered the air, his blue eyes flaring with a peculiar light.

A pulse of energy rattled Celeste's ears and smashed her and Soursop back against the bulkhead. Mathias was flung down the passage like a furry rag doll. Even Anguillithek reeled from the onslaught, a warbling cry rising from its throat. The few remaining windows shattered, spraying glass into the sea.

Yami lay staring at his mangled arm, the glow in his strange blue eyes fading.

"By the stars, no!" Celeste stared in horror. She'd been right; pain or trauma must have been the key to unlocking Yami's peculiar power.

The weapon had been triggered.

16

From the Depths

B ombs away!" Snick cried gleefully.

Torius ducked reflexively. Anything that made the gnome that joyous had to be dangerous. He glanced back to see Snick and her ballista crews at the main hatch coaming, each heaving a gallon-sized ceramic jar over the heads of the defending Stargazers. The jars—the detached warheads of her ballista bolts—flew into the ranks of Chelish marines and shattered, spewing forth sticky resin. The gooey mire glued the enemy to the deck, effectively stopping the momentum of the Chelish charge.

"Brilliant, Snick!" Torius dodged the slashing sword of a marine and brought his scimitar down on the man's wrist. His foe stumbled back clutching the spurting stump. "Push 'em hard, Stargazers!"

He and Grogul lunged forward, forging through blades and blood. Under the coordinated defense, the raking fire of Thillion and his archers, and Vreva's devastating spells, the Chelish were meeting far more resistance than they'd expected. Half their sails were on fire, their archers had been devastated, and a third of their boarding force was stuck to the deck. There had been casualties among the Stargazers, certainly, but they'd dealt far worse than they'd received. Now they had to finish the job.

The deck shivered under his boots, and Torius's ears popped an instant before a wave of pressure slammed into him. Half of the sailors and marines were knocked flat, and the others staggered, shaking their heads in stunned awe. The turbulent seas around the ships were blasted to a glassy sheen, concentric rings of wavelets expanding outward. For a moment, both sides stared at one another, unsure of what had happened.

Torius took a step back from the fight. "Snick, was that one of your surprises?"

"Not one of *mine*, Captain."

The lack of elation in her voice sent a shiver of fear up Torius's spine. Only one other answer came to mind.

The weapon.

The deck lurched under his feet as if the entire ocean shook from some deep-sea tremor. The adversaries stepped back from the battle, some pulling away wounded comrades, others looking around for the cause of this strange phenomenon.

Without warning, the sea surged up beneath the ships as if an enormous bubble had risen from the depths. The vessels heaved and ground against one another, several grappling lines snapping with the strain. Most of the sailors kept their feet, but a few fell. The mound of water dropped suddenly beneath them, casting out more concentric waves like the surface of a pond after a stone is thrown in, but immensely larger. As the bulging wave receded, the sea around them started to swirl, first slowly, then faster and faster, forming an immense vortex. The embattled ships began to move with that torrential flow.

"This can't be good!" Grogul bellowed.

"Avast boarding! Back to the ship! Cast off!" Captain Lance sheathed her sword and raced up to her quarterdeck. The Chelish retreated in haste, and the grappling lines released their hold. The two hulls screeched horribly as they parted, splinters flying. "Haul sheets and braces! Bear off!"

"I think she agrees with you!" Torius sheathed his sword and stumbled again as both ships began to spiral down into the building maelstrom, the deck heeling so hard that corpses skidded to the downside bulwark. "Everyone hold fast!" He grabbed an injured sailor and clapped her hand to the main hatch coaming.

"Captain!" Grogul pointed off the port beam, and for the first time in his life, Torius saw fear in the half-orc's eyes.

Looking into the depths of the whirlpool, he saw a black pit opening into a huge maw. Teeth taller than sailors lined that gaping hole, and a roar so deep that Torius felt that the sea itself would be torn asunder shivered the deck beneath his feet. This was what they'd had in mind for Augustana, and it seemed intent upon eating his ship.

My ship. A grim resolve pierced his terror, galvanizing him into action. *Not today, beastie!*

"Man the sheets! Windy, on the helm!" He lurched toward the quarterdeck. "Bear off, or we'll be pulled in!"

Stargazers scattered like leaves in a hurricane, some dropping their weapons in their haste. Snick took one glance down into that pit of gnashing teeth, yelped in alarm, and jumped back down into the hold. *Fury's Crown* bore away, her remaining sails billowing, but *Stargazer* was caught in the deepening spiral of the maelstrom.

Torius clawed his way to the quarterdeck, envious for the first time of Windy's hook hand. She drove the steel spine into the wooden handrail and hauled herself up like a lumberjack climbing a pine. Behind him, Grogul bellowed orders and the sailors responded, hauling on lines to bring the ship's sails back into position.

Torius gripped the wheel with Windy, and together they struggled to keep the helm hard over. The rushing water wanted to pull the ship into the vortex, and every time they made a half revolution around the whirlpool, they had to jibe or tack the ship to keep the wind in the sails. The mainsail boom swept past above his head, and the sail filled with a horrendous crack, lurching the ship over, deeper into the pit despite their best efforts. *Fury's Crown*, having a taller rig, and still more sail area despite the damage Vreva had inflicted, won free of the maelstrom on the first rotation, filling her topsails and tearing off downwind. *Stargazer* barely managed to hold her own, and the great cone of swirling sea became deeper with every rotation. The hull groaned under his feet, and Torius cringed.

"What in the name of all the gods is that?" Vreva lurched over, clutching the binnacle to keep from sliding across the deck as she stared down into the tooth-lined vortex in stark terror.

"The weapon!" Torius gauged their turn and bellowed, "Ready to tack ship! Now!"

The sails swept overhead again and filled, now pulling them up the increasing slope instead of down. But still, *Stargazer* couldn't break free. In moments they would be forced to jibe once more, and they'd be pulled deeper into swirling pit.

"We can't sail free!" Torius gritted his teeth in frustration. Despite all their struggles, all their pain and effort, everyone he cared about would be pulled to their deaths.

"Wait! I've got an idea!" Vreva let go of the binnacle and slid across the steeply inclined deck to the downside rail. There, she raised a hand and shouted out arcane words that were whipped away on the wind. A spark formed on the tip of one finger, and she sent it streaking down into the toothy maw at the base of the vortex.

The spark detonated deep within the gaping mouth, expanding to fill it with searing fire. A roar unlike anything Torius had ever heard issued from that throat, gouts of water, cooked meat, and gooey black phlegm spraying into the sky.

"Yes!" They weren't out yet, but Vreva had given him an idea. "Snick! Fire incendiaries into that Gozreh-be-damned thing!"

He heard a whoop from forward, and a moment later the port-side ballistae fired a broadside. The warheads detonated on impact, the alchemical fire spewing forth to stick to the sensitive tissues within. The immense mouth closed, and the maelstrom collapsed.

"Yes!" Torius cheered as *Stargazer* lurched free on the rebounding wave.

Anguillithek lunged forward, trying to force its way past Celeste to reach Yami, but she wouldn't have it. Coiling and flaring her upper body in defiance, she shot another flight of energy bolts into it. The bolts struck unerringly, gouging holes in its flesh, but the devil seemed not to notice the injury. It lashed out with both hands, trying to knock her down, but her shield of starlight kept its tentacles at bay. It couldn't get past her, and she wouldn't relent.

The deck lurched beneath them, and the devil slid into the wreckage of the chart table. The view outside the shattered windows canted to an alarming angle, but Celeste had more pressing matters at hand. Anguillithek lashed out at her again, but she ducked under the blow. Its hand smashed into the cabinetry above Yami, sending shattered glass and porcelain raining down on the boy's head. The cabin was being destroyed around them, their home reduced to splinters and shards. The thought of it brought Celeste's temper surging forth in a hiss of rage.

"Celeste!" Soursop had recovered, and now balanced precariously on the angled deck, clutching his knife and cleaver. He threw the butcher knife at Anguillithek's head, but the blade glanced off.

"Get Yami out of here!" Celeste screamed, ducking under the devil's sweeping blow and firing off another volley of missiles.

Soursop blinked and stared at her with a quizzical look.

He can't understand me. Blast this curse!

The deck canted even farther, and Celeste heard shouts from above. Something dire was happening outside, but she couldn't abandon Yami to find out what it was. Of course, if Yami's curse was dreadful enough to destroy an entire city and a fleet of warships, then they didn't stand much of a chance. She thought briefly of her recent prophecy—good and bad both—and wondered when the good part was going to happen.

Anguillithek surged forward, forcing her back with its greater bulk, stinging tentacles reaching out to grasp. She buried her fangs in its wrist, more out of desperation than any cognizant strategy. Soursop bellowed and charged, his cleaver held high. The devil met the charge with a sweeping blow from its free hand that sent the cook flying. Soursop's head cracked against the bulkhead and left a red smear as he slumped to the floor.

Yami screamed something, but Celeste still couldn't understand. She tore at Anguillithek's wrist, but its other hand grasped her. Its tentacles stung like fire, encircling her throat and lifting her, ripping her teeth free. Celeste whipped her sinuous body around the devil's, refusing to be thrown aside. The two serpentine adversaries coiled and writhed, fighting for supremacy.

"Yami! Run!"

Whether he understood her or not, the boy finally seemed to grasp the notion that this was not a healthy place for him to be. Cradling his injured arm, he lurched to his feet and dashed out the door.

Anguillithek bellowed in rage and tried to throw Celeste, but she tightened her coils like a constrictor. She struck again, but her fangs just skittered across thick scales, her strength waning from the devil's stinging poison. She reared back to cast a spell, but Anguillithek finally tore her loose. The naga flew across the cabin just as the entire ship lurched upright. She reeled from the impact for a moment as the horizon shifted outside the windows, unsure once again if she was dazed, or if the ship was actually being tossed around like a cork in a bottle.

Finally free of her entangling embrace, Anguillithek waved one writhing mass of tentacles at her and uttered an incomprehensible command.

Celeste tried to call forth her magic, to summon the flying motes of energy to pierce the devil's scorched and bleeding coils, but she couldn't speak. Agony lanced through her upper body like before, but unlike the last time, she hadn't the strength to retch up the foul water. She would have screamed, but she had no breath left in her body. Celeste fell to the deck, writhing, choking, fighting to cough up the vile tide, to take one more breath.

The ship lurched yet again, and she heard a rending crash, but it meant nothing if she couldn't draw a breath. Darkness closed in around her, dimming her sight. As Celeste rolled and convulsed, fighting to expel the water, she caught sight of Anguillithek for an instant before it vanished. The devil had escaped her yet again, and she lay here struggling to breathe, unable to follow, fight, or even save herself.

Good and bad. She found her mind wandering as consciousness waned and her strength ebbed. *What good, Desna? What good can come from this?* The shrieks of terror, smashing wood, and bellows of rage from overhead meant nothing now. There was only darkness, and it was quickly dragging her down into a pit she could never escape.

17

Hell and High Water

Vreva gripped the railing for dear life as the ship was flung free of the spiraling maelstrom, glad to simply be alive. *So that was Yami's curse.* She didn't know how the boy had been triggered, or even exactly what it was that he had summoned, but something didn't make sense. If the creature could be killed by one fire spell and a broadside of alchemical fire, how had Bushatra and Ronnel expected it to destroy the entire Augustana fleet and the city to boot?

"Sheets and braces! We're not out of this yet!"

Vreva turned at Torius's orders to see *Fury's Crown* already turning to renew her pursuit, her crew scrambling to replace burned canvas. But *Stargazer* was free, and with Calistria's blessing, they might just escape.

A crash and cry through the broken skylight shattered her hope. Celeste still battled Anguillithek below. If they didn't kill the devil, they would never escape.

"Torius! We have to help Celeste!"

Torius drew his sword and ran to the skylight as if to leap down, but a call from above stayed his action.

"Captain! Off the port beam!"

All eyes turned at Thillion's warning call.

A rising mound of water approached the ship, a building swell that was clearly no natural wave, but something immense beneath the surface. And it was coming fast. Higher it grew, rushing straight toward them, shifting its course to follow *Stargazer* like a cat chasing a fleeing rat. A shaft of sunlight through the cresting wave illuminated the vast shape below.

"What in the name of . . ." Vreva glimpsed a distorted multitude of glowing blue eyes. Her heart froze in her chest, her gaze fixed upon the onrushing horror.

Fortunately, Torius wasn't so transfixed. "Snick! Swimmer bolts!"

"Aye, sir!" came the gnome's shrill reply.

A moment later, six ballista bolts flew out from *Stargazer*'s side, plunging beneath the surface just before they reached their target. Whether the bolts struck true or not, Vreva couldn't tell, for the rising swell didn't slow. The wave rose until it broke, a great froth of white foam curling at its crest.

"No!" The anguished cry snapped Vreva's attention, drawing her gaze to the main deck. Yami knelt near the main hatch coaming, one arm cradled to his chest, his strange blue eyes fixed on the looming swell. "No, no, no!"

"Yami!" Vreva rushed down from the quarterdeck.

"All hands, hang on!"

The ship heaved with the breaking wave, hurling her against the rail. Seawater doused the middeck, knocking sailors flat. Grasping the balustrade to keep from plunging the down the stair, she gaped at the shape that rose from the wave.

A mountain of mottled armor broke the surface, a cliff of spiky chitin similar to the hue and texture of Yami's skin, yet vast beyond imagining. Toothed plates the size of barn doors shifted aside to reveal a mouth that could swallow the ship's longboat. The thick armor had been pierced by several of Snick's ballista bolts, but they seemed not to have injured the colossal monster at all. A claw the girth of a tree rose from the water to swipe the shafts away like bothersome flies.

The beast rose higher, the water around it churning and roiling. More claws emerged, lesser ones beneath its mouth flailing the air as if searching for something to thrust into that cavernous maw, and greater pointed spurs thicker than *Stargazer*'s mast spread wide as if to embrace the ship. Only the creature's underside was not armored, but undulated in thick folds of pink blubber.

"Fire!"

At Snick's shrill cry, six more bolts shot from *Stargazer*'s side. These, however, weren't meant to pierce. Their warheads detonated on impact, splashing liquid flame across the moist pink flesh.

Brilliant, Snick! Fire had run the creature off once, maybe it would work again. Vreva called forth her last flame spell and sent the spark hurtling at the beast's fleshy underside. It blossomed into a searing conflagration, adding to the inferno already cooking the blubbery flesh. Rivulets of fat oozed and flowed like melting wax in the heat, but the creature simply dipped down into the sea, extinguishing the flames. As it rose again, the seared flesh pinked up, blisters already healing. It came on, undeterred from its prey.

Didn't I tell you going to sea was a bad idea? Mathias yowled from the sterncastle door, his fur standing on end, his yellow eyes wide.

"Yes, you did! Now stay back!"

You don't have to tell me that twice! He darted into a corner, vanishing in a heaped coil of rope.

A wail of sheer terror from Yami caught Vreva's ear. The boy stared, transfixed by the beast, his nightmare made real. She stumbled down the rest of the steps and rushed toward him.

"Hold fast!" Torius bellowed from the quarterdeck.

The beast struck the ship, slamming *Stargazer* sideways through the water. Timbers groaned with the impact, and the deck careened sharply, knocking Vreva to her hands and knees. Yami was flung against the hatch coaming, clinging with one arm, the other obviously broken. The ship shuddered again as a great claw lanced down through the deck near the foremast.

This isn't good! Mathias yowled. *I'd rather be chasing rats and tumbling kitty cats!*

"Frankly, so would I!" Vreva scrabbled across the deck, trying to reach Yami as the Stargazers rallied to the attack.

Arrows and bolts flew. Though most glanced off the chitinous armor, a few pierced the softer skin of its underside, and one shaft struck one of the blue eyes. Grogul hacked at the claw piercing the deck like a lumberjack felling a tree, gouging a deep furrow with his axe. Thin blue blood poured forth, but it slowed and stopped as the gaping wound sealed. Nothing seemed to faze the monster.

Belowdecks, the ballistae cracked. The creature shuddered and wrenched its claw free of the deck, emitting a thunderous roar as it backed off. Six ballista bolts were embedded in the soft pink belly. Finally, something had hurt the beast.

As if in retribution for the injury, the creature ripped a claw through the rigging, shredding canvas, parting cordage, and sending a rain of wreckage falling to the deck. One of the beast's smaller claws impaled an archer and lifted him toward that horrible maw. The sailor vanished with a shrill scream, swallowed whole.

"Hull breach!" Snick's shrieked. "Water coming in!"

Vreva crawled toward the main hatch coaming, wary of falling debris. "Yami! Take my hand!"

The boy turned to her, eyes blank and wide. After a moment, he regained some measure of cognizance and reached out with his good hand. Their fingers touched.

Anguillithek materialized right behind Yami, enfolding the terrified youth in one tentacle-hand. The devil wrenched him from Vreva's grasp and rose into the air.

"No! Yami!" Reaching over her shoulder, Vreva pulled her hand crossbow from its holster, flicking an envenomed bolt into the slot. For an instant, she wondered why Anguillithek didn't just teleport away with the boy. It wouldn't worry about triggering the curse again. Maybe it couldn't.

Whatever the reason, it gave her a chance. She couldn't allow Yami to be taken, couldn't risk a beast like this ravaging Augustana.

Dear Calistria, forgive me! Vreva raised the weapon and took aim. Her heart ached, but she had no choice. Thousands of lives hung in the balance. *Do it! Kill him! You have to!* Her finger tightened on the trigger.

The tiny bolt flew, but lodged in one of the devil's thick tentacles rather than Yami's chest. She groaned and reached for another bolt, never taking her eyes off of her target, oblivious to the crack of shattering wood and screams of sailors as the beast continued to pummel the ship.

Overhead, Yami fought the devil's grasp, wrenching at the clinging tentacles with his one good hand. Anguillithek clapped its other hand on the boy, and Yami opened his mouth in a bloodcurdling scream. His broken arm had been twisted in the devil's grasp, the shattered bone ripping through the skin.

With his cry, another thundering pulse of energy knocked Vreva to the deck.

Convulsing with the wave of force, the looming sea monster opened its maw and let loose a howl so deep it shook Vreva's very bones. It thrashed its claws madly, driven into a frenzy by the call that had summoned it from the depths. One claw struck the mainmast, shattering the thick spar like a piece of kindling. Ropes snapped under the tension, cracking like whips, and the great mainsail collapsed. The upper portion of the mast toppled and started to fall.

Above, Anguillithek dodged falling debris. Vreva scrambled to one knee, raised her crossbow, and took aim. The deck shook beneath her with the rending crash of the falling mast striking the quarterdeck. *I'm sorry, Yami.* She pulled the trigger.

266 CHRIS A. JACKSON

Anguillithek jerked, but not because she'd hit it—the bolt flew wide of both boy and devil as an enormous claw lanced through the devil, piercing its body like a dagger transfixing a snake. Anguillithek howled and writhed, smashing one huge hand against impaling claw, but to little effect.

New hope blossomed in Vreva's heart. If the devil perished, it would drop Yami. That hope was immediately dashed, however, as Anguillithek's free hand grasped the claw and pulled, inching the devil toward the bloody tip. Bit by bit, it moved closer to freedom. Vreva braced herself as the ship lurched again. She could try to take another shot, but both Anguillithek and Yami were being flung around so violently, she had no chance of hitting the boy. She needed help, and she could only think of one person crazy enough to get to Yami.

"Torius!" Vreva looked to the quarterdeck, but could see nothing through the tangle of canvas and rope. The fallen mast stood out of the deck like a war banner. "Torius, are you alive?"

Torius grabbed the binnacle to keep from falling as another pulse of energy shook the ship and flattened the seas. "Gozreh's guts, not again!" *If Yami summoned a second monster . . .*

The sea monster conjured by the first blast went berserk with the impulse, flailing its huge claws wildly, the deck shivering with its sonorous bellow. One great claw lashed aft, the tip ripping through the mainsail to crash into the mainmast. The spar shattered under impact.

"We just *fixed* that, you gods-damned monster!" Torius roared. Then he saw Thillion.

The elf had been perched at the topmast bracings, using the elevation to fire at the frigate. Now he fell with the toppling mast, flailing for something to grasp to slow his fall.

"Thillion!"

Torius lost sight of his friend amid the tangle of cordage and canvas. The mainsail gaff broke free from its bracket and plummeted down, trailing shredded black sails. The shattered topmast fell toward the quarterdeck like a spear. Torius stood in a deadly rain of splintered wood, rope, and blocks, unable to do anything but stare up helplessly.

His ship, his beautiful *Stargazer*, was being destroyed before his eyes.

"Captain!"

Someone snatched his belt and jerked him off his feet. They rolled in a tangle of arms and legs as debris smashed to the deck all around them. As canvas draped them like a burial shroud, his savior landed on top of Torius with a grunt. Something slammed down hard on them, knocking the breath from his lungs.

Torius blinked, but it was dark under the black sail. He could barely breathe. "Windy?"

"Yes . . . sir."

"Windy! You saved me!"

"Someone's gotta . . . look out for you . . . when Celeste's not around." Her breathing was shallow, her words edged with pain.

"Can you get up? You're squishing me."

"Something's got . . . me . . . pinned. I . . . can't . . ."

"Hold still, Windy." Torius reached around her and felt a heavy piece of wood pressed against her back. Bracing his arms, he pushed. The wood moved just enough to allow him to squirm out from under the woman. Windy slumped to the deck, gasping in pain.

Through the thick shroud of fallen sailcloth, Torius could hear the crash and groan of tortured wood, and the cries of his crew as they battled the sea monster. A howl like nothing he had ever heard pierced the air.

I've got to get out there!

"Windy, can you stand?"

"Standing's okay . . . I think." She wheezed. "It's . . . breathing . . . that hurts."

"Torius!" Vreva's urgent cry barely reached him above the din. "Torius, are you alive?"

What the hell now? The captain freed his scimitar and thrust it skyward to slice through the sail, fighting his way out from under the draping canvas. Reaching back, he pulled Windy to her feet.

She gasped and clutched her side. "Think I . . . broke a couple of ribs."

"Drink this!" Torius pulled a potion from his jacket pocket and pressed it into her hand, then called, "Vreva, what—"

"There, Torius!" Vreva thrust her finger skyward. "The devil's got Yami!"

"Gozreh's guts!" The sea monster towered over the ship, flailing its horrible claws, ripping poor *Stargazer* to shreds. One claw impaled Anguillithek, but the devil was pulling itself slowly free. If it succeeded, it could fly away with Yami.

"Not if I can help it," Torius vowed. "Thillion!" If anyone could put an arrow in the flailing boy, it was his first mate. Then he remembered watching the elf fall.

"He's here, sir." Windy pulled aside the sail to reveal the elf. His eyes were closed, and blood darkened his hair. "Unconscious, but he's breathing."

"Give him this." Torius tossed her his last potion. *I'll just have to do this without getting hurt.*

Torius glanced at the wrecked middeck. Sections of the bulwarks were torn off, and holes pocked the deck where the creature had thrust its claws. Blood and splintered wood made treacherous footing, and the downed cordage created a rat's nest. By the time he traversed that mess, Anguillithek would be free. Besides, the sea monster held the devil high over the deck. He'd have to go up.

Looking aloft, Torius quickly picked out a path. He sheathed his sword and leapt onto the forward quarterdeck rail, then shinnied a few feet up the truncated mast. At the first set of blocks, he grabbed the forebrace line and climbed hand over hand up to the foresail yard.

So far, so good. Below him, his crew battled for their lives. Above him, Anguillithek inched his way toward the end of the claw. Torius picked up his pace.

He hurried along the yard, his feet finding easy purchase on the reefer's footrope. Next, he vaulted up onto the foremast and scrambled up a halyard. Finally, he hauled himself into the crow's nest.

Below, the claw upon which Anguillithek was impaled swept toward him. Before he could consider the insanity of what he was about to do, Torius drew his fighting dagger and launched himself into the air. He landed hard, jamming the dagger's keen point into the thick chitin and wrapping his legs around the claw as best he could.

The huge claw tilted, the devil now below him, and Torius made his move. He pulled out the dagger and slid down the blood-slicked claw, clutching it with arms and legs and silently cursing the knobby protuberances that bruised the tender parts of his anatomy.

Thankfully, Anguillithek was too intent on making its escape and keeping hold of a struggling Yami to notice Torius approaching from behind. Mere feet from the devil, Torius jammed the dagger back into the claw, slamming his palm against the pommel to drive it in to the hilt. Clutching the dagger with one hand and praying to Gozreh that it held, he released his legs and swung free. Yami was now within range. One cut, and their mission would be accomplished, Augustana safe. Torius drew his sword and prepared to strike.

Yami struggled against the devil's grip, beating against the tentacles with one hand. The other arm hung twisted and bleeding, white bone protruding through the skin. The boy's wracking sobs reached Torius's ears and, for a moment, his tear-streaked face turned toward the captain.

Torius blinked. Yami could have been Torius as a boy, screaming and crying as he was torn from his mother, sold into slavery for a brick of pesh.

Not today.

Torius blinked again, and swung his sword.

The scimitar's razor edge sliced through Anguillithek's tentacles. The devil roared, and Yami started to fall. Torius dropped his sword and snatched the boy's flailing hand. He gripped his dagger desperately and kicked his legs. *If I can just swing us out over the water . . .*

Looking up, he saw the devil's massive bloody fist coming at him—and even more alarming, a second claw just beyond Anguillithek scything down. Releasing his grasp on the dagger, Torius felt the breeze of the devil's fist overhead, then a warm rain of fiendish blood as the sea monster's claw sliced through the devil. Anguillithek's two halves spun away in opposite directions.

Torius wrapped his arms around Yami as they plummeted toward *Stargazer*'s deck. He braced for the impact, doubtful that they would hit anything soft enough to break their fall.

Vreva was right. I couldn't murder an innocent boy.

Wood shattered, and they plunged into darkness.

18

Abandon Ship

"Miss Celeste!"

Arms like thick bands of iron wrapped around her and squeezed hard, expelling a torrent of foul water from her lungs. Celeste coughed and retched, gasping for breath. The hard rim of a bottle pressed to her lips.

"Drink!"

Liquid filled her mouth, and she swallowed. Magical healing flooded through her like a cleansing tide, washing away the agony in her lungs. Blinking, Celeste found herself staring into the plump, distressed face of Soursop. Blood trickled from a cut on his forehead, and his hand gripped an empty potion bottle from her harness.

"You okay?" He dropped the bottle and took a step back. "I thought you were dead!"

"I thought I was, too!" She looked around the shambles of the cabin, panicked to see that both Anguillithek and Yami were gone. "What happened?"

"After that bloody blue devil cast some kind of spell on you, it just disappeared into thin air!"

"We've got to get—"

Celeste's ears rang as a second pulse of energy shook *Stargazer*'s timbers and rattled the few unbroken items on Torius's shelves. Yami had somehow been triggered again. The ship lurched, and a thundering roar shivered the air. From outside came the sound of tearing canvas and shattering wood, then a horrendous crash. Celeste flung herself aside as the ceiling caved in, wincing as splinters raked against her hard scales. When she dared to raise her head, what she saw took her breath away.

"By the stars!"

The topmast transfixed the cabin from top to bottom, piercing both the quarterdeck and the cabin sole into the compartment below. It had snapped an overhead beam, collapsing half the ceiling. The heavy beam lay across Soursop's lap, pinning him to the deck. One leg jutted straight out, and looked uninjured, but the other hadn't fared as well. A splinter the diameter of Celeste's telescope pierced his thigh just above the knee. Blood pulsed from the wound at an alarming rate. His lower leg was bent back under the beam, pinned down by the crushing weight. Soursop struggled to rise, but his face paled and he gasped in pain.

"Soursop!" Celeste ducked under the high end of the fallen beam and slithered to his side. She pulled a potion bottle from her harness and floated it to him. "Here! Drink! You're bleeding badly!"

"I . . . yes, ma'am." The portly cook drained the bottle, and his color improved. The bleeding slowed and stopped. Unfortunately, the splinter still pierced his leg. The wound would reopen when she moved the beam, but at least he wouldn't bleed to death before she could free him.

"Now hold still. I'm going to lift the beam off, and I need you to crawl free."

"Okay." He looked dubious. "I'll try."

Celeste slithered under the beam, pressed her coils against it, and flexed. The beam didn't budge. Wedging herself lower, she tried to use her coils as a fulcrum, but still the heavy beam wouldn't move. She strained until her head pounded, but couldn't budge the thing. The effort left her panting and weak. She looked around the destroyed cabin for something to help her, a lever or crowbar, but saw nothing. Without a mechanical advantage, she was simply too weak to lift that much weight.

"I need arms to do this right." Celeste pictured the strongest person she knew and cast her transformation spell. Long, gray-green arms and legs bulging with muscles sprouted from her sinuous body. Her chest expanded against the straps of her harness until she released the clasp.

In Grogul's form, she braced her legs, grasped the beam anew, and heaved. Her legs trembled with the effort, shoulders straining, but still the beam wouldn't move. Soursop tried to help, pushing against the timber with his good leg, but even together it wouldn't budge.

Celeste looked forward. She could try to get help, but it sounded as if the battle was raging even more hotly than before. If she left Soursop, and something happened to her, he would die here.

The ship lurched again, and Celeste reeled. Although quite accustomed to humanoid form by now, she found it difficult to balance on two relatively small feet instead of her own stable coils.

"Miss Celeste, we're sinkin'!" Panic tinged Soursop's voice.

"What?" Celeste glanced through the fallen wreckage out the aft windows. Soursop was right. The sea was higher than it should have been by several feet. *Stargazer* was taking on water.

"Get my cleaver!" The cook pointed to the fallen blade just out of his reach.

She shook her head. The cleaver was heavy and razor sharp, but it wasn't an axe. "I can't cut through the beam with that, Soursop. It'd take hours!"

"Not the beam, maybe, but my leg'd come off right enough, and I'd rather walk on a peg than drown!"

"Nobody's going to drown! I've just got to figure out how to get this thing off you, that's all." Regardless of her claim, she grabbed the cleaver and handed it to Soursop. If she couldn't move

274 CHRIS A. JACKSON

the beam, the decision might just come down to amputation or death.

"Promise you'll not let me drown!" He clutched the handle of the cleaver in a white-knuckled grip. He looked ready to cut off his own leg rather than remain trapped as the ship sank.

"I promise, now just relax for a second and let me think!" Celeste reviewed her spells and cringed. She might have fractured the beam with a lightning spell, but she'd cast her last. She doubted if setting it on fire would help, and her lesser spells wouldn't damage the hard oak enough to make a difference. As far as spells on scrolls went, she had a number of them, but nothing that would help here. She considered Snick's jugs of acid, but deemed that too dangerous. Besides, they were stowed forward, and who knew what mayhem raged between here and there.

Something heavy smashed into the door, and Celeste whipped around. Was Anguillithek coming back to finish her off? She plucked a scroll from her harness and turned to face this new threat with a sinking heart. She had almost no spells left, and could barely maneuver in the shattered confines of the cabin. If it was the devil, she feared the fight would be very short indeed.

Vreva gasped as Torius leapt from the crow's nest to the beast's massive claw. She had watched his traverse of the rigging with bated breath, fearing at every moment that he'd lose his footing or grip and crash to the deck. Those acrobatics, however, were nothing compared to leaping onto the creature.

I knew he was crazy, but I didn't think he was that crazy!

She held her breath as he slid down and then swung free to dangle by one hand. He drew his scimitar and swung forward. She forced herself to watch as that blade came down. She could have avoided all of this if she had simply murdered Yami when she had the chance. All of this was her fault. She dared not look away. But the scimitar severed Anguillithek's tentacles instead of Yami's head. The blade fell from Torius's grasp to clatter to the deck, and he snatched Yami by the arm before the boy could fall.

"Torius!" Vreva's brief elation gave way to horror as another of the beast's huge claws came sweeping down. Man and boy fell an instant before the claw scythed across the drowning devil. Anguillithek perished in a spray of gore.

Everyone on deck watched their captain fall. Torius pulled Yami into a protective embrace an instant before they smashed through the main hatch grating and plummeted into the depths of the hold.

Incongruously, Vreva heard a splash.

"Captain!"

At Snick's screech, Vreva scrabbled across the deck and peered down through the broken grating into the hold. As her eyes adjusted to the gloom, she beheld Torius and Yami floating motionless in the water that had flooded the lower hold.

Snick leapt down from the main hold. The water was shoulder-deep on the gnome, and littered with splinters and floating debris. She grabbed her captain, lifting his head from the water.

"Is he alive?" Vreva called down, fearing the worst.

"Think so!" The gnome's voice was heavy with relief. Reaching into her satchel, she pulled out a small bottle. "Took a nasty crack to the head, though. A potion should—"

"Look out!"

Something snatched Vreva off the deck. A scream tore from her lungs, images of being plucked up by the monster and swallowed whole flashing through her mind. Then she hit the deck, and felt a thick arm around her waist. She looked down in relief at the familiar gray-green hue of Grogul's forearm. An instant later, a claw as thick as her waist lanced down right where she had been kneeling, plunging through the shattered grating into the hold. Snick's horrific scream jarred her out of her relief.

"Torius!" Both she and Grogul cried out, scrambling up to look.

"Oh, please no!" Vreva stumbled to the hatch and looked down into a swirling pit of seawater and blood.

Torius fought up through the pit of blackness that was suffocating him. His ears rang, and his head pounded with every beat of his heart. Then fluid filled his mouth. *Drowning! I'm drowning!* But it didn't taste like seawater, and he felt water lapping against his chest, not over his head. *A potion?* He swallowed and gasped for breath. The pain in his head receded and his vision cleared. A concerned gnome face hovered only inches away.

"Snick? What the hell—" Light poured in through a hatch above, pieces of the shattered grating sagging at the edges, and a huge spar thrust down through the hole. They were in *Stargazer's* lower hold, in water. *What the hell happened?*

"Torius?" called a woman's voice from above, one of two faces at the edge of the hatch.

"He's alive!" Snick proclaimed, casting aside an empty potion bottle and trying to lift him up.

"Of course I'm alive! What in Gozreh's name—" Then the spar that had plunged through the hatch moved, and he realized that it wasn't a spar at all. It all came back to him in a flash: the fight with the devil, his rescue of Yami, their fall. *The sea monster . . .*

Torius struggled to his feet, steadying himself as the ship lurched. Water red with blood sloshed against his legs. He lurched forward and saw Yami.

"Gozreh, no!"

Torius collapsed beside the boy. Yami's face was just above the surface of the water, one hand outstretched to grope at the immense claw that impaled him just below the ribs. Torius grasped his hand and Yami looked at him, mouth gaping as if to ask for help, to plead for his life. The captain knew instantly that there was nothing he could do. No potion, no magic would save the boy. Torius had tried to save Yami, and failed.

Yami's eyes fluttered closed and his grip went slack.

The massive claw shifted and rose, and Yami rose with it.

"No!" Torius gripped the boy's hand hard, unwilling to let his body be taken by the beast. But as he stood, his foot found the hole in the planking left by the claw. He fell in up to his knee, water closing over his head for a moment as Yami was lifted. Shattered wood scraped his leg, snagging his pants and boot. "No!" His grip on the boy's hand failed, and he fell back into the water.

Snick was there in a flash, helping him out of the treacherous hole. He stared up in futile desperation as the claw that bore Yami's body cleared the hatch and disappeared. The ship rolled, and the sound of rending wood and shouting sailors fell to an abrupt and surprising silence.

"Captain!" Snick's eyes were on the hole in the deck. Water boiled up, rising visibly, and *Stargazer* heeled with the shifting burden, timbers groaning. "We gotta get outta here!"

"Right!" Torius grabbed the gnome and boosted her up to the upper hold, then scrambled up the ladder. "Snick, see what you can do about the water. We've got to get under way!"

"She's goin' down, Captain! Can't you feel it? Her back's broke!" His engineer wrung out her sodden hat, then cast it aside, her face twisted in misery. She had put more loving care into *Stargazer* than anyone.

"Do what you can, Snick. Slow the leak and buy us as much time as possible while I figure out what to do." As he reached for the ladder, the sailors on deck began to cheer. "Grogul!"

The bosun grabbed Torius's hand and hauled him up over the hatch coaming. Handing over his captain's fallen scimitar, he pointed to the receding form of the sea monster.

"The beastie's movin' off, Captain, but we're in bad shape. Mainmast is a loss. Still got the foremast and some sails, but without a backstay for support, we can't put much stress on her."

"Rig a pair of running backstays! We've got to get as far away from that monster as possible."

As Grogul relayed the orders to Kalli and Dukkol, Torius snapped his sword into its scabbard and looked to the east. The sea monster had backed well away from the ship. It held Yami's mutilated corpse up to one of its many eyes, inspecting the body like a child looking at a broken toy. He could only hope that the beast would lose interest in them entirely. *Maybe it's gotten what it came for.*

To the southwest, *Fury's Crown* approached. Though well short of her full complement of sails, she was on a brisk tack. It wouldn't take them long to close.

But why? He squinted suspiciously. *Why are you still here? Your devil's gone, Yami's gone, so what—"* He glanced behind him at the sea monster, then back to the frigate. *Maybe . . .* A desperate plan began to form in his mind.

"Orders, sir?" Thillion approached, picking his way through the wreckage, looking healthy despite the blood matting his hair.

"Thillion, Grogul, get the crew organized. Snick says *Stargazer's* sinking and there's nothing we can do about it. We're going to take *Fury's Crown.*"

The first mate raised an eyebrow. "Captain, if you think we can storm their deck, you must have hit your head harder than I did."

Torius waved off the elf's skepticism. He knew he could count on Thillion not to balk, and Grogul would walk into a dragon's mouth if his captain gave the order. But Thillion was right about one thing: boarding the frigate would cost too many lives. They'd never manage it by force, but if they could get aboard without losing anyone . . .

"I'm thinking of something slightly more devious, Thillion." Glancing around, he spied Vreva kneeling on the deck, leaning over the splintered bulwarks to stare at the distant sea monster. Tears ran in rivulets down her face. Unfortunately, they didn't have time to mourn. Torius grabbed her by the arm and hauled her to her feet. "Up, Vreva! I need your help to take *Fury's Crown*."

The sorcerer stared at him as if his words meant nothing. "How? I might cause a little mayhem, but I've used up most of my best spells. Maybe Celeste—"

"Celeste!" Torius scanned the deck, sudden panic seizing his heart. How could he not have thought of her earlier? She'd been fighting the devil. *Gods, what if she* . . . He looked aft at the main-mast sticking out of the quarterdeck. "Gozreh's guts, I've got to—"

"I'll get her, Captain." Grogul's huge hand closed on his arm before Torius could dash aft. "You've gotta figure out how to get us aboard that frigate."

"They're bearing down hard, Captain," Thillion said, assessing the frigate through a spyglass.

"I . . ." Torius longed to find Celeste—she could be injured or dying beneath the fallen mast—but he knew Grogul was right. "Get her, Grogul! Thillion, all hands on deck." As Grogul hurried aft, Torius leaned over the main hatch coaming. "Snick! I need you and your people on deck! We're abandoning ship, so grab anything you think we'll need."

"Abandoning ship?" Her voice sounded incredulous. "Where we goin'?"

"There's only one place *to* go, Snick. We're taking *Fury's Crown!*"

The gnome whooped in delight and started snapping orders to the ballista crews, confirming in Torius's mind that taking a Chelish warship with a bedraggled crew of pirates was completely insane. If Snick liked it, the plan had to be crazy.

Vreva grasped his arm. She wiped away her tears, her face set in grim determination. "What are you planning, Torius?"

"I'm going to offer them a deal: I give them what they want if they take us aboard."

"But . . ." Vreva's eyebrows shot up. "You think they'll fall for the same trick *twice*? Captain Lance is no fool."

"Our mission is accomplished, but they don't know that! All we've got to do now is survive! They wouldn't be sailing over here if they didn't think Yami was still alive. That thing," he jerked a thumb toward the sea monster, "is far enough so they can't get a good look at what it's holding, if it hasn't already . . . you know."

Vreva winced. She knew what he meant all too well. "Fine."

"We have to do this right. You can bet they have spyglasses on us right now. If you just transform into Yami, they'll see." He glanced around at the shambles of the deck. "Step into the stern-castle with Thillion. Come out as Yami being held captive."

"Good. Okay." Vreva went aft with the elf, and emerged a moment later looking exactly like Yami, right down to the boy's broken arm. "How do I look?"

"Perfect." Torius looked around at his amassed crew, gauging their stoicism. He knew they would fight to the death for him, but this ruse would have to be played carefully, or they were all dead.

"Stargazers, our ship is lost! Snick says her back's broken. She won't make it to shore, even if that beast and the Chelish let us sail away, which they won't." Drawing his scimitar, he pulled Vreva close and held the edge to her throat, making sure that they were visible to the approaching Chelish ship. "This ruse should get us aboard, but I need everyone to play this close to the vest. We're pirates desperate to make a deal. I want them to underestimate us, to think we can't put up much of a fight. We're going to take that ship! They're not going to hand it over without a fight, but surprise is worth more than their numbers and their broadside. Their devil and their caster are dead, so it's steel against steel."

"We're with you, Captain!" Snick piped as she popped up from the hold, wearing a bulging satchel over her shoulder. She shook the water from her hair and grinned like a maniac.

Torius nodded as the crew echoed the gnome's words. *We might just pull this off.* His crew certainly looked like a bunch of undisciplined pirates, bloodied and beaten into desperation.

"Good, now everyone be ready. When I give the word, we take them!" Up on the quarterdeck, he saw Windy Kate at the helm. "Windy, put her bow into the wind and tie off the wheel!"

"Aye, sir!" She hauled the wheel over, and *Stargazer* answered sluggishly.

The ship was perilously low in the water and getting lower by the minute, waves lapping at her ballista ports. The foremast groaned with the strain of rounding into the wind. The jury-rigged backstays were the only thing keeping the foremast upright. *Stargazer* lost speed until she lay dead in the water, waiting for the approaching frigate.

Torius spoke low into Vreva's ear. "Do you have anything else that might give us an edge?"

"I'll charm their captain when we get close. That should get us aboard. Then I unleash my secret weapon." She turned her head toward the nearby coiled lines, and Mathias came trundling out, his fur sticking up as if he'd been run through a clothes wringer.

"Mathias? What can he do?"

As the cat rubbed up against Vreva's leg, the sorcerer murmured softly and Mathias vanished. "No time to explain, Torius. Just get us close to the captain." Vreva nudged him with her elbow. "Play the brigand. You know, be yourself."

"Nice."

19

A Deadly Bluff

Celeste tensed as the cabin door gave way, splitting down its length. Slithering between the trapped Soursop and the danger, she readied her scroll, considering the wisdom of conjuring a mass of sticky spider webs in the confines of the cabin. A muscular arm thrust through the splintered door and wrenched half of it away. The hand sported fingers, not tentacles, which allayed her fears slightly, then Grogul's worried visage poked through the gap.

"Miss Celeste?" His eyes fixed on her and widened. "Miss Celeste! You're . . . you're *me!*"

She stowed her scroll and breathed a sigh of relief. "I needed arms, and yours were the strongest I knew of. Come on! I need your help to get this beam off of Soursop!"

"I don't mind you takin' my form, Miss Celeste." The half-orc kicked the remains of the door against the fallen wreckage, and widened the gap enough to squeeze through. "But couldn't you have magicked up some clothes, too? It's a little embarrassing!"

"Sorry. The spell doesn't come with clothes, and I was in a hurry." She gestured to the beam pinning Soursop to the deck. "Come on, help me lift this."

"Just don't go on deck like that!" He wrapped his arms around the beam and nodded. "Snick'd never let me hear the end of it."

"Just lift!"

They grasped the fallen beam and strained together, but even with the both of them and Soursop, the beam remained in place.

"No good! It's wedged tight." Grogul limbered up his axe. "I'll have to cut through it."

"Well, at least it wasn't just me." Celeste backed away as the bosun attacked the beam. Chips flew, but the weapon wasn't a woodsman's tool. The blade was made to cleave flesh, not oak, and the going was slow. Soursop winced as the splinter through his leg quivered with each stroke.

"Best grab whatever you can't leave behind," Grogul said between strokes. "Ship's goin' down."

"Sinking?" His words hit her like a kick in the stomach. Celeste looked around the cabin that had been her home for so many years. The thought of never sharing this space again with Torius broke her heart.

"Nothin' we can do. Captain's got a plan."

"What kind of plan?" She wasn't sure whether to be heartened or dismayed by the prospect of one of Torius's plans.

"He wants to take the frigate before that monster comes back to finish us!"

"Monster? Anguillithek?"

"Nah, the devil's dead. This one was summoned by the kid."

"Yami summoned a monster? What *is* it?" Canceling her transformation spell, Celeste rebuckled her harness and slithered to the shattered cabinet. Snatching up an old knapsack, she quickly tied it to her harness and started stuffing it with scrolls and bottles from her stash of magical supplies.

"Dunno what you call it. Big bug of some kind. *Really* big." With a final crack, the beam fractured, and Grogul hung his axe back on his belt. "We gotta hurry, though."

Wrapping his arms around one end of the beam, Grogul set his legs and heaved. Soursop yelled in pain as the splinter wrenched free of his leg, but managed to squirm free. Grogul let the beam fall, then hauled Soursop to his feet, looking dubiously at the cook's bleeding leg.

"Any more potions in there, Miss Celeste?"

"Yes, but no healing ones. Snick should have some." The ship lurched, and she heard shouting from forward. She tried to hasten her packing, but the cabinetry had been reduced to kindling by her fight with the devil. Some of the scrolls and bottles were buried in wreckage, and some were torn or shattered. "Go!"

"Gotta stop that bleeding first!" Grogul drew one of his kukri and sliced Soursop's pant leg up to the bleeding wound. He split the cloth and tied it around the cook's thigh in a makeshift bandage. "Good enough for now. Come on." He put Soursop's arm over his shoulders, and the two worked their way through the gap in the shattered door.

"Right behind you." Celeste slithered for the door, but turned to cast one final glance upon her home, now destroyed. With a jolt, she remembered her observation of Eox the Dead in the Stargazer constellation. The prophecy of death was coming true. *Stargazer* was dying.

Her vision blurred with tears. They'd had so many happy moments here: the first time she and Torius kissed, the first time she transformed into human shape so they could make love. She surprised herself with a laugh, recalling her clumsy, fumbling attempt to manipulate arms and legs. She'd been so awkward, and he had been so gentle.

Torius . . .

Celeste realized that there was one more thing she had to rescue from the wreckage. She slithered to the shattered chart table and rooted through the splinters until she found her silver sextant. The sextant had been a gift from Torius, and she wasn't about to leave without it. She stuffed the treasured instrument into her pack and turned back toward the door.

Something hit the ship so hard that Celeste was flung across the cabin. She curled protectively around her pack as the deck overhead collapsed in an avalanche of shattered timbers. Pain lanced through her head, and her world went dark.

Fury's Crown bore down on *Stargazer*, then suddenly turned to windward, expertly backfilling the sails to stop the ship only a short stone's throw away. *Damn, they're good.* It was the most impressive act of nautical intimidation Torius had ever seen.

"Give us the boy or we sink your ship!" Captain Lance stood on the frigate's quarterdeck looking all too ready to carry out her threat. The tips of ballista bolts nosed out of the frigate's ports, and archers stood on the charred remnants of the crow's nests. Marines stood in ranks near the rail, ready to board while the rest of the crew still labored to replace burned canvas.

Torius pressed the edge of his scimitar to Vreva's throat. "My ship's already sinking, Captain, and I don't intend to sink with it. If you want the boy, you need to strike a deal with us!"

"We don't deal with pirates!" Lance shouted back.

"Then you don't get your weapon!"

Vreva muttered under her breath, hopefully casting her charm spell on the captain, then called out in an imitation of Yami's voice. "Please don't let them kill me!" The likeness was surprisingly good.

"Listen to him, Captain. We can both benefit from this. Take my people aboard your ship and put us ashore anywhere you like! Then you get the boy back. We have our lives, you have your weapon. Everyone wins! That's the deal! Refuse and the boy dies. Then you get to explain to your superiors what happened here, and why you *failed!*"

"Please, Captain!" Vreva called again. "I'll do anything you want! Just don't let them kill me!"

Torius watched Captain Lance closely. Her brow furrowed, and her knuckles whitened on the hilt of her sword. Was Vreva's spell working?

"Captain!" Lacy Jane's voice sounded convincingly panicked. "The sea monster's coming back!"

Torius glanced over his shoulder at the approaching mountainous wave, and thought that maybe Lacy's panic wasn't feigned. "We don't have time to argue, Captain! Decide now, or we all die!"

Captain Lance looked at Yami, then fixed her gaze on Torius, her eyes hard as chips of obsidian. "Very well. But I warn you, Captain: if you betray your word—if your crew tries *anything*—we'll cut you down!"

"Grapples!" an officer ordered, and the Chelish sailors threw their heavy hooks across the gap.

"Stargazers, secure those lines and haul!"

The pirates complied, setting the grapples and hauling hard. The gap between the two ships narrowed until the two hulls crunched together, rocking the smaller brigantine.

Stargazer's deck was now much lower than the frigate's. Consequently, Torius and his crew were staring right down the shafts of the frigate's ballistae. At this range, a broadside would rip through the Stargazers like a sword through parchment, killing dozens. Torius held his breath, praying that he'd gauged Captain Lance correctly.

"Boarding nets over the side!" Lance glared at Torius, pointing at him with her sword. "You crew will sheath their weapons before they board my ship! I see one sword out of a scabbard, and that pirate dies!"

"Except for the one at Yami's throat, Captain!" Torius brandished his scimitar and returned it to Vreva's neck. "I'm not about to give you a chance to break your word and shoot me down."

"All right, but my order stands! Weapons away!"

"Stargazers, go! Stow your weapons. Smartly now!" He hung back, not trusting the Chelish captain to keep her word. If he boarded first with Vreva, they might try to take Yami and strand his crew.

"Make room for them!" The Chelish marines and sailors backed away from the rail.

The door to the sterncastle slammed, and Grogul shouted, "Come on, we're boarding!"

Torius breathed easier. He knew he could trust his bosun to get Celeste. He longed to turn, if only to catch her eye, but he dared not look away from Lance.

The Stargazers swarmed up the cargo nets. Snick and her ballista crews hauled chests and bags with them, and Grogul helped an obviously injured Soursop climb the cargo net. But no Celeste.

Of course! She's disguised as a sailor. Torius suppressed a grin. *They're in for a surprise when she transforms into a naga right in front of them.*

"Come aboard, Captain, before the creature strikes!"

Torius turned to see the sea monster rising from the brine, looming over poor *Stargazer*, its massive claws poised to strike. Slamming his sword into its sheath, he handed Vreva up to Grogul, who put his axe to their hostage's neck. Torius leapt the narrow gap to the boarding net just as a rending crash sounded behind him. *Stargazer* yawed, her tortured timbers groaning like a dying man's last agonized gasp. Torius clambered up the net and vaulted over the rail, only then daring to look back at his ship.

"Gozreh's guts."

The beast lunged at the sterncastle, smashing through the stout timbers as if they were wicker. Its huge claws lanced down, peeling back sections of the quarterdeck while the smaller claws rooted down through the gaping holes, a predator feasting on its fallen prey. The grappling lines snapped taut as *Stargazer* was born down by the monster's weight, several parting under the strain.

"Cast off and bear away!" Captain Lance ordered. Her sailors hurried to comply, slashing the grappling lines and hauling on the sheets to swing the towering sails to draw. *Fury's Crown* heeled with the billowing canvas and bore away.

Torius stood at the rail, his knuckles white on the polished wood, eyes fixed upon the sight of his ship being destroyed. *Stargazer* groaned as the creature ravaged the aft portion of the ship. The foreshortened mainmast snapped, toppling aft, and water flooded through the scuppers to cover the deck. Torius had seen ships die before, but never his own. *Stargazer* was the only vessel he'd ever called home, the only ship he'd ever loved.

Love . . . At least all the people he loved were safe.

The captain of the dying *Stargazer* turned away and scanned his bedraggled and bloody crew, but didn't find the face he was searching for. He looked again, but couldn't spot Celeste in any of her familiar guises. He'd assumed she'd taken on the form she used in Ostenso, but he didn't see Cammy's face anywhere.

"Where's Celeste?" he asked Grogul.

"She was right behind me when we left your cabin." The bosun looked around in shock. "Wasn't she?"

"Celeste?" Torius called out, panic gripping his gut. "Celeste! Sing out!"

No answer. A cold hand gripped Torius's heart, and he looked back to his sinking ship. *Gozreh, please, no!*

"Who's Celeste?" Captain Lance asked.

"The woman I love! She's still aboard *Stargazer!*" Torius couldn't breathe, couldn't think. He had to get Celeste back! Timbers cracked, and *Stargazer* groaned in death. He imagined her trapped below, struggling to escape while that thing ripped the ship apart looking for something to eat. He had to give her a chance. "You've got to fire on that creature to draw it off and give her time to escape!"

"I'll do nothing of the kind!"

"You *will!*" Torius drew his scimitar and put the point against Vreva's throat. "You'll fire on that beast, or I'll kill your precious weapon right here and now!"

"Do that, Captain, and you're all dead!" At her signal, her marines drew their swords. "You're not that crazy."

"Don't *bet* on that!" Torius kept the sword poised, unsure of what he could do to force the captain's hand, but absolutely sure that he wouldn't abandon Celeste. *She's still alive. She* has *to be!*

"Please, Captain!" Vreva-as-Yami pleaded, struggling in Grogul's grasp. "He's mad! He'll do it!"

Lance stared at Yami, her resolve wavering under the force of Vreva's magic. "Damned bloody-handed pirates!"

"Guilty as charged, Captain. Now bring your ship about and fire on that monster, or you'll see just how bloody we can get!"

Muscles writhed at the captain's jaw, but finally she gave the order. "Bring her about and prepare for a port broadside as soon as we have a shot." She shouted to the helmsman. "Mister Webley, keep your distance from that thing! Once we distract it, bear off."

"Aye, Captain."

Orders rang across the deck, and the crew responded, the sailors on deck scrambling aloft or hauling on lines. *Fury's Crown* came about smoothly. The frigate handled remarkably well for her size, but even so, by the time her port side faced the monster, the beast had ripped up half of *Stargazer*'s quarterdeck, rooting inside like an anteater taking apart a termite mound. Water stood a foot deep over the middeck. *Stargazer* was foundering.

"Fire!" the ballista captain bellowed, and a dozen ballistae cracked in perfect unison.

20

Death of the Stargazer

Seawater lapped against Celeste's cheek, snapping her from unconsciousness. She jerked up, cracking her head on a fallen beam—and if the pain lancing through her skull was any indication, in exactly the spot where it had knocked her insensate. Her senses reeled, and for a moment she saw everything doubled.

"Stars and heavens!" Blinking away her double vision, Celeste took in her surroundings.

She didn't find anything at all encouraging. The entire quarter-deck had collapsed, burying her beneath a veritable landslide of shattered timber. She spied gaps above, but nothing near large enough for her to slither through. Then there was the seawater sloshing across the cabin sole. She had no idea how long she'd been out cold, but she no longer heard any voices from outside. All she could hear was the rending crash of broken planks and groaning timbers. A sharp tremor reverberated through the ship, galvanizing her to action. She had to get out before the sea claimed *Stargazer,* and her with it.

Celeste moved her long, sinuous body, assessing her condition. Fortunately, no bones felt broken, and none of the splintered timbers had pierced her scales. She was, however, badly bruised for her entire length. Hissing in pain, she slithered out from under the shattered wood into a space barely large enough for her to coil. She flipped open the knapsack and picked though the contents. *There!* She had no healing potions left, but this would do for now. Celeste floated a bottle out of the pack, popped the cork, and quaffed its contents. Immediately, her fatigue and weakness ebbed away like a bad dream. She still ached, but at least she no longer felt like fainting.

Now to get the hell out of here.

Unfortunately, she had no spells to move the broken timbers out of her way or teleport her to safety. Through the wreckage aft, she glimpsed the shattered stern gallery windows. The opening was large enough for her to get through, but a ton of fractured wood filled the space between her and the potential exit. The crack and crash of breaking wood from forward recalled to her Grogul's mention of a monster. The last thing she wanted was to meet up with whatever it was. *Got to try aft, then.* The deck lurched, and more water flooded up beneath her. There was no time to waste.

Celeste picked the widest aperture she could see and started to slither through. Immediately, her pack got hung up. Usually, she had no problem snaking her way through tight places. She tried again to shove through, but it was no use. The pack kept getting snagged on a splintered timber. She wiggled backward until she was once again in the open space.

"Blasted contrivance!" She unbuckled the harness and the pack dropped to the deck. With all of the potions, scrolls, and instruments, it was too heavy for her to lift with magic. "I'll be damned if I'm leaving it behind!" She gripped the straps in her teeth and tried again to slither through the gap. It was a tight squeeze, but she might make it.

A horrendous crash sounded from behind her, shivering the timbers of the maze she was negotiating. Thankfully, they didn't collapse to crush her. As she struggled forward, a cool breeze blew through the wreckage. Sunlight slanted in, warming her tail.

Celeste hazarded a glance back, and immediately regretted it. With a roar of shattering timber, a vast claw tore away the cabin's forward bulkhead, and through the widening gap, an eerie blue eye peered in at her.

By the stars! Celeste had no idea what the creature was, and no desire for a closer look. With a surge of adrenaline, she slithered forward, but her harness caught on a beam and halted her progress. Something scraped along her tail, and she glanced back again. A smaller claw raked at her, its tip unable to pierce her tough scales. A basso growl reverberated through the hull, and the creature lurched forward, tearing through the deck with renewed vigor.

No! Celeste squirmed frantically as the smaller claw lanced down, missing her by only inches. Once again, the blue eye peered in at her, unnerving her with its scrutiny. Celeste mumbled a spell around the pack in her teeth, sending a flight of magical projectiles streaking toward it. The motes of energy plunged into their target, darkening the blue orb. The monster reared back.

Celeste took the opportunity to remove the harness from the pack. With renewed energy, she slithered on, trying to keep her head above the ever-rising water. The demolished stern windows were just ahead. She pressed forward, gritting her teeth against the pack's leather strap as sharp splinters scored her bruised scales.

I can make it. I can get out!

A deep howl shook the ship, and the harsh cracking renewed with such a ferocity that Celeste could barely hear herself think. Her stomach lurched as the stern of the ship dipped, and the sea poured in through the windows. Her escape was flooded.

No, no, no! Celeste gasped in a deep breath before the water surged over her head.

She thrashed, trying to get above the surface, and cracked her head again. Stars exploded in her sight, and a vision flashed in her mind. *Stars . . .* Eox, planet of the dead, among the shining constellation of the Stargazer, the sign of her birth. She had thought the significance clear, that the alignment referred to the death of their beloved ship. Now she thought that she might have been mistaken.

My prophecy . . . my death.

Vreva watched the volley of ballista bolts streak toward the towering monster. Several struck its thick armor, and a few plunged deep into its fatty underside. The barrage got the beast's attention, just as Torius had hoped. Unfortunately, instead of driving it off or luring it away from *Stargazer*, the attack seemed only to provoke it. The creature turned its attention toward *Fury's Crown* and emitted a gut-wrenching howl. Heaving its huge body forward, the beast lurched over *Stargazer*, forcing the damaged ship even further down into the sea.

The clatter of a scimitar hitting the deck broke Vreva's fixation upon the spectacle.

"Celeste!" Torius vaulted to the rail.

"Torius, don't!" Vreva warned.

Kalli echoed her sentiment. "Captain! No! I'll get her!" The gillman pulled her captain off the railing and dove into the sea, vanishing beneath the waves.

Unfortunately, Vreva's concern for Torius also caught the attention of Captain Lance. "What the devil . . ."

Vreva realized she'd blown her disguise. Yami was supposed to be terrified of the pirates, and she'd just shown concern.

The captain's confusion turned to narrow-eyed suspicion. "I don't know what deception you're playing at, but I'll have none of it! All hands, make all sail. We're getting away from this monster!"

Torius flicked his dropped sword up with his toe and caught it by the hilt, his face as grim as Vreva had ever seen it. "You'll turn this ship back, Captain. Right *now*!"

"I will *not*!" Lance drew her sword. "Furies, stand ready!"

The marines snapped to formation, shoulder to shoulder and bristling with steel. The Stargazers drew their own weapons.

With most of the Chelish sailors swarming over the rigging, piling on more canvas, the opposing forces on deck were nearly equal. Torius and Captain Lance squared off.

It was time for a distraction. Vreva had no idea where her familiar was, but hoped he was ready. "Mathias," Vreva said in their secret language, "now!"

Captain Lance screamed as Mathias materialized on her face, his claws raking bloody tracks across her cheeks. Grasping the cat, she peeled him away and flung him high over Vreva's head.

"Mathias!"

Behind her, Grogul reached up and snatched the flying feline by the scruff. "Got him!"

What did I say about no catapults? Mathias howled as Grogul dropped him to the deck. He scurried away in a panic.

Vreva sighed in relief. Not only was her familiar safe, but Mathias had had the presence of mind not to scratch Grogul with his poisoned claws.

Captain Lance was not so fortunate. The Chelish captain collapsed to her knees, her hands clutching her chest as her heart succumbed to the deadly toxin. Gaping in surprise, she toppled forward.

The crew of *Fury's Crown* stared at their fallen captain in shock.

That was all the distraction Vreva needed. She plucked two of the tiny golden charms from the bracelet she'd recovered from the dead witch, Keah. Uttering the command word, she cast the charms to the deck. As two full-sized lions sprang up from the gold figurines, Vreva cast another spell on herself and vanished from sight.

"Kill the Chelish!" she ordered the summoned lions, and dashed toward the quarterdeck as mayhem erupted behind her.

I guess the little furball's not completely useless after all, Torius thought, as Captain Lance toppled to the deck. Then he staggered back as two huge lions sprang up from nowhere. When he asked Vreva if she could come up with a surprise, he had expected some sleight of hand or illusion, but the lions looked quite real. All eyes were on the huge felines as Vreva vanished and shouted her order. With a roar that shook the deck, the beasts leapt forward, scattering Chelish marines.

Now time for our own surprise. "Snick! Now!"

"Bombs away!" the gnome shrilled with glee as she and her ballista crews hurled the ceramic warheads they'd smuggled aboard.

Gozreh, please don't let those be incendiaries! To Torius's relief, the shattered warheads spewed sticky resin all over the deck, gluing the marines' boots to the planks.

"Stargazers!" Torius bellowed, sending his pirates surging forward. "Thillion, aloft! Grogul, with me to the quarterdeck!"

"Aye, sir!" The elf scrambled up the ratlines.

As the Stargazers clashed with the immobilized marines, Vreva's lions ravaged the free, throwing the organized Chelish lines into chaos. Overhead, Chelish sailors called out in alarm, scrambling down to join the fray. Bolts and arrows whistled past, some sheathing themselves in flesh. Torius parried a sword stroke and slashed the marine's wrist. The man didn't even have time to yelp before Grogul's axe split him from collar to crotch. They forced their way aft, skirting the ravening lions toward the quarterdeck stairs.

"Pikes and archers!" bellowed a Chelish officer, but his command died in a scream as one of the lions took him down.

The stair to the quarterdeck was blocked by a small knot of sailors led by a nervous midshipman. Torius and Grogul hit them like a battering ram. Torius took a deep cut to his left arm, but made the sailor pay with his lifeblood. Ducking under another stroke, he barreled into the man, his shoulder to the sailor's midriff. The captain winced as the sailor bashed him between the shoulders with the pommel of his sword. He slammed the man against the sterncastle wall and planted his fighting dagger hilt-deep in the sailor's groin.

Whirling to face his next opponent, he found Grogul standing among three sailors sprawled in a welter of blood. The terrified midshipman scrabbled back, his hand clenching the hilt of a broken cutlass. The weapon's blade stood out from Grogul's thigh. With a snarl, the half-orc wrenched free the bloody blade and cast it aside. Eyes filled with murder, and knuckles white on the haft of his axe, Grogul took a menacing step toward the young officer.

"Grogul! Come on!" Torius grabbed his bosun's arm. "No time! We have to take the helm!"

"Aye, sir!" Grogul spat on the deck at the midshipman's feet and followed his captain.

As they climbed the stairs to the quarterdeck, Torius cast a glance at *Stargazer*, and his heart surged into his throat. The vast weight of the beast had pushed all but the bowsprit underwater.

"Celeste . . ."

"Kalli'll get her out. Come on!" Grogul's huge hand propelled him up the steps. "We can't get her unless we take the helm!"

Torius knew Grogul was right. *Focus! Take the helm, take the ship, evade that bloody great monster, and sail back to pick up Celeste and Kalli. Simple!* He flung another glance at his foundering ship and gritted his teeth in determination. *Hang on, love. I'm coming!*

They charged up the stairs, but then skidded to a halt. Six marines stood in a line before the wheel, crossbows leveled and ready to fire.

"Maybe this wasn't such a good plan after all," Grogul muttered.

"You think?"

21

Drowning Time

Constellations of flotsam floated around Celeste like some bizarre dream, a three-dimensional ballet of torn charts, clothing, blankets, broken wood, and a nebula of feathers from a shredded pillow swirling in the currents. Bits of her life hung shattered around her, sinking into darkness, fading like the dwindling breath in her lungs.

Out! I've got to get out!

Light shone beyond the gaping stern windows, tantalizingly close. Celeste surged forward, but the blasted pack hung up again. She tried dislodging it with a few jerks, to no avail. *Leave it!* She let go, looking for some way past it, but she'd already chosen the only path wide enough to let her through. The rest were too narrow, even if she transformed into Twilp Farfan. She wriggled back, looking for another way. *Any way but back into the jaws of that monster!* Debris shifted around her with the surging water, planks pinching her like the jaws of a vise.

Damn it! Desperate, she writhed free, momentarily disoriented. The creaks and pops of tortured timbers vibrated through the water from behind her. Visions of the monster's staring blue eye and those rending claws came back to her. *Any direction but back! Maybe the skylight.*

Thanking the stars for her flexibility, Celeste bent backward and worked her way up. The shattered skylight hove into view through the morass of wreckage.

Too dark outside! Why is it dark?

Her heart pounded in panic as she realized that the opening was covered by the rippling black canvas of a fallen sail. A heavy spar lay fore and aft across the skylight beneath the sail, but there was a gap. *The spar should float! Maybe I can push it aside and worm my way out from under the sail.* She wriggled between the casement and the spar, knives of broken glass scraping against her scales. Wedging her body through as far as she could, she pushed. Glass raked her, salt water stinging in the scratches, but the spar wouldn't move.

Need air! Got to breathe! She pushed harder, screaming in frustration, wasting precious air in a stream of bubbles. *I'm not a damned sea snake!* She writhed backward again, back down into the destroyed cabin, blood eddying in the water around her. She forced the panic down

Think Celeste! What about magic? The only spell she had left that could be remotely useful was her transformation spell, but changing into a human wouldn't help her. Even if she changed into a gillman, she wouldn't be able to breathe underwater. The spell changed her physical form, but it wasn't advanced enough to give her functional gills.

Gills . . . A transformation might not give her gills, but there was another spell that would let her breathe underwater. *That's it!*

Celeste slithered back through the maze of debris and found her pack, her lungs burning for air. *Please, let it be here!* She flipped open the pack with her magic and peered in. She had bought dozens of scrolls and potions in Almas, determined to be prepared for any need. Now she had plenty of need, and she couldn't find the right scroll. She knew she'd bought a scroll some time ago that would save her life now, but couldn't remember if she'd put it in the pack. *Please don't let it be one of the ones that were torn to shreds!* Rifling through the scrolls, she discarded one after another until the water around her was littered with floating parchment.

Celeste coughed reflexively, her lungs insisting that she take a breath. She bit down hard, knowing that if she opened her mouth she wouldn't be able to resist inhaling. Her ears ached as the ship sank deeper, the pressure building until she thought her head would implode. Squinting, she tried to read the next scroll, but couldn't make out the letters. Was it getting darker, or was her vision failing from a lack of air?

No! I can't die like this! I won't!

Through the pounding in her ears, she wondered how many drowning sailors had thought that very thing as the sea closed over their heads forever. *Thousands? Millions? Do their bones litter the sea floor as thick as stars in the sky? Will mine join them?*

The inscription on the scroll before her blurred, and the muscles of her jaw relaxed. She coughed again, bubbles tickling her face as they floated up, feeling like the caress of Torius's fingers. Her lungs screamed for air, an inescapable urge. *One breath . . . Just one breath . . .*

Her vision swam in the fading light. All she wanted was to close her eyes and breathe. *I'm sorry, Torius.* Celeste pictured her lover's face, that rakish grin that she so loved. She felt his fingers clutch her hair, his lips urgent on her mouth. She blinked, and gazed one last time into his bright violet eyes.

Wait! Torius has brown eyes. Who's kissing me?

Air flooded into Celeste's lungs—the kiss of life. Gasping, the naga drew in all the breath Kalli could give her. Her vision cleared, and with it, her thoughts. *The scroll!*

Celeste snatched up the scroll she had been trying to decipher, the arcane inscription now clear. *Yes!* The spell burst from her mouth in a torrent of bubbles, and the urge to draw breath immediately eased.

Smiling triumphantly at Kalli, she mouthed, "Thank you!"

The gillman grinned in response. Gesturing for Celeste to follow her, she turned and started toward the forward portion of the ship.

Celeste tugged on the woman's shirt with her magic, shaking her head wildly when Kalli looked back. "The monster," she mouthed. The gillman shook her head and pointed through the tangle of crushed wood. The gaping hole where the monster had torn into the cabin was clear. The huge beast was gone.

Well, that's convenient.

Feeling foolish, Celeste gathered up her scrolls and stuffed them back into her pack, taking the time to disentangle the bothersome straps before following the gillman out into the open sea. The surface shimmered overhead, startlingly far away. Through the crystal-clear water, she saw the sea monster swimming away from them, its vast bulk propelled by thrashing rows of swimmerets the size of galley oars. Below them, *Stargazer* sank into the depths, broken and torn. The celestial prophecy had come true, but not, thankfully, as Celeste had dreaded.

Kalli gestured again and headed toward the surface, swimming through the water with the ease of a bird soaring on the wind. Celeste undulated after her, lagging behind her impressive pace. Envying the gillman's effortless grace, she had a revelation and cast her transformation spell.

If the situation had been any less dire, Celeste would have laughed at the startled look on Kalli's face when they broke the surface as twins. She cast her gaze around the choppy sea strewn with flotsam and worked her arms through the pack's straps. "What happened? Where's Torius?"

"Aboard *Fury's Crown* with the rest of the crew." Kalli pointed to the pyramid of sails that marked the ship. "He has a plan to take the ship."

So that's his plan. Celeste squinted, and even from her poor vantage she could see a battle raging on the frigate, and in between them the foaming wake of the sea monster.

"What *is* that thing?"

"A charybdis. The biggest one I've ever seen." Kalli frowned. "Lucky it didn't gobble you up. Some . . . well, some weren't so lucky."

Celeste felt a pang of guilt that she had survived while others had not, but then realized that the matter wasn't decided yet. She was, after all, swimming miles from shore near a monster that ate entire ships. Unfortunately, she could come up with no good strategy for not being gobbled up. But if Kalli had seen one of these beasts before, maybe she knew how to evade them.

"So, what do we do?"

"For now, we swim *that* way." Kalli pointed away from the ship.

"But we've got to get to the ship! Torius—"

"The captain can handle himself. Charybdises are always hungry, and right now we're at the top of the menu! If the captain takes the frigate, he'll come back for us, but we don't want to be here if the monster decides to turn around!"

Celeste wanted to argue, but saw the logic. "I hope you're right!"

They raced away, dashing through the choppy sea like a pair of dolphins fleeing a shark.

Vreva crept up the stairs to the quarterdeck as the battle broke out behind her. She was no fighter, but she knew Torius would need to capture the helm in order to take the ship. She could help him with that. At the top of the steps, however, she paused. Six Chelish marines stood before the binnacle with crossbows at the ready, guarding the helmsman. *This might be harder than I thought.*

She readied her crossbow and drew a dagger, creeping along the railing and skirting behind the opposing force. Her flame spell hadn't done as much damage here as she hoped, scorching instead of incinerating, but it had left an inconvenient layer of soot. She stepped carefully, knowing that mysteriously appearing footprints could give her away despite her invisibility. Luckily, the marines kept their eyes and weapons trained on the stairs to the middeck.

They weren't expecting stealth, not with a crew of pirates raging over their ship.

Vreva studied the helmsman as she crept up behind him, picking a spot for her dagger just above the collar of his leather corslet. Vreva drew back for the lethal thrust, and bit her lip. It wasn't like she had never killed in cold blood before, but slavers and the heat of battle were one thing. Poor saps like a helmsman just doing his job felt like murder.

Suddenly Torius and Grogul pelted up the steps onto the quarterdeck, bloody blades in hand. The Chelish started to raise their crossbows. There was no time to debate morality.

Stupid conscience! Vreva reversed her dagger and brought the pommel down hard on the back of the helmsman's head. He collapsed like a poleaxed steer. Stepping over his body, she thrust her dagger into the binnacle to free a hand, grasped the enormous wheel, and hauled it over with all her strength.

The frigate yawed hard to port quicker than she expected, the deck tilting beneath her feet. Overhead, sails snapped in the wind, spars swung and sailors cried out in alarm. The marines on the quarterdeck stumbled, two of their weapons discharging harmlessly over Torius's head.

"Webley! What in the—" One of the marines glanced back over his shoulder, eyes widening as he saw Vreva standing behind the wheel. His countenance shifted from surprise to rage, and he brought his crossbow around.

Vreva shot him in the throat.

The man's fingers clutched at the small bolt in his neck, his mouth gaping in shock, but the poison stopped his heart before he could pull it free. His eyes glazed over, his legs folded, and his crossbow clattered to the deck.

The next marine in the formation stared down in surprise at her fallen comrade, but then caught sight of Vreva. Without a moment's hesitation, the woman brought her crossbow to bear and squeezed the trigger.

Vreva ducked behind the wheel, but the bolt grazed her cheek like the lash of a whip. She dropped her crossbow and reached for her dagger as the marine drew her sword and charged. With a sickening crunch, the marine's ferocious snarl drooped and she pitched facedown on the deck, a handaxe lodged in the back of her skull.

Thank you, Grogul. Vreva hauled herself upright on the spokes of the wheel just in time to see Torius and his bosun engage the surviving marines.

The pirate captain parried and slashed with dagger and scimitar in a deadly whirlwind of steel. Grogul employed a more direct approach, slamming his shoulder into one opponent hard enough to bowl the man backward into the binnacle. Vreva stabbed the reeling marine in the back of the neck, and he went down. The other ducked under a sweeping stroke of the bosun's axe and thrust his sword through the half-orc's shoulder, but the agile move did him little good. Grogul ignored the injury and drove a kick into the man's groin. As his opponent folded over, the half-orc brought his axe down on the back of the man's head. He turned to help his captain, but Torius's two foes lay sprawled in spreading pools of blood.

Vreva swallowed hard as Grogul wrenched the sword from his shoulder without flinching. She fingered the shallow gash in her cheek and felt suddenly dizzy. *An inch to the right . . .*

Torius dashed forward with a snarl on his face. "Why the *hell* did you heave to?"

"Why did I *what*?" Vreva clung to the wheel, trying to banish the dizziness by sheer force of will.

"You hove the ship to." Torius pointed aloft at the fluttering sails as if that should mean something to her. The bow pointed into the wind, and they seemed to have come to a stop. "We're dead in the water!"

"I haven't the foggiest idea what you're talking about." Vreva sheathed her dagger and picked up her hand crossbow. "I just turned the wheel. I was trying to save your *life*!"

"And you did, but—"

"Captain!" Lacy Jane pounded up the stairs onto the quarterdeck and pointed off the port bow. "Look!"

The sea monster surged toward them, gaining fast now that they weren't moving.

Vreva cringed. "And apparently, I may have killed us."

"No! Beyond the bloody monster!" Lacy pointed. "In the *water*!"

A slick of flotsam marked *Stargazer*'s grave like a grim memorial. Vreva squinted and caught sight of two shapes splashing beyond the wreckage. "Kalli and Celeste!"

"Thank Gozreh!" The relief in the captain's voice spoke volumes.

"Thank your bosun's mate, Captain!" Lacy corrected. "Now we've got to pick them up."

"We've got to get away from this monster first!" Torius glared aloft. "Keep an eye on them, Lacy. Grogul, hard astarboard. Get us underway."

Vreva stepped back from the wheel as Grogul grabbed the spokes. He spun it to starboard, looked up at the flapping sails, and muttered a curse. The ship remained motionless with her bow pointing into the wind.

"No steerage! The ship's in irons, Captain! We need to cross sheet the headsails to get her moving."

"There's still a battle going on!" Torius brandished his bloody scimitar and grimaced. "How the hell do we convince the Chelish to stop trying to kill us and help?"

*Is he *kidding*?* Mathias howled as he raced onto the quarter-deck and leapt into Vreva's arms. *Just show them that *monster*!*

Vreva held her familiar close, trying to calm her pounding heart. It wasn't easy with the cat's panic amplifying her own. He had a point, however. Fighting each other while that monster approached seemed as foolish as arguing about the decor in a burning house

"I agree with Mathias." When everyone looked at Vreva for an explanation, she pointed to the approaching hulk of the sea monster. "Just tell them to sail or die."

22

The Lesser Evil

Torius dashed forward and leapt to the quarterdeck rail. The fight still raged forward, but Snick and Vreva's surprises seemed to have tipped the scales in the Stargazers' favor. Most of the marines glued to the deck had been cut down, and although one of Vreva's conjured lions had vanished, the other was chasing a Chelish sailor up the mast, scratching and clawing the wood as the man scrambled to evade the predator's jaws.

"Stargazers! Furies! Avast fighting, or we're all dead!"

Disappointingly, Torius's bellow didn't provoke the sudden truce he'd hoped for. A few combatants disengaged, backing warily away from their opponents with their weapons still at the ready, but most just kept fighting, either not hearing or ignoring the command. That wouldn't do. He needed all hostilities to end.

"Vreva, call off that beast of yours! Grogul, lend me your voice! We don't have time to muck about!"

With a single word from Vreva, the lion vanished. Grogul strode to the railing and cupped his hands to his mouth. "Avast fighting! The ship's in irons, and the monster's on us!"

Torius's ears rang with the volume of the bosun's voice. Whether by sheer force or due to the threat of the sea monster's wrath, his pronouncement had the desired effect. The fighting ceased and every face on deck turned aft.

Torius took over, pointing his bloody scimitar for emphasis. "The ship's in peril!" There was no mistaking the cresting wave and glowing blue eyes rushing toward them. "We'll settle our differences later, but for now we've got to set sail or die! Topmen aloft! Cross-sheet the jibs, and haul sheets and braces! *Smartly* now!"

With wide-eyed glances at the approaching horror, the sailors obeyed, some dropping their weapons in their haste. Topmen scrambled aloft, others grabbed the lines that controlled the frigate's newly replaced headsails, hauling them frantically to port until the canvas cracked and filled to pull the ship's bow off the wind. The deck crew hauled new canvas from the hold to replace the sails burned by Vreva's spells. Dukkol took charge of the deck, overriding his Chelish counterpart by the sheer volume of his voice. Windy Kate charged up the stairs and took over at the helm, blood dripping from her hook hand.

"Windy, bear off as the sails fill. We need speed to get out of that thing's reach." Torius wiped his sword clean and sheathed it while he scanned the deck and picked out a mop of sea-green hair. "Snick, get the ballistae manned and give that monster a broadside when it surfaces!"

"Aye, Captain! Ballista crews, with me!" She vaulted the main hatch coaming and vanished below, a dozen Stargazers and Chelish sailors at her heels.

"Thillion, get down here!"

"Here, Captain." Thillion slid down a backstay, descending like some kind of wingless angel.

"You and Grogul man the aft-mounted ballistae!"

"Aye, sir!" The two raced to the siege engines mounted on the taffrail and started cranking the mechanisms that drew back the great bows.

The frigate slowly bore off the wind.

Torius looked back and forth between the advancing monster and the sails. *Come on, baby, give me some speed.* The headsails were sheeted home, and began to draw properly. Topsails cracked and filled, heeling the deck over. *Fury's Crown* began to slowly pick up speed—too slowly.

The ship lurched as the sea monster's bow wave slammed into her side. Cries of alarm rang out across the deck as up from the waves the massive creature rose, lifting its immense claws high to impale the ship.

"Snick! The beast rises!" Torius pictured poor *Stargazer* ravaged by those claws. *Not again!* "Fire!"

A rippling crack shook the deck as the ballistae fired. At this close range, all the bolts plunged deep into the beast's blubbery underside, some vanishing to their bitter ends. The monster staggered back with the impacts as one great claw scythed down. It clipped the port-side bulwarks, sheering through a half-dozen planks and sending chips flying. If the monster got a good hold, it would stop the ship dead. If that happened, it would all be over except for the screaming.

"Gods damn you, I will *not* lose a second ship today!" Torius looked desperately around for some way—any way—to stop the beast, but short of leaping down its cavernous maw with his sword, he had nothing.

On the far side of the quarterdeck, Vreva flung motes of energy at the monster from the tip of a silver wand. Unfortunately, the magical attack seemed utterly impotent.

"Vreva! Don't you have any magic better than *that*?" He nodded at the wand. "Anything at all?"

"Nothing I'm sure about." Frowning at the silver wand, she shoved it into her belt, then plucked something from a pocket and held it out. Two small dice engraved with strange runes lay in her hand. "I have these, but I don't know what they'll do."

Torius cringed as another claw struck amidships. It pierced the deck, but didn't plunge deep enough to violate the ship's hull. The creature did, however, have a grip on them. Its other claw rose like the blade of a huge guillotine. "Right now I'll take anything I can get!"

"All right, but I warned you!" Vreva stepped forward and cast the tiny dice at the creature, crying out a single word lost on the wind. The dice erupted into a billowing swarm of bright blue butterflies, enveloping the beast's head in a cloud of fluttering wings.

Torius stared. "*Butterflies*?"

"I *told* you I didn't know what would happen!"

Despite the seemingly benign effect, the creature reeled back, emitting an ear-splitting roar. Wrenching its claw from the deck, it flailed at the swarm of blinding insects.

Fury's Crown sailed free.

Cheers rang out from aloft and alow as Stargazers and Furies alike heralded their narrow escape. Torius wasn't so optimistic. He had little doubt that the beast would be after them in a flash.

"Avast cheering, Gozreh damn you all! We need more canvas aloft!" Torius assessed the ship's rig. Vreva's flame spells had destroyed half of the ship's sails. It took time to cut down charred remnants of a square-rigged sail and bend another to the yard, even with both crews working as quickly as they could. He knew they could outpace the beast once all the sails were up and drawing, but that would take time he didn't have. Time Celeste and Kalli didn't have.

"Bend new courses! We need speed!" Behind *Fury's Crown*, the sea monster finally evaded the blinding swarm of butterflies by diving beneath the surface. To everyone's dismay, it resumed its pursuit, charging right up their wake. He looked to windward, but couldn't spot the two swimming figures in the choppy seas. "Lacy, where are they?"

"Still got them in sight, sir!" She pointed into the distance. "There!"

"Don't lose them! Let me know when we're good to tack and come upwind of them. Windy, bear upwind as far as she'll manage and still make speed." Torius turned to the deck. A new forestaysail soared aloft, and sailors were wrestling the new square foresail up the mast to replace the charred one. "Dukkol! Trim to windward! We'll tack soon."

Two ballistae cracked behind him, and Torius looked back at the advancing beast. It swam barely a ship-length behind, gaining on them every second. "Keep firing! I don't know if ballista bolts will stop that thing, but we've got to try."

"Aye, captain!" Grogul fitted a bolt into his ballista, aimed, and yanked the firing lever. The heavy bolt slammed into the beast, piercing the thick armor, but the creature seemed not to notice.

"Torius! Here!" Vreva hurried to his side, proffering a small vial from her belt pouch. "We can put this on a bolt. It's my deadliest toxin."

"Do you think that'll kill it?" Torius eyed the vial dubiously.

"It works well enough on people."

"My arrows were envenomed, but they didn't seem to affect it at all," Thillion said without turning from the ballista he was reloading. "Even when I shot it in the eye."

"Lethality is dosage dependent," Vreva explained, "and different tissues absorb it at different rates. If we could get a heavy dose deep into it . . ."

"It's worth a try." As Grogul cranked the ballista's cocking mechanism, Torius grabbed one of the heavy bolts and held the head out to Vreva.

She popped the cork from the vial and tipped it over the iron head, pouring only a few drops at a time. Glancing up, Torius saw that the creature had reduced their lead to a few yards. It started to heave its bulk from the water, raising its massive claws to impale the ship, that horrible mouth gaping wide as if anticipating a meal. "Hurry up, Vreva!"

"I can't rush this! The tincture has to dry or it will drip, and you do *not* want this on your skin." She poured more and blew on it. "Rotate the shaft."

As he complied, a claw smashed into the water, missing the transom by mere feet.

"Vreva!"

"Not helping!" She poured again, tapping the last of the toxin onto the bolt's tip and blowing it dry. "Done!"

Torius loaded the shaft and stepped back. "Now, aim for something soft."

Grogul squinted at the armored beast. "Like *what*?"

"Like that!" Torius pointed down the toothed maw.

Grogul aimed the ballista and fired the envenomed bolt right down the beast's throat.

The sea monster shuddered, its huge mouth gnashing and the smaller claws flailing. Falling back, it plunged, churning the sea with its convulsions. Its broad back arched above the surface like a mountain rising from the depths.

"It's sounding!"

The creature's broad tail rose and thrashed, once, twice, and a third time, sending a sheet of seawater over the quarterdeck. The tail vanished, the sea roiling in its wake as it dove.

"Yes!" Torius thrust a fist into the air and pounded Grogul on the back. "Perfect shot!"

Grogul grimaced and sagged against the ballista. "Thanks."

Torius realized then that Grogul was still bleeding badly from the sword wound in his shoulder, his complexion paled to a sickly shade of gray. Tearing a swath from his shirt, he pressed it into the wound to staunch the flow. "Why won't you carry a potion like everyone else? Is it out of some misguided sense of orc—"

"Here, sir." Thillion pulled a small bottle from his tunic. "I still have one."

"Drink this!" The captain thrust the bottle at his bosun.

"Aye, sir."

While Grogul drank, Torius looked behind the ship, but there was no sign of the monster. His hopes that it might float belly up were dashed, but at least it was gone. Maybe they had killed it, but he wasn't about to bet his crew's lives on it.

Or Celeste's and Kalli's . . .

Torius snatched his spyglass from his belt and peered in the direction Lacy Jane was looking. There, far off the port beam, were two swimming figures. But something was wrong . . .

"What the hell? Where's Celeste?" Both figures swam using arms and legs, with the fluid grace of gillmen.

"I think she's the one without clothes, sir," Lacy Jane said with a crooked smile.

"Oh, well, of course!" Celeste must have transformed to match Kalli's pace.

"I think we've got our angle, sir!" Lacy pointed at the swimming pair and looked aloft to the pennant streaming from the top of the mast.

He gauged the angle and agreed with her assessment. "Prepare to tack ship!"

"Aye, sir!"

Sailors scrambled to their stations with only minor confusion. The Stargazers were unused to handling so many square-rigged sails, and Torius could hear the Chelish sailors cursing, but things sorted out quickly and Dukkol bellowed their readiness.

"About ship!" Torius commanded

Windy hauled the wheel to port, and Dukkol ordered the yards and sheets hauled over for the opposite tack. The frigate came about like quarter horse under the flick of the reins, not hesitating the way many large ships would have as her bow came through the wind.

"Damn, she's responsive!" Windy sang out with a grin.

"Get used to her, Windy," Torius told her in a low voice, "because I'll be *damned* if I'm giving her back to Cheliax."

"I'm with you there, sir!"

They settled on their new course, heading just upwind of the swimming gillmen. The new foresail was drawing, and the frigate picked up speed. Torius watched the integrated crew haul aloft a new mainsail, then noticed Snick hurrying up the steps from the middeck

"All secure belowdecks, sir!" She gave him her usual exaggerated salute. The gnome's right eye was swollen shut, the bruise darkening to purple, but she sported a grin.

"What happened to you?"

"Had to convince the Chelish quartermaster that he should shut the hell up and play nice, but he's no problem anymore."

"Well done." Torius wondered if the quartermaster was still breathing. Snick was deadlier than she looked, and if the man had given her that shiner, the gnome had probably repaid the assault with interest. He leaned down to her height and lowered his voice. "I still want to take the ship from them once we're out of this mess. Can you help me out with that?"

"No problem, sir. Already got my people collecting all those hastily dropped weapons." Snick winked, but then winced.

"Good." He turned back to the deck. "Dukkol, rig a boarding net. We'll heave to upwind of Celeste and Kalli to break the seas while we pick them up."

"Captain, I don't think that's a good idea."

Torius turned toward Thillion. "Why not?"

The elf pointed forward. The sea around the swimming pair churned and roiled, then began to rotate in a building maelstrom.

"Gozreh's guts, no!" Torius leapt to the rail, grabbing a shroud for support as he squinted into the spray.

The sea monster had not been killed by the poisoned bolt after all, and had beaten them to their quarry. The deadly whirlpool deepened and widened even as they bore down on the fleeing pair.

"Windy, a half point to port!"

"*Port*, sir?" Windy Kate stared at him wide-eyed. The new course would take them closer to the building maelstrom.

"Yes, port! And don't you dare deviate until I give the order!" Torius looked forward again and tried to gauge their approach. Though Celeste could probably do the calculations in her head, he was working on instinct. "Thillion, get up to the mains'l yard. It's mostly Chelaxians up there, and I need someone I can trust. Once they've got the new mains'l bent on, don't let them drop it until I give the word, then do it smartly and sheet it tight."

"Aye, Captain!" The elf scrambled up the ratlines, as nimble as a spider in a web.

"Grogul!" Torius turned to find Grogul still pale, but no longer bleeding. "I need you to rig some heaving lines. We have to pick up Celeste and Kalli on the fly, and it's going to be close. If we don't break out of that monster's maelstrom on the first pass, we're in trouble."

"Since when are we *not* in trouble, sir?" Grogul reached for a coil of heavy line.

"Good point." Cries of alarm from forward drew Torius's attention. The Chelish sailors manning the foredeck had spotted the maelstrom and were calling to their comrades in the rigging. "Now if we can just do this without a mutiny on our hands . . ."

The sea heaved and roiled beneath Celeste, startling her from her steady strokes. Currents clutched her like invisible hands, wrenching her off course. "What—"

"We're in trouble!" Kalli dipped her head below the surface, then came up wide-eyed and pale. "*Deep* trouble!"

Celeste looked below and instantly wished she hadn't. Far beneath them, the charybdis gyrated and thrashed its huge tail. As she watched, the churning water began to spin, spiraling down and down toward the creature's cavernous mouth. She popped her head up and wiped the water from her eyes. "I don't get it. Why doesn't it just swallow us whole?"

"I think it's smarter than that!" Kalli pointed to the approaching frigate. "It's laying a trap for *Fury's Crown*!"

"Torius?" Celeste looked toward the frigate, its grim figurehead glaring as it charged through the waves. At this angle of approach, the ship would sail near the edge of the maelstrom. "He's coming to pick us up!"

"Swim for it, or we'll be drawn in!" Kalli grasped her arm and jerked her toward the ship. "Come on!"

"Wait!" At a glance, Celeste estimated the size of the maelstrom, the speed and course of the ship, the rate of the whirlpool's rotation, their swimming speed, and all the relevant angles and velocities. Her mind flew through the calculations, and she had the answer.

"No! Swim *with* the rotation! If we swim outward or against it, we'll miss them!"

"You're sure?"

"Trust me!" Now Celeste grasped Kalli's arm and tugged her into motion. "Match my pace!"

Celeste set their speed according to her calculations. The pack of scrolls and potions on her back dragged through the water, slowing her down and sapping her energy. She stole glances at the ship with every stroke, constantly gauging their position to match the arrival of *Fury's Crown*.

Or so she hoped.

It was difficult to both swim and calculate at the same time, and it was also getting harder to glimpse the frigate. The wind-driven seas raged against the fast-moving water of the maelstrom, creating a confused wall of tossing spray. Celeste dove briefly, then arched and kicked hard, leaping above the surface enough to glimpse figures at the quarterdeck rail. Grogul and Torius both stood there grasping coils of line.

Is he crazy?

Unfortunately, she knew the answer to that question. Picking someone up while underway was a tricky maneuver in the best of conditions. In the midst of a maelstrom, it seemed impossible.

Gauging speeds and angles once more, Celeste ran the calculations. The equation in her mind balanced perfectly. Their courses would converge to within easy reach of thrown ropes. Now all they had to do was catch them and hang on.

Easy . . .

Celeste struggled to maintain her pace as the maelstrom steepened. If they missed, there would be no second chance.

As a wave slammed against her, Celeste harbored a brief, horrific thought—*The charybdis has us!*—before realizing that it was the ship's bow wave. The huge hull thundered past, and she heard snatches of Torius's voice above the rush of water.

". . . fall . . . mains'l . . . Grogul . . . *now!*"

Two coils of rope flew toward them, hitting the water only feet from their outstretched hands. Celeste and Kalli each grabbed one, latching on for dear life.

Celeste's relief was short-lived as the ship's momentum jerked them forward so hard that she thought her shoulders would be pulled out of their sockets. Rough hemp burned through her hands, saltwater stinging her torn palms. The two swimmers thumped into one another before they settled on their own paths, trailing in the ship's wake but dragged sideways by the maelstrom.

Celeste thrust her head above the water to glimpse the frigate's huge mainsail unfurling. *Fury's Crown* surged forward as the sail was sheeted home. She understood the maneuver—the ship needed all the speed it could get to break free of the whirlpool's currents—but cursed it just the same as the rope pulled even harder on her arms. Unaccustomed as she was to having limbs, she wondered if hers could be torn off.

"Hold on!" someone bellowed unnecessarily from the deck.

You think? Celeste swore that if she ever made it up there, she would find out who yelled that brilliant bit of advice and bite them, even if it was Torius.

The contrary currents subsided as the frigate pulled them out of the maelstrom. Celeste was no longer being pulled sideways, but straight behind the ship. *Like a fishing lure* . . . She regretted her analogy immediately as the charybdis surged up from its failed trap after them.

The beast breached like a vengeful sea god, half of its entire bulk clearing the surface. The wave from its impact crashed over them like an avalanche, tumbling them and jerking the rough hemp line again through Celeste's palms. She gritted her teeth against the pain as blood streamed from between her fingers. Desperate to take some of the strain off her tortured hands, she whipped one leg around the rope and clamped down hard with the other. Unable to see through the froth, she surfaced and looked for Kalli, hoping the gillman fared better. She caught a flashing glimpse of Kalli's face contorted in determination, and the line she clutched wrapped around her forearms to keep from slipping.

Panicked shouts from the ship heralded the beast's pursuit. A massive claw smashed into the sea between Celeste and Kalli, missing the naga by mere feet and spinning her like a spiral streamer in the wind. Teeth the size of greatswords gnashed only yards behind her trailing feet. If she let go now, she'd be swallowed whole.

"Haul, damn you! More sail! Hoist more sail!"

Celeste welcomed the sound of Torius's voice as much as the rhythmic tugs that pulled her up beside the ship. The rope lurched with the turbulent water at the stern, and she thumped hard against the hull, rasping her shoulder on the barnacle-encrusted wood.

Almost there!

Celeste glimpsed a claw scraping down the side of the ship, shearing the entire quarter gallery away as it plunged toward her.

318 CHRIS A. JACKSON

She lashed out with a foot to push away from the hull, and the immense limb brushed against her in passing, amid a landslide of shattered glass and ornate woodwork falling into the sea. The charybdis seemed to be tearing the frigate apart around them.

The line pulled her up the side of the ship, and now she could hear clearly.

"More sail!" Torius commanded from above. "Jettison anything not nailed down!"

Crates, barrels, and corpses flew past Celeste, splashing into the sea as she ascended foot by precarious foot up the side. Kalli hung only feet above and forward, blood streaming down her forearms from the rough rope. The din of splintering wood and lashing spray subsided. The quarterdeck still seemed a mile away, but she allowed a flicker of hope that she might actually make it

Then a barely perceptible itch threatened that hope. It quickly progressed into a telltale tingle that she knew all too well.

"No, no, no!" Her transformation spell was expiring. She'd been too busy swimming and calculating to keep track of how long it had been since she last cast the spell. The rope slipped from between her fusing legs, and her grip on the rope weakened as her fingers receded.

Celeste shouted out her spell, picturing a different form in her mind. She no longer needed to swim, but climbing sounded like a great idea, and being small and nimble would make that easier. Sighing with relief as arms and legs reformed, she shrugged her shoulders to center the pack and scrambled the rest of the way up the side of the ship. She grasped Torius's outstretched hand and shimmied over the rail into his arms.

"Celeste!" Torius pulled her into a crushing embrace, kissing her hard.

Celeste wanted to melt in his arms, but it hardly seemed prudent. She thrust her hands against his chest and pushed away. "The charybdis!"

"The what?" The captain looked at her quizzically, then blinked and stared. "You look like—"

"The sea monster! Kalli said it was a charybdis. Aren't we still battling it?"

"It's distracted." Grogul leaned heavily on the rail and nodded off the stern. "When we started throwin' over dead Chelish marines, the critter decided to stop for lunch. No accounting for taste."

In their wake, the charybdis bobbed among the jetsam. Its smaller claws picked through the wreckage, scooping up the bodies and feeding them into the great maw.

Celeste swallowed hard at the grisly sight. "I don't care what it eats, as long as it's not trying to eat us!"

"Good to have you back aboard." Torius reclaimed her attention. "For a while there, I thought I'd lost you."

"You almost did." Celeste kissed him hungrily, but laughter from the crew brought her up short.

"Hey!" Snick's indignant shout broke their clinch. "You can't be kissin' the captain lookin' like that! Couldn't you pick someone *else* to mimic? Or at least get dressed?"

"Sorry, Snick. I needed to be smaller so they could haul me aboard more easily, and you were the first person I thought of." Celeste banished her transformation, resuming her natural form with no small relief. It felt good to have scales again. Her water-logged pack fell to the deck with a clank, and she cringed. She retrieved her sextant and inspected it for damage.

"You bothered to haul along a bag full of junk with that thing chasing you?" Torius lifted the dripping pack and peered inside.

"You gave me this sextant, Torius!" Celeste glared at him. "Don't you *dare* call it junk!"

"I understand, but it's not worth your *life*." He pulled her close again, warm against her damp scales. "I'd buy you a new sextant."

"Well, at least we're a *happy* ship again." Vreva leaned on the rail, stroking a disheveled but purring Mathias.

"Yeah, and it's about damned time those two got together," Grogul muttered.

Celeste didn't understand the bosun's comment until she turned to see Kalli and Lacy Jane locked in an amorous embrace, oblivious to anyone else on the quarterdeck. Her surprise was curtailed by the arrival of Thillion, who dropped to the deck from the mizzen ratlines and handed over a bundle of red-and-black cloth.

"I took the liberty of striking the Chelish colors, Captain. We'd better fly something else before our friends arrive."

"Friends?" Celeste asked. "What friends?"

"Gray Corsairs," Torius answered. "Vreva's called them in."

"Yes, and I'll breathe easier once they get here. Our hosts are starting to get upset." Thillion pointed to the foredeck, where a large group of Chelish sailors huddled together, glaring at the heavily armed pirates surrounding them. "But do we *have* any other colors?"

Torius's face fell. "I'm afraid they're all on the bottom of the sea."

"Wait!" Snick scrabbled through the bag she had brought over from *Stargazer* and fished out a bundle. Grabbing one end, she let it unfurl. A long black pennant with Celeste's likeness sewn in silver thread fluttered in the wind. "I thought we might need an extra."

"Thank you, Snick." Torius took the pennant and stared down at the cloth for a moment before handing it to Thillion. "Run it up the mizzen halyard. No Chelish captain in their right mind would fly *that* flag."

Celeste bit her lip as she watched the pennant soar aloft. She remembered watching the ship she so loved sinking into the void of the deep, and felt a sharp pang of loss. "I miss *Stargazer* already, Torius. What are we going to do?"

"Do?" The pirate captain smiled at her and ran his fingers through her wet hair, pulling her close. "We'll do what we've always done. Keep sailing, keep fighting, and keep watching the stars."

"That sounds good to me." Celeste leaned against her captain, swaying with the motion of this new ship, and taking solace in the warmth of his arm around her.

23

Spoils of War

Good to be back, isn't it?* Mathias leapt up onto the banister and rubbed against Vreva's arm.

"It is." She looked down over the room full of boisterous Chelish naval officers. The scents of smoke, sweat, liquor, and wine filled the air, laughter and the thrum of music loud enough to render quiet conversation challenging. Business as usual. "Calistria help me, but I missed this place."

I knew you would.

Vreva admired the new stage act Kelipri had hired while her boss was out of town. The staccato percussion accentuated the perilous gyrations of the performers juggling burning swords. A gasp rose from the crowd as one of the jugglers feigned a mishap, then laughter as she showed them it was just a trick. Then one of the men blew forth a volatile mixture, igniting it with his flaming blade. Fire billowed into the air.

The officers gasped and applauded. Well, most of them applauded.

Vreva's practiced eye picked out a few who averted their gazes or hastily downed their drinks. One older lieutenant paled and wiped sweat from his brow with a scarred hand. A burn-scarred hand.

Swallowing hard, Vreva flexed the hand she'd thrust into live coals to burn away ravenous green slime. She recalled the scent of seared flesh in the witch's cellar, the screams of sailors trapped under burning canvas.

I'm a soldier. This is war. People die. Sometimes innocent people.

Maybe the fire show's not such a good idea after all. Mathias bumped her arm with his head, and she felt a wash of empathy from him. *You okay?*

"I'm fine." He'd been asking that a lot, and she knew she would be, given time. "Just glad to be home and alive."

I'm glad to be off that gods-damned ship! He licked his paw and flicked his tail. *Promise me you'll never make me go to sea again.*

"You know I can't promise you, love, but I'll do my best." She scratched him under the chin, and he seemed to accept the compromise.

Truth be told, the overland trip from Augustana had been almost as horrifying as their time at sea. Four days huddled in a farm wagon disguised as a peasant girl, sleeping in straw, shivering every night, and then dodging patrols of border guards, had left her longing for a warm bed. They'd arrived safe and sound in Ostenso two days ago, and already the unpleasant memories were receding. It was amazing what a hot bath, wine, and good food could do. Now she was back at work. Last night she'd arranged a clandestine moonlit walk on the waterfront. Tonight she would listen for any rumors about the disappearance of *Fury's Crown*.

Trouble! Mathias's tail twitched, his sharp eyes focused on the club's front door where Nonny the bouncer spoke to a tall figure in chainmail. The armored woman turned, her surcoat displaying a familiar crest.

"Lothera Cothos?"

Why would she come back here?

"I don't know, but I doubt it's to see the floor show. I better talk to her."

*Well, it's a cinch she's not here to talk to *me*!*

Vreva flounced down the stairs, preparing herself for the encounter. Concealed by the cheering crowds, she murmured her thought-reading spell, then, once she had Lothera in sight, whispered another incantation to soothe the woman's mind.

She greeted Lothera with a smile and a curtsy. "Harbormaster Cothos. What a surprise!"

"I . . . yes, I suppose it is." Lothera bowed stiffly, her motions precise, though her red eyes and roiling thoughts betrayed her state of distress. *Gone . . . he's gone . . . he can't be . . .* "I . . . didn't know if you had heard the horrible news."

"News?" Vreva painted on a worried look. "What news?"

The harbormaster's eyes darted around the room. *Damn the navy! If they did their jobs . . .* "Might we have some privacy?"

"Of course. Would a corner table suffice?" Vreva motioned to her head waiter.

"Yes. Yes, that would be fine." Lothera followed her to the very same table they'd used before. Unclipping her sword, the harbormaster slid into the booth without a word.

The waiter arrived with a bottle of wine and two glasses. While he drew the cork and poured, Vreva concentrated on her guest.

Gone . . . he can't be gone . . . Lothera took a hasty gulp of wine before the waiter even finished filling Vreva's glass. *Gods and devils, how can he be gone?*

When the waiter had finished and left, Vreva assumed a concerned expression. "I'm afraid to ask what dreadful news you've heard, but putting it off won't make it any easier. Please, tell me what's happened."

"It's *Sea Serpent*." Lothera reduced the remaining volume of her glass by half and drew a gasping breath. "I . . . heard from a merchant captain that the ship was . . . lost."

"Lost?" Vreva tinged her voice with panic. "You don't mean . . ."

"Lost at sea. Sunk by devil-damned *pirates*!" Lothera drained her glass and reached for the bottle. Her hand trembled so badly as she poured that wine spilled onto the table. *He's gone . . .*

"Dear gods, no!" Vreva put everything she had into the performance. "But what about the crew? What about Captain Akhiri?"

"Gone." The harbormaster bolted down her wine, then choked back a sob. "I don't know what . . . why . . . I can't believe . . ." Lothera lost her battle with tears and hung her head. "Oh, gods and devils! I . . . I can't . . ."

"You poor thing." Vreva grasped Lothera's hands and gripped them tight. She'd already known the news, of course. She'd concocted the rumor herself, and charged Twilp Farfan with circulating it through every waterfront tavern in the city. It had been her parting promise to Torius, freeing him of his relationship with Lothera. Trellis might have arranged some way for him to attain a different ship and resume his role as Abidi Ben Akhiri, but Vreva had nullified that potentiality. She owed the Stargazers that much for the loss of their beloved ship and the deaths of their shipmates. Strangely, she now felt a pang of sympathy for Lothera. "I'm so sorry."

"Sorry?" Lothera's head came up and she sniffed, withdrawing a hand to wipe away her tears. "I thought you'd be . . . I mean, you knew him longer than I did."

"I knew him for years, and he was a friend, but I wasn't in *love* with him, my dear."

"I wondered if you ever . . . if you and he were ever . . . together." Lothera reached for the bottle and refilled her glass.

"No, never." Vreva smiled ruefully, surprised by how well the truth wove into her web of lies. "Not for lack of trying on my part, you understand, but he always turned me down."

"You? He turned *you* down?" Lothera stared at her in blatant disbelief. "But you're . . . I mean . . . why?"

"Two reasons. The first was my profession, which he didn't care for, and later," Vreva raised her glass in toast, "he said he wouldn't betray the woman he loved."

Lothera's mouth dropped open. "He *said* that?"

"Yes." Vreva declined to mention that it was Celeste whom Torius loved and would not betray. This could work out well. Building a friendly relationship with Ostenso's harbormaster would certainly benefit her mission. She sipped her wine and smiled at Lothera. "I envy you in that regard, you know."

"You . . . you shouldn't." Lothera drank more wine, her eyes cast down.

"Why not? You've had something I've never known, and likely never will: the love of a good man." *True also.* Vreva had known love, but it had been a woman she'd given her heart to.

Lothera stared at her, new tears wetting her cheeks. "Because if losing someone you love feels like this, you're better off without it."

"Don't say that." Vreva put her glass down and fixed the harbormaster's gaze. "Never regret loving someone. Abidi Ben Akhiri enriched your life. Take that and remember him for what you had together." *Even if it was a lie.*

"But . . . it *hurts.*" Lothera downed her wine once again. "Nothing's worth hurting like this."

"Nothing?" Vreva shook her head. "Tell me that in a week or a month. The pain fades, but the memories, the good ones, remain." *True again. I'm just full of truths tonight.*

"I . . . hope so." Lothera took up the bottle again, and poured the last of the wine into their glasses. "I wanted to thank you. For your advice the last time we spoke, I mean. You were right."

"Oh?"

"Yes. I tried to show Abidi how much I really appreciated him, and . . ." A sad smile graced Lothera's mouth, softening her angular features. "He was . . . our last night together was like nothing I've ever experienced."

Well, well, Torius . . . Vreva smiled. "I'm glad for you, then, and even more envious." She raised her glass. "To Captain Abidi Ben Akhiri, may our memories of him sustain us, though he has passed from this world."

"Thank you for that, too." Lothera drank her wine down and pushed herself up from the table. "I'd better leave before I drink too much and make an even bigger fool of myself."

"Nonsense." Vreva stood and extended a hand. "I thank you for coming to tell me. I'd rather hear it from a friend than through the rumor mill."

"Yes, I . . ." Lothera shook Vreva's hand and picked up her sword. *Maybe she could be a friend. She's so nice . . .* "I knew you'd want to know, and I needed to speak to someone about him. Someone who knew him."

"Please come by whenever you feel like talking." Vreva walked with the harbormaster to the door, and curtsied formally. "I know we're both going to miss Abidi very much. Sometimes talking to someone who shares your pain helps ease it."

"I will." Lothera gave her another sad smile and bowed with the formal courtesy appropriate to their disparate social standings. *She is nice, and maybe she can tell me what she hears from these navy prigs.* "Thank you again, Mistress Korvis."

"It's been my pleasure." Vreva hid her mirth. *I'll sign a contract with Asmodeus himself before I spy for you, Lothera.*

Lothera walked out of the Officers' Club with her back ramrod straight and her stride long, the stoic Chelish bureaucrat once again. Vreva watched her go and smiled to herself. Yes, she could do much worse than to cultivate that friendship.

"She seemed distraught," Nonny said as he closed the door. "Hope it wasn't anything serious."

"She lost a friend." Vreva patted her employee on his huge shoulder and smiled. "We both did." *One more truth.* Abidi Ben Akhiri was truly dead, and Torius Vin could never dare to show his face, however disguised, in Ostenso again. *I'm going to miss that crazy pirate.* "The harbormaster is always welcome here, Nonny. Make her feel at home."

"Of course, ma'am."

Vreva sauntered back into the fray, thinking about her friends and wondering if she would ever see any of the Stargazers again. They may have worn out their welcome in Cheliax—perhaps in the whole Inner Sea—but Andoran had interests elsewhere, and a captain of Torius's experience would not be wasted.

She felt a surge of urgency from Mathias and worked her way across the floor toward him. She caught a glimpse of her familiar under a table crowded with Chelish officers, and cast a quiet spell to eavesdrop on the group.

"Can't believe the old man's dead."

"Found floating in the bay with his pants down's what I heard."

"Wonder how the hell that happened."

"Crossed the wrong woman, if you ask me."

"Know who they're going to promote to replace Ronnel?"

"No idea, but there's no shortage of candidates."

Vreva walked past without a glance. *Old news.* She knew all about Ronnel's unfortunate slip off the pier. The speculation that he'd crossed the wrong woman was more accurate than any of the young lieutenants would ever know. She thought of the sinking Stargazer, dead crew members, and poor Yami, and felt a cold satisfaction.

"Payback's a bitch," Vreva murmured, remembering the look of surprise on Ronnel's face as her poison gripped his heart, "and Calistria knows, revenge can be sweet."

Celeste coiled comfortably by the frigate's taffrail, gazing up into the star-studded heavens. For the first time in a week the racket of hammers, saws, and chisels didn't invade upon the silent glory of the cosmos. The repairs and modifications were done, the crew—exhausted by their frantic labor—finally resting. Peace reigned. The night was hers once again.

She knew that the work had been necessary. Sailing the Inner Sea in a stolen Chelish frigate was just asking for trouble, and they certainly couldn't sail into Almas as they were. Fortunately, like most warships, *Fury's Crown*'s lower hold fairly overflowed with spare timber, spars, canvas, paint, and cordage. Snick had had the time of her life directing the squibbing, exhibiting a joyful enthusiasm that buoyed the crew's spirits and distracted them from the loss of their shipmates and their beloved *Stargazer*. Now, with her hull freshly painted, transom and forecastle modified, rig altered, and masts re-stepped to a proper rake, the newly named *Wandering Star* could never be mistaken for *Fury's Crown*. The grim erinyes figurehead had been re-crafted into a pastel-clad beauty, with glorious butterfly wings and a crown of blue swallowtails upon her golden hair. Snick had spent days on the carving, and Celeste hours painting the figure, manipulating a finely bristled brush with her magic while stretched out on the bowsprit netting. She thought of the labor as a thank-you to Desna for her gifts.

Thanks, but no promises. She felt that she'd come to terms with her gifts and her relationship to the goddess. They had common goals and shared a love of the cosmos. If nothing else, they had solid grounds for friendship and mutual respect.

Other than painting, her duties had been few. Plotting a lazy course back and forth across the Inner Sea to avoid shipping lanes had required little navigation. Most of her time had been spent exploring their new home: cabins and holds, nooks and crannies, the huge galley, and the palatial aft cabin claimed by the captain. Captain Lance had owned an impressive library, and Celeste had spent hours reading the eclectic volumes, her ears stuffed with beeswax to dampen the clamor of carpenters and riggers.

"Gotta say, the gnome's really outdone herself." Grogul's baritone shattered the peace, but Celeste didn't mind. She knew with a flick of her forked tongue that Torius accompanied the bosun.

It must be near midnight and the captain's watch.

"That she has." The two strode aft, their steps slow and relaxed. "Though I think she went overboard with the paint. I mean, *purple* trim?"

Grogul laughed. "Well, it was either that or *pink*! All we had was red, blue, and white for woodwork. Gotta admit, Besmara herself wouldn't think we were *pirates*."

"Well, at least no one's going to recognize her as a Chelish warship."

The two men joined Celeste at the taffrail—the *purple* taffrail—and she smiled at their banter. "Good evening, my captain. Grogul, how's your shoulder?"

"Oh, right as rain." Grogul shrugged as if to demonstrate. "Nice to be done with all the hammerin', though."

"To that, I agree." She leaned against her captain's shoulder.

The three of them stared into the sky, lost in their thoughts, interrupted finally by the soft pad of bare feet on the deck behind them, and a quiet, "Pardon me, Captain."

"Good evening, Kalli." Torius turned to the gillman with a grin. "How's my new second mate doing?" The larger ship would require a larger crew, so he had appointed a new officer to help manage them.

"Fine, sir!" Kalli saluted smartly. "All's quiet. Sailing eight knots at zero-two-zero for Almas. Just coming up to midnight, so I thought I'd get a fix." She nodded to Celeste.

Celeste smiled. "Right away."

The gillman's promotion had been a surprise to some, but not to Celeste. Grogul had once again refused an officer's rating, and had recommended Kalli without reservation. She'd shown a new sense of confidence and leadership since their harrowing escapade, and already had the respect of the entire crew. There was just one catch . . .

Grogul straightened his shoulders, held his head high, and snapped a salute. "Bosun Grogul reporting for duty, ma'am!"

Kalli blushed and glared at the half-orc. "Oh, stop it."

The half-orc chuckled. "Hey, I'm the one who put you up for promotion, so I've a right to be proud."

"Only because *you* didn't want the job."

"Better you than me." Grogul grinned to Torius and pointed Kalli forward. "Let's see if you remember all I taught you about tyin' a monkey's fist."

As Grogul and Kalli went forward, Celeste raised her sextant and took two careful sightings. Torius called the time at her mark, his new pocket watch having been calibrated to the frigate's fancy chronometers, and she jotted down the numbers. Her calculations put them eighty miles south of Almas. At a leisurely eight knots, they'd make port by midmorning. She stowed her instruments and logbook in their case and closed it against the night air.

Torius wrapped her in his arms, breathing in the scent of her hair. "Kalli seems to be settling in well. It's nice to have one more officer aboard, and Thillion certainly appreciates her."

"Grogul will have to take up a hobby to fill his free time."

"Maybe he'll take up knitting." They both laughed quietly at the image.

"What do you think Trellis will say about the mission?" Celeste worried more about Marshal Trellis than she did about the Chelish navy.

"The weapon was neutralized, so she can't complain."

Despite the captain's mild words, Celeste felt the tension in his embrace. She knew that he'd been plagued by nightmares. She remembered her own near-drowning often enough, but had no bad dreams. Torius hadn't told her exactly what his were about, but she could guess. He'd lost a ship, and Snick had told her about Yami's death. Others might think it strange that a battle-hardened pirate would so mourn the loss of a boy he'd not even known, but Celeste knew there was more to Torius Vin than the brash persona he assumed on deck.

"I take that back," he amended after a pensive silence. "She'll probably complain about having to babysit the Furies for the next few years. They can't go back to Cheliax, after all."

They'd handed the prisoners off to the Gray Corsairs with Vreva, who had assured them that this was nothing unusual. They knew too much to be set free, but they would be taken care of. In a few years, when the secrets they harbored no longer mattered, they'd be released, or exchanged for Andorens held by Cheliax.

"I hope Vreva made it back to Ostenso safely." Celeste scanned the heavens. "I'd try to read her stars, but I don't even know what sign she was born under."

"Don't worry about Vreva." Torius pulled her close. "She's a survivor. She's probably already back at the Officers' Club, spreading rumors of our untimely demise."

"That's right!" Celeste gave him a playful nudge with her tail. "No more dalliances with your harbormaster lady."

"No, thank Gozreh. Trellis will have to find someone else to be Vreva's intermediary. She'll probably complain about that, too." Sighing, he gazed up into the star-filled sky. "So, do you see anything in our future?"

"Do you really want me to look?" She twisted around in his arms and eyed him skeptically, suspecting some joke.

"Sure. I'll take any advantage I can get, and what better advantage than knowing the future?"

"But what if it's dire?" Celeste recalled her prophecy of *Stargazer*'s death.

"We've got to take the good with the bad, just like these new gifts of yours."

Celeste considered that for a while. "It's all about balance, isn't it?"

"Exactly." He ran his fingers through her hair. "We lost *Stargazer*, but we gained *Wandering Star*. You were gifted with the ability to predict the future . . ."

Celeste picked up on his thought. ". . . and the curse of a twisted tongue every time we get in a fight."

"Think of it as a challenge." Torius chuckled. "We'll figure something out. And if something dark looms on the horizon, I think I'd rather know about it than blunder into danger."

"But you're so *good* at blundering into danger!" Celeste wrapped her tail around his legs.

"Well, there's *that*, too!" He held her close, and she felt the tension ease from his shoulders. "Maybe Desna's telling us to start looking before we leap."

"Caution from a pirate?"

"Even an old sea dog can learn new tricks, you know."

"Oh?" She playfully nipped his ear. "Maybe *I* could teach you a few new tricks."

"See, there you go again, looking into the future." Their laughter mingled on the breeze.

Feeling more at peace than she had in months, Celeste gazed up at her beloved stars, reveled in the warmth of her lover's arms, and listened to the song of the heavens.

About the Author

Chris A. Jackson has been sailing and writing full time since 2009. As a sailor, writer, and gamer, nautical and RPG tie-in fantasy came naturally. His *Scimitar Seas* novels won multiple gold medals for best fantasy novel of the year from *Foreword Reviews Magazine*, and his Pathfinder Tales novels, *Pirate's Honor* and *Pirate's Promise,* have become fan favorites. His non-nautical magical assassin series, the Weapon of Flesh Trilogy, has become a Kindle bestseller, spurring international interest and spawning the Weapon of Fear Trilogy. He's also branched into contemporary fantasy with the recent release of *Dragon Dreams*, a novel set in the fantasy world of Hellmaw. His shorter works include a nautical Iron Kingdoms novella, *Blood and Iron*, and stories in various anthologies, including a Shadowrun short story, "Sweating Bullets," in the *World of Shadows* anthology, and "First Command," in the acclaimed *Women in Practical Armor* anthology. Drop by **jaxbooks.com** for updates, or follow along as he sails the Caribbean at **http://sailmrmac.blogspot.com**.

Acknowledgments

Special thanks, as always, to my wife Anne for her energy, editing, and unfailing support. Many thanks, too, to her family for their hospitality while our beloved sailboat, *Mr. Mac*, was being refurbished this winter. New England in winter is not the Caribbean, but memories of snow will make me appreciate warm water and white sand all the more. Also many thanks to James Sutter for invaluable editorial input, and to the Paizo family, for making work fun. Lastly, thank you to the fans of these novels for letting me know I've hit the mark. Sail on! Game on! Take no prisoners!

Glossary

All Pathfinder Tales novels are set in the rich and vibrant world of the Pathfinder campaign setting. Below are explanations of several key terms used in this book. For more information on the world of Golarion and the strange monsters, people, and deities that make it their home, see *The Inner Sea World Guide*, or dive into the game and begin playing your own adventures with the *Pathfinder Roleplaying Game Core Rulebook* or the *Pathfinder Roleplaying Game Beginner Box*, all available at **paizo.com**.

Absalom: Largest city in the Inner Sea region, located on the Isle of Kortos in the middle of the Inner Sea.

Alamein Peninsula: Coastal region in northern Osirion.

Almas: Capital city of Andoran.

Andoran: Democratic and freedom-loving nation. Formerly controlled by the Chelish Empire, and before that by the Taldan Empire.

Andoren: Of or pertaining to Andoran; someone from Andoran.

Arch of Aroden: Enormous viaduct that once connected the continents of Avistan and Garund across the Hespereth Strait. Currently broken.

Aroden: The god of humanity, who died mysteriously a hundred years ago.

Asmodeus: Devil-god of tyranny, slavery, pride, and contracts; lord of Hell and current patron deity of Cheliax.

Augustana: Port city in Andoran known for its shipyards.

Avistan: The continent north of the Inner Sea, on which Cheliax, Andoran, and many other nations lie.

Azir: Port capital of Rahadoum, an atheistic nation south of the Inner Sea.

Bretheda: Gas giant planet in Golarion's solar system.

Brevoy: Frigid northern nation famous for its duelists.

Calistria: Also known as the Savored Sting; the goddess of trickery, lust, and revenge.

Castrovel: Lush, inhabited planet in Golarion's solar system.

Cecaelia: Aquatic monsters with the upper bodies of humans and the lower bodies of octopuses.

Charybdis: Massive sea monster that can create its own whirlpools.

Cheliax: Powerful, devil-worshiping nation north of the Inner Sea.

Chelish: Of or relating to the nation of Cheliax.

Cleric: A religious spellcaster whose magical powers are granted by his or her god.

Coast of Graves: Treacherous stretch of coast north of Osirion.

Corentyn: Port city located at Cheliax's southernmost point, from which the nation can restrict passage between the Inner Sea and the Arcadian Ocean.

Cosmic Caravan: Series of constellations important to astrologers.

Cynosure: Golarion's pole star, believed to be a residence of Desna.

Desna: Good-natured goddess of dreams, stars, travelers, and luck.

Devils: Fiendish occupants of Hell who seek to corrupt mortals in order to claim their souls.

Djedefar: Stepped tower on the Osirian coast, home to a community of Irori-worshiping monks.

Drowning Devils: Four-eyed, serpentine devils usually devoted to guarding Hell's waterways.

Dryads: Fey creatures that resemble human women and bond with trees.

Dwarves: Short, stocky humanoids who excel at physical labor, mining, and craftsmanship.

Egorian: Capital of Cheliax.

Elves: Long-lived, beautiful humanoids identifiable by pointed ears, lithe bodies, and pupils so large their eyes appear to be one color.

Familiar: Small creature that assists a wizard, witch, or sorcerer, often developing greater powers and intelligence than normal members of its kind.

Fey: Creatures deeply tied to the natural world, such as dryads or pixies.

Fiends: Creatures native to the evil planes of the multiverse, such as demons, devils, and daemons, among others.

Garund: Continent south of the Inner Sea, renowned for its deserts and jungles.

Gillmen: Race of amphibious humanoids descended from an empire that sank into the sea.

Gnomes: Small humanoids related to the fey, with strange mindsets, big eyes, and often wildly colored hair.

Golarion: The planet on which the Pathfinder campaign setting focuses.

Gozreh: God of nature, the sea, and weather. Depicted as a dual deity, with both male and female aspects.

Gray Corsairs: Naval division of the Steel Falcons, a branch of the Andoren military organization known as the Eagle Knights, primarily focused on combating slavery.

Half-Elves: Children of unions between elves and humans. Taller, longer-lived, and generally more graceful and attractive than the average human, yet not nearly so much so as their elven kin. Often regarded as having the best qualities of both races, yet still see a certain amount of prejudice, particularly from their pure elven relations.

Half-Orcs: Children of unions between humans and orcs, usually distinguished by green or gray skin, brutish appearances, and short tempers. Mistrusted and mistreated in many societies.

Halflings: Race of humanoids known for their tiny stature, deft hands, and mischievous personalities.

Hell: Plane of evil and tyrannical order ruled by devils, where many evil souls go after they die.

Hor-Aha: Lighthouse on the northern coast of Osirion.

Imps: Relatively weak devils resembling tiny, winged humanoids with fiendish features. The most commonly found devils on the Material Plane. Often used as familiars.

Inner Sea: The vast inland sea whose northern continent, Avistan, and southern continent, Garund, as well as the seas and nearby lands, are the primary focus of the Pathfinder campaign setting.

Irori: God of history, knowledge, self-perfection, and enlightenment. Popular with monks.

Katapesh: Mighty trade nation south of the Inner Sea. Also the name of its capital city.

Kellids: Nomadic human ethnicity from the northern reaches of the Inner Sea region, traditionally viewed as violent and uncivilized by southern cultures.

Kortos: Island upon which Absalom is located.

Lunar Nagas: Race of nagas obsessed with the stars and astrology.

Nagas: Intelligent, magical creatures with the heads of humans and the bodies of snakes.

Ogres: Hulking, brutal, and half-witted humanoid monsters with violent tendencies, repulsive lusts, and an enormous capacity for cruelty.

Okeno: Island port city controlled by Katapesh; major hub of the slave trade in the Inner Sea region.

Orcs: Race of aggressive humanoids from deep underground who now roam the surface in barbaric bands, recognized by their green or gray skin, protruding tusks, and warlike tendencies. Almost universally hated and feared by other humanoids.

Osirian: Of or relating to the region of Osirion, or a resident of Osirion.

Osirion: Ancient nation south of the Inner Sea renowned for its deserts, pharaohs, and pyramids.

Ostenso: Port city in Cheliax.

Pesh: Narcotic drug made from a type of cactus.

Qadira: Desert nation on the eastern side of the Inner Sea.

Scarab (currency): Gold coin from Katapesh.

Sail (currency): Gold coin from Andoran.

Scroll: Magical document in which a spell is recorded so that it can be released when read, even if the reader doesn't know how to cast that spell. Destroyed as part of the casting process.

Sorcerer: Someone who casts spells through natural ability rather than faith or study.

Squib: To refit a ship for the purposes of disguising it.

Taldan: Of or pertaining to Taldor; a citizen of Taldor.

Taldane: The common trade language of Golarion's Inner Sea region.

Thuvia: Desert nation on the Inner Sea, famous for the production of a magical elixir which grants immortality.

Twilight Talons: Top-secret espionage division of Andoran's Eagle Knights, thought by many to be merely a legend.

Verces: Rocky, inhabited planet in Golarion's solar system.

Witch: Spellcaster who draws magic from a pact made with an otherworldly power, using a familiar as a conduit.

Wizard: Someone who casts spells through careful study and rigorous scientific methods rather than faith or innate talent, recording the necessary incantations in a spellbook.

Turn the page for a sneak peek at

Hellknight

by Liane Merciel

Available April 2016

3

The Heartless

In twelve years as an investigator, Jheraal had seen her share of horror.

The Hellknight had witnessed the worst that arsonists' flames and spurned lovers' knives could do to flesh and bone. She'd seen the ruin of children beaten beyond recognition by drunk fathers' fists. She had uncovered the remains of innocents subjected to the occult rites of Urgathoan cultists, and stood expressionless beside the gallows as the executioners of House Thrune tortured criminals to death in showy displays for the crowd's jeers.

She had thought there was nothing left that could frighten her. And then she had seen what the rundottari had found in that stinking, mud-floored hovel among the ruins of Rego Cader.

The dead man bothered her the least of the four bodies in that shack. The fast-spreading fungus that had consumed his flesh was troubling, but more for what it might signify than for its own sake. Jheraal had seen decomposed corpses before, and while she was concerned about the implications of the mold that fuzzed the dead man's bones, the sight itself didn't disturb her. Not compared to the others in that place.

Slumped behind a tattered curtain were three hellspawn, each with a fist-sized, cauterized wound burned into the center of his or her chest. Two, presumably the missing servants Chiella and Nodero, wore the colors of House Celverian. The third was a more obviously devil-descended woman dressed like a fishmonger from one of the poorer districts.

All three were missing their hearts—Jheraal had held a light to each of those gaping wounds and looked closely to be sure—and yet they lived. Their mutilated chests rose and fell in steady breaths. A ghostly pulse beat in their wrists. When the Hellknight brought her light to their eyes and held open their eyelids, their pupils contracted under its glare, and then dilated when she put the light away.

They seemed to be comatose. Jheraal pricked each hellspawn's fingertips with the tip of her dagger, prodding them hard enough to draw beads of blood from the pads of their thumbs, but none of them flinched. She clapped her hands sharply next to their heads and shouted into their ears, but none stirred. Their faces remained slack, their breathing slow.

"What do you want to do with them?" one of the rundottari asked. Two ruin wardens armed with swords and crossbows had accompanied her out of the Obrigan Gate to meet the one waiting to show them the bodies. As formidable as the Hellknight was, even she wasn't expected to venture into Rego Cader without protection.

"They need a healer's attention," Jheraal said. "These servants may be innocent victims."

The rundottari spat on the muddy floor, displeased by her answer. "Or they might not. No offense meant to you, but they're hellspawn. And whatever killed that moldy fellow might be contagious. This whole thing might be a trap."

Jheraal gave him a flat stare. She was taller than the rundottari, and she used that to her advantage, looming over him in the scarred steel of her Hellknight plate. "If Durotas Tuornos believed that, he wouldn't have sent for me. Those servants are wearing House Celverian's colors. You will, of course, have heard what happened at their vaneo last night. These two might have seen something, or might have other leads to offer. If we can't get them healed, we'll never know. And if I lose valuable information about the Celverian murders because you were afraid of a little mold, well, I can't imagine your durotas will be pleased. Nor will his superiors. What you should be wondering is not whether this is a trap, but where you might be able to keep these people."

Licking his lips, the rundottari looked away. "There are cells in Keep Dotar that might serve, and a few under the Obrigan Gate."

"I'll take the ones under the gate." Keep Dotar, where the rundottari were based, was located in the northeastern part of the Dead Sector, far from the rest of the city, and was too remote to be useful. Jheraal didn't want secrecy. She wanted a full investigation that would force the killer to light. But she also didn't want to keep them at Taranik House, where rivals in the Order of the Rack might try to interfere with or claim credit for her work. The Obrigan Gate was neutral, but more accessible.

She unslung her pack and took out a large, flat box. It was much heavier than it looked. Although only plain wood showed on the outside, the interior was lined with a half-inch of lead and a thin coating of silver over the base metal.

Perhaps the precaution was unnecessary, but she didn't want to risk bringing some Urgathoan contagion into the city. Holding her breath and working quickly, Jheraal stacked the moldering bones into the lead-lined box. When the last of them had been tucked inside, leaving only a fuzzy shadow of white powder on the floor, she took out a long cylinder of soft white wax and held it over the rundottari's lantern.

It took only a few seconds for the cylinder's end to sag and start dripping. Quickly, while it was pliable, Jheraal scrubbed the wax against the box's seam. The molten wax flowed into the crevices and hardened in place.

After a few more rounds of softening and scrubbing, the seal was complete. Not a breath of air would get out of that box until she'd taken it safely back for inspection.

The Hellknight took a card out of her pocket and handed it to one of the rundottari. "Deliver this to Havarel Needlethumbs in Parego Spera. The card has the address. He's expecting the package."

The rundottari lifted the box, holding it as far away from himself as the length of his arms allowed. "I'll wait for you. Safer if we all go back together."

"Fine." It was cowardice, but she couldn't fault him. No one wanted to walk through Rego Cader alone. Jheraal hoisted the unconscious hellspawn man and slung him over her shoulder, motioning for the two remaining rundottari to grab the other hellspawn. It wasn't the gentlest way to carry them, but it was the fastest, and dusk was rapidly approaching. "Let's go."

They made their way back to the Obrigan Gate in silence but for occasional grunts and curses when one of the rundottari stumbled over a gap in the rutted streets while carrying the senseless devilspawn. Around them, the crumbling shells of Westcrown's former grandeur cast ever-longer shadows, while the red sun sank down between their broken towers.

For eight hundred years, the city of Westcrown had been the capital of Cheliax and one of the wonders of the world. Clad in shining white marble and gold, it had been renowned from sea to sea for its beauty. Beyond its architectural splendors, the city had been famed as a place of art, learning, and the high glories of religious faith.

Then Aroden, patron god of humanity and the nation of Cheliax, had died and cast his people into turmoil. Civil war tore the country apart, and when the fighting ended a generation later, the devil-binding House Thrune was ascendant. Queen Abrogail I, new ruler of the empire, moved her capital north to Egorian, and Westcrown entered a long decline.

Its population shrunken, its splendors diminished, its streets and historic buildings scarred by years of civil war, Westcrown pulled back to its central islands and abandoned the poorer districts along the north shore to ruin.

Today the sculpted fountains that had once flowed with fresh water for Westcrown's poorest citizens were filled with weeds and cobwebs. Nothing remained of the sculpted angels that had once ringed the basins except empty plinths bearing mottled crowns of bird droppings. The angels themselves were gone, having been stolen and sold to art collectors who wanted the masterworks for themselves. It was, Jheraal supposed, a fitting symbol of the city's decline that the marvelous public works that had once served its most vulnerable had been scavenged and hoarded away by a wealthy few.

The other signs of Westcrown's deterioration were less poetic but more dangerous. The wooden bones of taverns, inns, and dilapidated stables lined the pocked streets around their little party. No law-abiding citizens lived among them, but some of those ruins were the lairs of squatters and bandits. Others were infested with all manner of bloodthirsty beasts. On their way out, Jheraal and the rundottari had seen nothing more dangerous than a pack of starved dogs, but not all visits to the Dead Sector were so peaceful.

The Obrigan Gate marked the point at which civilization began again in Westcrown. Until they passed through its portcullises and put Rego Cader safely on the far side of its wall, they remained vulnerable.

She hefted the senseless hellspawn on her shoulders and trudged along a little faster. The man's weight compressed her armor, and the edge of her chestplate was digging into her flesh, but Jheraal forced the pain out of her mind. She'd chosen to carry the male servant for a reason. As long as she carried a heavier weight than the rundottari, and did so without complaint, they wouldn't dare shirk their own burdens.

A Hellknight she might be, and devil-blooded to boot, but she was also a woman. None of the three men behind her would let themselves fall behind. It might be pure chauvinism that drove them, but if it drove them, Jheraal would use it. She hadn't survived fourteen years in Citadel Demain, and then in the wider world, by being blind to the levers that moved people's souls. And she wanted to get out of Rego Cader before dark.

Smoke drifted through the weeds that fringed the mouth of an alley to her left. Jheraal's skin prickled. There *were* relatively harmless transients living in the ruins, and the smoke might be from something as simple as a squatter's cookfire. But there were arsonists, too, and madmen, and creatures of shadow that crept out with the night.

And something that stole the hearts of its victims and consigned them to a living death.

She hurried her pace. The thirty-foot-high wall surrounding the Obrigan Gate was visible now, rising above the skeletal rafters and chimney stumps that made up the crumbling skyline of the Dead Sector. Torches and lanterns lined its parapets in golden ribbons of fire.

Jheraal led her companions into the swath of clear space that covered the last hundred feet around the wall. They were within crossbow range of the Obrigan Gate's defenders. Behind them, dusk blurred the ruins and filled every empty doorway with black menace, but it didn't matter anymore. They were safe.

One of the small portcullises in the gate's base opened. A rundottari waved them hastily through, peering into the twilight with his lantern raised high. As Jheraal ushered her escort into the Obrigan Gate, then followed them inside, worry slid off her shoulders like a blanket of lead. The thud of the portcullis closing behind them was the most welcome sound she'd heard in days.

"See anything dangerous out there?" the gate guard asked.

"Not as such." Jheraal lowered the comatose hellspawn to the ground. Her shoulders ached, but she refused to stretch them or adjust her chafing armor where the rundottari might see. Hellknights admitted no weakness. "Do you have a spare cell big enough to hold all three?"

The guard hesitated, but after a glance at the rundottari, he nodded. "This way. The cells under the Gate have held worse than hellspawn."

Another small insult. Accidental, probably. Ignoring the rudeness, Jheraal picked up her living burden once more and followed the guard down a set of winding stairs to a niter-streaked dungeon. Twice she bumped against the cramped walls, jolting her armor into bruised flesh, but she refused to wince. *You do not feel pain. There is no pain.* "Send a messenger to the Qatada Nessudidia." The Asmodean cathedral was the largest temple in Westcrown, and would have the most powerful clerics to be found in the city. "Durotas Tuornos was correct: there is some unholy magic in this. I require a wizard and a cleric, the best that they have, to examine these poor souls. Immediately."

"We shall send the request at once," the rundottari assured her, opening an iron-barred cell door. Damp and littered with moldy straw, it was far from welcoming, but Jheraal had stayed in worse. She didn't think her insensible charges were likely to complain.

She laid the hellspawn on the straw, cradling the man's head against her gauntleted forearm. Removing a roll of bandages from her pack, she spread the gauzy cotton over the wound that disfigured his chest. It would do nothing for his missing heart, but she felt the man deserved that much dignity. "Good. Send word to Taranik House when they arrive."

After ensuring that the heart-stripped hellspawn had been settled safely into their barred beds at the Obrigan Gate, Jheraal returned to Taranik House alone.

Night had drawn its cloak over the city, and in Westcrown that meant that the main streets were lined with pyrahjes, enormous torches as high as men, that filled the avenues with fiery heat. Smaller lanterns hung from the doors of respectable private homes, and lines of torches or enchanted spell-lights drew cordons of radiance around the viras and vaneos of the wealthy. Anything to keep the dark at bay.

Fire was a perpetual hazard in the city, and walking between the pyrahjes on a summer evening could be uncomfortably warm, but the Wiscrani had deemed these costs worth bearing in exchange for safety from Westcrown's nightly curse.

From dusk till dawn, throughout the city, shadows hunted the unwary. Those who broke the nocturnal curfew and ventured beyond the streets protected by torch and lantern took their lives into their hands.

The way to Taranik House was well lit, however, and Jheraal walked the streets without fear. She was deadlier than any hunter in shadow, and she knew it.

So did they. No challenges came from the night.

Back in the garrison, the Hellknight returned to her quarters, locked the door, and finally allowed herself a sigh of relief as she took off her heavy plate. The padding underneath was soaked with sweat, and the fine, soft white scales on her skin had been dented and deformed where the armor pressed into her. Some had chafed off entirely. They floated to the floor like snowflakes when she pulled the padded jerkin over her head, leaving angry pink lines behind.

Jheraal daubed a soothing ointment onto the raw spots along her shoulders and under her right arm, where the armor had bitten in, then tied a soft sleeping robe around herself. In the morning, when she had to put on her public face again, she would be as stoic as the honor of the Hellknights required. For now, she could allow herself a small measure of comfort without shame.

At her desk, she sprinkled a few drops of water on the block of compressed ink she carried with her. While waiting for the ink to soften, Jheraal sharpened a new quill and took out three sheets of good paper: one for the nightly report she sent back to her superiors in Citadel Demain, and two for a letter to her daughter.

The report took little time to write. In quick, broad strokes, Jheraal summarized her visit to Rego Cader and her interactions with Durotas Tuorno's rundottari. She detailed the condition of the heartless hellspawn as carefully as she could, keeping her opinions out of the factual descriptions.

As an afterthought, Jheraal included a request for a consultation with the most skilled wizard that the Order of the Scourge might be able to offer. Udeno of Abadar, the cleric who had examined the late Othando Celverian's body, hadn't impressed her, and she wasn't sure any Wiscrani wizard would be better. Durotas Tuornos had thought it best to request a wizard from the capital, and perhaps he'd been right. Even if she could find someone uninvolved in the local nobles' scheming, indifference and fatalism seemed to rule the day in Westcrown. Anyone with real ambition would have sought a post in Egorian, so her odds of finding a wizard capable of unraveling this mystery were likely better there.

She sealed the letter and set it aside. Then, more slowly, Jheraal dribbled another trickle of water across the eroded slope of her ink block and smoothed a new sheet between her white-scaled hands.

Dear Indrath, she began, *I hope this letter finds you well, and that the summer is not too hot in Egorian.*

Then she stopped, at a loss for what to add. The flame of her lantern crackled in the silence. A bead of ink grew bulbous on the tip of her quill. She caught it and moved it back to the block just before it would have spattered on the near-empty page.

What could she write to a daughter who didn't even know who she was?

The truth, a small, plaintive voice whispered, as it had since the day Jheraal had brought her infant daughter to Citadel Demain, claiming the girl was a foundling.

And just as she had then, and as she'd done every day for the fourteen years since, the Hellknight pushed that voice aside. The truth would do her daughter no good.

Indrath had been born with the blessing of a fully human appearance. No hint of her mother's infernal heritage showed in her face, her speech, or her soul. She was a strong, gifted, *good* child, a child who could live her life free of the prejudices that had hobbled Jheraal's own life—as long as the truth remained unknown.

Jheraal would have given anything for that blessing herself. She would not deny it to her daughter.

She scratched her quill against the block's softening ink. *I saw this book in a shop window,* she continued, agonizing over every word, *and thought you might be entertained to read it. A collection of tall tales and outright lies, I don't doubt, but perhaps someday you'll get to see for yourself, and tell me if there was any truth to such fancies.*

She stopped again, her mind as blank as the rest of the page. What could she write next? Was that enough? Jheraal had barely begun, yet she couldn't think of a single thing to add. Her current investigation was nothing that needed to trouble an innocent child's thoughts, and she'd done little else in Westcrown. She had no amusing anecdotes, no profound insights, nothing that she imagined other people wrote in their clever letters. The Hellknight felt like a hammer, all bluntness and force, when she wanted to be deft as a scalpel in dissecting the world into bites that could fit a child's mouth.

Even her gift suddenly felt too clumsy. It was a collection of the adventures of Durvin Gest, infamous Pathfinder, and his recovery of the legendary Scepter of Ages. Jheraal had seen many versions of Gest's adventures over the years, but this volume, unique among them, included numerous detailed descriptions of his travels into the ruins of lost Ninshabur. The accompanying illustrations were lavishly colored and easily tripled the cost of the book. She'd spent half a month's wages to buy it, and then she'd paid an extra silver for the shopkeeper to wrap the book in paper pressed with tiny, exotic dried flowers.

Since she could first read, Indrath had loved stories about Durvin Gest. She'd been particularly fascinated with the far-off continent of Casmaron, where the fallen empire of Ninshabur was said to be located. Once, she had delighted in telling Jheraal about how someday she was going to travel to Casmaron and chart its territories as an envoy for Imperial Cheliax. One of her most prized possessions was a small ivory elephant, supposedly carved by an artisan in those far-flung lands, which Jheraal had purchased for her in the markets of Kaer Maga.

But that had been three or four years ago, and Indrath was fourteen now. Almost fifteen. Maybe a storybook was too childish for her.

Jheraal didn't know. Her own daughter, and she didn't know. It had been months since she'd last seen Indrath.

I hope you'll like it, she finished, and signed: *Your friend, Jheraal.*

"Your friend." She stared at those words, so small and inadequate to carry the burden she wanted to put on them.

There was so much more she wanted to say, and nothing else she could.

Sighing, she sealed the letter with a daub of wax and tucked it under the string that the shopkeeper had tied around the paper-wrapped book. She stacked the parcel next to the report she was sending back to her order. It, too, would go out in the morning.

Then Jheraal leaned back in her chair, folded her hands into her lap, and closed her eyes, trying to imagine who would tear the hearts out of hellspawn, and why, and what might be gained by leaving those maimed unfortunates alive.

Larsa is a dhampir—half vampire, half human. In the gritty streets and haunted peaks of Ustalav, she's an agent for the royal spymaster, keeping peace between the capital's secret vampire population and its huddled human masses. Meanwhile, in the cathedral of Maiden's Choir, Jadain is a young priestess of the death goddess, in trouble with her superiors for being too soft on the living. When a noblewoman's entire house is massacred by vampiric invaders, the unlikely pair is drawn into a deadly mystery that will reveal far more about both of them than they ever wanted to know.

From Pathfinder co-creator and award-winning game designer F. Wesley Schneider comes a new adventure of revenge, faith, and gothic horror, set in the world of the Pathfinder Roleplaying Game.

Bloodbound print edition: $14.99
ISBN: 978-0-7653-7546-9

Bloodbound ebook edition:
ISBN: 978-1-4668-4733-0

PATHFINDER
TALES

Bloodbound

A NOVEL BY
F. Wesley Schneider

Mirian Raas comes from a long line of salvagers—adventurers who use magic to dive for sunken ships off the coast of tropical Sargava. With her father dead and her family in debt, Mirian has no choice but to take over his last job: a dangerous expedition into deep jungle pools, helping a tribe of lizardfolk reclaim the lost treasures of their people. Yet this isn't any ordinary dive, as the same colonial government that looks down on Mirian for her half-native heritage has an interest in the treasure, and the survival of the entire nation may depend on the outcome.

From critically acclaimed author Howard Andrew Jones comes an adventure of sunken cities and jungle exploration, set in the award-winning world of the Pathfinder Roleplaying Game.

Beyond the Pool of Stars print edition: $14.99
ISBN: 978-0-7653-7453-0

Beyond the Pool of Stars ebook edition:
ISBN: 978-1-4668-4265-6

Pathfinder
Tales
Beyond the Pool of Stars
A Novel by Howard Andrew Jones

Rodrick is con man as charming as he is cunning. Hrym is a talking sword of magical ice, with the soul and spells of an ancient dragon. Together, the two travel the world, parting the gullible from their gold and freezing their enemies in their tracks. But when the two get summoned to the mysterious island of Jalmeray by a king with genies and elementals at his command, they'll need all their wits and charm if they're going to escape with the greatest prize of all—their lives.

From Hugo Award winner Tim Pratt comes a tale of magic, assassination, and cheerful larceny, set in the award-winning world of the Pathfinder Roleplaying Game.

Liar's Island print edition: $14.99
ISBN: 978-0-7653-7452-3

Liar's Island ebook edition:
ISBN: 978-1-4668-4264-9

PATHFINDER
TALES

Liar's Island

A NOVEL BY Tim Pratt

Count Varian Jeggare and his hellspawn bodyguard Radovan are no strangers to the occult. Yet when Varian is bequeathed a dangerous magical book by an old colleague, the infamous investigators find themselves on the trail of a necromancer bent on becoming the new avatar of an ancient and sinister demigod—one of the legendary runelords. Along with a team of mercenaries and adventurers, the crime-solving duo will need to delve into a secret world of dark magic and the legacy of a lost empire. But in saving the world, will Varian and Radovan lose their souls?

From best-selling author Dave Gross comes a fantastical tale of mystery, monsters, and mayhem set in the award-winning world of the Pathfinder Roleplaying Game.

Lord of Runes print edition: $14.99
ISBN: 978-0-7653-7451-6

Lord of Runes ebook edition:
ISBN: 978-1-4668-4263-2

Pathfinder Tales

Lord of Runes

A NOVEL BY Dave Gross

Years ago, the dwarven warrior Akina left her home in the Five Kings Mountains to fight in the Goblinblood Wars. Now at long last she's returning home, accompanied by Ondorum, her silent companion of living stone. What she finds there is far from what she remembers: a disgraced brother, an obsessive suitor, and a missing mother presumed dead. Yet the damage runs deeper than anyone knows, and when Akina's brother is kidnapped by ancient enemies from the legendary Darklands, she and Ondorum must venture below the surface—and into danger as old as the stones themselves.

From debut novelist Josh Vogt comes a tale of love, redemption, and subterranean battle, set in the award-winning world of the Pathfinder Roleplaying Game.

Forge of Ashes **print edition: $9.99**
ISBN: 978-1-60125-743-7

Forge of Ashes **ebook edition:**
ISBN: 978-1-60125-744-4

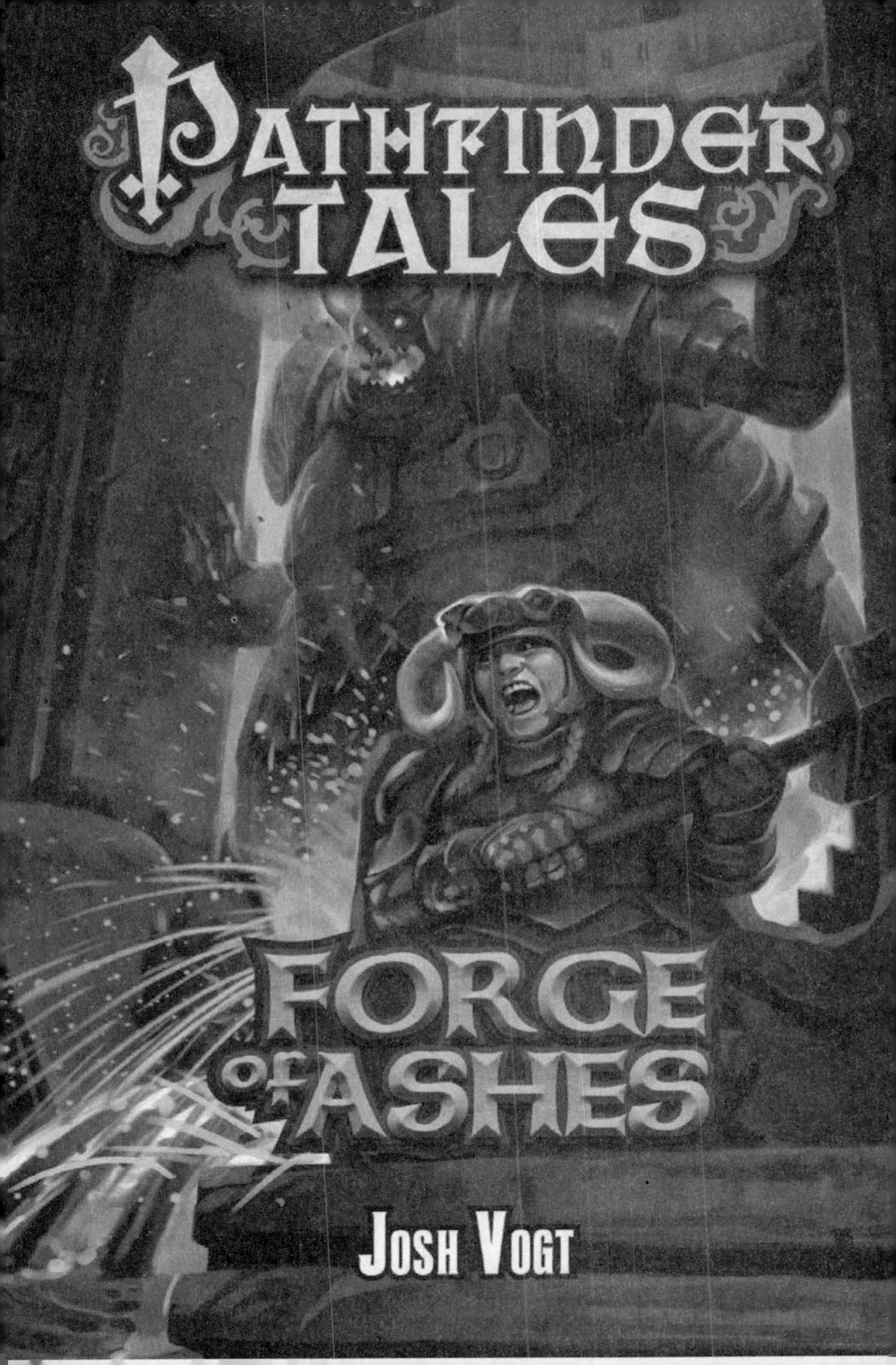
Pathfinder Tales
Forge of Ashes
Josh Vogt

PATHFINDER
ROLEPLAYING GAME
BEGINNER BOX

THE ADVENTURE BEGINS!

Designed specifically for beginning players and packed with must-have accessories including dice, monster counters, and a slimmed-down, easy-to-understand rules set, the *Pathfinder RPG Beginner Box* gives you everything you need to set out on countless quests in a fantastic world beset by magic and evil!

AVAILABLE NOW!
$34.99 • PZO1119-1
ISBN 978-1-60125-630-0

Photo by Carlos Paradinha, Jr.